THE PIANO TUNER'S SONG

KARENZA GRANT

L'Ours

A L'OURS BOOKS publication

Paperback first published in 2022 by L'Ours Books

Cover: Stuart Bache

Copyediting: Toby Selwyn

Proofreading: PS Livingstone

ISBN (ebook) 978-1-915737-00-7

ISBN (paperback) 978-1-915737-01-4

www.karenzagrant.com

To the two souls who stole my heart

The Piano Tuner's Song

Lo Boièr

(*The Oxherd*)

Traditional Occitan Folksong—Abridged

When the oxherd from plough returns
And sets his staff upon the ground
A, E, I, O, U
And sets his staff upon the ground

He finds his wife rested by the fire
Sorrowful and disconsolate
A, E, I, O, U
Sorrowful and disconsolate

When I am dead do bury me
In the deepest of all caverns
A, E, I, O, U
In the deepest of all caverns

When the pilgrims that way do pass
They will drink of sacred water
A, E, I, O, U
They will drink of sacred water

They will ask who departed here
Here lies the poor Joanna
A, E, I, O, U
Here lies the poor Joanna.

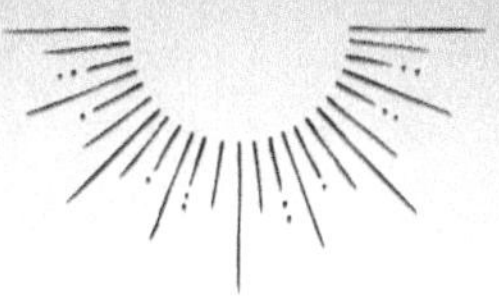

The first thing that ever there was, before the passage of days, before the light of stars, before the movement of planets, before the existence of man and before the composition of song, before all of these things there existed a single resonant sound. And as is often so paradoxical, this one sound contained within itself all other sounds. It was a euphony, a polyphony and a melody in one, and yet it was also a bud possessing growth and life and movement. It was possibility, it was promise, it was potential unbound and as yet unexpressed.

It was harmony.

Chapter One

I shifted the car into a low gear as the lane curved then descended, my chest tightening at the sight before me. There, almost at the foot of the valley, lay the village of Sarrat. The hotchpotch houses and the broad river curled around an immense peak of weather-hewn limestone spotted with box trees and heather—the pog, we'd always called it. And on the summit of the pog stood the ruins of the chateau fort.

As I took the next bend, the village and chateau disappeared from view, and I could have been driving in any part of the Pyrenees, with vivid sky, sheltering rock and autumn-yellowed hawthorn. At that moment Sarrat was just an image conjured more by imagination than memory, as it had been so many times at Eveline's and afterward, when I'd curled under my duvet at night and wished I were back... here.

I was here.

I turned the car again. There was the village—my imagination brought to life. I let out something between a laugh and a choke, and a smile extended across my face. I'd wanted to return for so long.

The early-afternoon sun cast a warm glow upon the crimson and amber woodland that surrounded the village, and the grey roofs amidst the trees grew before me as I approached, the tightness in my chest becoming an ache.

I drew a deep breath. I could do this—of course I could. There was no use sinking into pointless emotion. The past was the past and, more than that, I needed to be here. The peace and quiet was a necessity, and that ruled out Paris. I fixed my attention on the road, the scattering of fallen leaves at the sides, the ridge of earth in the centre. All I wanted was to be home, to walk through that door, to touch the walls I'd only been able to imagine.

The lane headed away from the village for a moment, then curved back, and there it was ahead, the first house from town—a rustic barn conversion tucked between October-bronzed hornbeam. Two figures stood beneath the branches. Each time I'd imagined coming back, I'd not pictured meeting anyone at this point. I shook my head, trying to fling off the fantasy. This was real. I was here.

I slowed into the pull-in and turned off the ignition, taking in the figures. An elderly man holding a wheelbarrow was in discussion with a familiar steel-grey head. Sylvie. A little piece of me melted at the sight of her.

Climbing out, the wind tugged at my clothes. I pulled my jumper down over my jeans, breathing in leaf mulch, woodsmoke and a hint of ice in the air.

"Violette, it is you!" Sylvie strode toward me. "Earlier than expected."

It was strange how in my mind's eye her hair was rich

chocolate, as dark as mine, even though I'd seen her in Paris recently crowned with grey. But her umber complexion, the upright posture of her broad frame and her hazel eyes sparkling with enthusiastic confidence were the same. "It's good to see you," I replied.

She engulfed me in her arms, then drew back and we exchanged kisses, the old man gazing on with interest from behind. Sylvie's hands grasped my shoulders as she studied my face. "Dear, as always, you are the very image of your mother. It could be her standing right here with those Prussian-blue eyes."

I wanted to reply, but I was unable to put into words all she'd been in my under-the-duvet imagination—everything I'd held dear, especially those warm hugs and her stalwart ability never to be fazed. Her friendship had meant so much to all of us, particularly Maman, and now that I would be living next door to her once again, Sylvie would be a part of my life as she always had been.

"And we have a great deal to catch up on," she continued, not noticing my hesitation. "I want to hear all your news. How was the drive, for a start?"

There was no doubt I could answer that one. I grinned. "Quick, eventless. I still feel like I'm part of the car."

"You must have left Paris early—"

"Sylvie," the gravel voice of the old man burst out. "I need away with this thing right now." His chalky moustache and thick sideburns shook as he spoke. He picked up the wheelbarrow, and its load, a covered triangular bulk, teetered to one side. He nodded curtly to me. "Nice to see you, Violette."

"Bonjour." I smiled back, but I didn't recognise him.

He turned to Sylvie. "I've absolutely no space for it. I can't keep it any longer."

"One moment, Violette." Sylvie stepped over to him.

"You know I have the builders in, Nico." Her voice was low. "This is completely inappropriate. Just one more night."

I headed to the car, pulled out my jacket and shrugged it on, then took the keys from the glove compartment and turned to the barn. The weathered oak door hadn't changed, with its eye-level window—the tourbillon of glass had made it almost impossible to tell who was at the door as I'd stood on tiptoes intent on seeing through.

"I've already had it much too long. Put it in your garage." I vaguely registered Nico's grumbling as my gaze followed the tendrils of ivy that twisted along the stone walls of the house. I needed that stone under my hands. I needed to be in there. I'd needed not to leave seventeen years ago. I'd make my excuses and catch up with Sylvie later.

"You know what Edgard is like," Sylvie continued. "The garage is packed to the brim."

"Can't Violette take it, for goodness' sake?" Nico muttered. "She's right here."

"What's this got to do with me?" I shut up the car and walked over to the wheelbarrow, surveying its load.

Sylvie placed her hand on my arm. "Don't worry about it now, dear. You have enough to be getting on with. I'll sort something out." She glared at Nico.

But I recognised the faded cloth that surrounded the bulk, the floral calico print wadded with protective padding. Whenever Maman had finished playing, I'd taken pride in sliding the cover over the worn curves of her lever harp. I'd thought it was long gone. I stared at the fabric—I'd forgotten how the pattern came together in small posies.

"Coming back after so many years would be a lot for anyone," Sylvie said, her face lined with concern. "I didn't want to overwhelm you with this when you'd just arrived. I was going to leave it a few days then mention it, rather than wheel the thing under your nose straight away."

"No, it's fine." I reached out and placed my hand on the cover. Even now, the soft cotton was familiar under my fingers. I swallowed, my throat dry and raw, the ache in my chest much too deep. "I thought Eveline had auctioned it off with all of Maman and Papa's things."

"Most of it went, but I took on this beauty. I couldn't bear to see her go. She was a part of your maman. I had no storage space, what with all of Edgard's mess, but she was passed around the village for various children to learn on. I like to think of her as your maman's legacy."

Sylvie always had been generous. "This is, uh, beyond belief." My words were completely inadequate. The harp and Maman had been inseparable—this was a small piece of her.

"You see," Nico said with a smug look. "Violette is perfectly happy to take it."

"Yes, I am." I nodded at Sylvie's still troubled face.

"The thing's not had any attention for a few years now," Nico added, "but you could get one of the Rabastens to tune it for you, or do any repairs. They'd be happy to help."

"I'll sort something out." I glanced at the door once more. "I don't mean to hurry you both, but it's been a long drive."

"Of course." Sylvie glared at Nico again.

He seemed impervious. "Come on then, let me be rid of this thing. I'm supposed to be helping Agathe with the garden."

The cracked path lay unchanged under my feet as I

strode to the house, the garden on either side overgrown and strewn with fallen leaves. Nico's and Sylvie's footsteps thudded behind me, the wheelbarrow rattled and my heart drummed. I'd been away for too long. I pushed the key into the lock, turned it and pulled down the handle, just as I'd always done.

The door opened and behind me the wheelbarrow clanked, the harp releasing a muffled discord of buzzing strings. A surge of colours cut across my vision, thick, dense—smothering my senses, filling my head, invading me. I gasped, my heart racing, my body shaking.

"Violette!" Sylvie placed her hand on my back. "Are you alright?"

I gripped the door frame. The colours merged into an ugly brown, then a lifeless black, pressing inward, stifling, suffocating. Through the deluge I could just make out the step beneath my feet, the mottled and fissured stone. I focussed on its surface, blocking out everything else, and the colours began to dissipate. My pulse eased, and with it a thread of dismay rose within me—I'd let my guard down, I'd been distracted by the barn, by coming home, and the sound had caught me unawares. But it wasn't going to happen all the time here—not in the peace and quiet of the mountains. It was going to be better. It had to be. I just needed to keep my wits about me until I got to know the place again.

The last of the colours faded to nothing. I forced my breathing into regularity, put on my perfectly collected face and looked Sylvie in the eye. "I'm fine," I said. "I'm tired and I need to get in and settled."

She examined me and nodded, but she wasn't convinced.

"Watch yourselves," Nico said as he hauled the harp from the wheelbarrow.

"Let me—" I moved in to take it from him.

"Nonsense." He pushed past into the hallway. "Where do you want it?"

Chapter Two

I closed the door on Sylvie and Nico, their figures twisting through the tourbillon as they headed up the path. Sylvie had promised hot food later and I wanted to catch up with her, but for now, they were gone and I was home.

Being inside felt less real than my imagination. The house was so still, so quiet. I'd never been here without people, without life busy around me. My fingers trembled, still unsteady from the barrage of colours, and I shivered from the cold.

The hall was as I remembered, the terracotta tiles, the wooden stairs, the coat rack in the same place by the study door, but the smell... it was the stale odour of old age. Yet it wasn't as if I'd expected the scent of Maman and Papa and home, the scent I could never remember but could occasionally glimmer from certain kinds of clean linen or baking bread, or the occasional origin of surprise. Once it had been wild irises—like Maman's face cream.

I took a deep breath. Staying focussed would help me get through this, and right now I needed to unpack to the point where I could eat, sleep and hopefully keep warm before nightfall. I zipped up my jacket. The first look in each room would be the worst.

The house lay empty but for my boxes and a little furniture, most of it piled in the living room. I braced myself against the pat of my footsteps as I walked about, holding the awareness I needed to keep my colours away, even though expected sounds rarely triggered a reaction.

Memories filled the bare spaces—Maman singing softly as she laid emerald wall tiles in the kitchen, Papa behind his desk in the study examining some old thing he'd collected for the musée, me sliding perilously down the stairs upon a blanket sled. Upstairs I could still see Maman and Papa's neatly made four-poster, and my bed under the window of the room next door, books and toys scattered across the floor. My chest grew raw with each recollection. I paused on the landing. The broad space was as big as a room itself, with a circular window that framed the view of the chateau. The walls had been lined with books and I'd curled up in the armchair by the window reading *Ariol* or *Alice au Pays des Merveilles*, while Maman gave music lessons below.

I opened the last door to what had been the spare room with its slanting ceiling, oak beams and sense of space. The removal company had reassembled my carved bedstead in the centre. I would be comfortable here. I ran my fingers over the pitted wall. Soon the house would become a mundane part of my daily existence. Being here would work. It had to. Taking a hold of my tangle of a life started at this moment.

As I headed downstairs my phone buzzed. I pulled it out

and stared at the screen, not quite able to integrate a message from Esprit Obscur demanding their proofs with this long-ago place. I still hadn't finished the designs for their rebrand, and they would have to wait.

Stepping into the living room, I pushed past the contents of my Paris apartment and gazed through the glass doors that extended along the far side. The valley and the chateau stood before me, the sight I used to take for granted every day, the sight that was home all by itself.

Tugging open the doors, the room became an extension of the sweeping, stone-studded land. The wind blustered in, the stale smell replaced by crisp mountain air. I inhaled deeply as I absorbed the view. The rough ground and fields below the garden led down to patchwork forest, flood meadows and the river. Amidst it all stood the pog, the chateau crowning its peak, the sturdy crenellated walls an organic part of the limestone from which they were hewn.

The chateau looked different, though. In my memory it had been brighter, more welcoming, yet now it appeared cast in shadow. But perhaps the impression was caused by the sun lowering behind the pog. And, anyway, the last time I'd seen this view it had been through the eyes of a ten-year-old.

I pulled the doors closed and turned back to the room. The dark wooden furniture, the piano and a family's clutter were long gone, replaced by my turquoise two-piece suite, my contemporary standard lamps and piles of boxes, all of it jumbled together, yet the harp stood by the hearth where it always had. I pushed through the disarray and bent down before the patterned calico. "Thank you, Sylvie," I murmured.

The years fell away as I pulled off the cover. The instrument's honey patina shone, the column carved into a tangle of branches that swept over the head and along the neck, as though one of the hornbeams had sprung up from the parquet. I'd always loved the delicacy of it, rather than the overbearing proportions of concert harps I'd seen Maman's friends playing.

A small iron tool had been tied to the base of the column with a faded blue velvet ribbon. I caught the tuning key between my fingers, its head cast with miniature interwoven branches, its shank tarnished with russet—it was a work of art all by itself.

I untied the key and placed the ribbon over the shoulder where it had always hung, then I drew an old wicker stool from the pile of furniture and positioned it before the sound-box. As I sat down I instinctively wrapped myself around the frame and curled my fingers into position, just as I'd done as a child. I could almost sense Maman's arms around mine, her gentle fingers adjusting my hands, her soft whispers of instruction in my ear, her warmth.

Staring at the yellowed strings, my eyes pricked, my chest holding so much. Breathing the emotion away, I lowered my arms and stood up. I would play the harp, but it wasn't sensible right now—I was tired from the drive and, going by earlier, holding back my colours might take too much effort. No, I needed to get on with unpacking and sorting. But there was no doubt that my colours would be easier to control here. The house was so still, I wouldn't have to maintain a constant vigil as I'd done in Paris.

Over the next few hours I lit the range, and finding logs by the side of the house, I lit the fire too, then I hauled boxes to useful places, cleaned the kitchen and the living room, and set about arranging the furniture, unrolling the cream rug before the hearth and positioning the sofa and armchair toward the fire. More memories surfaced, but I allowed them to arise as facts without feeling. It was better that way, better to enjoy being home rather than drown in sentimentality.

Occasionally I glanced at the chateau. It really did look different, and I couldn't decide how. As I tried various positions for the lamps, the words of one of the old songs came into my head, a song the musicians, Maman and Papa included, used to play in the chateau for the tourists on summer evenings. I sang under my breath, "*Quand lo boièr ven de laurar*"—when the oxherd from plough returns, "*Planta son agulhada*"—plants his staff upon the ground, then, "*A E I Ò U*", the vowels repeated in each verse—the song never had made sense, but it was fitting now I was back.

A knock rang out. Unable to restrain a smile, I abandoned the lamps, headed to the hall and pulled open the door. Sylvie stood there, her broad frame wrapped in a gilet, a covered tray in her arms. "Violette, dear, this isn't too early for dinner, is it?"

"It's perfect timing. I'm ravenous and I was beginning to flag. Come in."

She stepped past. "I'm sorry about Nico earlier. He really could have waited."

"Honestly, I'm just happy to have the harp back." The aroma of what hid under the cover tugged at my senses. "Onion and thyme. You remembered."

She beamed. "You used to beg for my onion soup. Where do you want it?"

"The living room. The kitchen is piled with boxes."

She followed me in, placed the tray on the hearth before the fire and glanced around. "Well, it looks like you're making progress."

"If you call progress putting everything in other rooms to

be sorted later. I'll get some water." I found two mugs, filled them and headed back in.

Sylvie had settled on the hearth. The deep stone step made perfect seating. As I walked over I was unable to take my eyes off her. She was a living piece of my past, part of that comfortable, warm, stable childhood world. Yes, we'd met once recently, but seeing her here was different—the years rolled away. I placed the mugs with everything else, then took off my coat and joined her by the fire. Finally, the place was beginning to feel warm.

Sylvie drew the cloth from the tray, revealing a plate of buttered pain de campagne and two bowls of thyme-and-gruyere-encrusted soup. She placed a spoon in each and handed me a bowl with a tea-towel folded underneath. "There we go, my dear. Enjoy."

"Delicious, thank you." I broke the gruyere and brought a little to my lips, wary of the heat. The cream, herbs and salty onion were exactly as I remembered. I closed my eyes, absorbing the flavours. "I think I've been transported back seventeen years."

"Oh, my dear." Sylvie lowered her bowl.

I glanced at her, unsettled by the tone of her voice.

She reached over and placed her hand on my arm. "I wanted to say it in Paris, but there wasn't the time or the place. Violette, I'm terribly sorry. I tried to keep in touch."

"I guessed you would have." I didn't want this conversation—it was hard enough holding everything back without going into more of the past—but once we'd cleared the air, we wouldn't have to return to the subject again.

"Damned Eveline." Sylvie's irritation was clear. "Why on earth she was appointed as your guardian, I'll never know. I tried to make the woman see sense, I told her you needed the village and your friends." She pulled herself upright, her soup clasped between rigid fingers. "I told her it was what your parents would've wanted, but she wouldn't listen. She insisted it was better for you to have a clean break."

"In hindsight I can understand that," I said, forcing away the emptiness that threatened to build. "I think it would have been much harder to come and go from Sarrat, always seeing what I'd lost, seeing my home lived in by another family."

"But Eveline wouldn't even let me keep in contact." Sylvie's eyes blazed. "She blocked my calls. I presume you never got my letters, birthday cards, presents?"

I shook my head.

"Violette, that wasn't right. You needed to know that your friends still loved you, that we were there for you, even if coming back to Sarrat was too much."

"Eveline never told me what she'd done, but I overheard the occasional phone call and gathered what was going on."

"Utterly unbelievable."

"It was. But I hardened pretty quickly." I studied Sylvie's face, her forehead furrowed, her lips tight. "I sometimes wonder if I should have contacted you sooner—when I was eighteen and legally out of Eveline's charge. But I didn't want to think about my old life then, not until there was a possibility of returning."

"I understand." Her expression softened. "I'm glad you got in touch when you did, and that you're here now."

"Me too." I took a mouthful.

"Anyway, what's done is done." She smiled and pointed her spoon at me. "And we have something much more important to focus on. The here and now."

"My sentiments exactly." I dropped my shoulders. The

discussion was over, and I could focus on what was in front of me.

"Tell me what your plans are now you're back." She sipped a spoonful of soup.

My plans were to control the bursts of colour that had been preventing me from doing most things in the bustle of Paris, but she didn't need to know that. "I have two weeks off work"—at least when I'd completed the proofs for Esprit Obscur and some updates for Sablier, the loose ends I hadn't managed to put off—"and I intend to decorate every bit of this place. I'd like to get back into village life too, perhaps meet up with some of the people I used to know."

"But it's a big change from Paris. It's quite a step."

"I've waited for the chance to come home for years. Going freelance was partly in preparation. And"—I glanced out at the chateau—"I've looked forward to the sense of really being rooted somewhere. I missed the community we had here."

Sylvie raised her eyebrows. "Well, that's not always a bed of roses."

I smiled at her through a mouthful.

"Won't you miss your friends and your life in Paris?"

There hadn't been a life since I'd quit as design director at *De Nouveaux* magazine, thanks to sensory overload. Working from home hadn't exactly been a social activity. Going out was always a challenge and my confidence had suffered. I shrugged. "There are a few people I will miss very much, but we will keep in touch." And it would be worth it a thousand times for the peace and quiet.

"What about you?" I asked as I scraped up the last of my soup.

"I'm retiring from the municipal in two months." Her lips pursed. "It's been almost thirty years."

I tilted my head. "Any plans?"

"Absolutely not one single thing." A wry smile drew across her lips. "And it's going to stay that way. Edgard retired last year. I intend to take a leaf out of his book and relax, read, do the garden and not much else."

We talked a little more about Sylvie's family and how Edgard was still the same literature-obsessed tyrant he'd always been, then with another warm hug she left and stillness descended.

Standing in the centre of the living room, I gazed around. The walls had been a warm sandy shade all those years ago, but now they were pink. With the dove-grey limestone hearth, the room was a pastel washout, at odds with the bolder colours of the wild landscape beyond the doors. But that could be changed. I should be able to decorate the whole place during my time off, and then I'd need to unpack fully and pick up some more furniture.

I stepped over to the armchair, angled it to face the pog and sank into the cushions. My phone vibrated. I pulled it out then stopped. I didn't want the interruption, not now, not at this moment. I held my thumb against the side button until the screen went blank, then I tucked my legs under me and gazed out at the view. Silence drew about like a protective cloak. This was the right place for me. I needed quiet, I needed to be home.

The sky behind the pog glowed with the remnants of the setting sun. I'd spent so many hours there with Maman and Papa amidst the chateau's sturdy walls when we'd played with the musicians, or charging around the slopes and swimming in the river with the village children. Now the pathway to the summit was barely visible, the chateau dark, the doorway only perceptible as a black hole into which the last of the light sank. My gaze drew to the blackness, and it spread outward until it was a presence in the room, until it enfolded me. My breath grew shallow as the certainty I'd felt seeped away.

The house was empty. They weren't here.

Chapter Three

PAINT, BRUSHES, DUST SHEETS, MASKING TAPE—I'D NEED to go to Foix for those and I could pick up some shopping at the same time. I should probably update my toolkit too, then I could attempt to fix the broken bedroom door handle and the loose pipework in the bathroom. What else?

I leant sideways over the warm range and propped myself up on the worktop, twisting the pencil between my fingers. I'd slept well and everything felt better this morning. It was so peaceful. The only sounds were the wind, birdsong and the gentle hum of the range. Already the knots in my shoulders were unravelling, the constant wariness that my colours could be triggered at any moment easing. My relaxation was aided by the baggy sweats and the woolly jumper I'd thrown on, the clothes soft against my skin. I didn't need to worry about what I wore here—no one would care.

In the morning light it was clear that the place required a coat of white paint—white to allow the limestone hearth to speak for itself and the oak doors, woodwork and parquet to come into their own, delineating the negative spaces. But before I could go to town for everything, I needed coffee. I still had some of the car to unload, and that included the moka pot. Picking up my keys, I headed out, still not quite convinced I was here.

It was a luxury to step outside not having to brace myself against the onslaught of the city. The wind brushed my face and stirred the hornbeams, the sound pleasant, welcoming. Pausing halfway up the path, I took in the vivid sky and the mismatched lines of the barn almost buried amidst an unruly tangle of golden hazel and shocking-pink spindle. I would have to tame the garden, even if just a little to let the light through the windows, but I had decorating and work, and then the snow would come. The undergrowth would have to wait until spring.

A movement caught my eye, breaking the congruity of the wilderness around me. A man stood at the side of the lane facing the opposite way—probably a hiker looking for the track to the chateau. I walked to the car and opened the boot. He turned at the thunk, glancing at me and then the house. He certainly wasn't dressed like a hiker. He looked completely out of place—his well-cut waistcoat over a dark blue shirt and a black tie would have been inconspicuous in Paris.

"Can I help you?" I called.

"Uh, I'm not sure, I..." He walked over, his eyes searching around, his gaze framed by carefully groomed dark curls, a resolute, shadowed jaw and a straight mouth that held a familiarity. I'd seen him before, but it couldn't have been here—that was too long ago.

"I know you, don't I?" I asked.

He raised his brow. "I... don't know."

It came back to me. "Rémy Rabasten. You were in *Le*

Monde a fair bit a few years ago. A master piano tuner for the Paris Opera, right?" I'd followed him with interest because he'd been a part of my life before—one of the boys with whom we'd created infinite variations of Pris du Drapeau in the meadows at the foot of the pog.

"Yeah." He looked around as though he were unsure of his surroundings, but he had to know where he was—he'd grown up in the village and his family's farm wasn't far. "Do I know you?" he added eventually.

"Violette Romèu." I extended my hand. "We used to play together down by the river, and you took harp lessons from my mother. I remember you with her in the living room on Saturdays." I nodded to the house.

He took my hand, studying my face intently, his irises light, crystal blue, his eyes set with intelligence and an appealing softness. "I remember," he said. "But I've not seen you since you were..."

"Ten. Yes."

"Your parents..."

The subject was inevitable, and although everything had happened so long ago, with the emotion of coming home, the answer was raw. "Yes, they died. I went to live in Paris and I've not been back since."

"Oh. Of course." He paused briefly. "Monsieur and Madame Durocher lived here then, didn't they?"

I nodded. "He died a few years ago. She has just moved to a nursing home, and I decided to return."

He appeared absorbed in thought for a moment, his gaze on the road, his curls shifting in the breeze.

"It's good to see you," I said, attempting to glimpse in him the gangly and rather gaunt boy he'd been, but all I could see was a tall, well-built and rather striking adult. "Do you want to come in? I would love the chance to catch up on everything that's been going on in the village, and I was about to make coffee."

"Uh, yes, thanks, coffee would be good." He spoke with hesitation, almost as though he were asking a question. I studied his face, wondering at his uncertainty. Then he shook his head as though dispelling something, his level mouth drawing into a warm smile. "Sorry, coffee would be great."

"Good. Come in, then." The shopping could wait a while. I leant into the car and hauled out the book box between me and the moka pot.

"Let me help." He took the weight with ease before I'd managed to lift it over the rim. I pulled out the crate I needed.

"You have the heavy one," I said as he followed me down the path.

He smiled. "No problem."

Pushing the door open with my back, I stepped inside.

"Down there is fine." I nodded to the floor by the stairs.

He obliged and gazed around the hall. "I've not been here for ages."

"That makes two of us." I placed my crate next to his, drew out the moka pot and pushed off my shoes. "Make yourself at home—I'm attempting to."

I headed into the kitchen, filled the pot and set it on the range. When I came out, Rémy had made his way into the living room and was standing stock still, gazing at the chateau, his expression something between dread and confusion. He really wasn't quite with it, and it was a little unnerving. I cleared my throat.

He turned on the spot and his face eased. "I, uh, haven't seen that view for a while."

"Aren't you staying at your farm?" I'd been there many times years ago. They had a similar prospect, although they were further around the pog.

"No, not at the moment." He looked confused again, then he glanced toward the corner of the room and his face lit. "You still have it!" He strode to the harp.

"Sylvie kept it—or at least organised its keeping. It came back at the same time I did, yesterday."

"Do you mind if I have a look?"

"Go ahead."

He extended a hand, paused as though he dared not make contact, then unfurled his fingers and touched the harp as if it were hot or terribly fragile. Seeming satisfied, he placed his hands upon the wood and, after a moment, ran them over the arm and down the column.

"It appears to be in good condition," I said, watching his movements with curiosity. "I haven't had a chance to clean it and it's bound to be out of tune. I don't think it's been played for a few years."

"It's absolutely beautiful." There was awe in his voice. "I have wonderful memories of this thing." He peered at the interlace of branches. "Alderwood, isn't it?"

"I'm not sure."

"The sound box is small but, if I remember rightly, remarkably resonant. Thirty-two strings. How old is it?"

I liked his enthusiasm. "I don't know. I never used to take much interest in dates."

He knelt down and examined the column. "Unpatterned, completely organic in form, unlike anything I've seen elsewhere. And the tuning key"—he picked up the iron tool, the velvet ribbon trailing across his hand—"is utterly unique."

"Someone recommended I get a Rabasten to tune it, so it's strange you're here," I said without thinking, then winced. It sounded like I'd asked him in to tune the harp. "But I'll pick up a digital tuner in town," I added in an attempt to undo my words.

Rémy stood up and turned toward me. "Alright, you've offended me now." His eyes gleamed. "You've got an expert here and you want to use a thirty-euro electronic device?"

I smiled. "I didn't ask you in to sort out my harp."

"Are you going to stop me?"

He didn't look obliged—the opposite, in fact. "So you want to do it?"

He shook his head. "I can't keep my hands off the thing."

I laughed. "Alright, then. Thank you. But coffee first."

He grinned and followed me into the kitchen.

I lifted the steaming pot from the range and poured. "I've no milk or anything. I haven't had a chance to go to the shop yet."

"Black's just fine." He'd leant back against the wall by the table, watching me, a faint smile at his lips. Perhaps he was trying to place me in his memories.

I held out a coffee. He leant forward and took hold of it, then flinched back. The cup dropped and burst against the terracotta, coffee dousing the floor, the cupboards, the table legs.

He stared at the debris, then at me, his mouth parted as though he couldn't believe what he'd done. "I am so sorry. It was hot." He was completely perplexed. There was obviously something wrong.

"Freshly made coffee tends to be hot," I said with a smile,

making light of it. "Stand still and I'll get something to clear it up." I stepped over the devastation and filled a bucket in the utility.

"Let me," he said as I came back in. "Of all the stupid things to do." He took the bucket and cloth and began cleaning up.

I gathered the broken pieces and dropped them in the bin, then found another cup and poured what was left of the coffee.

The last of the mess wiped away, Rémy stood up, dismay covering his face. "Your trousers."

I'd noticed. "I've just returned home for the first time in years, and I'm having my harp tuned by an expert—I can lose a cup and a pair of trousers for that."

He smiled. I passed him the fresh coffee and he clasped the cup cautiously, then pulled it toward him and breathed in the aroma.

I couldn't hold back any longer. "I hope you don't mind me asking, are you alright? You seem a little... unsettled."

He released a short laugh accompanied by a shake of his head. "I'm sorry. I know I'm out of it. I'll do my best to act like a normal human being." He took a mouthful and closed his eyes, savouring the taste.

"I remember you down by the river when we all played together. You were one of the older ones who used to make up all the games. If we didn't follow your rules, you would charge around possessed, desperate that we should get your instructions perfectly right. You were never normal."

He laughed. "You've got me there. I used to be pretty intense. Then my brothers would drag me home and tell my parents what an idiot I'd been. And you were one of the quiet ones. I don't remember you at school."

"You must be at least five years older. When I started primaire, you'd already gone to collège." I sipped at my coffee, watching his expression flicker, taking in the warmth of his eyes.

"That explains it. But I used to see you on Saturday afternoons here for lessons, and in the evenings in the summer when everyone played at the chateau."

"I remember you with a violin up there."

"Yep, and you played the..." He screwed up his eyes.

"You can't remember," I said with mock consternation.

He shook his head, a broad grin on his face, his gaze set on mine.

"I get it." I placed my cup on the worktop. "We all looked up to you and your brothers, brilliant musicians, even then. And I was an insignificant little kid who played the... tambourine."

He broke out into a full, resonant laugh, his eyes alight. I couldn't help but smile in response. "But you played other things," he said, and gulped his coffee.

"The harp, of course, and the piano. It used to be there." I nodded through the doorway to the back wall of the living room. "But I've not played anything since I left. And you?"

"Various instruments. I studied piano at the conservatoire, got into tuning, did an apprenticeship at Steinway, then went out on my own."

"And now you work at the Palais Garnier, and you are wanted by every high-profile pianist in the world."

"On good days."

I met his gaze for a moment and smiled. He'd relaxed, solidified. Without doubt an improvement on earlier.

He drained his coffee. "I'd better get to work. It's going to take me an hour or two."

"Are you sure I'm not keeping you from anything?"

"Not at all. Have you got another cloth? I'll clean the harp as I go. And a set of allen keys would help."

"I have both somewhere." The cloth was an easy find, the allen keys took a little longer. Once I'd unearthed them, Rémy disappeared into the living room with an enthusiastic smile.

I stared into the air where he'd stood, not really seeing anything. I wanted the harp tuned—of course I did—but I needed to be ready when he plucked the first string. Some sounds were more demanding than others, loud noises worse than quiet, the city bustle harder to manage than the organic stir of nature, and for some reason the odd unexpected sound broke through my defences completely. Like yesterday. But I wanted to play this harp and I wouldn't let my colours get in the way. I listened for that first note, but all I could hear was the soft scraping of what was probably an allen key.

"Can I have a bucket of warm water and another couple of cloths?" Rémy called through.

I flinched at his voice.

"I need to wash the strings," he added. "Years of sticky fingers have left a layer of grime, but we can probably get away without replacements."

"Just one moment." I gathered myself together and thoroughly cleaned out the bucket we'd used on the floor, then filled it, found some tea-towels and carried everything in.

He knelt before the harp, his tie and collar pulled loose, his sleeves rolled up above his elbows, the sinews of his arms flexing as he unscrewed the levers that changed the key at the top of each string. As I watched, there was something about him, something different, but I couldn't quite put my finger on what. That aside, and despite his initial strangeness, he'd been relaxed and easy company, and I had to admit, I was a little drawn to him. He looked up, grinned and nodded at my load. "Thanks."

"You're welcome," I replied, conscious I'd been staring. I placed everything on the floor by his feet, then headed back to the kitchen. I had more important matters to focus on. It wouldn't be long before the harp rang out, and I needed a job I could lose myself in. There was plenty to do—the utility needed cleaning before I could unpack the kitchen boxes, so best I get on with that.

I started work, vigilant for the first note, but it didn't come. The cupboards and shelves were covered in thick dust. That and my relentless listening made the cleaning laborious, my neck stiffening. An hour passed and there was still another cupboard to clean when Rémy came in.

"Fresh water?" He raised the bucket.

"Of course." I took it from him and stepped to the sink, allowing my shoulders to drop. There was no need to listen while he was here. As I poured away the grime, my phone buzzed against the draining board. Glancing over, I caught *Esprit Obscur* and *fin de contrat*.

"No," I muttered. Abandoning the bucket, I tapped on the screen and scrolled through the email.

"Trouble?" Rémy asked.

Esprit Obscur were not impressed with my work or my inability to return their calls. It wasn't really a surprise that they were terminating our contract. My designs had been consistently lacklustre—I'd never been able to interpret their branding requirements into something that jumped off the page. I just couldn't understand them. I put my phone down, closed my eyes and shook my head. They were one of my biggest clients and the account was worth a lot of money.

"Violette?"

"It's nothing. Just work." I rinsed the bucket, filled it with clean water and handed it over. But it wasn't nothing. Work was a part of my life that blended with the general disarray. I needed to pull myself together and produce some quality design.

We returned to our tasks, and once the utility shone, I unpacked the kitchenware, trying not to think about how losing Esprit Obscur would affect my bank balance, and trying not to think about the harp, even though every part of me stretched taut like one of its strings.

My head was in the cupboard by the range when the first note rang out. I rose and stared at the wall, running my eyes along the tiles, fixing on one and taking in the depth of its glaze, the shimmer of light on its surface. All it took was concentration, a rigid meditation that strained rather than soothed, and I would be fine. The note sounded again and again, no doubt middle A, each time vibrating at a slightly different pitch until Rémy was satisfied with the tone. The edge of my vision flickered in an indistinct halo as impressions attempted to unfold. I scrutinised the hairline cracks in the tile. Pressure built behind my eyes as I forced myself to focus, and the flickering dissipated, the impressions fading into nothing. Another note, then another, then two in combination—and no colours. Nothing.

Turning to the pile of kitchenware on the table, I redirected my attention to a mottled metal baking tray. I placed it in the cupboard and returned for something else, an old cake tin with a fluted rim. All the time Rémy's notes rang out without colour.

It was working. I was in control.

I transferred more of the pile to the cupboards, still wary, still concentrating on each item, my head throbbing. Rémy worked up and down the harp strumming octaves and intervals and... I was fine. I almost didn't need to make the effort. It was almost normal.

His tuning took form and the notes meandered into a delicate air. I smiled despite myself. It was the first time I'd heard the harp for years and the timbre was warm and mellow, familiar like evenings by the fire.

As I picked up a pile of plates, the tempo changed and the melody fell away to something rounded and sweeping. In my mind I could see Rémy sliding his fingers over the strings with deft precision, as though he were satisfied with his work and had launched into something accomplished to reveal the beauty and scope of the instrument.

I placed the plates on the worktop and leant back against the range rail to listen. The notes rolled and swelled and rippled—building and building again. I'd heard the arrangement before—perhaps not exactly, perhaps he improvised, but like the turning points in Tchaikovsky's ballets, the glissando evoked indescribable beauty, mysterious dreams and unexpected magic. It was startling and utterly, utterly heavenly.

Colour flooded my vision. I winced and gripped the rail, trying to centre on something—the wall on the other side of the kitchen, the ceiling, anything. I'd been careless. Each note flickered in its spectrum colour, muted by a gentle blue and then indigo—the bass notes of Rémy's chords. The resonance filled my vision and my hearing. My breathing grew shallow. What was I doing? I couldn't let this go any further. I should distract Rémy for a moment. I should ask him to stop.

I stepped toward the living room, placing my hand on the

wall to steady myself. Through my colours I could see Rémy seated upon the stool, the harp pulled against his shoulder, his fingers trailing back and forth across the strings. He tilted his head upward, his eyes softly closed, his neck lined, his face lost in concentration and rapture, the colours almost a part of him. The music continued, undeniably sublime, absolutely breathtaking, and then there was only colour—the senses by which I gained a measure of the world, by which I defined who I was, were saturated by shifting shades and tones that denied all other impressions, engulfing me, suffocating me. I struggled for air, my legs shaking, my head spinning. I needed to ask him to stop, but I could only rasp.

"Violette, what's wrong?" Rémy sprang up, the melody dissipating through the air, my colours fading as the notes reduced to nothing.

"Migraine," I lied, the word scraping from my throat as I stumbled toward the sofa. He caught my arm, steadying me as I sank into the cushions and dropped my head between my knees. I felt him sit down next to me.

"Is there anything I can do?" he asked, his voice a rich midnight blue.

"Quiet. I need quiet."

"Sure," he whispered.

I shut out everything but the sight of the thick rug pile shaping around my feet. As I studied the way the wool fibres lay against one another, the focus I needed to keep myself rooted to reality grew and my breathing settled.

Sitting up slowly, I turned my head toward him, forcing my expression into something I hoped was an approximation of normality. "I'm alright now." But anger twisted up within. I'd let my guard down, left myself exposed again, and now I had to make some excuse. My head pounded. At least I didn't have to lie about the migraine.

Concern lined Rémy's face. "What happened there?" he asked softly, his words colourless. I was in control again.

"It's nothing. The migraine caught me by surprise."

"Can I get you some water?"

"That would be good."

He disappeared into the kitchen, returned and handed me a glass.

"Thank you." I put on a reassuring smile and took a sip.

"For a moment there, you were almost white."

"I'm sorry, I really am fine now." The thumping in my head and annoyance with myself aside. I was always better when my colours were under control.

Rémy looked as though he were deciding whether to believe me. "Good," he said finally, and glanced at the harp. "It's all finished. I've tuned it to C. I guessed that would be an easier key to start in as you haven't played for a while. But if you'd rather go for another tuning, I can—"

"No. That's great. Thank you so much. I hadn't expected you to take the whole thing apart and clean it."

"It was a pleasure to handle such a beautiful instrument." His gaze swept beyond the window to the chateau, then returned to me. "Are you sure you're alright now?"

"Perfectly."

"Because I, uh, think I had better be off."

"Of course." I rose steadily.

Rémy stood up and studied me, probably for signs of imminent collapse. Forcing my irritation into purposeful, sound steps, I headed into the hall and turned to him. He'd done so much and he'd been so kind. "It was good to catch up. And thank you again for the tuning. Now I have no excuse not to play."

"Absolutely." He grinned as he pulled on his shoes.

I opened the door. "And come for another coffee sometime."

"Yes. If I can, I will. It's been..." He stared at me for a moment as though unsure what to say, his gaze intense, the light playing along his jaw on one side of his face. "It's been lovely to see you again."

We exchanged kisses, and as his cheek brushed close, I caught the delicate scent of myrrh and pine and earth after rain. We pulled apart and his mouth drew into a warm smile, his eyes shining.

"Au revoir," he said, and he strode off in the direction of the village.

The handle dug into my palm as I thrust the door shut behind him. I'd allowed my colours to completely overwhelm me. It was his playing—it had been incredible, and I'd not acted quickly enough. I'd listened instead of holding my guard, but I would not allow my synaesthesia to undermine my life here.

I strode over to the harp. It glowed from Rémy's care— the wood shone, the levers glittered, even the grooves in the twisted branches were dust free. It was so generous of him. I sat upon the stool and drew the frame toward me, my hands folding around the smooth wood.

With absolute focus I plucked a C, concentrating on the movement of the string, just the movement, just the vibration. The note rang out and nothing else. I plucked the string again and then once more a little harder. Nothing, no colour, just sound. Rémy's playing had caught me unawares, that was all.

I stood up, satisfied. I could do it. I could hold my colours away.

Chapter Four

Blackthorn, beech and briar hedgerows lined the lane, glittering with hoar frost, ornate against a canvas of incandescent sky and woven branches. As I strode along, the wind played about me, attempting to permeate my mountain jacket and woolly hat, but only managing to sting my cheeks and chill my legs where a single layer of denim was scant protection. It was already a cold year, but last night, after I'd returned from Foix with food and decorating supplies, the temperature had plummeted.

I passed Sylvie and Edgard's elegant old farmhouse, which despite the scaffolding, skip and builder's rubble managed to look as welcoming as I remembered. Along the lane, homes huddled closer until they formed pastel terraces three stories high, the shutters painted in complementary blues, pinks and yellows. I'd always walked this way with Maman and Papa for supplies on Saturdays, and this time Sarrat was no different.

It had been an exhausting week. Now that the house was unpacked to a functional level, today meant time to return to myself, time to exist without organising or cleaning or unpacking. I would start decorating first thing tomorrow.

As I strode onward, my thoughts circled to Rémy—his stunning playing, the rapture in his face as he drew his fingers over the strings, then my colours. I'd let my guard down too easily. The last two days had been much easier than Paris. I just needed to keep watch and I'd have my synaesthesia under control. I'd always managed to force the sensory overload away when it reared its head, apart from during the last couple of years, which had been so much worse. Being back in the quiet of Sarrat meant I would be able to manage again.

The clustered townhouses opened out and I paused beside the last one, the square bustling before me. The poste, the boulangerie-pâtisserie and the épicerie were all busy with people coming and going, calling to one another, laughing. Others were deep in conversation under the red-and-white-striped awning of the café.

I stiffened, waiting for the inevitable onslaught of colour, but the rhythm of the village formed a gentle lull, a reassuring murmur of the past, and the deluge remained mercifully absent. Realising my fingers were clenched into my palms, I loosened my hands and dropped my shoulders. But it wasn't only the worry of synaesthesia that had pulled my sinews tight, it was the magnitude of returning after all this time. I supposed it was expected to be nervous.

To my side, where the green swept down toward the pog, a group of elderly men bent together on the pétanque terrain, boules in their hands. I watched them for a moment before turning my gaze to the centre of the square and the thermal pool sunk into the cobbles, its steaming source rising constantly from the depths through a chute at the side then draining into the valley via a small stream that crossed the square, heading for the river. A group of children had abandoned their shoes and socks to paddle where the steps descended into the water, their parents looking on, talking with friends. A collection of old folk sat on the side, their legs dangling in, their eyes on the pétanque, as if they'd not moved since I'd left all those years ago.

I needed this, to be here absorbing this life, these sounds, my old normal. I could see myself playing in the deliciously warm water when snow had lain all around. I wasn't going to leave without wetting my feet.

Taking a breath of pâtisserie-scented air, I drew off my hat and headed for Boulangerie Amiel, receiving a few glances as I crossed the square. I was obviously something of interest—there weren't many tourists around between the summer and the ski season, and no doubt news of my return had spread.

I chose a pain de campagne and a pain aux noix and headed into the épicerie, tempted by the lavish window display of cheeses, strings of onion and garlic, and overflowing bowls of olives and artichokes. I picked out an Ariège goat's cheese wrapped in herbs and headed to the cashier. The shop was more extensive than I'd remembered, with plenty of fresh fruit and vegetables. It would make sense to stock up here next time, rather than at the supermarché.

As I scanned my card at the till, I felt a hand on my arm.

"Violette, n'est-ce pas?"

I turned to the voice—a tall woman about my age stood in front of me, her long straight hair draped over an open parka, a Scandinavian knit underneath. Her mouth was firm and her eyes were narrowed, assessing.

"Oui, hello?" I said.

"It is you. I heard you were back." The corners of the woman's mouth flickered up a little.

Her face held a glimmer of familiarity, and then it dawned. "Roselle! Of course!" I drew my hand to my mouth. She looked so different. "I can't believe it. I thought of you often over the years. I wondered if you'd moved away."

She shook her head. "Still here. No chance of getting out of this place. I intended to give you a few days to settle in, then make contact."

At a glance from the man waiting in the queue behind us, I picked up my bag. We drew to the corner by the deli jars and chocolate.

"But how are you?" she asked. "I wondered about you all these years. You know I wrote now and again, but I had no reply." The flickering smile was gone.

"I'm so sorry. Eveline was strict about correspondence. She thought it better I get on with my new life. But I'm well and it's incredible to see you." I examined her stoic face, not quite able to equate this woman with the grinning compadres who helped me dig up Sylvie's best flower bed to make mud pies. Not that Sylvie had minded—Edgard, on the other hand, had been furious. No doubt Roselle was thinking something similar about me, but her expression revealed nothing.

She shrugged. "Life happens. But, anyway, I have to pick up one of my kids in a few minutes and we're pretty busy for the next couple of days, but do you want to come around on Tuesday morning for a catch-up?"

I smiled. "I'd like that very much. Shall we exchange numbers?"

She nodded. "Let's do that."

She entered my number into her phone. We'd been the

only two girls of the same age at the village school, but our friendship had been much more than that—outrageous laughter, nonstop conversation, every moment spent together. I'd missed her so much.

"I have to go," she said. "I'll text you the address, but it's only just behind the square."

We exchanged kisses and she darted off. I stepped out into the bright autumn sunshine and stared after her. I hadn't been able to read her at all. Was she looking forward to Tuesday or was it a formality? Regardless, it would be good to catch up and piece together the broken connection.

Adjusting my shopping bag, I headed to the pool. The children were now sitting on the far edge, huddled together laughing. A stretch lay clear on the closest side between an elderly lady and Nico, his trousers rolled up, his feet dangling in the clear water, but most of him immersed in a newspaper.

Drawing in the sulphurous air, I sat down on the edge, pulled off my boots and rolled up my jeans. Nico hadn't noticed.

"Do you mind if I join you?" The low voice came from behind.

I twisted around. Rémy stood above me, dressed in the same clothes as yesterday, his eyes warm.

"Not at all." I smiled. "It's nice to see you again so soon." And it really was. I'd enjoyed his company yesterday. I moved along closer to the old lady.

He sat down between Nico and me, his legs folded before him, his dark curls sweeping one way and then the other as the chill breeze vied with the warm air that rose from the pool. "You look better today," he said, examining my face.

"I am." I would not let yesterday happen again, that was

for certain. I tugged off my socks and placed my feet on the warm cobbles.

He looked me in the eye. "Actually, I wanted to apologise for not being myself."

"I hadn't seen you for years—I thought you were probably always like that." The tease lightened my voice.

He laughed, the fullness around his eyes creasing. I smiled as I dipped a toe in the biting-hot water.

Rémy turned to Nico. "Monsieur Guérin."

Nico ignored him.

Leaning closer, Rémy waved his hand above the newspaper. No sign of acknowledgement. It hadn't taken much to gather that Nico was not the most observant person.

"I don't think anything is going to get his attention," I said as I eased my feet in, pulled them out and let them down again, the minerals immediately soothing my legs. "I'd forgotten how good this is."

I leant back on my hands. Relaxation spread through my body as I watched Rémy untie his well-made brown brogues. He pulled them and his socks off, rolled up his trousers and lowered his feet into the water. Propping himself onto his elbows, he angled his head back and closed his eyes. "You're right, this really is good. I haven't done it for years."

His sculpted neck flexed as his shoulders dropped, his lips pursing then relaxing. There really was something intriguing about him. I looked away over the pool. I'd always been drawn to men who were a suitable match on paper—career guys with a level of success comparable to my own at the magazine. Look how that had turned out. My long-term relationship based on our fast-paced Parisian lifestyle had fallen apart along with everything else. All that seemed shallow after being confined to my apartment with sensory overload for such a long time. But despite my attraction to Rémy, I had to admit I wasn't in the best of spaces for a relationship. I needed time to find my feet after Paris. Anyway, what was to say that Rémy was interested in anything more? I valued the beginnings of our friendship and that was plenty enough. "Thank you again for tuning and cleaning the harp," I said. "It looks unbelievable."

"Absolutely my pleasure. But how does it sound?"

I'd plucked one note. "Stunning."

He glanced past me, and I followed his gaze. The old lady to my side eyed me up and down, disdain swathing her face.

"What is that all about?" I asked Rémy softly.

He grinned. "I'm not quite sure."

She was looking at me as though I were mad. At my glare she turned away and so did I.

"Have I got breakfast all over my face?"

He pushed himself up, his shoulder close to mine. "Nope, you're perfect."

I couldn't help but notice the comment.

He glanced at the woman again. "Some people are just strange."

"I thought I'd get away from the stranger side of society moving from Paris, but first you, and now her." I unzipped my jacket—the heat of the pool had already warmed me through.

He smiled again. "Where did you live in Paris?"

"Rue des Fossés Saint-Jacques, in the fifth."

"I used to go to a club near there. Nice neighbourhood."

"Yes. My apartment was tiny, though, and the rent unbelievable. Coming back will be infinitely better. Here everything is so..." How to describe it...?

"So...?" He searched my face, a faint smile on his lips, like yesterday before he'd dropped his coffee.

"Paris is loud, full throttle, intense, but here the wind, the elements, the hot water bursting through the earth as it has for thousands of years—I don't know, it's raw, wild."

His smile was boundless now, but it was at odds with my explanation.

"What?" I asked.

"Nothing." He shook his head. "I agree completely."

I turned to the pool. Ripples rolled from the stirring of our legs. We were silent for a moment, the warmth soporific, my eyelids heavy.

"But why did you leave all those years ago?" he asked after a while. "I must have been a teenager and you were—"

"The latest village gossip?" Everyone had been so kind, but the nonchalant warmth I'd taken for granted from our friends changed in an instant to refrain, caution and sorrow. Yet even this subject couldn't pull me out of the delicious calm.

"No, it was never gossip. I remember my parents—they were devastated at your loss. I was too young to fully under-stand the repercussions. A car accident, wasn't it?"

I nodded, liking the fact he wasn't stepping around the subject as most people still did.

"Where did you go?" he asked.

"To Paris, to live with Maman's cousin, Eveline. She believed it would be easier for me to cut my ties with Sarrat, so I didn't return."

"That's hard."

I glanced at him. A shadow of indignation covered his face, his mouth fixed, his jaw firm. Strange how other people reacted. Usually with more affront to the situation than I felt.

"I missed Sarrat, but so many years have passed, and I'm back now."

"But if you missed it, couldn't you have returned before?"

The children lowered themselves into the pool again, setting the surface in motion.

"The house became mine when I turned eighteen, but the Durochers lived there, and they were in their eighties. I couldn't force them out." I knew what that felt like. "And I didn't want to come back and live somewhere else, or even visit, always wanting to be home."

"I get that. Well, you finally made it." He ran his feet back and forth through the water. "But what do you do? Or what will you do now you're here?"

"Design. Brand identity mainly." Esprit Obscur came to mind and my chest tightened. "I'm freelance, which will suit living in Sarrat."

"From your voice I'll take a guess you don't enjoy it."

I hadn't realised my tone had changed. "I used to, but now... I don't know. I've lost interest and my work suffers." To put it mildly. If I didn't get organised after this break, I would be lucky if I still had a business. "What about you? Are you staying in Sarrat for long?"

He paused for a moment. "I might be... for a little while."

I thought back to the articles I'd read about him a while ago. "You were something of a socialite, if I remember."

He screwed up his face. "I got dragged around by my friends. But it was always the music for me, and the perfectly tuned instrument. I worked for the Opéra de Paris mainly, but travelled too, New York, Tokyo, everywhere in between."

He spoke as if it were behind him. "Don't you still work?"

"It's been quieter lately." He looked away.

Had I hit a sore spot? But he'd been so enthusiastic about the harp. "I don't think I need to ask if you like your job."

He smiled. "I guess it was pretty evident yesterday." He studied me with soft, intent eyes, his gaze lingering for longer than friendship allowed, the space between us imbued with more than air.

"Yes, it was obvious," I replied. "So, what drew you to tuning rather than anything else?"

"The colour of music," he said.

I stared at him and swallowed, unable to think of a reply. But he was only being allegorical, and I was being ridiculous. I needed to respond. "What do you mean?" I asked stiffly.

"Sound can proportionally correlate to colour. If the frequencies of individual notes are multiplied and trans- ferred to the visual spectrum, the note A will be orange, B yellow, C green and so on."

My throat tightened as I recalled my reaction yesterday.

"I see tuning as a perfect balance of colour," he added. "If each note holds an absolute clarity of tone, the most beautiful music can be created, and that drives me in my work."

"I can understand that." I could wholly understand, but I would rather not dwell on it. I shifted, took a more comfort- able seat on the cobbles and paddled backward and forward, searching for a way to change the subject. "It's been good to see you again," I managed. "Do you want to exchange numbers?"

"I'd like that, but I've not got my phone." His brow narrowed and he gazed across the water, his silence clearly stating that he did not wish for contact in another way. The relaxing effect of the minerals dissipated. It looked as though I had misinterpreted his signals. A couple sat down on the other side of the pool and sent me steely glances. I was popular today.

"Can I ask you something, Violette?" he said, all serious now.

"Of course." I stared into the eddies, our legs refracting at odd angles.

He swirled his feet close to mine and turned his head toward me. I faced him. We were too close and neither of us pulled back. I could feel something between us. The curiosity and attentiveness in his eyes indicated that the sensation was mutual, but his rebuff had spoken otherwise. I didn't understand.

"When the wind blows," he said, "what colour do you see?"

My stomach twisted. "What?"

"The wind, what colour do you see when it blows?" he repeated, his face expressionless.

"I... what? What kind of question is that?"

He smiled a little. "Just a normal kind of question."

I raised my eyebrows. What harm could it do? It was just some silly game. "Blue, very faint, delicate like forget-me-nots," I answered truthfully, thinking of a gentle breeze, although I rarely saw the colour of the wind nowadays. "What has that got to do with anything?" I looked around the square, wanting to think about something else, but he watched me steadily, and I couldn't shut out the weight of his gaze.

"When water trickles, what colour do you see?"

"What are you getting at?" I pulled away from him and drew my jacket around me.

He didn't move. "Violette, indulge me."

I shrugged. "Silver." But I didn't want to continue.

"Yesterday, when I played the harp, what colours did you see?"

I stared at him. "I... what do you mean?"

"You know what I mean."

Rémy didn't know anything about me, and he couldn't know that. No one knew. The houses around the edge of the square, the people, the bustle, it all pressed in on me.

"Violette. What did you see?"

This wasn't right. I shook my head and pulled my legs out of the water. It took forever as I rolled down my jeans, peeled my socks over my damp feet and pushed on my boots.

"Violette?" He was still watching me attentively.

I don't know how he had the notion, or why he was being so persistent, but I wasn't going anywhere near the matter. I glared at him as I pushed myself up. "I saw nothing. Absolutely nothing at all."

I seized my shopping and strode home.

Chapter Five

The sour bread and creamy goat's cheese melted in my mouth, simple and delicious. I savoured the flavours as I stretched my legs along the length of the sofa, pushing my laptop to the side. Warmth poured off the stoked and blazing fire, enhancing the lingering effects of the thermal waters. I was unfurling here, undoing years of restraint.

The view was something else too. Low cloud hung above the pog, a dense slate disappearing into the valley. The sun slanted from the side, lining the formation with fiery gold, a stark contrast to the deep-green box trees that clung to the slopes. My gaze settled on the chateau, its rigid parapets, its sombre stone, and for a moment the shadow swathing its walls tugged at me.

Pulling myself away, I opened my laptop and, conscious to control my senses, clicked on the local radio. After a moment Dejango Reinhardt strummed softly and I sank into the cushions, my colours absent. Without the constant bustle of the city, my synaesthesia was barely perceptible, and I could relax, enjoy myself, live. I took another bite of bread.

But Rémy this morning—I cringed thinking of my overreaction to his questions about my colours, but his persistence had been, well, uncomfortable to put it mildly. He'd been so insistent when he knew nothing about me. I must have let something slip when I'd reacted to his playing, although I had no recollection of what. His awareness felt like an invasion—no one knew about my synaesthesia, and I wanted it to stay that way. One thing was certain—I wasn't going to be drawn on the matter again.

I could see him now, that soft but intent gaze, that strange combination of relaxed ease and intensity. I was attracted to him, I really was, but I'd misjudged his body language—although he had been giving off completely mixed signals. But there was no use dwelling on it. There had to be something else to think of... Roselle, she was here. It would be so good to catch up.

The track on the radio changed and the song I remembered the other day reverberated through the room, the tempo unhurried, the echoing notes forming mysterious harmonies. *Lo Boièr*—that was its name, *The Oxherd*. The melody was sublime arranged like this. I sighed and glanced at the harp. I wanted to play it, and *Lo Boièr* would be a good piece to start with—nothing too complicated.

I pushed the remains of my late lunch aside and walked over. Catching my fingers around the ribbon, I drew the key from the shoulder and placed it on the floor, blue velvet pooling around smoke-grey metal, all traces of rust removed by Rémy's cleaning.

Lo Boièr played on softly as I sat down upon the stool, a bright tenor singing the confounding words. It was a guess, but the first note of each verse sounded like an A—or a G.

Hopefully the song wouldn't require a key change, or I would have to adjust the levers. I'd tackle that if it came to it.

Tipping the harp to where it held a natural balance, I drew myself in so the wood lay gently on my shoulder, my knees supporting the frame. Maman surrounded me once again, but the memory was more comforting than raw.

The song chanted on. I raised my hands, all my attention on the strings—there would be no repeat of yesterday. The next verse began and I plucked an A to its opening chord. The note resonated through the room, not quite in harmony with the radio but close enough. Pressure built in my temples at the sound, but nothing more.

Lo Boièr continued. I steadied my fingers and plucked the C, the B, the G, floundering a little, missing the beat. Yet, despite me, the harp rang out with a sublime timbre. As I relaxed into the music, the pressure in my head eased. I smiled. What colours, Rémy? No colours at all.

The unhurried verses carried on and I managed more accuracy, my wrists curving away after each note with renewed familiarity—I'd played *Lo Boièr* many times all those years ago. Yet for all its beauty, something about the melody sounded... wrong. Not the music itself—the harp was stunning and the radio rendition enchanting—but something. I listened intently as I played. There it was, a disparity of pitch between the harp and the radio, the two slightly at odds with each other. Perhaps the harp had fallen out of tune since yesterday—it wasn't unknown after an intensive clean.

Lo Boièr ended and the presenter's voice filled the room. I tipped the harp onto its feet, stepped over to the laptop, clicked off the radio and searched for a video of the C major scale. Rémy had tuned the harp to C, so it should harmonise with the video. I carried the laptop over and placed it on the floor by the stool, then positioned myself around the harp once again.

The scale was instinctive, even after so many years, sunk into my subconscious through endless repetition. I walked my fingers between the highest and the lowest notes, but still the discrepancy between the harp and the laptop remained. Surely the strings couldn't have all gone out of tune by the same degree overnight. Perhaps it was something to do with my laptop. I would have to pick up a digital tuner next time I was in town.

I clicked off the video and attempted *Lo Boièr* without accompaniment—at least the strings were in tune with one another. My timing was out, I plucked numerous false notes and there wasn't a hope of me organising my fingers to attempt a chord, but there was something there. At the refrain I sang softly, "*A, E, I, Ó, U*"—I loved that part and, it dawned on me, I'd played the whole thing without a hint of colour.

I continued for a little longer, then hung up the key and went back to the sofa and my laptop to renew my decorating and DIY competency. A glimmer of orange caught my eye through the glass doors—a coat, bright under the cloud cover, twisted along the path to the chateau, and beneath it more movement—a group of people climbing the pog.

It couldn't be, could it? Were the musicians still playing this time of year? It was lovely there in summertime, but I could never figure out why either Maman with her small shoulder harp or Papa with his classical guitar had climbed two hundred metres to play with the core musicians every Saturday, no matter the season or the weather. By the looks of it, the tradition continued.

A smile shaped my lips. A hike to the chateau would be

perfect. The cloud cover had solidified to unbroken grey, all apart from a line of hard blue along the horizon. There would be rain, but hopefully it would hold off for a while. I banked the fire, switched on a lamp and hunted upstairs for my ski jacket, warmest boots and headtorch. Once kitted up, I headed into the bitter air. I'd thought the cloud cover might have brought some warmth. Obviously not.

I passed Sylvie's and took the drover's track just after her property, my feet twisting on the debris of the ancient walls as I descended into the valley. Woodland enveloped the path near the base of the slope, shrouding much of the light. It was a relief to break out onto the grassland. I crossed the meadows and strode along the side of the river. There hadn't been much rain lately and it flowed in low, steady meanders. The wind picked up a little and blustered about. I glanced around, wary of my open position—the result of spending too much time penned in between city buildings.

At the foot of the hill, I joined the old stone track that snaked back and forth across the pog, the alternation between ancient cobbles and exposed bedrock familiar, as though I'd not left. Stalwart and evergreen box arched overhead, the gaps between the branches affording brief glimpses of the chateau—a grey wall or part of a turret appearing then disappearing.

I glanced behind me at the indistinct path under the trees. Despite the familiarity of my surroundings, a thread of unease wound through me. I'd never felt even the slightest worry here before. The opposite, in fact—the pog had been a safe haven, a harbour amidst the massif, a warm place to meet friends. I ignored the sensation, tucked my hands in my pockets and pushed upward at a steady pace. I was reasonably fit, but I was soon out of breath. The people who lived here eight hundred years ago must have been a hardy breed.

As I broke out of the trees, the cobbles dwindled to mud and scree. The path grew steeper, turning only now and then, the last of the thicket giving way to scrubby grass and sheer limestone slabs that necessitated a scramble. The wind built, carrying scraps of a disjointed melody from the chateau. I paused and examined the sky. The cloud had densified into rotund billows lit from beneath by a glimmer of sunlight low on the horizon. I knew the signs—the weather was turning, and quickly. It hadn't been evident in the flat grey earlier, but it was clear now.

Wind buffeted into me. I was exposed, but this sort of weather wasn't unusual here, and mountain safety had always been a way of life, a constant consideration. I would need shelter. I gazed back at Sarrat and the barn nestled in the trees. I was about halfway up the pog, but it was much further back across the valley to home. If I returned, I would be unprotected on the floodplains. I glanced up at the chateau. It would be better to head for the refuge of the stone walls, and after all, the musicians were there.

Clambering around a limestone promontory, I headed upward. The wind bored into me. I pushed my weight against the gust to balance myself as the last of the sunlight vanished, the cloud darkening to charcoal. Thunder rumbled through the valley. Here it came.

As I doubled my pace, the wind rose to a shrill clamour, distorting hints of music as it skirted the pog. I focussed on the path with absolute determination to hold my colours away. A spear of lightning split, a thousand forks tearing the sky, followed by an almighty blast of thunder, and the rain began, but still I maintained control of my synaesthesia. I flinched at a thud to my side, unable to make out anything through the squall. Probably a fallen branch.

I never felt scared. No, that wasn't true, I felt scared a lot, but never due to the environment, be that the mountains or the streets of Paris at night. I was scared by what I couldn't control in myself. But now my skin crept. I was being ridiculous. It was the wailing of the wind—the sound was unnerving—and the air, it was darker, almost heavy. I drew my hood down tight and hurried up the last incline.

The chateau loomed ahead, its ramparts rain-soaked and shrouded in dusk. I stumbled along its flank toward the entrance, steadying myself against the wall as the rain drove into me. My jeans were already soaked through, and water trickled under my neck and seeped around my wrists.

Wrapping my hand around the doorway of the keep, I hauled myself in, the torrent ice-cold on my fingers. Lightning and thunder broke across the sky again and rain lashed down harder. Something that might have been *Lo Boièr* came from the far end of the courtyard. The musicians sat on rocks where the keep narrowed—the most sheltered point. They huddled together over their instruments, playing them at ridiculous angles as human weather shields. I could hardly believe they were making a coherent sound, and I couldn't understand for the life of me why they were trying. It wasn't exactly the *Lo Boièr* I'd expected, courted by the breeze and the evening birdsong. And, still, I couldn't shake the feeling of foreboding, not even here amidst the protective walls.

I moved in from the doorway and sank down where an outcrop of rock formed a barrier from the weather. The dusk aside, the air seemed thick, as though a miasma filled the keep. I peered toward the musicians and tried to listen, but thunder built to a constant rumble and the wind squealed as though it were composed of too many tones forced into an ear-splitting dissonance. I rammed my hands over my ears with little effect as I pushed away flickers of encroaching colour. But storms like this were quick to pass, especially in this wind, and the musicians obviously thought it would be alright. All I needed to do was sit tight and wait it out for a few minutes.

The light in the chateau dimmed further, and the air coagulated into something dark and traitorous. I had the ridiculous notion not to breathe, as though if I inhaled, I would take in fear itself. But, of course, I had to. The stifling air poured into my lungs and spread through my body, pulling my muscles taut as though fright were a possession of my blood. My throat constricted and my skin pricked with cold sweat. This was too much. I was experiencing some kind of panic attack and I needed to get home, dry and safe. I took another breath and started to choke.

The musician with the orange coat looked up, an accordion in his hands. He bundled his instrument under a cover and jogged over.

"What are you doing here?" he yelled above the wailing.

All I could make out in the murk was his massive fur-edged hood and full beard. I tried to reply but drawing in more of the fetid air made me choke again.

"Come on," he called, and pulled me by the arm across the courtyard, through the chateau door and into a blast of wind and rain. He drew a torch from his pocket, the light glaring through the dusk.

"Need shelter," I managed.

"No," he shouted, "we have to get you down."

He tugged me toward the path, but panic took hold and I

yanked my arm back. "What the hell are you doing?" I choked out across the storm.

Lightning forked toward us, the thunder deafening, much too close. We needed cover.

He stepped toward me, rain streaming off his hood. "I know this sounds counterintuitive," he yelled, "but we need to get you off the pog. Just trust me for now. I'll explain later."

It was completely counterintuitive. We needed the protection of the chateau. Lightning broke above us, so close I could feel the heat.

"Please," he said, his voice imploring, "trust me."

I tried to piece together why it was alright for a band of crazed weather-worn musicians to huddle in the chateau in a storm and not me, but my lungs burned and the sincerity in his voice seemed genuine.

"Alright," I yelled.

He grabbed my coat as though he were afraid I would get away and pulled me down the slope at a run, his torch lighting the path, the wind and rain buffeting us. He only slowed where the bedrock formed steeps and we had to inch down sideways.

We descended into the relative shelter of the box arches. My breath heaved, but the air was clearer here, and the fear sank away. I wanted to walk but the man pulled at my elbow. We ran out onto the meadowland, the deluge blasting us.

As we approached the woods, the storm lost its heart, the rain pouring rather than thrashing, the wind less of a wail and more of a bluster. The man slowed to a walk. I paused, leaning forward on my knees to regain my breath. I shouldn't have been so stupid, panicking in the chateau—and we should have stayed in its shelter.

"Come on," he called through gasps.

"What on earth was all that about?" Standing up, water poured off every part of me. I drew my headlamp from my pocket and clicked it on as I followed him into the woodland. It was completely dark now.

"You saw what it was like up there," he said, turning back. "The place is..." He thought about it. "Dangerous. It's ridiculous to go up there in a storm." His voice was firm, but his eyes were round, kind, the laughter lines in the corners accentuated in the torchlight.

I stopped and glared at him. "Then what was the merry band of musicians doing?" The whole situation was ridiculous.

He stared at me, his mouth open. Then, as though he didn't know what else to do, he said, "Joël Rabasten," and extended his hand.

I passed him and carried on up the path. He followed and drew to my side.

"Rémy's eldest brother," I said. "I remember you." Joël was about the same height as Rémy, but he carried more weight—he always had been stocky, but now it could have been the bulky coat that hung almost to the knees of his waterproof trousers.

"That's me."

I glared at him again. "Violette Romèu."

"I heard you were back."

No doubt from Rémy.

"Look," he added, "the pog is a dangerous place. It's best you keep off, especially if the weather draws in."

"I spent my childhood up there—I know what it's like. And I know how to shelter in a storm. We should have stayed in the chateau until it blew over." Why had he been so absurd?

He studied my face with his large brown eyes, and rain dripped off his nose. "Well, it's different now. Just take my advice." He stopped. "I'll have to leave you here. I'm going back for my accordion."

I shot daggers at him. "So, it's alright for you to walk back up there?"

"You'll have to trust me on this one."

I strode on up the hill, shaking my head.

"Nice to see you again, Violette," he called after me.

I didn't look back.

Chapter Six

Rain angled into me as I trod onto the road by Sylvie's. Lightning flickered to the faint roll of thunder, but the heart of the storm had moved away. Even so, I could barely see, I was so utterly drenched. My trousers clung to my legs, water ran down my neck and back, my feet squelched against my boots, my socks had deserted me to curl up in a corner somewhere, and now I'd recovered from our charge down the mountain, I was very cold.

A dark form stood in the shadows where Sylvie's property joined my own. The light of my torch illuminated the figure as I approached.

Rémy again. This was not a good moment.

"What are you doing here?" I was too cold to hold the defensiveness from my voice after this morning.

He looked me up and down as I drew closer. "I can't believe you've been out in this."

I strode past him. "You're not the first Rabasten to make that comment today."

"What do you mean?"

I could hear him following me down the path. "Joël was pretty insistent I shouldn't be at the chateau," I snapped, still confounded by his behaviour.

"You were on the pog?" Astonishment dripped from Rémy's voice.

I halted at the door and turned to face him. "Why is that so inconceivable?"

"Violette, you should keep—"

"You're barely wet." He had no coat and only a little rain mottled his shirt. "Where did you come from? I didn't see a car."

He ignored me and picked up my hand. "You're shivering. We need to get you indoors."

"I'm absolutely freezing." I fumbled in my zip pocket for the keys, opened the door with numb fingers and stepped inside, water trickling from my coat to the tiles. Rémy followed, and for a moment I considered asking him to leave. I didn't want to have more of this morning, but I was being ridiculous. If he mentioned my colours, I'd brush it off, and anyway, I was too cold to think clearly about it. "I need to get to the range," I stammered as I kicked off my boots. The fire would have died down by now, and I needed warmth.

"I'll get you a towel." Rémy disappeared upstairs.

"Make yourself at home," I muttered as I dripped through the living room. In the kitchen, I pulled off my jacket and dropped it to the floor, every part of me stiff with cold. Hanging myself over the range, I pressed my numb hands into the warm ceramic. My fingers defrosted a little, but my clothes were too wet for the heat to penetrate.

"Here," Rémy said from the doorway. He held out a bath towel and my robe.

Forcing my legs to move, I hobbled over and pulled the

bundle out of his hand. "Thanks," I replied through chattering teeth.

I pushed the door closed and staggered back to the range. As I stripped, my clothes peeled away, leaving my skin damp, red and goosebumped. I dried every part of me, then pulled the band from my hair and pressed out the water, the warmth of the range eventually easing my shivers.

I wrapped my robe around me and tied the belt, then cracked the door and peered through. Rémy crouched in front of the hearth, tending the fire. His visit was poorly timed, but he'd been considerate with the towel. As I stepped in, he turned his head and smiled—a small but exquisite smile that drew me. A notion I immediately pushed away.

In a moment he rose, strode over, pulled the rug off the back of the sofa and wrapped it around my shoulders. "Come on." He took my arm and led me to the fire, which he'd stoked to a fury.

"It seems the Rabastens are telling everyone what to do today." My words were stiff, my face muscles not yet thawed.

I sat down on the hearth and drew the rug tight around my shoulders, the warmth of the fire seeping through the mohair. Despite being much too aware of Rémy's presence, the beat of the rain and the faint thunder and lightning were almost soothing now I was on the other side of the glass doors. But I couldn't let go of Joël's senseless behaviour. "What right does Joël have to go ordering people off the pog?" I said, just about speaking coherently.

"Since my family built the chateau in the eleventh century, on our land, he has every right." He strode into the kitchen. From the sound of rushing water, he was filling the kettle.

"Oh, come on," I growled. "There's always been unlimited access."

"Well, now it's not a good idea." He came back in and looked me over, then sat down on the other side of the hearth, picked up my feet and placed them on his knees, wrapping his hands around my frozen toes. "These are much too cold," he said, his eyes flicking to mine.

Staring at him, I tried to work out if this was an act of friendship, but his gaze was intimate, the gesture even more so. I wasn't sure how comfortable I was with it after this morning, but his hands were deliciously warm, his fingers gentle as they surrounded my feet. For a moment, as I watched, there was a solidity about him, as though he were more substantial than his surroundings, as though his skin, opaline in the firelight, and the curls that hung over his forehead were more... present. I turned away and gazed into the flames. My imagination was particularly erratic today, what with panicking in the chateau and now this.

Anyway, I wasn't going to let this afternoon drop. "Why is it not a good idea to go to the chateau?" I asked, trying to hold on to my annoyance as his warm hands melted me.

He looked up and smiled, his eyes clear and faceted. "Once upon a time," he said, "before there were words..."

I frowned. What tangent was he going off on now? He was so capricious—I couldn't pin him down.

"Before there was music," he continued, "before there existed you or me, there was nothing but a sound."

Recognition dawned. "Oh, come on. I've heard this one before." A recurrent campfire story. Every child around here knew the old Occitan creation myth.

Shifting my feet a little, he drew toward me and placed his forefinger on my lips, the indication for silence clear, his proximity overwhelming, the scent of him subtle yet heady and intoxicating. After his confusing signals this morning, I had to raise some boundaries, but I didn't move.

"Before there existed you or me," he repeated, his finger remaining on my lips, "there was nothing but a sound."

I took in a breath to ask why he was giving me a rendition. He shook his head. I shut my mouth and frowned. I really couldn't figure him out.

"There was nothing but a sound," he continued, "a sound that broke into an absolute harmony, reverberating into the nothingness, creating all that was—the stars, the planets, the sun, the moon and creatures of a sublime nature. Every aspect of creation coalesced in one euphony." His hand returned to my feet. My lips tingled.

"The creatures existed in peace and joy and unending glory, serving the cosmic manifestation. But a few of them became curious. What if they took the great notes of the Harmonie and combined them in unexpected ways?"

As I watched him speak, his attention alternated between my feet and my eyes.

"The creatures began to experiment," he continued, "indulging in the power of their creation, and they became independent, autonomous from one another, great creators in their own right. But their tonal combinations were ever so slightly different to the Harmonie, and for the first time ever a Désaccord—a clash of dissonant notes—rang out."

The low singsong of his voice drew me. I shifted back and leant against the stonework by the fire. Lightning flickered in the distance, nothing more than flares in the darkness beyond the doors. My eyes sank to the motion of his lips.

"And for the first time, fear descended on the creatures. The Désaccord flowed through creation, carrying pain and confusion. The Great Harmonie could not allow such a thing to taint its manifestation, but the creatures had become elated with power and would not cease their creation. So the Harmonie cast the creatures and the Désaccord to a place of their own, the earth. And around the earth the Harmonie formed a void so that whatever the creatures should do, they would not affect the rest of existence.

"And so the creatures dwelt on the earth, and with them the Désaccord grew to a mighty power that bore fear and pain and confusion. But the Harmonie did not forsake the creatures. It dwelt with them, always offering joy and peace and fulfilment. The Désaccord raged against its abundance, wishing to cast the euphony into disarray, wishing to hold ultimate sway over the creatures that formed its first notes.

"In time, some of the creatures desired to return to the original manifestation. They found ways of drawing the Harmonie into their lives, they created great temples to its sublimity, the geometric architecture so perfect that the Harmonie dwelt amidst the walls, the formidable force of the Désaccord shrieking and wailing without. And for each of these temples they appointed a song, a song that augmented the harmony of that place, a song passed down through the generations as a key, as a formula to evoke the Harmonie, should the people have need."

Rémy drew in a steady breath. "And still today the Désaccord rages against the Harmonie at these sacred places. And when the two forces meet, the rumble of the Désaccord is heard throughout the land."

Thunder boomed in the distance, deep and sonorous. I smiled at his fortunate timing.

He grinned. "And still musicians play the appointed

songs in the sublime places built by the ancients." He placed my feet down.

"So what are you saying, Rémy? That the Harmonie and the Désaccord are battling it out on the pog?" I smirked.

"I'm not saying anything," he said softly. "I just told you a bedtime story."

"It was lovely, if incongruous, to be reminded of it, and my feet are warmed through. Thank you." I stood up, feeling more like myself. "I'm going to get dressed."

"I'll make tea," he called. He certainly was making himself at home.

Upstairs I attempted to brush my damp hair into conformity. Rémy made noises in the kitchen below. He really was something different, his thoughtfulness, that ridiculous story.

I threw on loose sweats and a long-sleeved top and headed down. He'd found the tray and was lowering the tea things onto the hearth, his shirt and waistcoat tight across his shoulders. My soaking things had been hung on the airer before the range.

"You really didn't have to do all this," I said. It was a lot considering we'd only just met again. "And I hope I'm not holding you up for anything."

He walked over, picked up a tendril of my damp, unruly hair and tucked it behind my ear. "No, believe me, you're not holding me up at all."

I stared at him, shaking my head. If I'd had any doubts about his body language this morning, there weren't any now. I scrutinised his face, the smooth surface of his cheek where it ran into stubble, the hint of a line above his chin. "Let's have tea, then." My words were rigid.

We sat back down on the hearth either side of the tray, the fire hot on my back.

Rémy poured and handed me a cup. "I promise not to drop it this time."

"Well, that will be an improvement on your last visit," I replied.

He smiled.

I brought the tea to my lips and savoured the fragrant linden, the heat warming every last part of me as my gaze settled on the harp. "You know, *Lo Boièr* was on the radio this afternoon and I tried to play along, but the strings seemed to be slightly out of tune." At least I could get this sorted.

He placed his cup down and strode over to the harp. I braced myself. I would be fine. I'd proved it earlier.

Supporting the frame with one hand, Rémy ran a glissando across the strings, then looked over at me. I maintained my poise, wincing only slightly as I held my colours at bay. There was something about his technique—it had more impact than mine.

He narrowed his eyes. "What's wrong with my playing, Violette?"

"Nothing at all. It's stunning. But what about the tuning?" If he was going to get insistent about my colours again, he could leave. I wasn't going there.

Rémy ran his fingers up and down the strings in varying intervals, then took the key from the shoulder, made a few adjustments and hung it back up. My head throbbed. I focussed on the rug, not daring to remove my eyes until the reverberations had dissipated. Even so, there was no colour.

He walked over and bent down in my line of vision. "What's going on?"

I looked up at him with the smile I'd perfected after so many years. "Nothing. What's going on with the tuning? Did it loosen after the clean? But all the notes are out to the same degree."

He shook his head, picked up his tea and sat down on the sofa, crossing one leg over the other. "It's fine. There were only a couple of very minor adjustments, but yesterday I tuned the harp to A at 432 hertz. I always tune to that frequency, and I hadn't considered doing it differently."

"What has that got to do with anything?"

"A is usually tuned to 440 hertz, occasionally 438 for certain concert orchestras. In 1940 it was decided to standardise the tuning of all instruments to A at 440, but it's wrong, the decision was made in error."

"I don't understand." I sipped my tea, relieved he'd obviously moved on from my reaction.

"Middle A naturally resonates at 432 hertz. When it does so it is mathematically constant with the patterns of the universe. At that level it vibrates with the golden ratio and with the Schumann Resonance—the electromagnetic beat of the earth—Plato's musica mundana. Music is, at that level, one with the planet and all life. But if A is tuned to 440, music is out of tune with everything around it, including the listener—we all have our own internal music, the noise of being alive, our musica humana."

The details went over my head, but I got the essence of his explanation. "Why would music be set at a different frequency than how it mathematically should be?"

He shook his head. "I'm not certain. When it's set like that, even the most beautiful music creates disharmony, and it's impossible to fully appreciate. I didn't consider that you might be playing along with the radio, or anyone else. I should have said."

"Well, now I understand. And it may be my unpractised ear, but the harp sounds stunning."

He smiled. "If you want me to tune it back to 440, I can certainly do that."

"I think I'd prefer music in its purest form." I could go without playing to the radio.

His smile grew into a grin for a moment and then fell away. "But, Violette, I have to ask you something."

This sounded like earlier today. My chest constricted. "Rémy, don't go there."

"I didn't mean to upset you this morning, which is why I came over," he said. "But you see things when you hear music, don't you?"

I stared at him, unable to move. I just needed to skirt the question, to brush it off.

"You see colours and maybe shapes," he continued.

"I, uh…" I needed to pull myself together, but I could only think of the suffocation of my colours, the submersion of my senses, the loss of myself. "What gives you that idea?" I choked out.

He uncrossed his legs and leant forward, his elbows on his knees, his cup between his hands. "And perhaps it's not just music and sound, but other senses mingle too. Violette, you have synaesthesia, don't you?"

Words abandoned me as I opened my mouth to reply. "What?" I managed eventually.

"Perhaps your senses blend in other ways—a smell causes a colour, or you feel the pain of another person's injury."

I stared at him. No one knew. Absolutely no one knew. "Why do you think that?" I stammered.

"A few reasons. Your reaction to me playing the harp initially. But after yesterday I remembered our parents talking together. I remember your maman saying you had synaesthesia."

My parents had known, of course. "But why would Maman talk to your parents about it... and why would you remember after all these years?"

"Because I have it too. I have well-developed synaesthesia. I guess our parents were comparing notes. I remembered because my synaesthesia was, and still is, important to me. Anything connected to it fixes in my memory."

He had what plagued me. I didn't know anyone else who suffered from the disorder—I'd never wanted to. But still, it seemed improbable. "What is the likelihood of two people in one area...?" Part of me sank away. I'd inadvertently admitted to the condition.

"It's not that uncommon," he replied. "Twenty per cent of the population."

Scouring his face, I attempted to take it all in. He must have mastered his synaesthesia, living in Paris, working with music. "But how do you cope—do you have any problems holding it back?"

He frowned. "Hold it back? Why would I want to do that?"

"Well, obviously, because of the disruption it causes, the interference to your senses. Not being able to perceive the world as it should be is... a struggle." That was an under-statement.

"No, I never hold it back. It's part of me and it doesn't interfere with anything. It augments my senses. When I hear sublime music, I also see colour and form. It's stunning—

another level of experience bringing me closer to the essence of music."

I shook my head, completely unable to comprehend. How could it not interfere with his life?

He peered at me. "That's it, isn't it? That's what you do. You hold it off, you hold it away."

I gazed at him, my shoulders rigid, tightness extending along my neck into my jaw. It was all so close to the bone. This was a part of me I'd hidden for years.

Incredulity spread over his face. "Violette, what does it matter? You're talking to someone who knows exactly what you experience. I know how it feels."

My breathing grew rapid. "Yes, I push it away."

"And it caused the migraine the other day?"

I nodded.

"But how can you hold back your own senses?"

"I do it because I have to. Because it completely over-whelms me."

He placed his cup on the floor, sat back and ran his hand over his forehead into his hair. "But you can't live like that, denying yourself."

He was making biased assumptions about me. I shouldn't have said anything. "What right do you have to judge how I should live?"

"Because I know synaesthesia. I know it's a gift, not a limitation."

"It's not a gift if it's tearing you apart." The anger in my voice was clear.

He stood up and stepped toward me. I rose in opposition, my eyes blazing, and he paused.

"It doesn't have to tear you apart," he said gently.

His proximity drew me, but at the same time he was

much too close to who I was, and he was judging me. He had no idea how I felt, what I had to deal with. "I don't want it," I growled.

"Violette, trust me. I can help you with it."

I shot daggers at him—the second Rabasten telling me to trust him in preposterous circumstances today. "No." It was almost a shout.

He took a step back.

"I don't want it," I repeated, my words cutting like knives. "Just because it works for you doesn't mean it is in any way, shape or form for me. You know nothing about me."

I strode over to the rain-spattered doors and stared into the darkness, attempting to see past the reflection of the fire, the lamps and Rémy, the occasional distant flicker of lightning illuminating the clouds beyond. I wanted my synaesthesia to be gone with every fibre of my being, and I didn't need this now, or ever. More than that, I didn't need to be angry—I'd made my decision, I just had to communicate it to Rémy clearly.

A calm certainty spread through me. "I don't want to talk about the matter again," I said, my voice firm. "If you can't respect that, please leave."

I turned around to see Rémy out, but he was gone.

"Rémy?" I called. I hadn't heard the door open. I walked over to the kitchen and peered in. He wasn't there. He must have left quietly while I stood at the window. After everything, a short sharp "fine", or "I'm going now", would have been... normal.

I poured some more tea and dropped into the folds of the sofa, the upholstery still warm where he'd sat. After the intimacy of the evening and Rémy's awareness of my colours, his misplaced judgement cut into me. But he had synaesthesia—

he knew what it was like to see the world in a different way, although we obviously had individual experiences. It was a shame he couldn't keep his opinions to himself. He had no right to tell me how to live.

I took a sip of tea and gazed into the fire. The logs glowed amidst the curling, sedate flames, just like when I'd sat in Papa's lap on the hearth, staring into the embers as Maman played the harp, her ballade swirling in crimson and copper, twisting and fusing with the flames. I'd never thought there could be anything more beautiful than firelight, Papa's warmth and Maman's music sending spirals through it all.

But in Paris my colours were something else—black, jagged, scraping, tormenting. The noise swamped me, suffocating my senses, making me want to be someone else, making me long to die. I would struggle through every day, every moment at school, every trip on the metro, stuffing my ears with tissue, trying to hide from the assault.

The occasional sound would bring such beauty—the song of a blackbird, a street band with flute and violins. But even those harmonies would inundate me until there was nothing left of myself.

It had been foolish to mention it to Eveline—or perhaps it had been the best thing I'd ever done. I'd stood upon the checkerboard marble in the hall staring at her closed study door, trying to decide what to do. It was quiet indoors and the murk that had bombarded me all day had washed out to a grimy veil, but it still covered me like a disease, my vision dull with it, my mouth thick with an ugly taste, my skin crawling with its texture—nothing like the colours Rémy drew from the harp. I dropped my collège bag onto the floor, glad to release the weight. It couldn't have been more than a year since I'd left Sarrat, and it had been a bad day, one of the worst. My colours had tainted everything, dark and rank. I hadn't been able to concentrate, at times I'd barely been able to see, and I'd fought the nausea back. The teacher scolded me continually, to the point of ridicule by the other children, and I'd been scared, so scared that it wouldn't get better, that it would only get worse.

Eveline was Eveline, but she was an adult, a lawyer, someone many people trusted to deal with all sorts of things. She would know what to do.

I knocked.

"Come." The impatience was steel nails in her voice.

I shuffled into the elegant study under her gaze. She sat behind her desk in her signature classic Chanel, her hair styled into a chignon, never out of place. I wished I could shrink from those cheekbones, that pitiless gaze.

"Violette. How may I help you?" she asked. "Corette has been taking good care of you, no?"

Corette prepared my meals as quickly as possible before disappearing to see her boyfriend. I nodded.

"Well, then?"

"I... uh... haven't been well."

She raised an eyebrow. Even now I could see the small creases upon her forehead, the disinterest in her eyes. She tapped a finger on her desk, once. A sign I needed to get to the point.

"I... I can see things, colours. But it's too much, I can't think straight. It's hurting me." The words spilled out.

She stared at me for a moment, her eyes probing. "Violette," she said, her voice poised. "People who see things have options. They may be given medication to help them function properly. If that does not solve the problem, if they remain ill and unable to be useful members of society, they may be taken into care."

It took me a moment to take in her words. I stared at her as they sank through me, and for the first time my situation was clear. I knew medication didn't work—I'd tried it for the headaches that came with the colours, it just made everything a thousand times worse—and I knew what care meant. I'd seen a documentary on mental institutions, the clinical white walls, the patients in varying degrees of torment, restrained if necessary, all freedom withheld. In that short moment I saw my life as two possibilities, only one of which I could bear.

Meeting her gaze, I swallowed and cleared my throat. "You misunderstand me—I think it may be my eyesight. Could I have an appointment with the optician?"

She studied my face for a moment, nodded, then returned to her work. "I'll have Corette organise it."

She didn't look up.

I walked out, steadily, calmly, all the way to my room on the third floor. I'd sat on the bare boards in the corner between the wall and the foot of the bed, and I'd stared at the cracked edge of the armoire. It took most of the night experimenting, forcing, and as the sun rose I was exhausted, but I had succeeded in my goal. I had a degree of control over my colours. I'd made myself normal, and I never spoke of the matter again. Until today.

My stomach tightened. What right did Rémy have to pull things out of me that had found their place, that were private, that had a reason to be concealed? Of course, most people suffered from synaesthesia without problems, sometimes not even realising they experienced the world differently, but it wasn't for me. It was no longer enjoyable, it was an affliction, a weakness, a lack of self-control.

And Eveline, she had been hard but fair. Of course, she could have handled my situation with sympathy, but that hadn't been her way. She'd shown me how to cope, not just with my synaesthesia but with the intense Parisian world—work hard, dress well, be organised, use the influence of society. And she was right. I'd forged a successful career on those principles, culminating with my appointment as design director at *De Nouveaux*—all until I'd no longer been able to hold back my colours once again in the jarring Parisian cacophony. Then I'd retreated into my apartment and freelance work until I took my chance to return to Sarrat. And here, back in the peaceful home I'd never wanted to leave, I could control my colours with ease.

Rémy was wrong. I could lead a full life without synaesthesia. I already had done, and I would continue to do so.

E

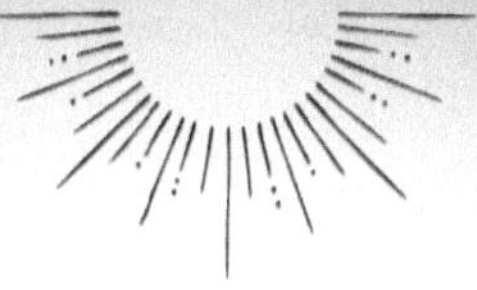

The Désaccord cast a shadow upon all that was, and with it came opposites. Shame met glory, pain met solace, and conflict met peace. But the Désaccord bore its own exquisite sublimity—not sublimity in the sense of the Harmonie's celestial manifestation but sublimity in the sense of indulgence, overarching yet fleeting pleasure, pleasure that begged to be satisfied, pleasure that had to end, and when it did end, its absence left a fathomless void of despair. With the Désaccord came such music—music that could express the greatest unbound joy and the darkest deathly depression, music that could move so far in both directions, it would rip the soul apart.

Chapter Seven

The harp lay against my shoulder, shifting a little as I adjusted my position to reach the strings. The last couple of evenings practising *Lo Boièr* had paid off and the melody was beginning to sound coherent. I still played single notes, no chords, but my tempo was regular, and I used most of my fingers. Moreover, I'd not seen a hint of colour for days, and I'd not had to think about holding my synaesthesia away. It was as if the resolve I'd built after the argument with Rémy had forced it into acquiescence. That and the delicious tranquillity of Sarrat.

"*A, E, I, Ó, U...*" I sang the refrain under my breath. It was peculiar—the vowels were played on the same note with the exception of the U, but each letter reverberated in a different way—the A in my throat, the E at the back of my mouth, the I in the roof, the Ó formed by the whole mouth and the U coming from deep within my chest. Each had a distinct quality, a unique timbre, and discovering the intricacies of the melody, I was drawn to the song over again.

I finished the verse and placed the harp down. It had to

be time to leave for Roselle's. As I rose and stretched my limbs, I was unable to restrain a smile. The room looked stunning, the parquet and the wood trimmings chestnut brown against the brilliant-white walls, the limestone hearth a happy intermediary. My bedroom was finished too, also in white, the bed for the moment the only furniture, a breath of minimalist fresh air. My arms ached from the repetitive effort of painting, but the place was coming together.

The scent of Bourbon roses and lilies pervaded the house. The two bouquets I'd positioned on the floor before the glass doors had been gifts from old friends who'd called in to wish me well. I'd also received a bake from Agathe, Nico's wife, which I'd guiltily accepted still not remembering them from before. Everyone had been so welcoming and I already felt at home. Life here was a huge improvement to Paris.

I strode to the hall and put on my mountain jacket and boots, unable to ignore the crate of proofs I'd stowed under the coat rack. I still hadn't completed the updates for Sablier. The sooner I finished, the better—I couldn't risk losing another client—then I could forget about work for what was left of my break.

Grabbing my bag, I left the house. As I turned onto the road, a car drew up and the window rolled down.

"Violette! I'm glad I caught you."

Joël Rabasten. Without the hood I could make out hair the same shade as Rémy's, but shorter and flecked with grey. He grinned and his eyes shone.

"Hello, Joël." My voice was clipped. I'd still not made sense of being dragged off the pog. But his grin was infectious, and I tried not to smile back.

"We're getting together for Sunday lunch at the farm.

Yves is down and we all want the chance to catch up with the village's newest arrival. Will you come?"

"What? As long as I don't go up to the chateau?"

He laughed. "Even if you go to the chateau, you're still welcome."

I studied his face. I wanted to see his family again. His parents, Clémence and Armel, had always been so lovely, as had his brothers. I wanted to see Rémy too. I had half hoped I'd bump into him again, wanting to know if he could respect my decision about my colours, but there hadn't been any sign of him. His persistence on the matter perplexed me—what did it matter how I saw the world? Despite all of that, there had been something between us, and surely we could clear the air.

I smiled. "I'd like that very much. Is there anything I can bring?"

"Just yourself. Make it about one."

"Alright. Thank you. I'll look forward to it."

"See you then." The window wound up and he pulled away.

If Rémy could keep his opinions to himself, it would be nice.

I strode to the village at a fast pace in an effort to warm myself—the sky was leaden and the cold wind biting. At the épicerie I bought a bouquet of dahlias, roses and milk thistle, then followed my phone to the address Roselle had texted through. It was one of a row of pastel townhouses behind the square, hers cream with sky-blue shutters and a sanded door and frame that appeared in mid-repair. I knocked and waited a few moments.

The door swung open. "Violette," Roselle said, the

corners of her mouth flicking up for a second, her eyes hard, the rest of her face lifeless. She really had changed.

"For you." I passed her the flowers.

"They're beautiful. Thank you," she said, her voice too even, but she almost smiled again. "Come in, let me take your coat and we'll go through to the kitchen."

I gave her my jacket, which she hung by the door, then she led me through a narrow hall, past the stairs to a modern kitchen extension flooded with light from patio doors and Velux windows. The room was a dichotomy of sleek lines and children's artwork taped everywhere.

"It's a lovely house," I said, feeling a little nervous. It had been such a long time and Roselle seemed so closed.

"We're still renovating, but it works for us. Have a seat." She nodded to the table. "I'll make the coffee."

I pulled out a chair and sat down as she busied with the kettle.

"How long have you been here?" I asked.

"Oh, about four years," she replied without turning around. "You know, I missed you terribly."

I stared at the back of her head. I hadn't expected that.

She brought over the coffee tray without meeting my gaze. "It took me ages to get over you leaving. I know it must have been terrible for you—so much worse—but I just wanted you to know." Her eyes flicked to mine as she placed the tray on the table and sat down opposite.

Her words stabbed at me. Even now it was hard to think back to those endless days without her. I'd never fitted in at school in Paris, my southern accent ridiculed endlessly, even when my colours weren't causing problems. I used to imagine she was there, sticking up for me, or that we were both in my room at Eveline's, exchanging secrets as we always had. "I missed you too—more than I could bear to think about. And I'm sorry we didn't keep in touch."

"How did you cope?" she asked.

"It was tough, but I adapted. I guess I shut down a fair bit in order to survive."

"Makes sense."

I didn't want to dwell on it. I gazed up at the children's paintings on the cupboard doors. "So, you have kids. And I guess that makes you possibly married?"

"Right on both counts. I have two children, Gy, seven, and Édith, five." She nodded to a home-print stuck to the fridge.

I got up and looked more closely. They were all blond hair, cheeky grins and sparkling eyes. "They're adorable. Absolutely gorgeous."

"Most of the time."

As I sat back down, she passed me a coffee and offered me a plate of jewel-coloured macarons. "Help yourself."

I chose pistachio. "And your husband?"

"Pascale. He's a good dad, a committed Garde-Moniteur du Parc."

"Well, you've obviously done something right." I smiled.

"What about you?" she asked after a pause.

I sat back and wrapped my hands around my coffee. "No children. I'm single and happy." The sensation of Rémy's finger on my lips stole into my mind. I ignored it. "I ended a long-term relationship a while ago. I wanted to come back here when the opportunity arose, and he was Parisian to the core. He wasn't the right person anyway."

"Have you been in Paris all this time?"

"Most of it. I studied graphic design there and worked my way up to design director at *De Nouveaux* magazine, though I became freelance in readiness to come back here." And so I could survive the constant barrage of colours. I took a bite of my macaron, the earthy nut, sweet honey and mellow cream breaking on my tongue. "Absolutely delicious," I said through the mouthful.

"*De Nouveaux*, that's impressive. It has to beat being a cashier at the bank in Ax." She stiffened a little and ran her finger around the rim of her cup.

"Not your ideal career?"

She looked up, her face expressionless. "It wasn't my first choice when I left uni. But, hey, the bills have to be paid. Pascale isn't exactly earning reams and the area has a low rate of employment. I guess I should be grateful."

I nodded. "What did you study at university?"

"Fine art with a focus on sculpture."

"You were always the one with paint under your nails and glue in your hair."

Her mouth tightened. "I carried on with sculpture for a year after uni, put together an exhibition that was quite successful. But then I... well, you know how it is. The bank was a more reliable source of income."

I sipped my coffee. I should have felt grateful for my job, the reasonable income, the flexible hours, the creative element, but I could barely push myself to return my clients' calls. What was the matter with me? I looked around the room again. I would have expected to see something of Roselle's creative past, her artwork on the walls, some sculpture, but there was only sharp-edged furniture and the children's pictures. There hadn't been anything in the hall either.

Roselle stared into her coffee and the silence drew out. I

needed to say something. "It's lovely to be sinking back into village life, and to have the peace and quiet."

She nodded, seeming relieved to have another topic of conversation. "I guess it makes a change from Paris. We heard from the estate agent exactly when you were coming home. You know what it's like here."

I nodded. I hadn't expected any different. I would be of interest for a few weeks and then I'd become part of the scenery again.

"Which is why you had Pascale's father at your house with the harp the moment you arrived," she continued. "Sorry about that."

"Oh, Nico?"

She nodded. "He's not the most sensitive person."

"I'd noticed," I replied with a laugh. "But it wasn't a problem. I was happy to have it back." So Nico was Pascale's father. All I had to do now was place Pascale in my memories.

"Good. I thought it might have been difficult for you."

"Sylvie thought the same. But I want to honour the past, take what I can from it and move into the future."

"I think," she said, meeting my eyes, "that is the perfect attitude."

Was this the "poor you, aren't you doing a good job coping" subtext that I received occasionally, more often when I was younger—the attitude I used to wonder at as the years passed and it all became distant? But Roselle didn't give that impression. It was more of an agreement, a consolidation. I nodded. "Absolutely."

I took a sip of coffee and thought of us playing by the river. "Remember how we used to spend every moment together?"

Again the flickering lips. "Swimming in the summer, playing with the others."

I grinned. "Sleepovers where we never slept. And what about when we bivouacked in my garden? We ended up abandoning camp, terrified by the hooting eagle owls."

"And when we created a den on the pog, the boys were desperate to get in. They launched regular raids to force us out," she replied.

"And you know what we always used to say to each other?"

She nodded, and for a second there was an actual smile.

"You betta," I said in English, complete with the terrible American accent we always used with the phrase. "Come and play tonight—you betta. Give me that chocolatine—you betta. See you tomorrow—you betta."

Her eyes sparkled.

The front door slammed and I winced, wary of my colours, but there were no impressions. Roselle's face closed up as footsteps sounded along the corridor.

"Forgot my lunch. I've got to get up to—" A head appeared around the door. "Violette! Lovely to see you." Presumably Pascale strode over wearing the grey Parc National uniform, his face clean and friendly, his blond hair cropped close, his physique that of a climber. I rose and he towered above me.

"Great to see you." We exchanged kisses, and as we drew back I studied his face. "There is something familiar about you, but I can't put my finger on it."

"We used to be in the same class at school," he said.

I put that in context, grasping at names and faces from the past. Still not coming up with anything, I glanced at

Roselle, hoping she would elucidate, but she gazed out at the garden.

Pascale stepped back and flinched as though he'd been stung. "Sorry," he said, turning away. He fiddled with something in his ear and pulled it out. A hearing aid. "The damn thing's been playing up all morning." He tapped it and placed it back in. "Anyway, can't stop. I'm on my way to record golden eagle numbers at Trois Seigneurs. I should be there already."

He looked at Roselle. "Where's my lunch?"

"On the side," she replied without looking at him, her voice hard. I glanced between them discretely. There was obviously something going on.

"Violette, let's catch up soon." His smile was forced.

"I'd love to," I said, as if my overly cheery voice would break the tension.

He grabbed his lunchbox, headed out, and a moment later the front door slammed.

Finally, I placed his name. "That wasn't tiny little Pascale Guérin, was it?"

Roselle nodded, her shoulders relaxing.

"Pascale who used to cry whenever Madame Robert spoke harshly to him?"

"The one and the same," she said without much feeling. "We both studied at the Université de Toulouse. We got together in our first year."

Now I could place Nico. "Well, Pascale grew." I couldn't quite believe it. "But he lost his hearing?"

She nodded. "A few years ago."

I shook my head. Despite everything I went through, I couldn't imagine a world without sound. "What happened?"

"Sudden sensorineural hearing loss. He woke one morning and he was deaf. As simple as that."

"What, nothing caused it?"

"Nothing that anyone could tell. It came back partially in one ear, but not in the other and not enough for him to manage without the hearing aid."

"I'm so sorry." I couldn't think what else to say.

"He manages," she replied.

We sipped our coffee in silence for a moment, a silence that yawned for seventeen years. I wanted to fill it, to find everything we'd lost, everything life had taken away.

"I can't believe the musicians are still playing up on the chateau this time of year," I said finally.

"Every Saturday." She pursed her lips. "All year round, no matter the weather."

"I can see why they play in summer—it's great fun and the tourists love it—but I can't understand why they continue in winter."

"It's the Rabastens taking tradition to extremes," she said. "And some of the others."

"Talking of Rabastens, I re-met Rémy the other day. He came in and tuned the harp."

"What?" She looked at me quizzically. It was a relief to see a different expression on her face.

"You know, Rémy Rabasten, the youngest Rabasten brother."

"Yes, of course I know who you mean, but you couldn't have. Haven't you heard?"

"Obviously not." What was there to know about Rémy that had passed me by?

Her eyes narrowed. "He went missing five years ago and he's not been seen since."

I stared at her. "No. I don't think so. Or he's back, because he did a great job with the harp."

She shook her head. "It must have been one of his brothers. There's a good resemblance between them."

"Well, I also met Joël the other day, and I saw him this morning. He certainly didn't look anything like Rémy."

"There's Yves. He's most similar. They're all musical, but Yves and Rémy made a career of it. Yves plays lead violin for the Orchestre Symphonique de Paris. And then there's Noé, but he's more like Joël in appearance, although taller. He lives in a house on the edge of their farm, married. His kids are at school with mine."

"No, it was definitely Rémy."

"Come on, Violette. Didn't you hear about it? It was all over the news." There was a hard edge to her voice now.

I shook my head. I hadn't heard anything. Then it clicked. "You said five years ago?"

She nodded.

"I was in Quebec. I went over for six months to help launch the magazine there." I was curious now. "What happened?"

Roselle's face clouded and she stared around the room for a moment, as though she didn't want to broach the subject. Then she took a breath. "I don't think anyone knows exactly. He was involved in some goings-on at the Paris Opera, infighting, that sort of thing. Rémy didn't turn up for work one day, and no one had seen him. They began a search and tracked his car down to the other side of the village, the parking area for walking to the chateau."

I nodded, wanting to know more.

"His car was left there and that was it. There's not been a sight of him since. It was said at the time that perhaps he disappeared to get away from his high-pressure lifestyle, but if so, why would he leave his car here?"

He must have been through something major to disappear for so long. It would explain him saying he hadn't worked much recently. But if he'd not seen his family in five years, why was he spending so much time with me? "Well, I guess he's back then," I said.

"Violette, for goodness' sake, don't go around saying things like that," she snapped, her face drawn into a scowl. "If he were back, we would have heard about it. His mother, Clémence, is distraught—the whole family are cut up."

"But I—"

"You can't just waltz in here after all these years expecting everything to be the same as it was, the perfect Sarrat of our childhood." Her voice was almost a shout now. "There are people who this really affected. Evidence was found that questioned Rémy's state of mind. Some people think he's taken his own life."

I gaped. It wasn't her mistake about Rémy—that was understandable—it was her vehemence. I was no longer the hopeful friend. I was the intruder, the stirrer, the enemy.

"No, it must have been Yves who tuned your harp. I think he's back home at the moment." She shook her head and glared out the window.

Glancing warily at her, I finished my coffee. There was too much beneath the surface and I'd become the target. Perhaps if I changed the subject... something... anything... to bring back that glimmer of a smile. "How are your kids enjoying school?" I tried. "Are the class sizes still small?"

She turned back to me, all closed up once more. "I'm sorry, Violette, I have some jobs I really must be getting on with." She piled the things onto the tray. "Perhaps we can continue another time."

I stared after her, speechless as she carried the remains to the sink then busied herself rinsing the cups. Our reunion was clearly over. I scraped back my chair and stood up. "Well, don't worry, I'll let myself out." I strode into the corridor, grabbed my jacket, pulled the front door open and stepped out onto the street. No footfall behind me, no words, nothing. I closed the door and walked away, too stunned to think.

At the square, I slumped against the side of a house. A midweek emptiness shrouded the place, steam drifting from the pool toward the café, where only a few deserted chairs and tables stood outside. A solitary elderly couple, well dressed against the weather, crossed the cobbles arm in arm. The cold seeped through my clothes. I pulled on my jacket, drawing it tight around me. I don't know what I'd expected from Roselle, but that really hadn't gone well. She was struggling with life, or herself, or something, and she obviously hadn't heard that Rémy was back, but even so, her reaction had been scathing.

I swallowed against the lump in my throat. I could see the tears in her eyes when her maman had scolded her for ruining her new dress. She'd worn it to the river when she'd been told not to, and she'd slipped in the mud, coating herself to the chest. I'd held her hand all the way back to her house, glaring at the other children who'd stared in shocked silence until smiles had taken shape in their faces. And, before that, when she'd had money from her grandfather, she'd insisted we spend it together on chocolate. We bought as many bars as we could from the épicerie, then hid in our den and ate until we were sick. We didn't use the den much after that.

A man hollered across the square at the couple, pulling me out of the past. The young Roselle was replaced by her face moments ago, the contempt after I'd mentioned Rémy. But what was Rémy playing at? He'd made his family suffer through a vanishing act, so something significant must have happened. And he'd kept his return quiet. Perhaps he wanted to avoid the public eye. Roselle had said his state of mind was in question—he'd been erratic when we'd first re-met, but he seemed fine now, completely sure of himself. The whole thing was a mystery, and my curiosity was piqued, but no doubt he would explain everything at lunch on Sunday.

Chapter Eight

I ran the roller over the wall where my bookcase had stood all that time ago, a fresh streak of white replacing the garish yellow the bedroom had acquired in recent years. Every painted wall, every fresh surface, every filled crack flooded the house with light and possibilities.

There was little over a week to complete the rest of the barn and I was pacing along. I'd had an early start, picking up more supplies first thing, and I'd already given Maman and Papa's old room a coat. If I kept on, I could finish both bedrooms and prep the hall and landing today. But my thoughts repeatedly returned to everything that had happened at Roselle's yesterday. Surely her reaction hadn't been surface irritation. She'd seemed submersed in a very dark place. And Pascale's hearing loss... So many times I'd blocked out the jarring hustle of Paris, desperate for silence, but the thought of not being able to hear familiar voices, or music, or the rustle of leaves—it was inconceivable. All of that had been taken away from him. Yes, he had a hearing aid, but a digital amplification of the world couldn't be the same.

Stopping mid-roll, I stared at the stippled surface. Did I deny myself a sensory experience when I pushed away my colours? But hearing and synaesthesia were completely different—hearing was a normal sense, synaesthesia was a distortion that took me to the edge.

I still hadn't experienced any colours since that evening with Rémy, and although it was early days, it appeared I'd mastered the disorder once again. It was a huge relief not having to always be wary, not having to focus constantly or struggle through repeated headaches, but it was also... disconcerting, I supposed. There had been so many changes lately and I needed time to adjust.

Paint dripped off the roller onto the dust sheet and I turned back to the wall, glancing through the window to the garden. The dull cloud cover drained the undergrowth of colour. It just looked cold. I noticed a movement to the side. Edgard crouched by a flower bed in his and Sylvie's garden. I still hadn't greeted him and, the recluse that he was, he probably wasn't going to come over here.

I swapped the roller for a brush and worked paint into the corners, seeing the line of Rémy's neck in my mind's eye not for the first time this morning. His disappearance was intriguing. My thoughts had returned to him constantly and I'd only resisted trawling the internet to find out more because of the notion I'd be prying, but my resolve was faltering. There was no reason I shouldn't be as informed as anyone else. In fact, I had more reason than most.

Releasing a sigh, I placed the brush down. I needed lunch, and most of all I needed to stop thinking. Hopefully finding out some facts would put my mind to rest. I stepped out of my overalls and headed downstairs, shaking out my limbs in the process.

After cleaning myself up, I made a thé au citron and grabbed some bread and butter, then settled at the table with my laptop and entered *Rémy Rabasten disappearance* into the search.

The results consisted of reports from newspaper and gossip sites. I scanned through an article from *Le Monde* that included a publicity photo of Rémy, his curls brushed back, his mouth straight, his neck strong. A confirmation that I had the right Rabasten, not that I'd ever questioned it. But considering the piece had been written over five years ago, he'd not changed much. I took a bite of bread and skimmed through the article.

The disappearance of Rémy Rabasten is the latest in a host of intriguing events surrounding the Palais Garnier and the Opéra national de Paris. After Bénédict Roy's stunning composition Les Profondeurs du Monde *provoked critical acclaim, with reports of the audience having been "stunned" and "enraptured", the orchestra was thrown into confusion by infighting and the sickness of several members. A few days later, Roy passed away from a heart condition. Rabasten disappeared only weeks after his close friend Roy's death.*

I'd been so absorbed by the magazine launch in Quebec, I'd missed all of that. I sipped my tea and clicked on an article from *Le Figaro*.

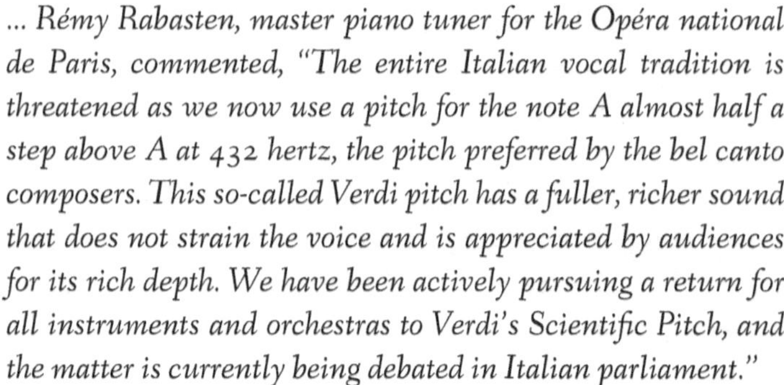

... Rémy Rabasten, master piano tuner for the Opéra national de Paris, commented, "The entire Italian vocal tradition is threatened as we now use a pitch for the note A almost half a step above A at 432 hertz, the pitch preferred by the bel canto composers. This so-called Verdi pitch has a fuller, richer sound that does not strain the voice and is appreciated by audiences for its rich depth. We have been actively pursuing a return for all instruments and orchestras to Verdi's Scientific Pitch, and the matter is currently being debated in Italian parliament."

He really was committed to this 432 tuning. But apart from Rémy the other day, it was the first I'd heard of the matter. Returning to the search results, I scanned the titles. *Mystery at the Opéra de Paris* from *Le Parisian* proposed that attempts of ancient rituals, performed in the depths of the Palais Garnier, were connected to the death of Bénédict Roy. I raised my eyebrows, but there was no doubt that people messed around in the catacombs near there—they always had.

I clicked on another picture of Rémy outside a red-carpet event at the Palais Garnier. On his left stood a tall man with an attractive, youthful face, and on his right, a shorter, overweight man who'd made a failed attempt to look well dressed. The caption read, *left, Alex Chaufourier, assistant music director of the Opéra national de Paris, centre, Rémy Rabasten, master piano tuner, right, Bénédict Roy, composer.*

Continuing with the search, the same information repeated over and over. Rémy certainly led an interesting life, but there wasn't much beyond what he and Roselle had told me. I snapped the lid down, still burning with curiosity. I would just have to wait until the weekend. It would be better to hear what had happened from Rémy in person, anyway. I needed something to distract me. Stretching my legs would help. I'd see if Edgard was still outside.

As I headed into the hall and put on my coat, I pushed away thoughts of Rémy by scanning the walls to assess their need for filler. One particular indentation by the study door caught my eye. It was slightly larger than the others, but flat so it hadn't stood out. I pulled up my zip, stepped over and ran my fingers across the broken plaster. It crumbled a little. I was sure I'd been here when the hollow had been made, but I couldn't quite grasp the memory. It would come, no doubt.

Outside, I strode up the path. The cloud bore down low and heavy, promising rain. The storm on Saturday had cast another layer of leaves over the front garden, although a few still clung to the branches. I would need a rake, and at some point, a shed to put it in. But all of that would have to wait.

Edgard was still in the garden, kneeling on an old cushion, his silver head bent low, his fingers in the earth. I called his name and hurried to their drive to meet him.

"Violette." He rose slowly and walked over with a stiff stoop.

There were a few more lines on his stern face, but he wore the same grown-out stubble and still held an air of shagginess. A grimace of a smile inhabited his face for a moment. "So glad you're back," he said as we exchanged kisses. "You've certainly grown."

I laughed, relishing in his years-ago familiarity. "I haven't heard that one in a while. I think I stopped growing about ten years ago."

"How's the decorating?" he asked.

"Monotonous, but I'm getting there."

"Good, good. That house needed a lick of paint. You're not still wrecking flower beds, are you?" He looked warily back to where he'd been working.

"No." I smiled. "I stopped that a little while back too."

He replied with a sort of huff that I interpreted as a laugh.

"Oh, Violette," Sylvie called as she came around the side of the house carrying an armful of building rubble. "Lovely to see you." She threw the rubble into the skip then headed over. We exchanged kisses. "I'll try not to get dirt on you, dear. How are you settling in?"

"Don't mind me," Edgard said. "I've got a bit more to do, then the garden's set for winter and I can hibernate by the fire with a book."

"Nothing's changed there, then." I smiled.

"Nope, never will." He walked back to his bed.

"So, how is it all going?" Sylvie asked.

"The decorating is getting there. Oh, and I met up with Roselle yesterday and I've had an invite to the Rabastens' for Sunday lunch."

"Lovely. You're getting back in contact with everyone."

"Roselle seemed a bit... stressed."

She studied my face with those confident, caring eyes. "Difficult visit?"

"You could say that."

She wiped her hands on her trousers. "Give her some time. She's been through a lot in the past few years."

"Oh?"

"Their first child, Théo, they lost him down by the river maybe five or six years ago. One minute he was with them, the next he was gone. It was presumed he'd drowned, but his body was never found. The poor thing was only four years old."

I gaped at Sylvie, her words cutting through me. I couldn't comprehend what it must be like to lose a child. I saw Roselle's ten-year-old face again. She'd been so carefree. It seemed none of us had the chance to remain innocent, unaffected by life's onslaughts. Dear Roselle. "I had no idea," I managed.

"She won't talk about it, that's how she is. But I think she makes it harder for herself."

I nodded. But the timeframe didn't fit. "She must have been young when she had Théo."

"She became pregnant in her first year of university. She and Pascale did a great job getting through it all with a baby in tow, and afterward her sculpture really took off. But Théo's death knocked them both. Pascale got himself together after a while—I suppose he had to go to work—but Roselle just stopped and turned in on herself."

Gazing into the bushes, I tried to take it all in, vaguely registering Sylvie talking about Pascale and Nico, then, "You look pale, Violette. Tell me you've been getting some fresh air."

I pulled my thoughts back to Sylvie. "Uh, yes. I had a walk to the chateau on Saturday and I've been stretching my legs between painting sessions." Hopefully that would appease her.

"I'm glad to hear it," she said. "But, dear, I don't think it's a good idea to go up to the chateau at the moment."

"Not you too." I scrutinised her face. "What's wrong with the chateau these days?"

"Has someone said something to you?" she asked.

"Joël Rabasten. He told me to leave the pog. He even came back down with me."

She took in a breath. "I don't know what the Rabastens think they're doing up there. It's not a good place anymore."

"Places don't change. It was a bit creepy, but the weather didn't help."

"The Sarramauca." She peered at me. "You know the old folk tale?"

"The evil mist that suffocates people while they sleep?" I raised a disdainful eyebrow.

There came a groan from the flower bed. "Get a grip on yourself, woman," Edgard hollered.

Sylvie shot him a glare.

"A load of old rubbish," he murmured into the soil.

She turned back and shrugged. "I don't know what else to call it."

I stared at her for a moment. Sylvie, the sensible one, the rock. This wasn't right. She wasn't going to unravel before me. "You don't believe that," I said.

"Of course she doesn't," came Edgard's cry.

"No, not really." She let out a fragile laugh. "But perhaps the Sarramauca was only ever the name for something people didn't know how to explain."

I released a breath. That was more like her—finding the logic.

"All I can say is, it used to be a beautiful place, and now it's different, unwelcoming."

"Oh, come on." Even this was too much. I didn't want it —from her of all people.

"I'm serious, Violette. Please don't go up there, give the chateau a miss for the moment. There are plenty of other lovely walks."

She meant it. Her expression was clear. My chest tightened and for a moment everything swamped me—Rémy's opinions and his disappearance, Joël's insistence on the pog, Roselle's contempt and the hell she must have gone through with Théo, and now this. Perhaps Roselle was right—perhaps I had expected everything to be the same, a part of me yearning to return to our childhood idyl. But it was clear now, so much had changed.

Chapter Nine

In the days that followed I rose early, turned in late and spent the hours between painting, filling and sand-papering until my shoulders ached and my fingers stung. I managed to finish the bedrooms, the hall, the landing and some of the study as I listened to music or old films. When I needed a break, I drifted to the harp and experimented with *Lo Boièr, Se Chanta* and some of the other old songs. I still hadn't been bothered by my colours. It was certainly a relief, yet the disturbance had been so consuming for the last few years, and now it wasn't. I couldn't deny there was a space within me, and pushing on with the decorating helped fill it. By the time I drove to the Rabastens' for Sunday lunch, I was glad to have the afternoon off and looking forward to the company.

As I pulled up in the farmyard the old house formed part of the autumn-tinted fields and forest that enveloped the mountainside. Parts of the walls were inlaid with grey stone, other parts were painted and supported by massive oak beams. The place held a solid, enduring quality, as though it would always be there.

I climbed out of the car with a bottle of Mourvèdre in my arms, then straightened my skirt, tucked my hair behind my ears and strode across the dirt yard to the farmhouse, drawing in the scent of leaf mulch, fungi and mud.

Laughter rang out through the worn wooden door as I approached. I gripped the Mourvèdre tighter, preparing myself to see Rémy. I'd been preoccupied with his disappearance, attempting to make sense of everything, and it would be a relief to have an explanation. But more than that, in the brief time we'd spent together, we'd built a sort of momentum that, after our argument, had suddenly ceased. I hoped Rémy could see past my synaesthesia so we could continue where we'd left off.

The door opened a little before I had chance to knock. A girl and a boy peered out, one head above the other, both with caramel curls and shining eyes. The girl giggled and placed her hand over her mouth.

I smiled at them. "Bonjour."

"Bonjour," they replied in unison, and ran off.

A hand pulled the door open and a man of about Rémy's age loomed above me, his frame broad and strong, his hair cropped short. His face held a severity about it, but his eyes were gentle, like Rémy's. He smiled and his face softened. "Violette, welcome. I'm Noé."

We exchanged kisses.

"I remember you," I said, "from when we all used to get together at weekends. Weren't you always messing around with Rémy, Joël trying to keep tabs on you both?"

"That pretty much sums up our childhood," he said with a wry smile.

I laughed.

"And I remember you with your parents at the chateau," he added.

"Every Saturday evening in the summer."

"It's great to have you back. Come in." He stepped to the side.

I passed him the Mourvèdre.

"Thank you very much." He took my coat.

A hot and ever so slightly sticky hand wrapped around mine. I looked down and the boy grinned up at me.

"My son, Seb." The girl peered out from behind Noé's jeans. "And my daughter, Emmie."

"Enchantée," I said, smiling at them both.

They giggled.

Seb tugged my hand again and pulled me through the coat-and-boot-strewn entrance hall after Noé, the aroma of roast beef and herbs drawing me as much as the small hand.

We emerged into a broad flagstoned room. At one end a fire blazed in a massive hearth, a comfortable seating area arranged in front, the couches piled with cushions. A huge oak table extended across the rest of the room, beautifully laden with mismatched china, autumn foliage and a row of candelabra. There was no sign of Rémy, but a woman laid the final touches to the arrangement. She looked up and headed over, a smile blossoming on her warm face, her mass of shoulder-length curls the same shade as the children's.

"Orianne, my wife," Noé said.

"Lovely to meet you, Violette." We kissed and she squeezed my arm. "It's very good to have you here. Hopefully now we shall have something other than music and cattle to talk about."

Joël strode over from a doorway at the far end. "Violette!"

he boomed. "Come and meet everyone else." He wrapped his arm around my shoulders and led me away, his eyes sparkling. I caught sight of the chateau through the window on the other side of the room, the end battlements distinct. The perspective was different here.

We entered an old-fashioned kitchen. "Maman," Joël said.

Clémence crouched in front of the range, prodding at what had to be the source of the aroma. She rose gradually, closed the oven door, then brushed back her short grey hair and walked over, stooping a little. Her face glowed with the same merriment as Joël's, and yet as she neared, I could see Rémy in her too.

"Violette, we are so glad to have you. Armel and I still miss your parents very much. We missed you too, but now that ends." She kissed me on both cheeks. "You look well, my dear. How is Sarrat suiting you?"

I bathed in her warmth. "I'm loving it. I'm so glad to be back. And thank you for having me—"

"Violette," came a gruff voice. A bent old man appeared from the doorway, his clean-shaven face too chubby to be lined much. "Welcome. We're very happy to see you and so glad you could make it for lunch." More kisses, then he turned to his wife. "Are we ready to eat?"

"We are ready," she replied. "Everyone, à table."

"Let's get you seated," Joël said. I followed him back into the other room. He pulled out a chair at the centre of the table. I sat down and he settled to my right.

Noé finished lighting the candelabra, and despite the daylight, the glow was mellow and intimate, reflecting in the glasses and china. Everyone took their seats, Clémence and Armel at each end, Noé on my other side and Orianne opposite with the children. There was an empty chair in the corner, no doubt for Rémy.

"Violette. Good to see you." The voice curled from behind, accompanied by a hand on my shoulder.

I turned. "Yves." It wasn't difficult to deduce from my memories and his slight similarity to Rémy—although his gaze was very different and he wore his hair longer, swept back and parted on either side of his face. "Very good to see you," he said with a small smile. "I had better take my seat or I will be holding us up."

Joël rose and served the entrée of ham, asparagus, boiled eggs, olives and aioli while Armel poured the Mourvèdre. Yves made himself comfortable in Rémy's chair, and the table was full.

Disappointment sank through me. Rémy wasn't coming. But I was sure he'd said he was in Sarrat for a while. Perhaps he was staying somewhere else. But why would he be in the vicinity and not come home?

Joël settled and Armel lifted his glass. "To Violette's return."

"To Violette," everyone chorused.

I pushed away my regret and tried not to sink back as the focus of this lovely family descended upon me. Instead, I met their eyes. "Thank you," I said as I chinked with them all.

"So, Violette." Armel had seated himself again. "How are you finding it back here?"

"I'm loving the peace and quiet, and being in the house again."

"I'm glad to hear it. If we can be of assistance in any way, do let us know." There were nods all around.

"Most definitely," Clémence added.

"I appreciate that very much." I took a bite of asparagus

and aioli, the combination creamy, bitter and sharp, entwining on my tongue.

"There's so much for us to catch up on," Joël said between mouthfuls. "What are you doing for work?"

"I'm a designer, corporate branding mainly."

"I suppose you can do all that over the internet these days." Clémence glanced at me as she forked up some egg.

"Yes, absolutely." I turned to Joël. "What about you?"

"I have a bar in Ax—L'Ours, near Bassin des Ladres. I live above."

"Nice location," I said.

"Come by sometime."

"I will." I could certainly imagine Joël the all-attentive bar-keeper.

"He should come back and live on the farm," Clémence said, a pained expression on her face. "And settle down with a nice girl."

Yves emitted a shallow laugh and smirked at Joël. "I'm sure Stephan would have something to say about that."

Noé and Orianne chuckled.

"No stirring," Joël replied with a faux black look.

"Maman doesn't care about your orientation," Yves said. "She only wants more grandchildren, and she's given up on me."

Clémence ignored them both. "Noé and Orianne live in a cottage on the edge of the estate," she said.

I nodded as I finished my apéritif.

"They do most of the work around here these days, with a bit of help from these two." She smiled at the children, who grinned back, Seb with half an asparagus stalk hanging from his mouth.

"It must be a lot of work," I said.

Orianne nodded. "The farm keeps us constantly busy."

"Completely," Noé said through a mouthful.

"And Joël and Noé are members of the mountain rescue team," Armel added proudly. "Family tradition, but I'm years past it now."

Joël laughed and glanced at me. "You're getting to hear all about us today." He pointed a finger at Noé. "Night training changed to Tuesday."

"Got it," Noé replied.

"Yves, I heard you are lead violin for the Orchestre Symphonique de Paris," I said, leaning to the side to avoid a candelabra that stood between us.

He glanced at me before returning his attention to his plate. "Correct."

"So, the laid-back lifestyle of Sarrat isn't for you?" I added.

"No. I like to be involved in more of the arts than playing with the local musicians."

Joël looked at him with narrowed eyes. Yves returned a sarcastic grin.

We'd all finished our entrée apart from Emmie, who was chasing olives around her plate with a fork. Joël and Clémence got up and cleared away the dishes. I rose to help.

"No need," Clémence called. "We have it under control."

"Hey, I heard Nico brought your harp back," Noé said as I sank back down. "Are you playing?"

"A little, yes. In fact—" I was about to say Rémy had cleaned and tuned it but stopped, thinking of Roselle's caution. Yet the family must know that Rémy had been back. Whether he was still here was another matter. And if Rémy hadn't wanted me to talk about him with his family, surely he would have mentioned it.

"You were going to say?" Noé asked as Clémence placed the roast on the table, the beef tied with string and set amidst a platter of potatoes, parsnips, carrots and broccoli. Joël passed around the plates.

I reined in my thoughts. "Yes, I'm getting a feel for it again."

"Well, wonderful," Armel said as he carved. "It was lovely that the harp stayed in the village. A number of children learnt on it, and in a very small way, it was as if your maman were still here."

There were comments of agreement.

The beef, vegetables and side of puy lentils with sliced merguez were passed around, more wine was poured, and the exchange turned away from me. I sat back, enjoying the food and the amiable conversation.

Eventually the roast was cleared and the cheese platter brought out accompanied by Carignan grapes and home-made bread. I helped myself to slices of Camembert, Roquefort and Comté as I listened to Yves's tales of playing in Vienna recently. Then the conversation fragmented into small groups, Orianne and Clémence laughing with the children, Noé, Armel and Yves discussing bringing the cows down from the high pasture, Joël and I chatting. I felt wrapped in their warmth, in the happy banter of a lovely family, far from the lack of conversation and the constant concern for etiquette at Eveline's, and far from my Parisian meals for one when I'd been secluded in my apartment.

"I heard from Sylvie, you've been decorating," Joël said to me, everyone else occupied with their conversations. He took a hulking bite of bread, a thick wedge of Camembert on top.

"Yes, I've almost whitewashed the whole place. A blank slate for a new start." The Roquefort rolled around my mouth, rich and delicious.

"I always loved your barn conversion. Very cosy and the view is spectacular. You have a better angle on the chateau than us here." He nodded toward the window.

"The chateau where everyone says I mustn't go." I looked at him out of the corner of my eye.

There was wariness in his face. "I'm sorry, Violette, it's just…"

"Just…?"

"Just that I don't recommend it at the moment."

"And you have no better explanation than that? Even though you and the musicians go there every week."

He looked as though he was searching for a reply.

"Even Sylvie came up with something," I said, then finished my cheese.

"What did she say?"

"That it was the Sarramauca." I grinned.

"I, uh…" Joël was lost for words.

"Forget it," I said. "I'm perfectly capable of making my own decisions about where to walk."

"Violette, don't—"

I needed to change the subject. "I thought Rémy might be here."

Joël's mouth dropped and silence ripped through the room.

I glanced around, unsettled by their faces. Clémence and Armel were statues staring at me. Orianne studied her napkin, Yves rolled his eyes and Noé took a deep breath.

"I... uhh, I'm sorry," I said. "I just thought—"

Joël shook himself. "No. No. You obviously don't know. Why would you? You've been away."

I couldn't shift my gaze from him. I knew what he was going to say, only I didn't want to hear.

He leant toward me. "Violette." His tone was low, as though we were the only people in the room, as though everyone else were not listening. "I'm sorry to say, Rémy disappeared five years ago. No one has seen him since. There is a chance he may have... passed away."

Clémence let out a sob and thrust her napkin over her mouth.

What was going on? What the hell was Rémy playing at? "I'm so sorry," I managed. "I didn't—"

"Of course you didn't know," Joël interrupted, changing my meaning. I was going to say I didn't mean to upset everyone.

"Oh, for goodness' sake," Yves said, brushing his hair away from his face and glaring around at everyone. "Can we please not have this catastrophe every time his name is mentioned? Rémy was completely wrapped up in himself, in what he was doing, no matter what anyone said to him. It was bound to end like that."

Armel stood up, his face burning. "Yves, I never want to hear you talk of your brother that way again," he shouted.

The children's eyes widened. Seb started to cry. Yves flung down his napkin and strode out the room. Clémence was trying not to sob.

Joël stood up. "That's enough, everyone. Violette didn't know."

But I had known. Roselle had warned me. Although how I could've taken the warning seriously with Rémy's visits and him strolling around the village square on Saturday for all the world to see, I couldn't fathom. "I'm so sorry," I murmured.

"Yes, Violette," Clémence added through sniffs. "You weren't to know. Just give me a minute." She rose and headed out through a door near the hearth.

Armel cleared his throat. "Very sorry, Violette," he mumbled, before hobbling off with some plates. Joël joined him.

I sat there in silence, twisting my napkin as I tried to make sense of it all. Orianne hauled Seb onto her knee and made hushing noises. Emmie had crawled under the table to Noé and was pulling at his jeans.

"Papa," she said.

Noé picked her up. She looked as though she too were about to cry.

"Everything's fine, sweetheart," he said. "Look, here comes Uncle Joël with the dessert."

Joël placed the tart on the table, pears sunk into what looked like frangipani, the aroma of sweet almonds reminding me of baking with Maman after picking cherries. I wanted to rewind, to erase my words, to bring back the happy family. My knuckles whitened around my napkin. How could Rémy do this to these lovely people?

Joël placed his hand on my shoulder and smiled as he sat down. "Forget it," he said quietly. "This is my family for you. One moment the jolliest lot in France, the next there's a heated argument raging or an upset about something. It'll blow over in no time."

Clémence returned. She drew in her chair and smiled around. "Time for dessert," she said, but her eyes were rimmed with red. She cut the tart and served it with crème fraîche. Armel reappeared and poured the white, and the children climbed up to their places between Orianne and Clémence. Yves's empty chair remained a blazing beacon of my mistake.

I had no doubt the tart would be delicious, but I couldn't taste it and I had to force each mouthful down. Joël, Orianne and occasionally Noé made efforts to restart the conversation, but each topic drifted off, unanchored, lacking enthusiasm. I couldn't leave without helping clear up, during which silence descended. As the last dishes were put away, Clémence announced tea. I made my excuses. They were a family sorely reminded of their grief, thanks to me. They would be better off alone—and who was I deluding? I couldn't wait to get away.

Joël showed me to the entrance, passed my coat and apologised for his family once more. By the time the door clicked shut behind me, I'd grown rigid, my pulse throbbing, a faint sense of nausea rising in my throat. I just couldn't understand any of it.

Chapter Ten

The wind whipped around the barn, howling through the chimney, stoking the fire into an incandescent roar, the reflection ablaze in the pitch-black glass doors. I thrust my laptop onto the cushions at my side and slumped back into the sofa, casting a sideways glare at the screen. I was exhausted. I'd worked on the designs for so long, I could barely separate the colours. Yes, I'd put off Sablier in favour of decorating, but it was my vacation. I only had a few days left and I didn't want to spend them working on this.

I scowled at the mess of shapes that imposed on my evening. If I couldn't come up with anything original, I would have to fall back on the basic rules of design and provide them with something very ordinary, like most of my work of late. Contract by contract, I was ruining my reputation. Perhaps I needed a break to try something else for a few months.

And I should be thinking of Maman and Papa. After all, it was Toussaint—All Saint's Day. I should pay my respects somehow or at least keep them in mind. But for some reason their memories were distant. I couldn't even see their faces tonight.

It was late. Too late. I should go to bed.

My gaze drifted around the room, the firelight glowing across the pristine walls. At least the house was painted. I still had to unpack, but I'd managed to finish everything I'd set out to do in the last few days. I thought I would feel settled, though, once it was done, yet I just felt on edge. The sensation wasn't helped by everything that had happened with Rémy. His continued absence was confounding, and the question of why I was the only one to know he'd been back gnawed at me. Those moments we'd spent together were distant now—almost dreamlike.

I lightly considered the possibility that I'd imagined him as some sort of compensatory device to cope with returning home. It wasn't as though I never saw things—my colours were a sort of hallucination. Rémy could have been a messed-up extension of my synaesthesia. But that was utterly ridiculous—I'd touched him, smelt him. He'd been as solid as anyone else. Anyway, my synaesthesia was caused by sensory stimuli. It wasn't the same as an out-and-out hallucination, and it never had been.

Incredulity twisted through me. I was actually beginning to doubt my own sanity because of a man who was too selfish to reassure his own family he was alive. Despite all that, part of me was sure that Rémy must have a good explanation for everything, and if I admitted it, I was deeply troubled. Something considerable must have happened to him, and it was strange I'd not seen him again after the argument. I shifted my legs. The sofa was bunched up in all the wrong places.

I should go to bed.

A knock rapped on the door. I flinched and turned

toward the sound, as if somehow I could see through the walls. It was too late for visitors.

I pushed myself up, walked into the hall and turned on the outside light. All I could make out through the tourbillon was dark hair and a skewed face, but even so, I knew.

I unfastened the lock, a gust of wind thrusting the door open in my hand.

"Violette," Rémy said, a cheerful smile drawn across his face, his eyes glinting.

Relief sank through me. He was alright.

And he looked... the same. His jaw was shadowed as usual. His waistcoat, dark blue shirt and black tie were unchanged. I fixed upon his face, his chin, the angle of his nose, the intensity in his eyes. I wanted to reach out and brush his cheek, to touch that solidity.

He smiled. "Aren't you going to say anything?"

Pulling myself together, I glared at him. He'd dragged his family through so much. "What the hell are you doing here?"

"I, uh." He stared at me, the wind tossing his curls in every direction. He looked lost, his face blank. "I... uh... wanted to see you."

My nails pressed into my palms, tension locking my arms. "Rémy, what the hell is going on?"

He searched my face. "I'm sorry, I have no idea."

"I need to know." My voice was a growl. I indicated for him to enter. He kicked off his shoes and we headed into the living room, pausing at the hearth.

"Now tell me," I said.

"Violette, please, what's the matter?"

I blazed at him. "How can you ask that?"

"Because I truly don't know." His jaw was firm, his neck ridged.

"You have been missing for five years, your family thinks you may be dead and yet here you are back in Sarrat, visiting me after midnight, without a care for what they are going through."

"What...?"

I stared at him. "What do you mean by 'what'?"

He shook his head. "I... don't understand."

"How can you not understand? Just answer the question."

"Uh... five years?"

"I need to know, Rémy. I need to know what's going on."

There was something like desperation in his eyes. He walked over to the night-black doors and gazed into the darkness.

"Rémy?"

"Could you just give me a moment?" He raked his hand through his hair.

Taking a breath through gritted teeth, I strode into the kitchen and, not knowing what else to do, put the kettle on. The wind clamoured around the walls and squealed in the range as I spooned too much chamomile into the pot, added steaming water and made up the tray.

"Violette," Rémy called.

I carried in the tea.

He stood in front of the doors, his back reflected in the glass, his eyes following me as I placed the tray on the hearth. I walked over to the sofa, closed my laptop, stowed it underneath and sat down. "I'm listening."

"I know this is going to sound strange." He looked into nothing for a moment, then refocussed. "But I need you to trust me."

"The famous Rabasten words." I smirked.

He stepped over, crouched down and fixed me in the eye, his gaze almost fierce. "Violette, I want you to know that I would never, ever hurt my family intentionally. I couldn't even consider it. But I'm in a difficult situation at the moment, one I haven't been able to solve. As soon as I can put it right, the very first thing I will do is go home." He laid his hand upon mine, his touch warm, light. "I swear to you that I will try to sort out this whole thing as quickly as possible."

I could feel myself scowling. "What could be so bad or so difficult that you can't go home?"

He shook his head. "I... can't tell you."

My scowl deepened.

"But I promise," he continued, "as soon as I can speak about it, I will."

"That doesn't explain anything," I said, searching his face.

He was silent, just staring at me.

"So," I added, "that's it. I'm supposed to maintain some kind of sham in front of your family, as though I haven't seen you? It's ridiculous."

"I'm sorry," he said.

"And you aren't going to offer me anything else?"

"I can't." There was a fragility in his voice.

"Are you involved in drugs, or something illegal?"

He looked me in the eye. "I can tell you in all honesty I'm not involved in anything like that. Please, just give me a little time."

He was asking so much and I couldn't imagine what kind of situation he was caught in. "So there is nothing I can do. I have to wait until you tell me what's going on, or whatever it is sorts itself out?"

He nodded.

I shook my head. I didn't like it at all. "You know, I went to your family's on Sunday. They invited me for lunch. Roselle warned me about you, but you so clearly weren't missing. I mentioned you to Joël and everyone overheard—your poor mother—and Yves said something and your father lost his temper. It was a total disaster, and the look on their faces—"

Rémy was staring into the air, his eyes wide. He swallowed. "Go on."

He looked... devastated, his pain disarming me a little. What had he gotten himself into? "They obviously miss you, that's all."

He nodded, stood up and, as if not knowing what else to do, walked over to the tea things and poured. He carried two cups back, passed one to me and sat down on the couch, his face composed once again.

"I need to apologise," he said, "for the way I acted last time I was here."

I raised my brow, wanting more than that. His persistence about my colours had been too much.

"I was out of line," he continued, his gaze steady. "I had no right to judge the way you live."

"You had no right at all." I glared at him. "You need to respect my choices. Your way is not everyone else's and I'm not going to argue about it."

He nodded. "Agreed."

Shifting, I pulled my jumper loose. I still wasn't completely comfortable with the absence of my colours, but that wasn't the point. At least he'd admitted he was out of line. It was a peace offering. "Then, apology accepted," I said.

"Good." His shoulders sank.

I cast my eyes over him as he sipped his tea, glad he was here despite everything. "I was worried," I blurted.

He scoured my face.

"That something had happened to you," I continued, "that I wouldn't see you. Rémy, I don't want you to disappear again under inexplicable circumstances."

"I don't want to go away," he said, his eyes soft and alight. "I like spending time with you very much."

I smiled.

"What are you doing tomorrow, then?" he asked, a grin extending across his face.

Accepting his invitation wasn't the wisest choice when I hadn't a clue what was going on. But I couldn't deny I wanted more of his intensity, his kindness, his laughter. I was drawn to that something between us I could feel even now, and I couldn't resist what felt so right. "I have some unpacking," I said. "But that can fit in anywhere."

"What about spending some time in the mountains? We could meet at Les Fonts."

Restraining my smile a little, I nodded. "I'd like that very much. Midday?"

He glowed with delight. "Perfect."

"I... uh... I was going to ask about exchanging numbers but..."

He shook his head. "Probably best we don't go there."

"I honestly don't know what I'm getting myself into." And that was the truth of it. I was becoming involved with someone who obviously had major problems and wouldn't confide in me. I never did that. "And I suppose it's too much to ask where you are staying?"

"Violette, I am so sorry." There was genuine regret in his eyes.

I shook my head and attempted to stifle a yawn.

The corner of his mouth turned up. "I shouldn't have come at this time. I had better go."

"Yes, I need to sleep."

We headed to the door and exchanged kisses, his lips brushing my cheek, the sensation shivering my skin.

"Violette, I can't wait for tomorrow," he said before drawing away. "Goodnight."

Chapter Eleven

A cloudless, saturated blue shone above the sawtooth mountains, throwing into contrast the slopes of deciduous forest that had been stripped of colour in the recent storms. The only compromise to the bright day was the bitter chill, and I was glad of the incline to warm me through. Surely it wouldn't be long until the first snow—the high mountains in the distance were already covered.

I'd always loved coming up here, away from everything after an endless drive of hairpin bends, yet Les Fonts was not so far from the road that it justified a hike or serious mountain precautions.

The path forked, offering a route that rose between the peaks or a switchback that ascended to the ridge. I took the latter, feeling the slope in my legs, my pack pulling at my shoulders, my breath spiralling before me. I turned near the top to see if Rémy was heading up behind. There was only one parking area, so it was likely, yet the pass lay empty but for an eagle circling low. Perhaps he'd had a lift and was already there—a lift with whom? I took a deep, unsteady breath and pushed on up the slope, trying to ignore the knots in my stomach. I wanted this, I wanted to get to know Rémy, but his disappearance to the world at large wasn't helping me feel at ease, nor was my discomfort at everything he'd put his family through.

The ridge levelled then sloped downward, and there below me lay Sarrat, the chateau and the rest of the world in miniature, a patchwork of browns and gold, interspersed with evergreen forest and twisting river. The occasional road made the wilds a little tame, but only a little.

I strolled down the path, clambered around an escarpment of limestone that sheltered a stand of trees then ducked between the branches. The rutted trunks dug into my hands as I slipped down the mulch into a rocky hollow, and there they were—three hot springs bubbled up in a stone pool, the water clear, the ripples capturing the light that slanted between the trees.

A smile came from somewhere deep within. I'd always loved this place—the heat spreading through the bedrock into the dry earth and, on still days like this, the steam warming the air under the canopy. There was something magical about it—there always had been—the sanctity of the water rising from the ground, not piped or restrained as in the village but unadulterated and alive.

My gaze followed the watercourse as it tumbled through a break in the trees, the vaulted boughs of hazel framing the valley and the pog in the distance. Rémy clearly wasn't here.

I stepped across the stream to a small clearing set between the rock walls of the hollow. Easing my shoulders back, I dropped my pack onto the earth amidst a multitude of tiny golden leaves, then I sank onto a boulder edging the pool and took off my hat and gloves, feeling the warmth of the steam on my skin.

Something clasped my shoulder. I flung around.

Rémy stood there, his eyes fixed on mine. "Violette."

I rose, my heart pounding, and for a moment I was at a loss for words. "Hello," I managed eventually, and grinned. "I didn't hear you arrive."

"Sorry for the startle," he replied with a smile.

We exchanged kisses and once again I could feel him, his closeness, his presence. I pulled back and took him in. "You're wearing the same thing." The same clothes as last night, as every time we'd met, all of him tidy and well groomed. The only difference was he'd pulled his tie loose and opened his collar. "Why are you wearing that in the mountains?"

He glanced sideways. "I didn't have anything else."

"It's freezing—well, not in here, but out there. Didn't you bring a coat?" I took his hand without thinking. He was warm, much warmer than me despite the fact I'd worn gloves. "You don't feel cold."

He curled his fingers around mine. "I'm fine, Violette. Just forget about me."

"What's going on?"

He shook his head. "I know this is an... unusual situation. But for now, could we spend the day together without thinking about anything but the two of us? Let's just be... normal."

I wanted to forget, I wanted there to be nothing standing in the way of getting to know him, but with everything that had happened, it wasn't easy to concede. Yet surely it wouldn't do any harm to have one day? "Alright. I'm sure I can put it all aside for that long."

"Good." He nodded and released my hand, which felt cool without his warmth. "How's the unpacking coming on?"

"The study is done, ready for work on Monday, but I'd rather not think about that for today either." I crouched down to my pack, pulled the blanket from its fastenings and passed him the bag. "See what you can find." I shook out the blanket. It fit well between the pool and the rocks.

Rémy knelt down, rummaged around in the bag and drew out the bottle of Beaujolais and two wine glasses wrapped in napkins, a bemused expression on his face. "Wonderful," he murmured as he planted the bottle in the pool. He pulled out the pain complet, more of the Ariège goat's cheese that was fast becoming an addiction and a pot of olives and artichokes, then arranged it all on the rocks.

I smoothed the blanket, sat down and took off my jacket, feeling perfectly warm from the heat of the springs. The view drew me, the expanse of autumn ochres glowing in the sun, the river sparkling. Only the chateau reflected the coming winter, the walls dim, as though light couldn't penetrate its depths. The place was as dark and foreboding as it had been bright and welcoming in the past. It had become easier not to look at it—to gaze out into the valley or enjoy the wilderness of the garden rather than have to tear myself away from the shadowy stone every time I glanced in its direction. Even from this distance it pulled me. Despite the balmy warmth, I shivered.

"The chateau is different these days," I said without looking away.

"Perhaps," I heard him say as my eyes followed the lines of the keep. He shifted over and took a seat beside me, blocking my view.

"Thank you, Violette," he said.

I leant around him to take in the walls without hindrance. His fingers brushed my chin and I turned toward him, thoughts of the chateau falling away.

"Thank you," he said again, his brow creased, his mouth set firm.

"What for?"

"For thinking of lunch. It looks delicious."

"Well, let's eat." I smiled.

He rummaged in the bag and drew out the corkscrew. "Shall I?"

"Go ahead."

He pulled the cork, poured and passed my wine, then met my eyes and raised his glass. "To your return to Sarrat. May you have many joyous years here."

"Thank you." We clinked and drank, all the time his gaze upon mine.

"Help yourself." I glanced at the meal.

He grinned and set his glass on a rock, then took the pain complet from the paper bag, tore a hunk onto his napkin and spread it with thick butter and goat's cheese. I placed my glass next to his and did the same, the pungency of the spring mingling with the sharp aroma of the creamy cheese.

I watched him as I ate. He broke off a chunk and placed it in his mouth, his eyes closing as he chewed slowly, then he bit into another piece and then another.

"You look as though you haven't eaten for a month," I said.

He glanced at me. "It's so utterly good." He made up some more bread.

"There's something about simple food well prepared."

"I couldn't agree with you more." He wolfed down another hunk.

"Wherever you're staying, they don't feed you."

He ignored me.

We helped ourselves to olives and artichokes, then satiated, Rémy settled on his side and sipped his wine. I finished my crust, conscious of his eyes covering me as though he were captivated. I couldn't help but smile, and his lips flickered in response.

"You know, I find you fascinating," he said.

"Really?" My face was set, but my stomach turned. I bundled up my napkin, cast the crumbs onto the clearing floor and discarded the cloth with the leftovers. "Why is that?"

"Your self-control, the way you've abandoned Paris and come home, the fact that you know what I see."

I tried to unravel the threads of what he'd said.

"And the fact that you see me," he added.

I couldn't keep up. "That I see who you are as a person?"

He shrugged and took another sip.

"So you make enigmatic statements and don't respond to questions about them." I thought for a moment. "Actually, you do that a lot."

He grinned. "Maybe I do."

"You know, I find you fascinating too," I said.

He studied my face. "Oh, yes?"

"Yes."

"What, just yes?"

I nodded. I desperately wanted there to be a good reason for his disappearance and the distress he was causing his family as there was so much that drew me to him. His passion and enthusiasm, his gentleness. But more than that—something about all the parts that made up him. His bearing, the way his shirt creased over his shoulders, the depth of his gaze, his deft, confident movements, his utterly stunning handling of the harp and, if I dared admit it, the fact that he experienced synaesthesia too. All of it melded into a dynamic whole I couldn't take my eyes off. But I wouldn't say that, not now, not yet, because despite everything, I barely knew him. "I want to know more about you," I said instead.

He smiled. "Like what?"

Where to start? I wanted to know what made him, him. And he'd found a spark for work that I completely lacked. That fascinated me too. "Tell me about what drew you to music." It seemed like a good place to start.

"The interiority of sound. Music is so intimate." He took another sip of wine.

I eyed him, wary this would return to synaesthesia again. Yet music being Rémy's occupation, I couldn't avoid the subject altogether.

"Music is story without words," he continued, "perceived by the ears and the mind, yet it speaks straight to the heart without the interference of the intellect. It has the power to affect people, to change them." He swirled his wine. "Music is subliminal, raw, pure."

"I can see that. Music always transports me." At least when I had my colours under control.

"Exactly."

"But then, how come you work in tuning, rather than playing, performing?" I asked.

"I still play, I always will. It's part of me, but I'm intrigued by the way sound works, the way the mind and ear collaborate, the mathematics of the perfect proportion. Toward the end of university I could see my life going in two directions. I could become a member of an orchestra, producing music as my daily grind, but I could see myself losing enthusiasm that way. My other option was to become a soloist. It was the more flexible path if I could make it, but I didn't want the limelight."

I thought of the pictures on the internet. He hadn't managed to avoid the publicity.

"But what about you?" he asked. "What made you choose design?"

"The interplay of colours, how they can be shaped and ordered, creating tension or balance." I thought about it for a moment. "I suppose it's similar to what you were saying in a way. Colour, texture and form speak to a person directly—they give an impression that can be used to convey a message."

"But you're not happy with it anymore?" He drained his glass and placed it on the rock.

"No. It's a mess. Even back at the magazine I was finding it difficult to enjoy the design process." Because of my colours.

He looked me in the eye. "Isn't design for you like working with something you're trying to get rid of? It's a strange choice of career, to work with colour, for someone avoiding their synaesthesia."

I scowled and picked at the broad weave of the rug, twisting it between my fingers. I didn't want to talk about it. Or perhaps I did. I'd not talked about it with anyone, and it felt uncomfortable, but a part of me wanted to share what I'd hidden for so long—if, and only if, Rémy could respect my perspective. "I love colour and form... and music. I just don't like it overwhelming me. I enjoyed the arts in Paris, the museums, gigs, concerts, the ballet. It felt so utterly normal to enjoy Scheherazade, to listen to the music and experience the spectacle of the ballet with no distortion of the senses."

"So you enjoy the ballet to feel normal?" His gaze pierced mine. "Like some kind of challenge to keep your synaesthesia away?"

Of course, I enjoyed the ballet for what it was, but it was true—I relished in not experiencing colour, in the security of being in control of myself. To be honest it was the same for design. There was a part of me that enjoyed being master of what threatened to overwhelm my senses. I liked to shape colour rather than it shaping me—until I could no longer hold back the deluge in the city noise.

I twisted away from his gaze and stared at the depressions in the rock. The subject needed changing. "And I didn't abandon Paris,' I said, thinking of his earlier words. "I wanted to come home to Sarrat." I turned back to him and took in his full, intelligent eyes. "Anyway, I thought you would be all in favour of the city considering you worked there, and"—I looked him up and down—"considering your clothes." I hadn't noticed before, but he also wore the same brown brogues. "How did you get up here in those? They don't even look scratched."

"Not today," he said, his lips curling up at the corners.

I had agreed not to talk about any of his peculiarities. I turned onto my back and the warmth of the earth seeped into my body.

"Bobo," I teased, wanting to lighten the mood.

He pushed himself up and leant over me, a glint in his eye. "What did you say?"

"You heard me, bobo."

"Bourgeoisie bohemian." He laughed. "Come on, I'm not that. I love my job—music is everything to me. I'm not worried about anything else."

"Well, look at it like this—you're an artistic free spirit

who wants to change the world of music and the production of all musical instruments to incorporate a change of tuning. You even put the matter before the Parlamento Italiano. Your family descends from the counts of Toulouse and you wear" —I glanced at his waistcoat—"this in Sarrat."

"My family and I don't recognise our heritage in that way."

"Exactly."

"Hey." He narrowed his eyes. "How do you know about the Italian parliament?"

"I searched you." I kept my face purposefully expressionless.

He raised an eyebrow. "Cyberstalking."

I laughed. "When Roselle said you were missing, I fished around a little. You lead a colourful life, Rémy Rabasten. It didn't look like you managed to avoid the limelight."

He flopped back down. "The limelight happened to me. It wasn't something I wanted." He turned his head to face me and grinned. "Parigot."

Parigot, tête de veau—Parisian, head of veal. I sprang up to sitting, the old rhyme in my head. He implied I was an arrogant, rude Parisian. But I couldn't help smiling at his tease. "I have to say, Eveline taught me to survive in that city —and how to achieve what I wanted. There couldn't have been a better role model."

"She sounds like quite a person."

"I forged a successful career by taking on her principles," I said.

"And what about passion for what you do, the joy of it? Did Eveline teach you that?"

I stared at him. Of course she hadn't. It was all about

hard work and status. Enjoyment didn't come into it. "Not exactly."

"And now you're back here."

Yes, I was back here. "On top of it all, I always wanted to go home. I missed the mountains, I missed Sarrat and I missed the silence. I'm Occitan through and through."

He scoured my face. "Was your synaesthesia worse in Paris?"

Wary of returning to the subject, I shrugged. "Yes. It's been so much better here and, thankfully, it seems to be gone."

"What?" His face became hard. I wasn't sure I liked the expression.

"You know that's what I wanted." A golden leaf no bigger than my fingertip twisted between us and settled on the rug.

"Yes, but I don't understand how it could go, just like that."

"It's been easier here, without the sensory bombardment of Paris." I tried to smile, but it wouldn't come.

"And life's better without it? You're better without it?" Indignation covered his face.

"I was completely overwhelmed," I said, my voice rising.

"If you hadn't fought it, if you'd accepted it, you would have found a way to cope." His tone met mine.

I glared at him. He didn't understand what it was like, and I couldn't believe we were having this conversation. "You agreed not to talk about it, and now you're telling me how to live my life again."

"I agreed not to argue, that was all."

"Well, what is this?"

He was silent. The trickle of the stream filled my ears.

Eventually he sat up and studied me, still the hardness in his face. "I don't think it's gone."

"Why?"

He shrugged. "And you're truly happy now?"

I propped myself up, reached for my wine and took a sip. The honest answer was no. I felt empty, lacking—although I couldn't for the life of me reason why when I'd been desperate to get rid of my colours for so long. It was almost as if I'd torn away a piece of my past, a piece that linked me to Maman and Papa and everything before.

"Violette?"

"Yes, I'm happy." I forced a smile and looked away.

He frowned. "I don't understand. Why were you so afraid of it? What was the worst it could do to you?"

"Drown me, take away my sense of self, prevent me from functioning."

"It doesn't have to be that way. It really doesn't. My synaesthesia has augmented every experience of my life." He took my hand and brushed his fingers across the back. My skin blazed with his touch. "I could help you experience it again. Help you manage it."

I pulled my hand away. "I've had enough of this conversation." I tried to look over his shoulder. "You're in front of the view. You've been there all the time."

"I wanted to have all your attention," he said with a smile.

I laughed despite myself, and he laughed too, the hardness gone, the tension broken as though he'd accepted my finality.

"I need to move." I placed my glass on the rock, stood up and stretched, taking in the valley. The sun had shifted and lowered, and now it streamed into the alcove, lighting the steam, casting the pog into even darker contrast.

Rémy rose and stood before me. "Come and sit back down." He took my hand and tugged gently. "I have another tale for you." His lips pursed.

I raised my eyebrows. "As if the last heretical interpretation of the creation of the universe wasn't enough."

He laughed and dropped to the rug, pulling me with him. "But you haven't heard this one."

"Alright." I slid back onto my side and he did the same, only closer than before, and there it was, that sense of him, as though he were more opaque than everything around us.

"Once upon a time, in a land far, far away…"

My eyes rolled.

"A very long time ago and just the other day…"

I shook my head and collapsed onto my back.

He grinned, took a strand of my hair between his fingers and looped it around them. "I'm drawn to you," he said in a low voice, "as though you have some kind of underlying harmonic that pulls me."

Glints of powder-blue sky filtered through the curls that hung over his face. I wanted to draw him closer, but resisted. "That wasn't part of the story," I said.

"No, you're too much of a distraction."

I laughed. But could he be any more provocative?

"Alright…" He looked up into the canopy for a moment and took a breath, still twisting my hair. "There once was a young man, a musician, some called him a troubadour. He played the…" He searched my eyes for a moment as if he could find the answer there. "The lute. He played the lute—"

"You're making this up as you go along."

"Maybe." The corner of his mouth turned up. "He

played the lute for the finest people in the land—the king, the queen, the princes, the princesses, the noble men and women. He captivated them with his exceptional articulation, his expressive phrasing and his unparalleled timbre. And he knew if he tuned his lute in a certain way, and combined this with his skill, his audience would be captivated, lifted to heights they only approached in their dreams. In fact, people were brought to the core of themselves by his playing." Rémy's voice, low and soft, lilted with the story's cadence, mingling with the gentle lull of the trickling stream. My eyes followed the wisps of steam that drifted through the tangle of branches overhead.

"Now, the great chateaus of the land had been built on the old places, erected by the ancient ones to reflect the perfect symmetry of the universe, built to hold and reveal the Great Harmonie, and the musician knew this. He played with such passion, such intensity, that he forgot himself, and his music joined with the Harmonie, creating sublimity that had never been heard before. And while he played in these chateau sanctuaries, the Désaccord howled and pried at the walls, it buffeted and cajoled the stone, it tore at the very foundations of the rock upon which these places stood.

"But the musician was only human, as are we all, and a thread of greed wove around his heart. He thought he could do more, he thought he could capture the hearts of his audience entirely. He thought that if the people of the land were under his spell, he would have endless esteem and prestige.

"The musician shaped the harmonies of music with his astounding skill, but the discordant notes that inevitably echoed out into the banqueting halls and chambers were unruly. They struck their own dark chords and echoed to the Désaccord howling without. The harmony was free to soar into the domains of beauty through the musician's fingers, but the discords were a power unto themselves. He wondered if the discordant notes could be shaped, given their own purpose and power, so that music would have unprecedented force.

"The musician considered this for a long time. He pondered on the nature of the Harmonie and the Désaccord and he saw that harmony was present amidst all the joys and sublimities that life could conjure. Indeed, it was love itself. In the same way the discord was present in conflict, in pain, in hate, in darkness and in death. He experimented with his own music, but still the discords were unruly and unpliable— they would not do what the musician wished. So the musician scoured the land for the knowledge he sought, and though he searched through every library, though he questioned every wise woman and every wise man, the musician found nothing.

"One day, however, after many years of searching, the musician was approached by a man hooded in a black cloak, red silk glimmering from the lining of its swirling folds. The cloaked one whispered that he had the information the musician sought contained within two books. The musician purchased the volumes and scoured the words that lay within. They explained how, with the aid of a ritual of a certain kind, the Désaccord could be tamed and shaped to form the most powerful music ever created.

"The musician could not wait. He gathered what he needed and performed the ritual right away. He evoked the Désaccord and found he could shape it to his bidding. When he played, the sublime heights of the harmonies were contrasted by a new depth, a depth that held power and enchantment. Such music had never been heard before, and the people of the land were enthralled.

"But the more the musician played, the more his newfound music gave sustenance to the Désaccord, and instead of buffeting around the chateau sanctuaries, the Désaccord reached out dark fingers to pry within, casting all light asunder. One day, when the musician once again evoked the most sublime heights and the darkest depths with his playing, the Désaccord reached into the chateau sanctuary and touched the king, the queen, the princes, the princesses, the noble men and women, filling them with fear, the kind of fear that is deathly and treacherous but also delights and entices and plays with sensibilities. They became mad with it, unfit to rule, and chaos ensued throughout the land.

"Apart from being a musical genius, the musician was clearly a fool, as so often is the case. Yet deep within his being, part of his heart remained pure, and seeing the pain that resulted from his music, he tore off his thread of greed and resolved to put right the trouble he had caused. He journeyed with his lute to the most powerful sanctuary of the Harmonie in all the land. In deep remorse he called upon the Harmonie to put right all he'd set in motion, and he played with such passion, such intensity, that he once again forgot himself.

"The Harmonie was evoked, but the Désaccord had followed him and it tore around the walls of the sanctuary, desiring to punish the musician who now wished to subdue its greatness. The Désaccord tried to seize the musician, but the Harmonie, in its endless grace, enfolded him, taking him away from the world into its protection.

"Now, the musician was humbled that the Harmonie

was willing to protect him, and he vowed to return to the rocks and the mountains and the sanctuaries to serve the Harmonie. But when he attempted to leave the sublimity, the enraged Désaccord lay in wait, ready to destroy its former master. The Désaccord could not harm the musician while he dwelt within the Harmonie, but it could prevent his return to the world, and in endless vengeance it vowed it would always do so. The musician was trapped in the sublimity that was his first muse, and he was never seen again."

I blinked, the cessation of Rémy's voice pulling me from the story world. Fairy tales always did have the power to transport me. I turned to him. He was still playing with my hair, smiling a little.

"You're right," I said, "I hadn't heard that one before. But you forgot something."

"What was that?"

"You forgot to say, 'The End'. All the best stories finish that way."

His eyes fixed on mine. "Perhaps it isn't the end."

I adjusted my position against the stones pressed into my back. "But I have a question."

He sat up. "What is it?"

"The king, the queen, all the noble people, they were driven mad. What happened to them and the land filled with chaos?"

He shrugged. "Without the musician's interfering, everything returned to normal pretty quickly."

I sat up to face him. "Well, you are certainly skilled in the art of storytelling."

He laughed.

"And the musician," I said, "do you think he deserved the protection of the Harmonie after all the trouble he caused?"

He frowned and looked agonised for a moment. "No, I think he's an absolute damned fool."

"But it was a beautiful story. What made you tell it?"

He reached out and tugged gently at my jumper, appearing fascinated with the merino, then he released it and looked up at me. "It was appropriate."

"Appropriate to what?"

He craned his head over his shoulder toward the sun lowering at the side of the pog. "We should get going. It's only an hour or so until sunset."

Glancing around him, I took in the globe of burnished orange, streaks of yellow fading into blue along the horizon. Despite the warmth of the springs, it was colder too. "Yes, we wouldn't want to get caught in the mountains after dark with you wearing that," I replied.

He managed to glare at me and smile at the same time, then his eyes softened. "Thank you for today," he said.

I smiled and looked down. I didn't do this. I didn't get caught up so quickly. But he was something different, his stories, his music, his opinions. I busied myself stowing away the contents of the picnic. He shook out the rug, rolled it up and passed it to me, still standing between me and the valley. I gave up on the view and put on my jacket and hat.

"Ready?" I asked, looping my arm through the pack.

"Let me." He took the bag and hung it over his shoulders, then held out the crook of his arm. I linked into him and we took the easy route, following the stream out of the hollow then striding up to the ridge, the connection of our arms intimate, as if we were an old couple, all apart from my heightened sense of him.

We topped the ridge and joined the pass, talking a little, our stride falling together. There was no doubt about it, we were headed for something more, but right now we were at that cusp where novelty was something to savour. Our arms were still linked when we reached my solitary car. He must have had a lift. It was absurd I didn't even know that small detail about him.

"Do you want a ride back?" I asked as we crossed the car park.

He drew to a halt, pulled me toward him and secured his arms around my waist. I relished in his solidity, his warmth, the intimacy a precious, delicate thing.

"No, I'm going to walk," he said softly.

I glanced down at his shoes, now scratched and caked with mud. They would disintegrate by the time he returned to wherever. The nearest house was a good few kilometres away, and it would be dark and cold. "Are you sure?"

"Absolutely. You don't need to worry." He brushed my cheek and smiled. "Today has been so very special for me."

"For me too." It was perfect like this, with none of his problems.

He drew close, our faces almost touching. I could feel his breath, the scent of him drawing me.

"I don't want this to end," I said softly.

"I never want this to end," he murmured, "but I must go." He pulled away suddenly, stepping back. "I really must go."

I scrutinised him. I'd been sure he was going to kiss me. Instead, more of his erratic behaviour.

"Tomorrow?" he offered.

I sighed. "Dinner?"

"Yes, perfect."

"Come early," I said. "Three or four if you like."

"Alright." He leant in to exchange kisses, and although he lingered a little, it was as if we'd not been close a moment before. He drew off the pack and handed it to me. "Until tomorrow." He smiled, then strode down the road and disappeared around the corner.

I unlocked the car and climbed inside, casting my pack onto the passenger seat. What was I so utterly caught up in? It was all so... intense.

My fingers were already cold as I started the engine. The readout showed the temperature at freezing. How warm was Rémy without a coat? It was preposterous. I thrust the car into reverse and turned around. He knew better than to dress like that in the mountains, and just like the situation with his family, he was putting me in a position to worry. Well, I couldn't leave him to walk home. I'd pick him up on the way.

I pulled out and took the first of the hairpins, and then another. I'd expected to see him almost straight away—after all, how fast could he walk? But nothing. I slowed down, assuming he'd be around the next bend. No. He must have taken a footpath.

Chapter Twelve

I turned the cup in my hands, staring at the caramel and ebony swirl, the grainy ceramic warming my fingers. I was aware of the square bustling around me—cutlery clattering at the next table, a group of girls splashing as they waded through the pool, friends hollering as they caught sight of one another, their calls carried on the blustering wind—but I could only focus on the thread of anticipation that twisted within. We would spend the evening together.

Yet elation met with something hollow right in my middle, a breach I didn't know how to address. He'd walked off taking a cross-country route inappropriately dressed, or perhaps he'd prearranged a lift, or I supposed he could have parked on the road for some reason—I wouldn't have been able to see his car behind the pines. But the point was, on top of the whole situation with his apparent disappearance, he'd put me in a position to be concerned about him without a thought. I rubbed my eyes and drew my hands over the sides of my face. I'd not slept well.

A scream tore through the bustle. One of the girls climbed out of the pool, dripping from the waist down. That had been me once. We all took turns—it was inevitable on the slippery cobbles. So much had changed, yet Sarrat's Saturday blueprint remained the same. The village was oblivious to the ordeals we'd undergone. In years to come, when I sat on the edge of the pool, my skin spotted with age, Sarrat would no doubt be the same, and we would all bear even greater burdens. And where would Rémy be then? Still hiding out?

"Violette!"

I scanned the square. Joël headed over from the boulangerie, all grand smile and twinkling eyes, his bulky jacket burgeoning his frame, bags hanging from his hands like counterweights. I forced myself to smile, but my chest tightened. I had ruined their meal.

"Joël," I said as he drew close. He leant down and we exchanged kisses.

"It's good to see you, Violette." He adjusted his bags. "I want to apologise for last weekend. You couldn't have known about Rémy."

Oh, but I did know about Rémy—I knew too much and yet so very little about Rémy. "No, it should be me apologising. I—"

"Absolutely not." He grinned. "The family is terribly excitable, especially when Yves is home. But we tend to steer around the subject of Rémy, at least when we're together like that."

"Please," I said, my voice a little too hard, "it's in the past now."

He nodded and smiled. "We want to invite you around again, to make up for it. I promise no arguments and no bad atmosphere. Maman wanted to make it next Sunday, but she's baking for a charity event in town, so the weekend after."

Clémence was so kind, and Armel too. I glanced at Joël's decent face. They didn't deserve Rémy's treatment. "Please tell Clémence it was lovely to be surrounded by her warmth, and the reaction was completely understandable. I would love to come again."

"Great, I'll let her know." Joël's eyes shone. "Oh, and bring the harp over, if you like. It would be good to play together."

The harp that Rémy tuned—Rémy, whom you think is missing and possibly dead. Pressure built in my jaw. "That's a lovely idea, but I won't be ready for accompaniment for a while yet."

"Well, as soon as you can. I can't wait to hear that marvellous thing again." He glanced at his watch. "I've got to go. I have to get this back to the farm before, uh... I need to get this to Maman."

He dove toward me and we exchanged kisses once again.

"Good to see you," he said, and dashed off.

Well, I would do everything I could to make sure my next visit would be pleasant for everyone. I called for the bill, gathered my bags and trod home, my scarf irritating me as though I had grit under its folds.

The aroma of slow-cooked garlic and sage met me as I entered the house. I removed my outdoor things and carried my bags into the kitchen. I'd asked Rémy to come around three or four. He would be here soon and I wanted to be organised, but hiding my knowledge of Rémy to Joël continued to rile at me. Why on earth couldn't Rémy just be straight about whatever he was going through? I pulled out the shopping, dropping the pain de campagne, the ceps and the Syrah hard onto the worktop.

I washed and dried a couple of my old hand-engraved Bourgogne glasses, then prepared the ceps and added them to the cassoulet. The haricot beans had melted perfectly into the garlic, sage and olive oil. It could simmer away gently in the warming oven to be ready at Rémy's convenience.

Checking the state of the living room, I noticed a chill in the air. I lit the fire, dusting my jeans with ash. I could change into something more appropriate, perhaps even a dress, but... did I want to get closer to someone who was so far away?

A knock rang out. No time to change then. I took a deep breath, strode to the door and drew it open.

Roselle stood there, her face blank, her parka buttoned to her chin, a large tin under her arm. For a moment I could only think about Théo, then I gathered myself. "Roselle, good to see you. How are you?" I could dismiss last week now I knew of her loss.

"Can I come in?" she asked, her voice flat.

"Of course, let me take your coat." No doubt Rémy would see her car and wait until she was gone. He could wait.

"I can't be too long, I'm due to pick up Gy and Édith soon." She placed the box on the stairs, hauled off her parka and handed it to me, then tucked the box back under her arm as though it were in need of protection. "What's that smell?" she asked.

"Cassoulet." I hung up her coat. "Like Maman used to make. I bought ceps in the village."

"I used to love it—the tender garlic."

"There was nothing like it." I led her into the living

room. "See what you think of the new colour scheme, or rather the lack of colour. I'll make tea."

I put the kettle on and prepared the pot.

"I like the white," she called through.

"Did you see it when Madame Durocher lived here?"

"Pink, wasn't it? This is much better."

"I didn't want to take anything from the view." I glanced at the chateau through the doorway. Cloud built from behind the battlements, dulling the sky. "I'll pour," I said, turning back to the tea.

Roselle stepped into the kitchen. "I'm not doing well with the whole chatty friendship thing at the moment," she said abruptly.

I put down the kettle and turned around.

The usual hardness filled her eyes. "When I want to express something, I... uh... bake. Talking to you the other day stirred up a lot of memories. I want to say, I'm sorry for my reaction." She passed me the tin.

I took it, absorbing what she'd said. That apology obviously hadn't been easy. I opened the lid. In the bottom lay four perfectly formed tartelettes, the delicate pastry cases bearing countless ever-so-thin slices of apple in a shiny glaze. She'd remembered my favourites. A hint of warm apple and vanilla rose from the tin, delicate and complementary to the garlic and sage. I looked up at her. "You made these?"

She nodded, the corners of her mouth flickering.

"And the macarons the other day?"

"Yes."

My eyes pricked a little. I hadn't been able to see it, but she'd really made an effort. I blinked, pushing the sentiment away—she wouldn't appreciate it. "I thought the macarons were from the pâtisserie. They were perfect."

Almost a smile. She was there—under it all.

"Thank you so much," I said, although words weren't enough. "Have a seat and I'll get these sorted." I poured the tea and plated the tartelettes as she sat down at the table and glanced around.

"Same old kitchen."

"Yes." I carried everything over. "I painted a little, but it's not noticeable with all the wood and tiles in here."

I settled at the table and forked up a mouthful, the caramelised apple melting on my palate. I couldn't help but close my eyes for a moment. "This is unbelievably delicious."

"Good." She took a bite and glanced over to the worktop. "You're expecting company."

I followed her line of sight—the wine stood with the glasses.

"I shouldn't have barged in," she added.

"He will have to wait," I said without thinking, then realised I'd implicated myself. This was ridiculous. I couldn't even talk about my life because of Rémy's secrets.

A slight glimmer lit her eyes. "Is he local?"

I smiled despite everything and took another mouthful. Perhaps I could talk around the subject.

"That was quick work," she added, before I could think what to say. An actual grin flickered on her lips. "Who is he?" She raised her hand. "No, let me guess... Rique from the épicerie? He's been single for a while."

I shook my head. "I've never met him. Roselle, I—"

"No?" Her eyes searched around the kitchen. "What about Edmond Guegan?"

I liked her enthusiasm but I needed to get some control over this. "I haven't got a clue who that is, but—"

"Oh, I know! Yves Rabasten."

The arrow struck too close to home. "No, absolutely not, though I went to theirs for lunch the other day."

"How was it?"

"The whole family were lovely." Until I dismissed her advice and mentioned Rémy. I cut into my tart.

"They're good people." She narrowed her eyes. "Well, who then?"

What could I say? "I'd really like to tell you, but in some ways... it's complicated." I stared into the finely sliced apple. "I just don't know about it all."

She sat up. "It's none of my business."

I shook my head. "No. I want to tell you. If it works out, I promise to reveal everything."

"I'll hold you to that."

"When we were little, we were just too young for the whole boy thing—apart from the idea that most of them were contaminated and we needed to run as far away as possible."

She pointed her fork at me. "I remember hiding from Pascale's big brother on the pog when he threatened to put mud down our necks."

"And the next day we were all friends again," I said, "playing loups-garous, which I think was the craze at the time."

"I remember that."

We ate in silence for a moment, but the thought of Théo played on my mind. I needed to say something so we could put it behind us. "I heard about your eldest," I said softly.

She placed her fork on her plate and stared out the window, her face set, her jaw tight. "I should have explained. I thought you might hear about it somehow, though."

"I am so sorry."

She turned to me, her face lifeless once more. "It's fine. I don't want to talk about it, but it's fine. Time moves on."

I nodded and struggled to finish my last mouthful, trying to think of something to say.

Roselle sipped her tea, the remains of her tartelette abandoned on her plate. She glanced at her watch. "I have to pick up the children in five minutes."

"Of course." I'd timed that terribly.

She rose and I walked her to the hall, wishing we'd left things on a better note. She shrugged on her coat, her eyes avoiding mine.

"Let's meet up again soon," I said as I pulled open the door. "Thank you for the tartelettes—and the macarons." I hoped she could hear the appreciation in my voice.

She nodded, her face set in stone. We kissed automatically and she walked to her car with steady, measured strides.

Taking a deep breath, I closed the door. "Sorry, Roselle," I murmured. And I didn't just mean for my poor timing. I meant for Théo and for all those lost years.

I headed to the living room, dropped onto the sofa and stared into nothing. Roselle and Pascale must have suffered so much. Rémy's family too—they'd also lost a son and brother. I rubbed my face. Rémy was way overdue.

My gaze drifted to the chateau—it always did. Instinctively, I pulled myself back to the room, as though it were safer to keep my attention anywhere else. But, then, what was I doing not looking at my own view? I'd let Joël, Rémy and Sylvie get to me. Perhaps they'd made their associations with the pog after Théo disappeared, but I didn't need to follow suit. Their behaviour was senseless—so much was senseless at the moment.

I rose and squared up to the chateau, glaring at it, challenging it, daring it to... what? There it was, dim in the fading light, leaden cloud billowing above the rock. My eyes drew to the shadowy crenellations—the place was curious, almost hypnotic, but that was ridiculous. All this talk of the Sarramauca, the Désaccord. I'd let their unfounded fears affect me. It was a chateau, that was all.

I grinned and turned away to sit down, but a pinprick of orange caught my eye. I swung back and stared. The musicians were heading up the hill. My heart thudded slowly, my muscles tensing. Joël had all but hauled me from the pog, and here they were again. And Rémy—he'd insisted I shouldn't go there, spinning flamboyant stories hinting at something sinister. Had the chateau become some kind of urban myth? I glowered at the rugged, broken walls. The whole situation was ludicrous. Not just the chateau, but Rémy. I was involved with someone who couldn't tell me why he was France's number one missing person. And the worst of it was that, despite this madness, I was completely beguiled by him.

I shot another evil look at the chateau, then flopped onto the sofa and scowled at the dancing flames, sparks of yellow and orange darting up the chimney.

"Violette."

I sprang around.

He stood there by the door, smiling, a boundless presence.

I glared at him, wanting him and not wanting him. Not wanting all this nonsense. "How did you get in?"

His smile vanished. "What's wrong?"

A short sharp laugh escaped me as I glanced over him. He wore the same clothes again. "What's wrong? You obviously have a resident tailor, barber and cobbler installed somewhere in the mountains at this mysterious place you're staying at, because you're so utterly perfect, not even a scratch on your shoes. Oh, and you took the mountain path with no coat—did you think I wouldn't worry?"

"Violette—"

Anger grated through me. It was all completely incomprehensible. "And your brother is on the pog again, despite no one else being welcome there, and despite it being home to the Sarramauca, the Désaccord and whatever the hell else." I seethed the words. Nothing made sense. Nothing. "And you know what?" I glanced at the chateau, its walls sombre in the gathering dusk. "I don't care what Joël says. Or what you say."

I strode into the kitchen, hauled the cassoulet from the oven and dropped it onto a board, then stormed past Rémy, up to my bedroom. I flung on a fleece, grabbed my torch and tore back down, my feet drumming on the stairs.

Rémy walked into the hall as I pulled on my boots. "Where are you going?" he asked in a low voice, his eyes wide.

I flung on my ski jacket, grabbed my hat and gloves and shot him another glare, my mouth twisting upward. "Wouldn't you like to know?"

He reached out and grabbed my wrist. I stared at his hand, his fingers around my pulse drawing me despite myself.

"Violette, please trust me," he breathed. "You said you would."

"It's not that I don't trust you, it's that I don't like this ridiculous situation." I pulled my hand away, strode to the door and tugged the handle, thinking I'd left it unlocked after Roselle. It didn't move. I undid the dead bolt and turned back. "The door was locked. How on earth did you get in?"

"I, uh—"

"I don't care." I stepped out, slammed the door and marched up the path.

The wind spiralled fallen leaves and tossed the hornbeams to and fro, the icy air slipping between my layers. Even so, I was hot—too hot. The situation wasn't right, any of it—Rémy's clothing, how he'd gotten into the house, his supposed disappearance. I paced past Sylvie's brightly lit windows. The Sarramauca indeed.

Clicking on my torch, I turned onto the drover's track, then headed down through the woodland and crossed the meadows, driving confusion and fury into every stride.

"Violette!" Rémy yelled from behind. I ignored him and took the old cobbled path onto the pog, the wind surging around me.

"Violette, wait!" Closer now, distorted by the gale.

I turned around.

He ran up to me, his breath heaving. "Please, Violette, don't go up there."

"This is absurd. You have to tell me what's going on." Lightning splintered across the sky to a peel of thunder.

"I'm trying to tell you—believe me, I'm trying."

"What do you mean? You haven't told me a thing. And you're doing it again."

"Doing what?"

"You're out without proper clothing and no torch. Do you think I don't care?" It was ludicrous—a life or death matter this time of year. But he'd just entered my locked house... his clothes were always the same...

"Please, just come back home."

"What? When I have a chance to listen to the musicians? When I have a chance to experience the Désaccord?"

A look of horror crossed his face. "Violette, don't be stupid."

That was a mistake.

I strode upward under the arches of box, the woody limbs flailing.

"Please, Violette, don't go any further. It's not safe."

Notes fractured around me, displaced in the wind. The musicians. Thunder and lightning broke again, this time casting a blast of hail.

"Violette, get down here," Rémy roared, his voice cast with an edge I'd not heard before.

Hail stung my exposed skin. I knew by the change in incline that the clump of box stood at the top of the next slope before the path curved again. I ran for it and ducked under the knotted branches. As I regained my breath, the air grew thick, almost palpable. Foreboding sank into my chest. Ice pummelled around me, the branches a poor shelter. I shone the torch back down the slope, the beam ineffectual in the deluge. Rémy was an idiot to be out dressed like that.

The wind swirled around the boughs, casting hail at odd angles, building to a squalling cacophony. The air condensed in my throat, gelatinous and ropy. As I breathed, it sank in like pure dread. But that was stupid—the last thing I needed was to panic like before. The hail lessened and my torch caught Rémy's figure on the slope. He had to be frozen. I ducked out of the bushes, concerned about him even now.

He strode up to me and grabbed me by the shoulders. "I won't let you go any further."

"You won't let me? It's not your choice." Obviously, he was fine—I shouldn't have wasted my time. I pulled away and carried on up the path.

He caught my jacket and pulled me back. I turned to

face him. With an unearthly howl, another barrage of hail belted down, pellets of ice springing off him. "You can't go any further." His face twisted with something I couldn't read. Perhaps rage, but more like desperation.

"Why?" I shook my head, unable to believe I was indulging him.

"Because I can't go any further."

"You don't have to come."

"I do."

He still wasn't making sense and he had no right to handle me. I yanked myself away and sprinted up the last incline before the chateau, cold shivering through me despite my pace. Thunder rolled continuously, lightning strobed all around and the wind caterwauled as though it were a tangle of pain and loathing and sickness. The air it carried thickened further, restricting my throat. I forced myself not to cough. I wasn't going to get carried away because of some insane superstitions.

"Violette! No!" Rémy called, his voice agonised.

I couldn't ignore that tone. I swung back. Rémy stood below me by the stand of box, my torch beam barely penetrating the billowing, teeming air that gusted over the surface of the pog, encircling Rémy, encircling me.

"You have to come back here," he yelled.

There was no way I would be drawn by his crazy angst. I took a step backward, a step closer to the chateau. He took a stride toward me and the swirling darkness descended upon him in a cutting shriek. I rammed my hands over my ears, but the sound pierced through all the same. The murk drove into Rémy's gut. He bent double with a scream. Then it pulled at his limbs, hauling him above the ground and ripping into every part of his body.

I was rooted to the bedrock. I couldn't look away and I couldn't comprehend what I saw. Rémy thrashed and cried in torment, unable to escape the glutenous embrace—the air, the wind, whatever it was, somehow it knew what it was doing.

Amidst the onslaught, Rémy managed to fix his eyes on mine. "Violette," he mouthed. Then the darkness forced in on him, encompassing him completely. It bawled and screeched and dissipated to nothing. Rémy was gone.

"Rémy," I yelled as I hurtled down the slope to where he'd stood. I spun around, attempting to scan the mountainside through the murk and the weather, but there was nothing—nothing at all.

Screams racked from deep within my chest. I yelled his name over and over again, the rank air filling my lungs. He'd just gone, he'd vanished. He'd told me he couldn't go any further, and then he'd disappeared. He'd left me. I screamed again and again and again.

Something seized my coat. "Violette."

Breathless, I swung into Joël.

"Are you alright?" he said, the musicians peering over his shoulders, their faces creased in concern.

I stared at Joël. Rémy was gone, and I couldn't say anything.

"We need to get you off the pog," he said, grasping my arm.

"No, Joël. Get your hands off me." I pulled away.

He took a step backward. "Okay, Violette, but—"

I turned and fled down the path, my feet twisting and sliding, my vision blurring with tears. Everything repeated in my head—he'd said he couldn't go any further and then he'd gone. But he couldn't vanish, people didn't just vanish. I stumbled to the base of the pog and made my way across the meadows, slowing from exhaustion as I entered the woods. My breath heaved as I trod up the drover's track, and still the tears wouldn't stop. Everything had been so confusing before, but now... now I couldn't even think straight. And he was gone.

Once past Sylvie's I paused, my heart pounding. He might just turn up as he'd done before, a shadow under the hornbeams. But no. The lane lay empty.

Chapter Thirteen

Shudders coursed through me as I let myself into the house. I was unable to focus, unable to grasp what had happened. The fire still blazed, the heat unrestrained without the guard, but it did nothing to ease the chill that seeped into my bones. He'd stood there by the door only a little while before, asking me where I was going. Maman and Papa had stood there too, before they'd left for their evening in Toulouse.

My chest ached and my clothes clung to me, cold and uncomfortable, soaked from melted hail. Barely aware of my actions, I tugged off my outdoor gear with trembling fingers, some invisible force guiding me through the motions of self-preservation. As I climbed the stairs, images of Rémy flickered through my mind, his hands on my shoulders, his insistence I should return home. I stripped off my wet things and pulled on a jumper, sweats and socks, yet still I could see Rémy, the fetid air ripping into his body, his anguish. He'd shaped my name on his lips moments before he'd...

My throat stuck. I tried to breathe normally, a small part

of me insisting I needed warmth. Following my instincts, I headed downstairs and dug at the fire with the poker, my hands trembling as I broke the flaming logs into charcoal pieces. I piled on more wood and it caught immediately, the clamouring wind dragging the inferno up the chimney. Even so, I couldn't feel the heat.

Still the images came, mingling with vestiges of lightning flickering through the glass. I didn't understand what I'd seen. I couldn't understand. Everything around me seemed unreal, everything but the images of him. I hauled myself to the sofa, pulled the rug from the back and curled underneath, my body shaking.

Where had Rémy gone?

The thought repeated over and over.

I opened my eyes. I must have slept. The fire had burned to glowing coals and the room was cold. Beyond the doors the first snow drifted across the night. As I pulled myself up, everything that had happened came back and a sinking emptiness filled my middle. My world had cracked around me.

For a moment I sat there, unable to move, then it dawned how very cold I was and practicality took over. I hauled myself up and stacked more logs on the fire. "What happened to you, Rémy?" I whispered into the ashes.

The floor creaked.

I spun around. He stood there by the wall, gauzy, a shadow of himself, his shoulders, his face, his body, all tinted diffuse twilight blue, the harp visible through him.

"Rémy?" I gasped.

His gentle eyes drew wide, his mouth parted, his chest rose and fell—all of him translucent, a poorly projected image. "Violette," he said softly.

This couldn't be my imagination—it couldn't. "What are you?" I stammered, my heart hammering.

"I'm just me." He raised his hands and gazed at them, then shook his head.

"You're... not real."

"I am real, Violette, I promise."

"No. I saw you attacked... screaming. And now... look at you."

"I know it's so completely implausible," he said steadily, his brow arched, "but please try to entertain the possibility that this really is me."

All I could do was gape, cold sweat prickling over my body. He had to be an illusion, a ghost, something...

"Please, Violette..."

I couldn't ignore the anguish in his voice, and I needed to respond. "What happened?" I whispered.

"I told you already," he replied. "I just didn't tell you I had."

His words set me further adrift. "You haven't explained anything."

He took a step toward me, a glimmer of desperation in his eyes.

I slid back across the hearth. Despite all of this, a part of me wanted to reach out and touch him, but I couldn't. He didn't come closer.

"The story," he said. "The musician."

I released a dry laugh. "The musician who raised the Désaccord to make the most powerful music? The musician protected by the Harmonie while the Désaccord tried to destroy him?" I shook my head.

"I'm the musician," he said.

"Don't be ridiculous."

"Violette. It was me. I messed with things I didn't understand. Me and Alex and Bénédict. We created the most awe-inspiring music with a depth that had not been heard before... and this"—he gestured to himself—"this was my price. We invoked the Désaccord and we couldn't contain it. Things were happening, strange things, the orchestra went out of their minds, we lost Bénédict." Rémy's face creased, pain and regret clear in his eyes.

"No," I said. It wasn't possible.

"Look at me, Violette. I'm barely... here. Is it too much of a leap?"

I tried to make sense of his words, but I was only able to stare.

"I always knew about the Désaccord and the Harmonie," he went on. "We—my family and some others—we've always known. It's why we play at the chateau every week. We play to evoke the Harmonie, to hold the Désaccord away. The chateau was built on ancient ruins astronomically aligned and built in perfect proportion to reflect the golden..."

He'd lost me, and it must have been written all over my face.

"The chateau was built to evoke the Harmonie," he continued. "It's one of the few remaining places that still reflect the intention of the ancient builders. Each of the surviving sanctuaries has a specific song tied to its dimensions, and I knew the song for the chateau because we'd always played it there." His voice wavered a little. "After what happened, I knew I had to do something to restrain the

Désaccord. So I went there—I picked up an old violin from the Palais Garnier and I drove to Sarrat. I climbed to the chateau and I played the key song—I played like never before and I evoked the Harmonie. But the Désaccord was linked to me somehow, it tried to seize me, to destroy me, and the Harmonie... it encompassed me in absolute..." He glanced around as though he were searching for a suitable description. "Absolute grace, warmth, beauty. It wouldn't allow the Désaccord to touch me. But when I attempted to return, the Désaccord was there, waiting, preventing me."

I narrowed my eyes. "You're saying you are still in the chateau?"

"In a way."

"Despite the fact I've seen you in various places, despite the fact I've touched you... despite all that, you've been sitting in the chateau for five years?"

"It's not quite like that. When the Harmonie protected me, I was taken up in it. I... I don't know where I am exactly. Somehow inside the Harmonie even though I'm here."

I frowned at him.

"The chateau also exists in the Harmonie," he added, "and time is different. I didn't know I'd been away for five years until you said—I had a sense of time passing, but it could've been an hour, a week, a year, all at the same time. It's hard to describe. And Théo is here too."

My breath caught. "What?"

"Théo Guérin, Roselle and Pascale's son."

"I'm sorry." I couldn't understand any of this, least of all what he'd just said. "Théo is there, with you?"

"Yes. I don't know what happened, but I think he must have been caught up in everything that day."

My eyes locked with his. "They think he's dead. Drowned in the river."

Pain drew across his face, his chest heaving.

"Is he alright?" I asked.

"Yes, he's fine, content. But he can't return because of the Désaccord. Because of me."

It was so utterly unbelievable. "This is why your clothes never change, you don't have a phone and you can't return to your parents?"

He nodded.

"No one else can see you?" I asked.

"It doesn't seem like it."

My stomach twisted. "Then why can I?"

"I've been trying to figure it out," he said. "The first time I returned, I found myself on the road outside your house."

"You acted as if you didn't know where you were."

"Because I didn't. It took me a few moments to recognise the place. And all the while we talked, I tried to work out what had brought me here. Then in the village, at the pool, Nico couldn't see me, and that woman thought you were talking to yourself."

My mouth hung open. "That's why. And the coffee?"

"I'd not had any... direct sensory experiences for a long time. The heat took me by surprise, and the taste, and the food yesterday." He smiled.

"So what is it? How can I see you?"

He took a deep breath. "I think it must be your synaesthesia."

I shook my head. My colours were my colours, nothing more.

"I can't see any other explanation," he said. "After the first time, when I tuned your harp and you were affected, I thought through everything and remembered I'd heard you had synaesthesia. That's why I questioned you at the pool. I honestly don't know how it works, but somehow, when you arrived, I was drawn to you, or you drew me... and you could see me."

"But I haven't got synaesthesia anymore." My voice quavered.

"I don't think that's true. I think you're controlling it, seeing what you want to—you want to see me, but you don't want to see sound as colour because it frightens you."

"Don't go into that again."

"I have to," he said. "I have to raise it as the most likely idea... the only one I can think of."

The possibility was too much to consider. I stood up, aware of the space between us, his body wraithlike, a not-quite-there deep, enigmatic blue, the scrollwork of the harp, the strings, the levers all showing through.

"Violette, it's still me." His gaze burned.

I took a step toward him, taking in the line of his nose, the softness around his eyes, the wave in his brushed-back curls. And despite his transparency, I could feel him. "Then why are you like... this?" I asked.

"When we went to the pog I basically walked into the Désaccord, right where it was waiting for me. It attacked."

"You disappeared."

"The Harmonie took me back. But I don't know why I'm like this now." He glanced down at himself. "Perhaps the Désaccord trapped me further inside the Harmonie—or it did something to you, to prevent you from seeing me properly. But really I've no idea."

I shouldn't have gone to the pog. He'd asked me not to. He'd asked me to trust him. I hadn't listened, but it had all been so preposterous—it still was. And despite everything, I didn't want to lose him. "I... we have something. I like spending time with you." I stammered out the understatement. I had to try harder. "Your touch... I want to be with you."

A smile drew across his face and his eyes lit. He raised his hand as if to touch me and stopped, obviously thinking better of it. "Violette, I want you, I want to get to know you, I want to spend every second with you. But I..." He glanced down at his filmy body.

I reached up, almost daring to touch his cheek, wanting to make a connection, but his skin was gossamer, lighter than before, I was sure of it. The lines of the harp showed more clearly, as though he were nothing but a layer of colour, an impression of himself. Fear gouged through me. "You're fading," I whispered.

He glanced down at himself and his lips parted. He was barely more than a shimmer.

"No," I stammered. "No. I don't want to lose you. We have to do something. Rémy, tell me what to do."

"I'm not sure." He shook his head.

"You said I see you because of my synaesthesia." I had to entertain the notion no matter how much I didn't like it.

"It's my best guess."

"Well, then, how do I bring it back?"

He opened his mouth for a moment, then closed it. "Violette, I can't ask you to do that."

"You're not asking. How do I bring it back?" I wasn't going to let him go, even if it meant subjecting myself to the thing I detested the most. What other option was there?

He scoured my face. "Your synaesthesia hurts you. I can't ask you to do something that tears you up."

The years in Paris had been too much. I'd lost my mind as colours swirled over me, blinding my vision, my senses becoming more than my thoughts. "Yes, it's horrendous, and I never want to experience it again, but I'm not going to let you disappear. If I can help in some way, of course I'll do it." There was no question.

He nodded, but he didn't appear convinced—and I was sure he was lighter again.

"Play the harp," I said. His playing had moved me and provoked my synaesthesia.

He turned and passed his hand through the strings.

My mouth dropped. "Then tell me what I have to do," I said, my voice rising. "Tell me!"

He released a breath, seeming to finally accept my decision. "I think," he said slowly, "you will have to open your senses. I think you will have to feel."

My throat tightened. There was so much I didn't want to feel. But I wasn't as vulnerable as I'd been years ago. I was willing to give it a go.

"We can try something," he said. "Sit down."

I stepped back and sank into the armchair. He positioned himself behind me. Even though he was barely... there, I could feel his presence as I always had.

"You need to relax," he said softly. "Let go of yourself."

"After all this?"

"Yes, after all this. Try to switch off. Listen to the fire and allow your senses to respond."

I gazed into the blaze. The glowing logs had settled together in the centre, the flames fusing as they drew upward. I couldn't really believe my synaesthesia would make Rémy solid but I had to try, and my stomach knotted at the prospect. I took a deep breath and released it slowly, attempting to let go. The room blurred as I relaxed my focus and absorbed the gentle cracking and hissing of the fire. I followed the variation in sound, and all the time I could feel Rémy standing behind me. Minutes passed, minutes of enforced steady breathing, minutes of listening—but nothing. I shifted around and glanced at him.

"Give it a while," he said. "Forget everything."

As if I could do that.

I sat back and listened, every flaming crackle confirming my synaesthesia was absent. "It won't come back," I snapped.

"You're trying too hard. Stop worrying about what you have to achieve and focus on what you feel as you hear the sounds. Let's try something different," he said. "The wind."

Dropping my head back onto the cushion, I opened myself to the rushing and gusting beyond the doors. Rémy had been tormented on the pog by that... whatever it was. It had been the wind and it had been something more, but the bluster around the house didn't shriek. It held an indistinct softness, deep and resonant, the vibrations reverberating through the walls.

"How does it make you feel?" he said, his voice barely distinguishable from the gale.

"I feel..." I searched inside. "A little too warm, there's tension in my neck."

"Can you take it further?"

Shimmying my shoulders to release the rigidity, I saw Rémy on the pog again. I didn't want to lose him. I didn't want him to vanish, yet this really wasn't working. I sprang up and spun around, my eyes blazing. "I can't do it."

He made a brief half-smile, the lines of the dark doors and the snow beyond clearly visible through him. "Yes, you can. You've done it before, so many times."

"And I've spent my life trying to shut it away."

"Sit back down," he said.

I dropped into the chair, clenching the arms as I forced myself to relax again.

"My guess is," he said into my ear, "for you to be able to see me, and for your synaesthesia to have bothered you so much, your condition is extreme."

Yes, it was extreme. I shrugged.

His hand covered my clenched fingers, his touch warm, weighty. I glanced down. He was a chimera against me and yet I could feel him as solid as before. I shuddered and closed my eyes. It was better if I didn't look.

"I think," he murmured as he withdrew his hand, "not only can you see sound, but you can see scents and flavours. Perhaps you can see touch too."

His fingers trailed over the back of my neck. My skin shivered, my attention immediately honed to his touch. I wanted him to be as solid as he felt. Slowly, he drew his fingers across my collarbone, over my pulse. I melted into his hand, my breath shallow.

"Perhaps," he whispered, his fingers brushing across my cheek and then my lips, "you can see all of me."

I gasped. His touch was fire, bursting into ripples of midnight blue tinged with silver. There was nothing but colour where he'd trailed, effervescent colour shimmering through my sinews. Releasing shallow breaths, I fought the impulse to push the luminosity away—this wasn't the assault that had so often consumed me in the past. No, it was strangely gentle and yet at the same time seductive. The colour of Rémy.

I twisted around.

There he stood, on the other side of the armchair, solid, tangible, whole. He looked down at himself and grinned.

I rose and stood before him, the echo of his touch upon my lips. My gaze covered every inch of him—the contour where his cheek met his curled locks, the familiarity of his always-the-same clothes, the flexing of his wrists as his fingers stirred. I stepped closer and ran my hand over his collar and along the neckline of his waistcoat, resting my palm on his chest, relief flooding through me, relief mingled with longing. He was here—somehow he was here—and I didn't want him to leave.

He placed his hand over mine. "You did it." His voice rippled night blue, enthralling, flourishing in meanders that diminished to nothing.

Reaching up, I cupped his cheek, his stubble appearing as dark points before me. I drew his face toward mine and kissed him ever so gently, relishing his yielding, welcoming lips. He wrapped me in his arms and reciprocated with tenderness then fervour. My sense of him grew until I was filled with his scent, his touch, his taste—all of him blending into colours that were utterly vibrant. I was consumed by him, and it felt so right.

We drew apart, his arms still around me, his eyes searching my face. "You really did it." More mesmerising ripples.

"With your help." I let out a burst of hesitant laughter. Struggling to pull my attention from him, I glanced around us. Undulating grey streamed through the room, jagged then smooth, the colour of the wind roaring around the house. A gust shook the walls and an explosion of black engulfed the grey, merging with the creaking umber of a rafter, the sparking scarlet of the fire, the stark white points of snow driven against the doors. All of it fused into a cacophony of colour that covered me entirely. I fought for breath, my throat constricting.

"Violette!"

I could feel Rémy shake me, but I could barely make him out.

"Violette, what is it?"

"Too many colours," I managed.

"Shut it out," he shouted. "You know what to do, you do it all the time."

Shut it out. I knew how to do that. Through the distortion I could perceive his face, the flush of his cheeks, those eyes. I fixed on him, refusing to take in anything but his crystalline irises. He was all there was, nothing else, just him.

"Violette!" He shook me again.

My breath evened out and I blinked. The colours were there, flickering in a halo around my vision, but they were restrained.

"What the hell just happened?" Rémy's voice—I wanted it. Not the other colours, just him, just a little.

"Violette, talk to me."

I centred on his colour, allowing it to come forth, holding back the others.

"Violette?"

There it was again, that intriguing blue. Through it all I registered his face lined with concern, his arms tight around me and the fact that I hadn't responded. "There was too much colour." I stumbled over my words. "I pushed it away, all but yours. And you're still here."

He smiled. "Here and solid."

His voice flickered across my vision. I fought to hold the

other impressions away, still focussing on his face. If I pushed his colours away too, would he vanish?

He unfurled from me and stepped back, his hands on my arms as though he were assessing my state. My legs wobbled without his support. I reached for the back of the armchair, but he took my weight before I could make contact.

"Come on." He guided me to the sofa and I dropped into the cushions. "The synaesthesia is too much for you," he said. "I'm sorry."

"Don't be." I touched his cheek. "Your colours are perfect, I want them. It's just everything else—it's taking a great deal of focus to keep it all away." I remembered his words from when we'd argued. "You said I needed to let go, to experience my synaesthesia fully, but I don't think I can." I stared at his waistcoat, focussing on each ebony button in turn.

"Of course you don't have to. I'm not the expert on these things and I didn't understand how hard it is for you. Don't do more than you can manage, if you even want to do that at all."

His colours were stunning. I followed them as they swirled and twisted, enhancing my sense of him. Even so, weariness flooded through me. I shifted around and leant my head against his shoulder. "This is all so new. I just need a moment."

I

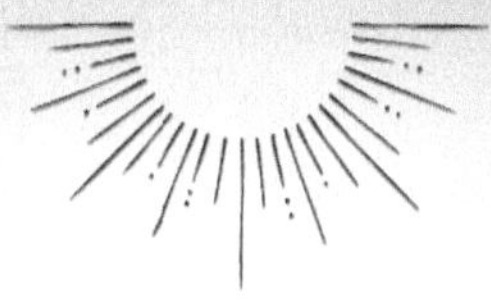

Humankind sculpts the Harmonie in many ways. What is matter but music solidified? And all of it is but an image of true form. It is illusion.

I, for my sins, sculpt music, I fashion vibration. I know the interval that inspires joy and the mode that provokes pain. I know the chord that bears profound love and the key that holds darkest fear. I know how to mould harmony and dissonance to reflect the antithesis that drives mankind ever onward without pause and without rest. I fathom the gaps, the pauses, the spaces in which assimilation and rebirth occur. I master the notes that combine to hint at all human experience. I comprehend how to sculpt the Désaccord, how to shape it, how to make it my own.

With knowledge comes power over minds and hearts, and the relentless drive to create, to order the world for selfish ends, the creation unto death—for how often does the created take control of the creator? Yet I have found form in matter to calm the torment, to quiet the urge, to still the ruthless compulsion.

I have found you.

Chapter Fourteen

I sprang upright, wincing at the brilliant light, the duvet balled in my fists. Images of Rémy tore through my head, the Désaccord ripping into him, the harp visible through his body, the colour of his touch.

He wasn't here.

My gaze settled on the landscape beyond the window. The first proper snow had fallen overnight and the valley was swathed in white, the pog and the chateau barely visible against the steel cloud. I shivered. It had been horrendous there—the thick, rank air, the shrieking.

A blackbird flew across the garden, its warning call breaking the silence, terracotta and orange flecking the glare. I winced and adjusted my position, the bed frame creaking in puce streaks joined by the grating grey of a car passing in the lane. I stared at it all, my throat closing in, my breath shallow, the sensation utterly terrifying. I wanted to tear it from me, but I had to cope. It certainly wasn't as bad as Paris.

I focussed on the bedstead, the sweep to the central curve, the detail of flowers carved into the wood. The colours became less intense until they were flickers at the side of my vision. I could hold them there, on the edge of awareness, but I didn't want to force them from me completely and somehow push Rémy away too.

"Rémy," I called, my voice sharp. He wasn't here now, so had he faded to nothing? I pulled off the covers and noticed my clothes. I wore the jumper and sweats I'd changed into yesterday evening. I couldn't recall going to bed—the last thing I remembered was resting against Rémy.

A piece of paper lay on the floorboards by the wall, my phone weighing it down. I hauled myself out of bed and picked it up. In curling letters was written, *You are beautiful when you sleep, as always x.*

He'd been here. I closed my eyes for a moment and released a breath, but I wouldn't be happy until I'd seen him. He'd said I'd drawn him to me. If I'd done that, perhaps I could do it again, but I hadn't the faintest idea how.

I strode into the bathroom, leant on the sink and gazed at my reflection. My face was pale, my hair tangled and matted. I felt as bad as I looked, my head heavy, my mouth dry. He'd written that I looked beautiful when I slept. A small smile crept to my lips.

I squeezed toothpaste on my brush and cleaned my teeth, holding the colour of the scrubbing away as yesterday evening repeated in my head—he'd tried to tell me what had happened through stories and... Théo. I gripped the sides of the basin seeing Roselle's lifeless face, her voice strained. She'd lost him. She thought he was dead. Poor Théo was caught in all of this, and he and Rémy were trapped, unable to return. We had to do something about it, but I couldn't do anything without Rémy here.

Turning on the shower, I gasped as a wash of blue smothered my senses. I needed to be aware of my surroundings at all times, aware of any potential sounds. Focussing on the ceramic rim of the bath, the colour dissipated. I sat down on the edge and dropped my shoulders, barely able to believe that after years of closing myself off to my synaesthesia, I was opening myself again. It was madness, but I couldn't risk Rémy.

I undressed, turned the shower to full and stepped in. The colour intruded again and I drove it back. Perhaps I would be able to manage now I had so much more control. I scrubbed shampoo into my scalp and washed the rest of me, thinking over Rémy's words. He'd said I'd drawn him to me. I'd stood outside gazing around the garden when I'd noticed him on the road the first time, and, as far as I could remember, I'd not done or thought anything. When I'd seen him next, I'd sat by the pool in the square. Later that day I'd seen him again. I'd been drenched with rain and intent on getting indoors. I couldn't see a connection.

I dried myself, wrapped the towel around me and stepped into the bedroom, gazing through the window to the pale silhouette of the chateau. Was Rémy somehow there at this moment? Well, wherever he was, I had to get him here.

Pulling myself from the pog, I blow-dried my hair, holding the encroaching colour away. The moment when Rémy had turned up at Les Fonts came to mind. I'd been staring into the water, doing nothing. But perhaps that was it... I hadn't done or thought anything each time Rémy arrived. I'd been staring at the garden enjoying the wilderness, and later as I trod along the lane in sodden clothes, I'd been too wet to think of anything. Perhaps I needed to not think to bring him back—it made sense because when I wanted my colours to vanish, I did the opposite, I focussed, I brought myself back to me. But I'd been furious with Rémy yesterday when he'd appeared inside the house. That didn't fit—or did it? I hadn't exactly been focussed.

Perhaps I needed to let go. My grip tightened around the dryer. What if I couldn't draw him? Yet there was something that always made me lose myself.

I threw on some clothes and headed downstairs. Despite the range's continuous efforts, it was too cold. Blinking away flashes of yesterday, knowing that if I thought about it I would probably not be able to do what I wanted to do, I knelt on the hearth and lit the fire. When the kindling had caught, I stepped over to the harp and drew the key from the arm, setting it on the floor, then I positioned myself on the stool and tipped the frame, resting it on my shoulder, where it had begun to feel like part of me.

It was worth a try.

As I ran my fingers over the smooth wood, I closed my eyes. Despite the crackle of the fire and the creak of my stool, the room bore a strange silence, the hush of the outer world that only snow can bring. I extended my forefinger and drew it back across the strings, releasing a glissando in a spectrum of colour that flickered at the periphery of my vision. Pressing away the sounds of the house, I allowed the vibrations of the harp to come to the fore. Yesterday I'd needed to open myself to solidify Rémy. I had no idea if I needed to do the same to call him back, but it was somewhere to start. If I could be selective, rather than let everything overwhelm me, perhaps I could manage my synaesthesia.

I curled my hands and swept my fingers over the first notes of *Lo Boièr*. Colour surged over me, seizing my breath. But synaesthesia was only a distortion of my senses, not reality, and Rémy was worth more than habitual fear. I steadied myself and played on. My movements were fluent now, my fingers finding the strings by memory, my hands even shaping the occasional chord. I let the music wash over me as I sang the baffling words under my breath, shaping my mouth around the vowels in the refrain, catching a shimmer of my own voice as I strove to harmonise with the harp. I played verse after verse, the old melody filling me with peace, transporting me somewhere beyond myself. As I drew to a close, I opened my eyes.

He stood by the fire.

I started, the sight of him drawing me from wherever I'd been. It had actually worked. I'd let go as I'd played and he'd come. Relief washed over me.

His mouth angled into a gentle smile. I stepped over, took his head in my hands and kissed him. He pulled me in closer, his solidity reassuring me he was more than the phantom of last night.

"I've been waiting to see you since I carried you to bed," he murmured as we came apart. His colours encircled me and I wanted more of them.

"Well," I said, "that's how I got upstairs. How long have you been standing there?"

He brushed my cheek. "Since what I'm guessing were the first few notes of *Lo Boièr*."

I tightened inside. I wasn't used to being listened to.

"It was absolutely beautiful," he added. "I didn't want you to stop."

"It wasn't meant to be beautiful, it was just meant to be."

"That's the best kind of music." His saturated blue rippled over me, tinged with the slightest hint of other colours when his voice varied in tone.

"I'm so glad you're back," I said.

He grinned. "I'm glad to be here. How are you coping with your synaesthesia?"

"Thankfully I'm able to allow in what I want to experience."

He drew his fingers over my throat, sending ripples of silver through me. "And what do you want to experience?" he whispered.

"I think you know."

He kissed me softly, his lips tantalising. I wanted so much more of him, but how much more could I have? I drew back.

He studied my face with a questioning gaze.

I couldn't risk him disappearing again. We had to sort this out. "You're trapped, you and Théo. I'm so sorry I went back to the pog—"

He opened his mouth to say something but I continued.

"—and I'm utterly relieved I could help you... solidify. But you haven't returned properly, have you? You're back to me, but not to everyone else." If he was... normal, he wouldn't have appeared suddenly again.

"No," he said softly with a shake of his head.

"Then we need to figure out how to get you and Théo back."

"Being in the Harmonie is barely describable. It's beauty and peace, but I don't belong there, it's not my place." His voice grew deeper, scored with frustration. "Life, the world, everything, it's all moving on, and until you called me, I didn't know what was happening. I want to come back and live again." He pulled back and ran his fingers through his hair. "And Théo shouldn't be there because of me. I wanted to ask you to help the moment I'd figured out what was going on, but it would have sounded ridiculous."

"Well, now I know, we can do something about it. Last night you said your family was aware of the Désaccord and the Harmonie—can they help?"

"My family wouldn't know any more than I do. No, we have to contact Alex. We were in this together, Alex, Bénédict and me. Everything we learnt we took from two old books that detailed the concepts of the Harmonie and the Désaccord in combination with all kinds of musical theory from as far back as Pythagoras and Plato. Amongst it all there were..." He narrowed his eyes. "Ways to influence the Désaccord. Alex studied the books most. Bénédict was busy with his latest composition and I was travelling everywhere for work. If anyone would know how to help, it would be Alex."

I kissed him briefly. "So how do we contact Alex?"

"When I... left, he was the assistant music director of the Paris Opera."

I pulled away from him, drew my laptop from under the sofa and sat down. He joined me, draping his arm around my shoulders. I brought up the website of the Opéra national de Paris with its elegant black-and-white schema and searched the staff list. "Alex... Chaufourier?"

"Yes, that's him."

I clicked on the link.

Alex stood before us, his boyish face, watchful eyes and broad shoulders framed by the pillars of a baroque building. He was styled in a white shirt and black jacket that, with his dark hair, coordinated with the colours of the website perfectly.

We scanned the text.

"He made music director while I've been away. He looks older. What else have I missed?"

I thought of the meal with his family and glanced at him. "Do you know Orianne?"

"Noé's wife. She was pregnant..."

"Emmie is almost five and Seb is three." I scoured his face, unable to imagine how it must feel to be away that long and not even realise.

He frowned. "I'm an uncle. I can't believe I missed their births." He closed his eyes and dropped his head back against the cushions. "Hell, what have I gotten myself into?"

"I'm going to call Alex." I grabbed my phone from the kitchen and stood behind the sofa to take the contact details. "The number is for the box office. It's the only one."

"The admin office won't be open today anyway."

I tapped in the number, strode to the doors where the reception was better and stared into a veil of lightly falling snow. With the cold we'd had, it wouldn't let up now, not until the spring.

"Do you mind if I look at the schedule?" Rémy asked.

"Go ahead."

He made a couple of clicks. "There's a performance of *Don Giovanni* on at the moment, accompanied by the Vienna Philharmonic. The Paris Opera orchestra are playing with a modern ballet for lunchtime short performances over the weekend. Alex is conducting that, so he'll be around."

"Opéra national de Paris box office, how may I help you?" came the clipped voice on speakerphone.

I glanced at Rémy. "Hello, yes, I'm trying to reach Alex Chaufourier. I know this isn't the normal route to contact him, but it's urgent."

Rémy raised his eyebrows. I shrugged. It was urgent to me.

"I'm sorry, I have no contact details for Monsieur Chaufourier. You will have to call the offices tomorrow morning."

"I need to get hold of him immediately. Is there anything you can do?"

"Just one moment..." I heard talking in the background. "The best we can offer is for you to leave a message."

"Alright. Please could you say that Violette Romèu is trying to get hold of him for an urgent matter concerning Rémy Rabasten." I gave her my number.

There was silence for a moment.

"I have the message. It will be passed on as soon as possible."

"Thank you." I clicked off the phone.

"The first step complete." Rémy smiled and glanced at the harp.

"Play it," I said with a laugh, guessing he couldn't keep away from it for long. It will be good to see if I can deal with my colours." I'd managed to play *Lo Boièr* with synaesthesia, so I could attempt to listen to Rémy, although I had to be careful.

Grinning, he walked over and picked up the key. "Let me know if it's too much," he said, wrapping the velvet ribbon around his fingers. Supporting the harp with one hand, he crouched down and plucked an A with the other. I was still open to the timbre of the strings from when I'd played, and a soft yet vibrant orange shone around me. It was... manageable. Beautiful, even.

Rémy strummed various intervals and made a couple of slight adjustments. Wary of the colour, I went into the kitchen and washed the plates from yesterday afternoon. The bottle of wine and the glasses were still on the side. Perhaps they would finally be used today.

"It's holding its tuning very well considering it wasn't used for years," Rémy called through. "Where was it kept?"

"I only know Nico stored it recently."

I lifted the lid of yesterday's cassoulet and inhaled the garlic and sage, now with the added dimension of the peaty ceps. It would be even better for dinner today. My hunger made me realise I'd not eaten since Roselle's tartelette yesterday. Watching Rémy's tuning scales with caution, I hacked the pain de campagne into thick slices and spread them with butter and jam, making enough for both of us. The notes became cohesive, stronger, more of the stunning glissando he'd played when we'd first met, more colour. My body tightened, but I exhaled and let the music glide over me.

The melody continued, the colours enthralling, somehow tinted with Rémy's own midnight tones as he shaped the notes. I left the bread and went to watch him, perching on the arm of the sofa. His fingers worked deftly back and forth, his eyes closed, his face poised between ecstasy and concentration as he played a combination of a delicate melody and rolling notes sweeping through the octaves. His curls shifted as he moved to and fro with the instrument, his shirt tightening and releasing as he positioned his arms, all of him alive with more colour, more intensity than everything around him. I resisted the desire to run my fingers through the dark locks of his hair, the dark locks through which I could see the wall.

I pulled myself up and scoured his neck, his shoulders, his arms, his elegant fingers at the strings—all of him was solid, opaque, normal. I let out a breath, but it did nothing to relax me. What if he faded again?

His eyes opened and met mine as he brought his composition to a close.

I gathered the key from the floor and studied the miniature branch work, remembering Maman tuning the harp as she prepared for Saturday lessons, her lips drawn into that pensive smile I liked so much. I grasped the ribbon and hung it over Rémy's head. He looked at me questioningly.

"Keep it," I said. "It means you have to come back and tune the harp."

He ran his fingers over the metal, then loosened his shirt and tie and tucked the key inside. "I will."

I leant forward and kissed him slowly before pulling away to allow him to continue. His gaze lingered on me, then he turned back to the harp and began a piece with medieval intonation. Almost used to the colour of his playing, I grabbed a slice of bread and jam from the kitchen, hunger getting the better of me, and sat back on the sofa arm, unable to stop myself smiling at Rémy's obvious pleasure.

He glanced at me, noticing the bread in my hand. "Give me some of that!" He jumped up and pulled me toward him, the notes hanging in the air.

I laughed.

"You know I haven't eaten for five years." He tried to snap at the crust, his teeth clicking.

"You ate two days ago, at Les Fonts, and rather a lot," I replied.

He raised his eyebrows and tried to snatch the bread from my hand. "It doesn't really make up for so long."

I swooped the bread behind my back. "Alright. Just have a little patience."

He looked at me out of the corner of his eye. I drew the wedge slowly upward toward his mouth. He lunged for it, but I drew it away with a shake of my head.

"I can't believe you could deny me food." He pressed his

fingers into my ribs, sending me into streaks of laughter, then he hauled me up, over his shoulder.

I hammered on his back with my free hand. "Put me down!" I demanded amidst giggles.

He spun around, slammed me onto the sofa and sprang on top of me. Remarkably the bread was just about in one piece. He lunged forward and took a bite, his eyes rolling to the back of his head. "Heaven," he said through his mouthful. He swallowed and kissed me with sweet lips, then pulled back a little as though he could see me better that way. "You know, I want you so much." His voice was low and throaty, dark and textured.

I reached up and drew him toward me. "I want you too." But I wanted him here, always, and I needed to make sure of that. "I don't want you to disappear again. How do we know you won't?"

He stroked my hair. "We don't know how this thing works. I didn't disappear before we went to the pog, and there's no saying I'll go again."

But I thought I'd seen through him as he'd played the harp, although it could have been my overworked imagination. I pushed him back and sat up. "Even so, we can't risk it. Alex may not get my message, or he might think it's a prank and not respond." There was only one practical solution. "I'm going to Paris first thing in the morning. I'll make contact with Alex face to face if he doesn't reply. It will be easier to explain the situation to him in person anyway."

Rémy searched my eyes as though he were thinking it over, then nodded. "Alright. Alex and I had an arrangement that if anything should happen to either of us, we would administer the other's property—we knew we were on thin ice with the Désaccord. It's been a long time, but it might be worth asking him if my apartment is available for you to stay in. It has parking."

"Otherwise, I'll get a room. If I'm there for longer I can stay with friends."

"But promise me one thing?" he said.

I scanned his face.

"That you will continue to do whatever you do to call me so I can be with you in Paris."

"Agreed." I nodded.

He kissed me and glanced out the window. "At least it gets you away from the chateau."

We made plans for the rest of the afternoon. I readied the house for my absence, then walked to Sylvie's and told her I would be away—she wrapped me in a warm Sunday roast-scented hug and wished me a safe return. Rémy and I ate the cassoulet with the wine and the last of Roselle's exquisite tartelettes. Afterward, I spent the evening trying to accomplish all the work planned for tomorrow. It was supposed to be my first day back, and with the loss of Esprit Obscur and Sablier barely content, I couldn't risk postponing any of it. I'd have to keep on top of everything while I was away.

At some point while I studied the marketing strategy of a small champagne producer in Sézanne, Rémy disappeared. He'd been clearing up the kitchen and I'd only noticed him gone by the lack of noise. I investigated, finding the house empty, a thread of panic twisting up inside. But we'd talked about it—we knew he might go. The plan was to call him somehow in Paris tomorrow. I had so much to get ready anyway.

It was after midnight when I'd finished work, packed a selection of Paris-suitable clothes and dropped exhausted into bed. I stared into the blackness of my bedroom, trying to let go of the past hours. It was snowing again, and the room was deathly silent.

Something brushed my hair gently from my forehead.

Rémy lay on the bed beside me. "I get to watch you sleep again," he said softly.

"Do I call you every time I think of nothing?"

"I think so. It was happening all the time when you arrived back in Sarrat. That's why you saw me so often in the first couple of days. I had to prevent myself from bumping into you more than I did, or it would have been even stranger. All until we had that argument."

"I got control of my colours after that and you disappeared," I said, barely able to form my words and keep my eyes open as he stroked my head. "I pushed you away with my synaesthesia."

"Obviously not hard enough, because I came back." I could hear the smile in his voice. "And you call me closer now. At the beginning I was on the road, then I'd find myself in your garden. Now I'm in your bedroom."

"Hmmm. What is it like there?" I murmured.

"Where?"

"The Harmonie. What will you do when you go back?"

"I'll make up the fire, sweep the snow off the path, let the cat in, that sort of thing."

I laughed without opening my eyes. "No, really."

It's... different, serene, but at the same time full of energy and movement. I don't really do anything because it's not my time to be there. I don't think in the same way, and there's no urgency. Sometimes it scares me that I might slip away completely."

I opened my eyes and he stopped stroking.

"I shouldn't have said that," he added.

"Yes, you should, if it's the truth."

"Well, I haven't gone yet."

I thought of yesterday and what I'd seen today—possibly seen. I had to hold on to him. He started stroking my hair again and I drifted away. After a little while he whispered, "Violette, there's something I want to say."

"Hmmm."

He kissed me softly on the top of my head. "Thank you for doing this."

CHAPTER FIFTEEN

Finding a space on Rue Boudreau, I parked, turned off the ignition and leant on the wheel. It had been eight hours from Sarrat, including stops. The sound of the engine still buzzed in my ears and my head ached from pushing it away. At least the snow had been confined to the mountains and the route had been clear.

Sitting back, I gazed around. The neo-classical limestone buildings that lined the narrow street were cast in grey by the dull, icy sky. Even so, the decorative wrought-iron balconies before the first-floor windows engendered typical Parisian charm. After all this time, I never tired of the architecture.

Being back so soon was strange. It was different being in Paris and knowing my home awaited me in Sarrat, no longer a childhood dream or a future possibility but an actuality.

A yawn escaped. I'd woken once in the night and Rémy had lain there upon the covers, still watching. In the morning he was gone. I'd expected him to appear during the hours on the autoroute, but he hadn't. Perhaps I'd been concentrating too much.

I drew my compact from the glove compartment, clicked up the mirror and tidied my make-up. It had been freeing to go without in Sarrat, but here appearances mattered, and I might be taken more seriously by Alex if I looked the part. The cold crept in now the engine was off and I shivered. I hauled myself out of the car and stretched every muscle, then pulled my black merino overcoat from the back seat, wrapped it around me and tied the belt. The droning background of the city sent dark flecks across my vision. I held the imposition at the margins of my sight as I changed into my Louboutin heeled boots—remnants of my design director days—and slung my bag upon my shoulder. Stepping back, I twisted my foot on the edge of the pavement. I hadn't missed my Paris colours at all, and I hadn't missed the heels much either.

As I scanned my card at the parking meter, I glanced around. The street was empty but for a man heading in the opposite direction. Tucking myself into an unused doorway, I stared into nothing, trying to ignore the distant rumble, the smell of diesel fumes and a grey smear of a shout from the adjoining road. I released a deep breath, and with it much of the journey.

"You look beautiful in Paris," a voice whispered in my ear, rippling through me.

I smiled. That hadn't been too difficult.

A hand lifted my hair and kissed the back of my neck. "How am I going to resist you any longer?"

The feeling was mutual. His arms encircled me and we fell back into the doorway and kissed again and again. After a few minutes we broke apart and I searched the street furtively. A woman approached from the corner. "If no one can see you," I said, "what do I look like kissing you?"

He grinned. "I have no idea."

"So, Alex." I drew out my phone and checked my messages. "Nothing yet." Only an email from my newest client, Aubépine, wanting me to get back to them straight away about my proposition. I would need my laptop for that. It would have to wait. "Let's get there and see if we can track him down."

At the end of the street we turned onto Boulevard des Capucines and the cacophony hit me—the black grind of stop-start traffic, the shrieking, serrating brakes of a lorry, the invasion of shouts, calls and conversation. My heart raced and the floor spun away, my vision obscured. I pulled in against the wall of a shop and thrust my hands over my eyes.

"What is it?" Rémy demanded, wrapping himself around me, a shield from the city.

"The colours," I breathed. "It's too much." And it wasn't just the colours, but a deep gash of fear, and the chilling suffocation of being buried under it all.

"You have got it bad," he murmured. "Push it away. Push it all away if you have to. You know how."

"I don't want you to go."

"To hell with me. You need to be able to handle this. If I go, you know how to call me back. Getting hold of Alex is more important anyway."

I peered at the wall, focussing on a limestone block. The colours began to recede, giving me more focus. Centring on the patina of the surface, the torrent retreated further. I dropped my hands and looked up. Rémy was still there.

"How is it now?" he asked.

"On the edge of my vision." I regained my breath. "It's so much worse in the city."

"That's why you left, isn't it?" He scrutinised my face.

"That and wanting to return home." I glanced around. Several people were staring as they passed. A man sitting outside the café opposite looked as though he was about to come over and help. I pulled myself away from the wall, straightened my coat and forced a smile. A fine sight that must have been with Rémy only visible to me.

"I'm alright now," I said. "Let's go."

Rémy wrapped a protective arm around my waist.

The Boulevard des Capucines merged with the Place de l'Opéra and the familiar sight of the Palais Garnier stood before us, the golden angels of Poetry and Harmony looming from the corners of the Corinthian-pillared opera house, the busts of Mozart, Auber and Rossini eyeing us as we took the pedestrian crossing toward the steps and archways of the entrance.

"Nice place to work," I said.

"Isn't it? We need to go around the back to the administrative door."

I nodded.

"Have you been inside?" he asked.

"For the occasional ballet and concert. I prefer it to modern theatres. It's another world in there, as though the architecture assists the music in transcending the ordinary."

An oversized grin drew across Rémy's face. "My thoughts exactly."

"Why are you smiling like that?"

"I like that we think the same way about some things."

He took my hand and we strode down Rue Auber, passing the west entrance of the opera house hung with a massive dropdown banner for *Don Giovanni*, red flames licking around a figure cloaked in black. As we joined Rue Scribe, a horn blasted on the other side of the road, flashing a rough, broken scar before me. I stumbled, cold running through my body. My colours still held the power to overwhelm me so suddenly. I focussed on the pavement and the warmth of Rémy's hand in the raw air.

We rounded the end of the opera house and Rémy led me through open iron gates into a courtyard, the city noise immediately a little softer. We headed up steps to glazed double doors.

I pressed the buzzer, feeling Rémy's hand on the small of my back.

"How may I help you?" a male voice said through the intercom.

"I'm trying to get hold of Alex Chaufourier."

"Monsieur Chaufourier is currently in rehearsal with instructions not to be disturbed."

"Could you please give him a message to call Violette Romèu as soon as he is finished—or if he has a break? It's urgent I get hold of him today." I gave him my number.

"I'll ensure he receives the message."

"Could you tell me what time he finishes rehearsals?"

"I'm sorry, I'm not at liberty to divulge that information."

The intercom cut out.

I turned to Rémy. "Well, what now? I can't just wait for him to call. Do you know when he might finish?"

"Around six if things still work the same way inside—which is highly likely as the place hasn't changed much since it was built."

"Then I'll wait." I checked my phone. "Two hours and I'm starving. I'm going to get something to eat. Do you want anything?"

"No. I'll keep an eye on the entrance while you go." He kissed me.

Dodging traffic and restraining my overwrought senses, I headed for a boulangerie across the street, bought a baguette sandwich and a coffee, then returned to the back entrance, pausing inside the gate. Rémy was gone.

Settling on a stone ledge opposite the door, I took a deep breath and released my tension with the exhalation—I'd done the same by the car and Rémy had appeared immediately, but relaxing allowed the cacophony to flood over me. I tensed up and pressed my colours away, my nerves raw. It really was too much. I'd been here under an hour and I was already fed up of feeling as though I was being torn asunder. Yet I had to remember that Paris was only temporary. My synaesthesia had been a lot better in Sarrat. Anyway, it wouldn't need two of us to watch the door or make contact with Alex. I'd call Rémy later, somewhere quieter.

I unwrapped the baguette and ate with ravenous bites, savouring the creamy mustard mayonnaise and sweet tomatoes. Keeping my eyes on the door, I gulped down my coffee, its heat warming my throat and my fingers. The light was fading, the streetlights flickering on, and it was bitterly cold sitting still. I drained my cup, drew out my phone and searched the Opéra de Paris site to have another look at Alex, my gaze shifting between the display and the door. Alex stared back at me from the screen, his face youthful, attractive, his short brown hair styled messy, his chin raised with an ever so slight look of superiority, or perhaps confidence—a professional at the top of his game.

A bald man followed by a young woman exited the building. I glanced back at my phone, tapped Alex's name into the search engine and scanned the summaries. There were plenty of results from a few years ago, around the time Rémy was there—*Alex Chaufourier, the life and soul of every party, dates a different woman every night... The assistant music director of the Paris Opera takes his social life more seriously than his professional life... Alex Chaufourier scandal as his ex-boyfriend speaks out about their relationship.* It was a wonder he ever had time to study those books, not to mention whatever else they'd gotten up to.

Then, dated more recently, *Alex Chaufourier, new music director of the Paris Opera, abandons his party lifestyle and devotes himself to the music he loves... Newly committed bachelor Alex Chaufourier places music above romance.*

My gaze flicked to the door. A man in a black suit pushed through, his face in his phone. He raised his head. It was him.

I jumped up and strode across the courtyard. "Monsieur Chaufourier."

He paused, his chin angled in a duplicate of the photo, his eyes scanning me. "Yes?"

"Sorry to approach you like this, but I need your help."

He frowned. "In what way?"

I took a deep breath. This was going to sound ludicrous. But he'd been involved in whatever they'd done with the Désaccord—surely it wouldn't sound too unbelievable to him. "I... uh, I'm a friend of Rémy Rabasten. I wonder if there is somewhere we could go to talk?"

"If you're from the press, I can tell you now that I will not be of any assistance." His voice rose in rigid black lines.

"No, no... Rémy speaks very fondly of you... and Bénédict."

"Rémy's gone," he growled, his eyes flashing.

A group of people passed. I stepped toward him. "Could we please go somewhere to talk?"

He studied me. "If you have something to say, say it here."

I took a breath. "From what Rémy told me, you know what happened before he disappeared."

"And?" he asked, his voice clipped.

"You know he evoked the Désaccord."

A flicker in his expression, then his face became inscrutable.

"Well," I continued, "when Rémy went missing, he was taken up by the Harmonie in protection from the Désaccord. He's been there ever since and he can't return."

His eyes moved now, assessing me, his jaw tight. "What?"

"He's been in the Harmonie for the past five years, and he's asked me to contact you to request your help."

"How do you know this?"

"I can see him," I said. "We think it may be because I have synaesthesia."

"Utterly ridiculous." He strode out the gates onto Rue Scribe.

I dodged through the crowd after him. I needed Rémy to be here—he would know what to say. If only I'd called him despite my colours. "Please, he needs your help."

Alex ignored me.

I tried again. "Rémy needs to get home."

"Leave me alone or I will call the police," he said over his shoulder.

I had to think of something... "Rémy told me about the books."

He stopped suddenly and turned around.

I drew up short in front of him. "He thinks there may be something within them that will help get him back—he said you'd studied them and you know them best."

He looked aghast for a second. "Only the three of us knew about the books."

"Rémy told me everything yesterday," I said.

"So you think he's not dead?" There was a minute waver to his voice.

"I know he's not."

He scrutinised my face. "You could have come across this information somehow."

"That's not the case. Rémy explained all about the Désaccord and how the three of you used it to influence Bénédict's composition."

His eyes opened a little wider. "If I entertain the idea that Rémy is alive, just for the moment, and I can tell you I'm struggling with this, do you think there is a chance of getting him back?"

"I don't know." I swallowed. "We were hoping you might be able to help there."

"What does Rémy want me to do?"

"He only said you knew the books, and if anyone could help, it would be you."

He continued to study me, commuters and tourists passing us on either side. "I placed the books in secure storage after Rémy disappeared. I haven't looked at them since." He stepped closer so there was barely any distance between us. "You have to understand my position. For all I know you've stumbled upon this, and you're trying to obtain the books or use the information against me. But part of me has always hoped that Rémy was somehow alive. So... if there is even the slightest chance that he might still be with us, I'm willing to follow it up. I'll give you an extremely cautious benefit of the doubt. But I really don't know if I can help."

My shoulders dropped. "Thank you."

"I'll need to retrieve the books and read them again. It should take me about a week."

"I... think it might be better if we try to sort this out sooner rather than later."

"He's been away for five years. Are a few days going to matter?"

I had to say it. "I don't know how much longer I can keep contact with him."

He looked quizzically at me for a moment and then nodded. "Alright. I'll get the books out of storage in the morning. Apart from rehearsal, I can spend the day reading to see if I can find anything to help. I'll meet you tomorrow evening. Are you based in Paris?"

"No, Sarrat. But Rémy wondered if you still have his apartment under your care."

His brow narrowed. "I do. I've been trying to sort out the place with his family for a while now, but as Rémy is officially missing rather than deceased, the paperwork is taking forever."

"He requested that you give me access while I'm in Paris, so if it's possible, perhaps I could meet you there?"

He stared at me.

I could imagine how it sounded. "I'm not trying to appropriate his apartment." I let out an exhausted sigh. What else could I say?

"Benefit of the doubt," he said, shaking his head. "If there is any chance of getting Rémy back, I'm willing to risk his apartment for a few days."

Relief flooded through me.

"When do you need access?"

"Tonight. Now."

"Alright. I'll meet you outside in half an hour, and we can take it from there."

A broad smile drew across my face. "Wonderful. Thank you."

"I didn't catch your name?"

"Violette... Violette Romèu."

He smiled for the first time, his features softening. "Call me Alex. Good to meet a friend of Rémy's. If what you say is true, it would be unbelievable. I hope we can help him."

He turned away and strode up the street. I watched him weave through the bustle, barely able to believe I'd convinced him.

Chapter Sixteen

The rush-hour traffic had been a challenge, causing me to pull into Rue Margueritte a few minutes late. Alex stood by a broad garage door, the building above elegant with golden limestone. I clicked down my window as I approached.

"Take bay six," he said, and pressed a fob. The garage rolled open.

I steered down the ramp and parked. Alex followed me on foot.

"So, you found it alright?" he asked as I climbed out.

"Yes, I lived in Paris for years, so it wasn't difficult. Just the traffic to contend with." Lived in Paris, rather than live. I smiled at the thought of Sarrat as I hauled my overnight case from the boot.

"Let me." Alex dove in and took the handle, then indicated to a door in the corner. "After you."

We pushed through into a hall with an old wood-framed elevator. Alex pressed the button and we squeezed in. The mechanism clunked and ground upward, the intensity of the noise startling, a thick layer of black smothering me. I grasped the side of the lift to steady myself.

"Are you alright?" Alex asked. "You look pale."

I pulled myself up, ignoring the colour. "I'm fine." And I was. Pretty much. Apart from a couple of notable moments today, I'd managed to control my synaesthesia reasonably well. "Thank you, by the way," I added, "for taking a chance on all of this."

"Rémy was one of a kind," he replied. "A unique talent full of passion and drive, with a laid-back quality that was difficult to resist. But together we were stupid, arrogant." His voice grew low. "We interfered with things that weren't meant for us, and we paid the price. I was the one who drew the information from the books—I should have been caught up in it, not Rémy and Bénédict." For a moment there was something vulnerable, almost desperate, on his face, the confidence gone. I couldn't imagine how he felt with Rémy missing and Bénédict dead.

"Rémy said you were a good friend."

He shook his head. "Not good enough."

The lift opened and we stepped into a vestibule with marble stairs and a baroque balcony spiralling downward. Alex entered numbers into a keypad by a door, unlocking the apartment. I followed him through a dark hall, only the street-lit glow of the building opposite visible through floor-to-ceiling windows. He clicked on the light, illuminating a stunning chandelier that hung in the centre of an expansive room, then placed my case down and opened his hands. "I hope you like it."

I stepped in slowly, turning around to take it in. An extravagant fireplace and seating area stood at one side, behind it a grand piano was angled before the windows, and in the nearest corner a dining table was adorned with candles. The room was decorated in various shades of grey and white, the floor a large herringbone parquet, all of it engendering a spacious, tasteful feel.

"How on earth did he afford this?" I murmured. Paris real estate was astronomical. I don't know what I'd expected. Something smaller, perhaps. Alright, bigger than my former apartment, but I was having to join the dots between Rémy in Sarrat and this.

"Rémy's tuning had a quality to it that others couldn't replicate," Alex replied as he adjusted a thermostat in the hall. "He was in such high demand that he could name his price." He stepped over to two broad doors in the centre of the far wall, threw them open, then flipped another switch, illuminating a second chandelier hung above a king-size bed perfectly made with countless pillows. My house really was the barn of its origins in comparison.

"I haven't been here for a while," Alex said as he opened two more doors, revealing a modern kitchen. "I only check it now and again, but the cleaner should have been. She's here every two weeks on a Friday now no one is using the place, so everything should be reasonably fresh."

I nodded. "Alright."

"I need to make a move. Shall we exchange contacts?"

"Of course." We took each other's numbers.

He tapped at his phone for a moment longer. "I've sent the door code through so we should be sorted. I'll bring the books over this time tomorrow." We walked to the entrance and exchanged kisses. As he drew away he wore that vulnerable look again. "I'm still finding it hard to take in everything you've said. You'll have to excuse me if I'm a bit... stunned, I suppose."

"That makes two of us," I replied.

He handed me the garage key fob and drew open the door. "Can I ask... how do you see him?"

I hardly knew. "He, uh, just turns up."

"And then he's... solid?"

"Yes, as you or me. But it seems I'm the only one who can see him."

The vulnerability grew into something more startled. He looked around cautiously. "Is he here now?"

"No, he's not."

He pulled himself up and brushed his hand through his hair. "Alright. Until tomorrow then."

"Alex, thank you so much," I said.

He nodded and jogged down the stairs.

I closed the door, headed back in and shook my head. I was certainly seeing another side to Rémy—and he would want to be here. I rubbed my face in my hands. Calling him meant relaxing, and relaxing meant opening myself to my colours and feeling as though I were being driven over by a train. Yet it was more peaceful here. I had to try.

Settling on the sofa alongside the fireplace, I wriggled to ease the restriction of my overcoat—it was still too cold to take it off. Drawing a deep breath, I sank down into the cushions and closed my eyes. Endless miles of motorway appeared before me, then the facade of the Palais Garnier, then Alex. A motorbike passed on the road outside, spanning my vision with black. I dug my nails into the sofa and screwed up my eyes. Letting go felt alien to who I was, to all the years growing up in Paris learning control, learning to maintain a semblance of normality. It didn't help that it was so cold—it wasn't exactly relaxing.

Trying again, more autoroute and city traffic formed in

my head. The congestion was bad enough around here without me imagining it. I sat up and took another long breath, then laid my head back upon the upholstery and stared at the chandelier. The glass sparkled with a hint of iridescence, sending a luminous glow throughout the room, individual crystals spinning in the warming air, the occasional chink scattering flecks of colour through it all.

I caught a movement by the door and turned my head.

He strode toward me, appearing a tone apart from the room. "Whatever you said to Alex, it was obviously the right thing." His voice rippled, deep and rich, the only colour I wanted more of. Even so, I pushed the impressions away to my peripheral vision. We wrapped our arms around each other and I ran my fingers over his cheek, reassuring myself he was solid. The corners of his mouth turned up and he kissed me tenderly.

We parted after a few moments and I scanned his face. "I don't know what you do to me, Rémy Rabasten, but you have me completely beguiled." The jest was clear in my tone, even though the sentiment was true.

He grinned. "It's my special power that ensures my victims never get away."

"I can believe it."

"How was Alex?" he asked.

"When he managed to get his head around the idea of you still being alive, he was pretty confounded. He certainly took some convincing. I was worried he wouldn't believe me for a moment." For longer than a moment.

He frowned. "Why didn't you call me?"

"I tried," I said, "but it was too difficult amidst the bustle."

"Will he help?"

I nodded. "He's going to go over the books tomorrow and see what he can find, then he'll come here in the evening."

He let out a breath. "Alright. That's good." He glanced around. "I can't believe I'm home."

We broke apart and he walked into the bedroom, then back again, trailing his finger across the top of the sofa as though he were reassuring himself he really had made it.

"It seems like yesterday and it seems like years," he said as he circled the grand piano, running his hands over the sleek ebony. "I've missed this beauty very much."

I smiled. "I can see I have competition."

He strode over, gathered me up and kissed me again. "Never."

"But you know I called you a bobo?"

He raised his eyebrows in mock consternation. "How could I forget?"

"But, come on," I said, glancing up at the chandelier and the plaster mouldings.

He headed to what looked like a draped window near the kitchen and beckoned me with his finger, a mischievous glint in his eye.

I walked over, staring at him. "What?"

"This is why I have the apartment." He pulled back the curtains and opened the French doors behind, revealing a rooftop terrace lined with containers of evergreen box and still-flowering roses growing a little wild around an arbour and along the walls.

"Come on." He took my hand and drew me outside. Below us Paris glowed in amber. A host of earthbound stars dropped away to the Tour Eiffel resplendent in golden lines and glimmering lights.

I breathed the frosty air, my exhale a spiral of mist. "This is stunning." I glanced at him.

He was staring at me. "There is only one thing I want to look at."

There was no doubt I felt the same way. Would I ever get used to the angle of his cheek, the soft fullness of his eyes? I traced the lines of his neck and flinched. The illuminations of Paris were visible through his skin and through his collar. I swallowed. He wasn't completely translucent, only barely, but I could make out the lights all the same.

"What's wrong?" he asked, touching my chin.

I forced myself not to pull away. He still felt solid, but he had to be fading because I'd spent most of the day controlling my colours. I needed to open myself more. I couldn't let him go, or Théo for that matter if there was a chance of helping that family. We had to get on with figuring out how to bring them back. How much longer was Rémy going to last?

"Violette?" he said, concern written across his face.

I pulled myself together. Alex would be here tomorrow with the books—we would do something about it. We would have to. "Nothing." I forced a smile.

He took my face in his hands and kissed me tenderly. I closed my eyes and shivered.

"You're cold," he said.

"A little. Actually, a lot. It was freezing waiting for Alex, and I haven't had chance to warm up."

"Come on, let's get inside." He led me in, closing the doors behind us.

In here with the lights on, Rémy thankfully looked as solid as usual. He drew me over to the sofa by the fire and unwrapped the belt of my coat, a playful smile pulling at his lips.

I raised an eyebrow, attempting to restrain the desire he provoked despite what I'd seen. "I have a client to get back to before I do anything else. I should have done it earlier." It certainly wasn't an excuse. If I didn't get to work as soon as possible, I would lose my clients and my living.

"They're not going to be at the office now," he said, his voice throaty.

"They need the information for first thing."

He grinned and held out his hand. "I just want your coat."

I laughed, wriggled out of it and sank into the sofa. "I had you down for ulterior motives."

"I can't say you were wrong." He draped my coat over the chair, then pulled a blanket off the back and wrapped it around me. "The place will warm up soon." He bent down by the hearth, took a match out of the holder and lit the already prepared fire. "This should help."

"Thank you." I drew the rug tight.

Still kneeling on the floor, he shuffled over and took my hands. "What about food? Are you hungry?"

"No, I'm fine. I had a baguette whilst waiting for Alex. I'll just warm up and do my work. But maybe some tea?"

He smiled, jumped up, grabbed my coat and hung it in the hall, then headed into the kitchen.

My shoes kicked off, I curled my legs under me and listened to Rémy's kitchen percussion, conscious that I still held my colours at the edge of my sight when I needed to be more open.

"Ginger," he said, carrying in a tray. "The bags must be at least five years old, but they look alright." He handed me a cup. I wrapped my hands around the ceramic, absorbing its warmth.

"How's your synaesthesia?" he asked. "Can you manage a little more noise?" He placed the tray on the table and took a mouthful of tea, glancing at the piano.

"It all appears to be under control," I said. And if the harp was anything to go by, his playing would be nothing like the city blast. "Go ahead."

He placed his cup down and stepped over to the piano. "It's a 1923 Steinway, Model A-III, crafted in ebony, evenly weighted with a clear yet warm tone and the richest colour palette I've ever seen."

I couldn't help but smile at his enthusiasm.

He lifted the keyboard lid, raised the music stand and pushed up the cover, propping it open. I sipped my tea, the ginger warming me through. The fire had come into its own and the room was starting to feel cosy, despite its size. I rolled the blanket off my shoulders.

Rémy played a saffron-toned A and a few notes at intervals and shook his head. "This is completely unacceptable."

It sounded fine to me. "What is unacceptable to you is probably perfectly alright for the rest of the world."

I finished my tea, found the bathroom and freshened up. Feeling much more myself, I sat down by the fire with my laptop and clicked open my emails. Rémy continued making adjustments to the piano, a leather bag on the floor, a wrench in his hand. I forced myself to the screen. Aubépine wanted changes to my initial proposals. I sent through some ideas and responded to a couple of other clients. There was so much to do, but the rest could wait until tomorrow.

Closing my eyes, I listened to Rémy's tuning scales, which were becoming more coherent, the hint of colour lining my sight. But through it all I pictured the city lights visible through Rémy's skin. I couldn't put it off any longer. I needed to be more open to my synaesthesia.

With trepidation, I attempted to relax, letting go of the defences I'd raised, allowing the sensory impressions to come forth. Colour poured over me, my heart thumping. I forced myself to breathe steadily. Rémy's playing was different.

As his fingers travelled down the octaves, the colours repeated themselves, only with more intensity, more saturation. I watched the impressions with wary curiosity. Rémy ascended to a higher pitch, and one of the notes stood out with a lurid hue. The colour should have been proportional to the others—the note before had been orange, so it should have been clear yellow, but it was darker and lacklustre, smeared with the remnants of its predecessor. "That one was out, wasn't it?" I called.

Rémy drew his head from the bowels of the piano and grinned. "Very good. I'm taking it you didn't hear that. Most people can't when the discrepancy is slight."

I followed the captivating ripples of his voice. "Pure colour," I replied, then I glanced at him out of the corner of my eye. "That's how you do it, isn't it? You can see the notes you're tuning."

He grinned. "My secret is out. I like to think there's a bit more to my competency than just that, but, yes, I usually work with colour. It's a lot easier to see when an instrument is in tune. Listen to this." He reached to the keyboard and played a note. A sunset of stunning orange spread through my vision.

"That was A. The piano is tuned to A at 432 hertz, like your harp, and..." He leant into the piano with his wrench, then played the same note again. "This, if I've adjusted it correctly, is A tuned to 440 hertz, the standard concert pitch to which most orchestras and instruments around the world are tuned."

The note was still orange but with more red, and it lacked the intensity of the previous A. "It's not so... alive," I said.

He placed the wrench on the piano stool and walked over. "Exactly. It's difficult for the untrained ear to hear the difference. But if you have synaesthesia, it's clear which tuning is preferable." He leant over the sofa and stole a brief kiss. "When the orchestra is tuned to A at 432, the music is vibrant, living—more able to convey its message because it is in harmony with everything around it."

"Hence the campaign for a return to 432 hertz."

"There are many arguments against tuning at that level, and some of them are valid, but when you can see what is going on, it's completely clear which tuning is—"

My phone buzzed, the colour an unwelcome intrusion. I hunted in my bag and drew it out. The screen displayed *Philippe*. "It's Eveline's son. I need to take this. He never calls and Eveline is not well."

I tapped receive, my shoulders stiffening. "Good evening, Philippe. How may I help you?" Rémy placed a kiss on my head and turned back to the piano.

"Violette, hello," Philippe said. "How's the house coming on?"

I pressed his colours away. I wasn't going to indulge him for a moment—not after years of him and his sister making it clear that the feral girl from Sarrat had cast their mother's life into disarray, even though they'd left the nest a long time before I'd arrived. "Very well, thank you. I'm settling in nicely."

"Good to hear it. But I'll get to the point."

He always did, very quickly.

"Eveline asked me to make contact. In fact, she's been extremely persistent."

"Oh?"

"She's been talking about your parents and getting quite distressed over the topic—her dementia is a little worse. Anyway, she says she has something important she wants to speak about in person next time you're in Paris."

Eveline had always made her opinions known clearly and repeatedly. There wasn't often anything new, so I was curious. "Actually, Philippe, I'm in Paris for a few days. I could probably manage tomorrow, if that's any use?" I had no idea what Alex and the books might bring, so best get the visit over and done with while I had the chance.

"Splendid, that should put her mind at rest. She's gone on about you for days with no sign of stopping. Isabelle and I will be there tomorrow—we have a consultation with her doctor—but we could meet you afterward at two o'clock."

All I needed was both Eveline's wonderfully successful children casting disdainful glances over me. And Eveline's script usually involved comparing my life to that of Philippe, who had followed in her footsteps by becoming an eminent lawyer, and Isabelle, a successful consultant oncologist. It had never been left to any doubt that graphic design was not, in her opinion, a proper profession. "Wonderful," I said. "See you then."

"Until then," he replied.

I clicked off my phone, took in a deep breath and glanced over to Rémy. The piano stood open, ready to be played, its reflection indistinct in the dark windows. The tool bag lay on the floor, the wrench resting upon the stool. He was gone.

My stomach sank. I must have been too occupied with

Philippe, but no matter, I could call Rémy. I closed the lid of my laptop and set it with my phone on the coffee table, then sat back into the sofa and arranged the blanket around me, allowing the tension in my shoulders to drain away. In my mind's eye I saw one of my designs, then the follow-up I needed to send to Sablier.

I shifted sideways and reclined, staring into the chandelier. I just needed to let go of everything. I focussed on my breathing, and the moment a thought entered my head I let it pass through. As minutes elapsed, tension coiled up from deep inside, slowly at first, barely perceptible, until I realised my body was rigid.

Pulling myself up, I twisted around to face the fire. The flames undulated gently, reminding me of Sarrat, drawing my thoughts to the harp. If only I had it with me—I'd managed to call Rémy because of its calming influence.

The warm glow of the logs was easier on my tired eyes than the chandelier. I sank onto my front, resting on the arm of the sofa, watching the flickers around the blackened wood. Surely the more colour I could summon, the easier it would be to do this. If I listened carefully, the fire made a gentle sizzle that speckled red around me, scattered with almost imperceptible yellow crackles, tiny pinpoints of light. But still no Rémy.

After a while a car drew along the street, smothering the pinpoints in ugly grey, then voices rose in brusque song, "*Alouette, gentile alouette...*", and laughter. My insides tightened, my breathing grew rapid, my heart pounded.

I sat up.

I couldn't do it. I couldn't call him back.

Chapter Seventeen

I clicked send on the third proposal, finishing my day's work early thanks to having started before dawn. At last I was reasonably up to date. I pushed the laptop across the dining table and dropped my head into my hands. If I could just let go, Rémy would come back. But what was the use of attempting to call him when I'd tried until late in the night, slept terribly and failed again in the morning?

Tiredness enticed me to close my eyes, but I needed to find some reserves for this afternoon. I hauled myself from the chair, wrapped up for the cold and headed out, choosing the stairs over an ordeal with the ancient elevator. In the street, snow swirled in ethereal spirals, the powder dusting my coat as I strode along. November was early for this kind of weather in Paris and it wasn't settling underfoot. No doubt the sky would revert to hard grey soon, but for now the place was a fairy tale.

Turning onto Rue Washington the clamour of the city struck, the traffic and the bustle ripping dirty streaks around me. I flinched at the onslaught, but not wanting to make

Rémy's situation any worse than it already was, I retained as much colour as I could bear.

Dodging traffic, I made my way to a small pâtisserie on the opposite corner and bought a chocolatine and a coffee. As I pushed out the door, a man headed across the road before me. The snow partially obscured my vision, but his beard and broad frame wrapped in an overcoat and scarf made me think of Joël and all that had happened since my return to Sarrat. I might have been back in Paris, the place I'd known for so long, but because of Rémy, I was in another world.

I hailed a taxi, settled in the back and ate my lunch, the rich chocolate lifting me as the city sped past, a snowy replay of my former life—a restaurant I'd frequented, streets in which I'd shopped. We passed the *De Nouveaux* magazine offices on Rue du Faubourg Saint-Honoré. I could see myself stepping out the door for the last time, barely holding back my colours and my tears, barely escaping with my reputation. In the months before, I'd battled to cope with my synaesthesia whilst functioning with any degree of competency. I'd wanted to stay, I'd loved it there, but that hadn't been an option. My resignation certainly had made my return to Sarrat simple. Now I was a visitor to the city. It was strange how one reality could replace another so quickly, and this wasn't the first time.

The taxi drew up outside the maison de repos, a tidy block of concrete opposite Hôpital Necker. I entered the glass atrium, pushing away a blast of ugly colours provoked by an information video that played in the seating area. The warm air was stifling, augmented by a medical smell vaguely disguised by air freshener. I pulled off my hat and gloves and loosened my coat.

Philippe and Isabelle stood by the reception desk talking

together. Isabelle glanced toward me, her hair styled perfectly in shoulder-length curls, her features hardened by her serious air. She looked me up and down. Philippe turned around, all corporate smile, dead eyes and receding hairline.

A sturdy wall already raised against their colours, I strode over. "Isabelle, Philippe."

Philippe stepped toward me and we exchanged kisses. "Violette, good to see you. What brings you back to Paris so soon? The house has not fallen down, I hope?" He chuckled.

I put a smile on my face. "No, the house is fine. I'm here to attend to a few matters. I'll be returning soon."

Isabelle bent forward and we kissed. "Then we were lucky to catch you. Maman's condition has deteriorated. We've just spoken to her doctor. He's not overly concerned considering her age, but she has been desperate to speak to you." She glanced at Philippe. "And we have absolutely no idea why."

Philippe sighed. "Whatever it is, she seems most upset about it."

"Alright," I said. "I'll go up and see what's bothering her."

Isabelle nodded. "I have to get back to work, but Philippe will be around for a little while longer in case you need anything."

More like in case I managed to upset Eveline.

Isabelle kissed me again and placed her hand on my arm. "Well, good luck in Sarrat. Let's keep in touch."

That wasn't likely. "Yes, let's."

She kissed Philippe and strode toward the entrance.

Philippe glanced at me. "Shall we get it over with?"

We took the elevator to the tenth floor and I followed him to Eveline's room. He paused outside. "Wait here. I'll see if she's receptive."

He made his way in and the sound of their conversation filtered through the door. I couldn't catch the words, but I could hear the cadence of Eveline's clipped tones and I was transported back to her townhouse a few streets from here, surrounded by orderliness, pristine decor and the rules she'd used to rise high in life. At first I'd thought she was an unfeeling monster, but as the years passed, it had become clear that her attitude to life was highly effective. And while I didn't want Philippe's or Isabelle's lives, it had been because of their maman that I'd mastered my colours, then school, then my career.

Philippe came out. "She's ready to see you. I'll be here, so call if you need me."

I stepped in. The room was more a hotel suite than a care home, the windows draped elegantly, the furniture antique, the view along the street opposite to the Tour Eiffel one of the most coveted in Paris. Her care must cost a small fortune, but that wouldn't be a problem for her. The only thing that detracted from the hotel air was the hospital bed in the centre, the back raised with Eveline propped up to almost sitting.

"Eveline. How are you?" I asked as I walked over.

Despite her circumstances, her white hair was perfectly coiffed in her hallmark chignon and she wore tidy lipstick in a muted claret. It wouldn't surprise me if she had someone in every morning to do her hair and make-up.

She peered at me, her eyes cold amidst those harsh features. "Violette. Thank you for coming. It is good to see you."

We exchanged kisses. She looked me up and down the same way Isabelle had. Eveline had passed that on to her daughter.

"You too. You look well," I replied.

She nodded. "Thank you for the compliment, but we both know I am not at my best. And you, my dear, appear pale and drawn. I thought the country air would have put some rouge in your cheeks, but obviously not."

The same Eveline, but this meant she was having a good day. I forced a smile. "The air in Sarrat is doing me good. I think it must be my return to Paris." More like my lack of sleep last night.

"How are you finding it back in the mountains?"

"I'm enjoying the peace and quiet. The house is coming on, I've decorated throughout, and I've reconnected with some old friends." I thought of Rémy and my skin tingled, then my stomach clenched. I'd not been able to call him.

"You're not finding it too difficult, all the old memories?" There was an unfamiliar softness in her voice and her glossed lips trembled ever so slightly, then conformed to their customary thin line.

"Not at all. After all, there's no point dwelling on the past. It was one of the things I learnt from you, and it has helped a lot."

She examined me through tapered eyelids. "You know I've never been one to use euphemisms..."

She certainly wasn't.

"My legs have not improved and no doubt Philippe has informed you"—she cleared her voice—"my dementia is worsening. Although I am feeling perfectly fine at this moment, it comes over me and I spout a load of old nonsense."

"I'm sorry—"

"No, Violette." She tapped her finger once upon the over-bed table, her nail clicking against the faux wood. "No plati-tudes, please. It is as it is."

I nodded. This was her way, and it was good to see her currently so coherent.

"But," she continued, "I have had plenty of time to reflect in here, and there have been a few things on my mind lately, what with you returning to Sarrat."

"Oh?"

"I really don't know that I did the right thing with you." Her voice wavered a little—so unlike her.

"What do you mean?" I frowned.

"I took you away from Sarrat, away from everything you had ever known, but I think I may have been wrong."

I couldn't believe what I was hearing. "Eveline, you always said to choose the best course of action and cast regret aside. That principle has kept me moving forward in life. It's stopped me dwelling on what is long gone and... to tell you the truth, I think I would have found it terribly hard occa-sionally visiting Sarrat, seeing what I was missing, seeing the house occupied by others."

"Yes, but, Violette." She raised her chin and her lips tightened. "I have realised something important. When faced with a challenging event in life, or if one makes a mistake, yes, it is necessary to pick oneself up and carry on, but there is no point in all of that struggle unless one learns from it."

That made sense. I nodded.

"And I had to move you to Paris—my work and my life were here. But I wonder about my decision to cut you off from those who wished to keep in contact with you, the mite that you were. But your parents... I had the sense they were involved in something."

I peered at her. "What?"

"Your maman spoke to me about your father just before the accident. They were having arguments over the antiquities he was dealing in. But your mother was wrapped up in him, life in Sarrat and her music. I couldn't glean the full picture. And afterward, the details of their accident never made sense. The coroner's verdict was accidental death. Your papa lost control of the car on black ice, but it was highly unlikely in the weather conditions that night as the roads were clear. I had a sense there was something going on and I didn't want you involved."

I shook myself. I'd never heard her talk like this. "Eveline, I'm sorry, what are you saying—"

"The other day," she continued, "Inès Deloffre brought me some delightful millefeuilles and such a beautiful spray of roses. My dear, I was overjoyed, I can tell you."

"What?"

"They were the most beautiful rosé with the palest of centres, such exquisite flowers."

What was she talking about? But of course. Her dementia had pushed her onto an alternate track. She'd been so together, I hadn't expected it. "Eveline, my parents, their accident. What were you going to say?" She'd been an extremely astute defence lawyer, one of the best in the country, and if she thought something had been amiss, I would, under normal circumstances, believe her.

"What car accident?"

"You were saying the events surrounding my parents' crash were unlikely."

"Oh, yes. You know how it can be with unexpected trauma. I was terribly upset losing Idette. She was a creative type, no money, absolutely no sense, married on a whim. But their daughter—Violette, wasn't it?"

I nodded dumbly.

She smiled at me conspiratorially. "She came to stay with me for a little while... I think. But you know there was something I never told Violette?"

"No?" I raised my eyebrows.

"I liked her very much. I think I was a little strict. She had an artistic streak like her mother that could have become out of hand. I think she thought I didn't approve of that, but I did. And do you know something?"

I shook my head, unable to prevent myself from gaping. Was this some kind of caring alter ego emerging from her dementia?

"If I ever saw Violette again, I would tell her, whatever it takes, she must be true to herself. After all, it is the only thing we have. I've learnt that much being stuck in this place."

She closed her eyes for a few moments. Was she asleep? I shuffled my feet a little and turned my head. Philippe peered in through the glass.

"Oh, Violette, it's you," Eveline said.

I started and twisted back.

"Yes, as I was saying," she continued. "You were different to us, you always were. I wonder if I tried to put you in our mould to make my own life more comfortable. You complied, but I don't think it was your natural state." She shook her head. "Our way was only one way. I should have been more accommodating. The reason I asked Philippe to call you was that I want to say..." She took my hand and squeezed it. "Be yourself, child. Your maman had that one thing right in her life."

I stared at her. Why on earth did she think I was anything other than myself?

I pushed through the doors of the maison de repos, the black traffic scarring my sight. Forcing the colour back, I crossed the street and strode in the direction of Rémy's apartment, not caring about the snow gusting into my face on the rising wind.

Eveline had been confused. Her dementia was worse, yet perhaps it only stirred thoughts that had lain within for years. She obviously doubted the validity of my parents' crash. I'd never questioned the accident—why would I? No, it was Eveline's dementia. Philippe thought she'd confused the accident with another case she'd handled. It seemed likely. If only I'd been able to get her back onto the subject.

And why did she think I wasn't myself? She'd been so rigid about her mode of life, the one right way. I'd adopted it to good effect, and now she was telling me otherwise. Not only that, she'd admitted she'd liked the girl I'd been. It was a shame she'd never shown it—a shame she'd stamped out every piece of that carefree child. What right did she have to force my life in one direction then refute it in an instant? Anyway, surely we were defined by our choices, what we'd made of ourselves and how content we were with the outcome of our lives? What else was there?

My feet pounded into the pavement. I drove myself on faster, not noticing where I was going, my insides twisting up. What else was there? Well, there sure as hell was my synaesthesia—it hadn't fitted into my life with Eveline and I'd forced it away. Rémy had asked me how I'd managed to live always denying a part of myself. And now, damn it, I was stuck between wanting my colours to hold on to Rémy and wanting to keep the hellish invasion away because, no matter how hard I tried, I couldn't cope with it. My hands balled in my pockets. I wanted to run, shout, roar, punch something, anything, preferably Eveline, Philippe and Isabelle. I wanted to tear them apart, just as I was split asunder.

Pushing on and on, thoughts whirred through my head until I'd had absolutely enough. Eveline was sick. She couldn't be held accountable for her words. As I blocked out the afternoon as best I could, my pace gradually returned to its regular stride and I found myself at the end of Rue du Bac by the Seine. I crossed the busy junction and took the steps down to the deserted river walkway, the tourists sensibly taking warmer refuge in the city. The leaves on the alders that lined the bank clung hopefully to the branches despite the wind. I walked beneath the boughs, watching the snow twist into the leaden water, the flakes disappearing amidst the torrent, and I let the afternoon swirl away with the river.

"Tough day?" Rémy strode along beside me.

I continued on for a few moments, my mouth open as I stared at him and the colour of his words, snowflakes settling in his tousling hair, his lack of coat at odds with the wintry weather. Then I stopped, grabbed his waistcoat and drew him toward me. His encircling arms were sturdy and warm. I scoured his face for transparency. He seemed solid, but that wasn't enough. I had to keep him. I had to open to my colours somehow.

"I... I tried to call you," I said, my voice rising, "but I couldn't. I tried all evening and in the morning. Rémy, I don't want to lose you."

"You're not going to lose me," he replied, "and you did just call me."

"Yes, but I can't control it. I don't know if it's me, that I'm stressed with my colours in Paris, or what, but—"

"Hey, we're seeing Alex tonight. We'll figure something out—and I'm here now."

This was so erratic.

He glanced around. "I know roughly where we are…"

"I'm heading back to your apartment. We're almost at the Pont des Arts. I've just seen Eveline and I… wanted to walk."

He touched my cheek. "You're cold, let's keep going." He held out his arm and I clasped hold.

"How was Eveline?" he asked as we continued along the walkway.

"Oh, different. She wasn't herself—which was to be expected. She even implied my parents' death wasn't an accident." I glanced up at Rémy. He looked directly ahead. "And then she told me to be myself. Ironic, coming from her. I don't really know what to make of it all."

He shot a kiss at my cheek. "Sounds like good advice."

"Yes, she must have been taking notes from you," I snapped.

He raised his eyebrows.

"I'm sorry." I let out a breath. "It's just… so much is going on at the moment."

"I know." He stared into the cobbles as we walked. "I'm sorry I've put you through all this."

I stopped and pulled him toward me. "Don't. Don't ever be sorry. I'm so glad we're together."

He smiled, but there was sadness in his face. What must it be like for him, away from everything he loved, unable to control when he returned? I tugged at his arm and we carried on.

"I need to feel my synaesthesia," I said.

He glanced at me and frowned. "But you are feeling it, aren't you?"

"Yes and no. I'm holding most of it away. If I can experience more without it overwhelming me, perhaps I can keep you here."

He looked out over the water, his brow creased in thought.

"How is it for you?" I asked. "How do you manage?"

"My senses blend most of the time—smell, taste, colour, touch. But I'm used to it. I know the scent of snow on the wind will be white—the two go together, it's not really separable."

"And what about less enjoyable impressions?"

"I let them wash over me."

I glanced at him. "I need to feel more. I need to try."

"Alright. I can think of a few ways we can explore the senses." His eyes glinted.

I laughed and barged into him. "Here is probably not a good place."

We walked on in silence, approaching the Pont des Arts, the feel of him secure against me.

"I love the way this place empties in bad weather," I said as we drew under the railings hung with thousands of padlocks sealing the love of countless couples. He dropped my arm. I turned toward him, but he was gone.

Rémy's apartment was still, empty. The steadily falling snow cast a glare against the open piano despite the fading light. I pulled off my outdoor things and clicked on a couple of lamps, my numb fingers fumbling with the switches. Despite the long walk I was frozen, and I needed to warm myself properly.

I lit the fire then headed into the bathroom and ran the bath, adding drops of pine oil. The apartment was almost warm by the time I undressed and eased myself into the water. The heady pine focused and relaxed me at the same time and I released a slow breath. I needed to find a way to call Rémy back, but how? As I sank lower the water engulfed me to my neck, the heat thawing my frozen limbs. I closed my eyes and laid my head against the rolltop, my muscles unravelling, the day thankfully drifting away. It wouldn't be long before Alex was here.

After a few minutes I reached for the soap and washed myself, faintly humming *Lo Boièr*, wishing I had the harp to call Rémy with. I paused, soap covering one arm. *Lo Boièr*—those strange lyrics, the entrancing melody. There was some-thing about it. They sang it on the pog, they always had, and it transported me, it lifted me completely. I'd played it the other day and I'd been so absorbed that Rémy had come back straight away, but could *Lo Boièr* itself somehow have helped?

I finished washing then stepped out of the bath, towelled myself dry and released the water. I wrapped Rémy's robe around me and walked into the living room, casting my eyes over the grand piano. I could still see Rémy bent into its depths, the wrench in his hand.

I sat down at the stool, ran my hands along the keys and placed my fingers over the central notes, my middle finger finding C. It had been years since I'd played, but it was worth a try. I'd worked out the notes for *Lo Boièr* on the harp, I only had to transfer them to the piano.

As I pressed the A with my thumb, vibrant orange flooded the room, my body tensing at the imposition. I ignored myself and reached for the E with my little finger, casting indigo across the orange, a transcendent sunrise. I found the other notes, picking out each with care, the sounds filling the apartment with colour. Once confident my fingers could find their way, I began again, this time managing the mysterious, unhurried tempo, each note having time to develop its clarity of tone. It was a novice's melody played simply, but it was a melody nonetheless. My thoughts dropped away as I continued, and the notes rang through me, clear and harmonious.

I glimpsed a shadow in the corner of my eye and looked up. He stood at the side of the piano, watching.

It had worked. Relief poured over me.

He strode forward, straddled the end of the piano stool and took my head in his hands. "You got me back," he whispered in a shimmer of captivating blue, his lips close to mine, his breath on my skin.

"*Lo Boièr*," I said, savouring his proximity.

"That makes complete sense." He kissed me slowly then drew back a little. "So you want to feel?"

"Yes, absolutely." I had to try.

He swung his leg around me so I sat between his knees, his chest firm against my back, his arms around mine. He kissed my neck then ran his fingers down to my wrists and clasped my hands, lifting them gently onto the piano.

"One of the most extreme forms of synaesthesia," he murmured in my ear, "is when one person feels the sensations of another." He splayed his fingers over mine. "Sense my movements."

I glanced back at him with a puzzled expression.

"Try it. Copy me," he said.

If he thought it would help.

I extended my fingers to imitate his positioning,

absorbing the warmth of his body around mine, relishing his presence. He pressed gently upon the ring finger of my right hand, the key beneath striking a delicate chartreuse. I held the colour at the margins of my vision—but what good would that do? I released a breath and allowed the impression to grow. He pushed on my thumb and a rich cornflower blue followed, then my little finger, and a delicate yellow added inflection. We played on and the beginnings of an enigmatic melody unfurled.

"Satie, *Gnossienne Number One*," Rémy whispered, and kissed my neck. "Now, close your eyes. Shut out everything but me."

"Alright."

He pressed his fingers softly upon mine, his muscles playing over my arms. We repeated the first notes, the melody shimmering before me even though my eyes remained closed. He slid his left hand along the keyboard. I followed instinctively, unsure how I'd known where to move. We played a chord then changed position for a deep indigo bass note. I followed again without thinking. It was inconceivable, but I'd known where to place my hands. I had to see what I was doing. I opened my eyes and my fingers fell on a jarring discord.

He paused. "Try to forget yourself."

I took a breath and closed my eyes once more. Forcing myself not to think, I followed him as though I could sense his desire to reach out and play each note. The melody developed, languorous and otherworldly, difficult to grasp like a hidden question at the edge of consciousness, and still I accompanied him. The swirling colour added depth and momentum to the melody, but it covered me, pulling at my sense of self. My throat narrowed and my chest tightened—it was too much. But Rémy's rough cheek lay against mine, his arms sturdy around me. The colour and the music flowed, and I breathed.

The melody descended an octave and changed expression, alternating high and low as though its duality was the answer to the fore-asked musical question, flashes of rouge adding force to the reply. And still we played together, Rémy's every intention somehow clear to me, his heart beating through my back. He kissed my neck again, sending ripples over my skin, and the melody changed once more. The pitch rose, my fingers scaling every colour but the rouge of before, as though the melody had more to say than the forcefulness of the previous phrase, as though there was something beyond its dichotomy. And all the time the alternating bass note and the chord grounded the melody, anchoring us here in the present with each other.

My perception of Rémy grew—the flexing of his arms, the tension and release of his fingers, his influence on the piece an unfathomable blue that tinted the melody. But there was more than that—music and colour flowed through every sinew of his being, dynamic and expansive, driven by his passion for the melody, and there, underneath it all, lay his need for me to experience what he'd always known, what was so important to him—his blended senses.

The music rose again, mysterious and unbound, and I knew he could feel me as I could him. Sensation spread through every part of us, born on the melody. I was alight with him, and he was everything.

He drew the melody softly to a close, our hands resting together upon the keys. I sat there in stunned silence, breathless, sweat beading upon my forehead. I was aware of myself, yet I was more aware of what made up him. I twisted around and scoured his face. My senses had expanded and merged with his and... it was utterly incredible. "We have the same interpretation of the world," I whispered, "but from different... perspectives."

"Different and the same," he murmured.

I kissed him, feeling every part of his being. He responded, his touch flaming through me.

A knock rapped out.

I pulled back, the reality of the room registering.

"Ignore the door," he said, drawing me to him. "I need you, not the door."

Somehow my rationality nudged to the fore. "I can't. It must be Alex."

The knock came again.

I rose, my eyes lingering on his, feeling his need for me. "We have to see Alex," I said.

He nodded. "Of course we do."

Chapter Eighteen

Feeling as though I'd stepped away from half of myself, I walked toward the door, adjusting Rémy's robe then scraping back my sweat-damp hair. I was completely underdressed, my feet bare, my make-up no doubt a mess, but more than that, I needed to gather myself. I paused in the hall. "Alex, could you just give me a couple of minutes?" I called.

"Of course," he replied through the door.

I strode into the bathroom, Rémy's eyes following. I could still feel him all through me. Staring into the mirror, I willed myself back to the here and now. My cheeks were flushed, my pupils dilated, my make-up had disappeared, but that was better than black streaks. I washed my face, brushed my hair and knotted it into a messy bun, then pulled on black jeans, a cashmere polo neck and ballet pumps, the mundane act of dressing bringing me back to myself. Feeling a little more grounded, I slipped through the bedroom door.

Rémy stood by the window, gazing out at the street. He turned and smiled. "Ready?"

"Ready." I nodded, but my stomach eddied. Alex had to be able to help. I strode to the hall and opened the door.

Alex stared wide-eyed over my shoulder, clearly agitated. "I heard him. I'd know his playing anywhere."

I flinched as the controlled city black of his voice spanned my vision. Being open with Rémy was one thing, but the rest of the world was going to take more work. I pushed Alex's colours away a little, allowing me to focus.

"Are you a musician?" Alex added, scouring my face. "It couldn't have been you, though—it was Rémy's expression. He loved that piece."

"Alex, come in." I stepped back. "And no, I'm not a musician." A couple of weeks playing the harp wasn't enough to count.

He stared at me and nodded slowly, as though he were trying to put everything together and not succeeding.

"Can I take your coat?" I asked.

"Uh, yes." He shrugged it off with his scarf as he juggled a leather document pouch, then he strode into the living room and gazed around. I hung up his things and followed him in.

"Where is he?" Alex said.

I didn't need any confirmation—I already knew by the emptiness in my gut, Rémy was gone.

Alex stood by the piano, staring at it as though it were alive. "Is he here?" he asked in a stronger voice.

"He was here. It was him playing a few moments ago." Him and me. "But when I let you in, he... went."

"And he does that? Comes and goes?"

I nodded.

"I had my doubts, but..." He let out a brusque laugh. "He's really alive, isn't he?"

"Yes, he is."

He looked bemused.

"I'm sorry I left you waiting," I added. "I hope I haven't held you up?"

"Not at all. I thought this might take some time, so I've nothing planned this evening." Alex's colours continued to press in on me, but his black wasn't the blast of Paris. It was a steady, secure, delineating black, clean and straightforward. I imagined people knew where they stood with him. But even so, I couldn't have my senses bombarded like this. I pushed Alex further away.

"And, anyway," he continued as he unbuttoned his suit jacket, "it should be me apologising for my reaction. Hearing Rémy playing..." He frowned. "It brought back a lot of memories."

"Well, I'm glad you heard him if it confirms his continued existence." I thought of Rémy's hands, his body wrapped around mine. "Have a seat," I said. "Can I get you a drink?"

"Water would be good."

Heading into the kitchen, I realised my stomach was painfully empty. "I'm going to phone for takeout," I called through. "Will you join me?"

"I've not eaten. That would be perfect."

I opened Rémy's wine cupboard. A card for Les Demoiselles was pinned to the inside of the door. I'd seen the restaurant near the boulangerie around the corner. It wouldn't take them long to deliver here. "I've not used this place before. Do you mind if I get a selection?"

"Sounds fine."

As I ordered I attempted to accept the lifeless brown voice on the other end of the line. Rémy said he let unwanted impressions wash over him. I tried to do the same but only succeeded in feeling faintly nauseous. After ordering the second dish, I'd had enough and I pushed the colour away. Putting my phone down, I gazed through the doors to the piano. Rémy needed to hear what Alex had to say, but I'd be too tense to play *Lo Boièr* with the music director of the Paris Opera in the room, or anyone else for that matter.

I carried in two glasses of water. Alex looked up from his phone and smiled as I passed his glass, his boyish face affable, a definite improvement on when we'd first met. "So," I said as I sat down opposite. "Where do we start?"

He took a sip and leant forward, his elbows on his knees, the glass between his hands. "I think it would be best if you tell me everything you know about Rémy's disappearance, which is where my knowledge ends." His voice flickered at the fringes of my vision, blending with the background noise of the apartment. His colour was actually quite pleasant. Was this a part of what Rémy had seen in him? "If I know what happened," he continued, "I may be able to relate his situation to what I've read in the books."

"Alright. Rémy said that when everything got out of hand, he had to do something to restrain the Désaccord. He took a violin from the opera house, drove to Sarrat and climbed to the chateau." Alex scanned my face attentively. "He played the key song but the Désaccord attacked. The Harmonie took him into safety, but when he tried to return, the Désaccord lay in wait, and it continues to do so. I don't think there's anything more to it than that."

"That explains Rémy's car abandoned in Sarrat." More black with a little agreeable grey. "The books are clear that should the Désaccord become too powerful, a key song can be played at a sanctuary to redress the balance. I wondered if that was what he'd tried there." He sat back. "We should do the same."

My stomach sank. "There's no point. Rémy's family play there every week while the Désaccord rages around. They don't appear to be doing anything effectual."

"But are they playing the key song?"

"*Lo Boièr*, right?" It had to be. The song and the chateau were inseparable, and the melody had such an unusual quality.

His jaw tensed. "Then, yes, they've been playing the key song, but I don't understand why it hasn't worked."

"There must be something else in the books." I couldn't keep the urgency from my voice.

"I'm not sure." He placed his glass on the table, took the document pouch from the cushion beside him and undid the clasp.

I twisted my fingers together. There had to be another way. We couldn't leave Rémy there—and it wasn't just Rémy. "There's someone else caught up in this too," I said. "A boy, Théo. He was drawn into whatever happened that day."

Alex looked up from the pouch.

"Théo is in the Harmonie with Rémy," I said. "His family believe he was lost in the river."

Alex shook his head. "Unbelievable. The poor kid. Even more reason to find a way." He drew out two small books and passed one to me.

My fingers ran over the textured black cloth covering the hardback. "It looks modern. Rémy said the books were old."

"They're copies that Rémy had made. He never did tell me where he found the originals. Did he mention it to you?"

"No, he didn't." I opened the book to the front paper, marbled in gold. The next page featured an antiquated diagram—what looked like the scroll of a violin with a heavenly hand adjusting the tuning peg. The scroll descended into interlocking spheres decorated with musical notes, symbols of the planets, an equator of stars and numerous Latin words. I frowned and turned the page around, trying to make sense of it.

Alex noticed my confusion and glanced at the diagram. "It's the mundane monochord with its proportions and intervals. A well-known illustration by Robert Fludd. The books are full of more or less arcane drawings. Some have been incorporated into modern music theory, and some I've only seen here."

There was a title above the diagram. "*In Musica Sphaerarum,*" I read out. "'The Musical Spheres'?"

"'The Music of the Spheres'."

I nodded. "My Latin is almost non-existent."

"And underneath is the subtitle, *Superum,* which means 'The Heavens'."

"Okay." I turned the page to what looked like a wolf formed from globes of indecipherable writing. Piercing the beast's centre was a staff on which musical notes were detailed. I couldn't make anything of this one either. There was another drawing on the following page, this time a mesh possibly denoting musical intervals. The main text began below, the first letter illuminated in jewel colours and gold, the rest of the passage a barely legible handwritten scrawl. Even so, the lettering looked familiar. No doubt I'd seen something similar at a museum or on the internet.

I studied the text. "Middle French?"

"On the very early end of middle, I would say."

"Great," I mumbled. I tried to interpret the script. "Only the immutable and worthy one may... find the secrets herein of the music of... the spheres." Half the words barely showed resemblance to their modern-day counterparts. I looked up at Alex. "I don't know what I expected, but that sentence was..."

"Hard-going, archaic, almost indecipherable?"

I raised my eyebrows and nodded.

He released a brief laugh. "Tell me about it. Try reading the whole thing."

"I can imagine." I met his eyes and they held a warm-hearted spark.

Returning to the book, I carefully flicked through fifty pages of recondite figures and plenty of writing, as much of it scrawled at angles around diagrams as making up the main text. Defeated by incomprehension, I placed the book on the table.

Alex handed me his copy. "This one is called *Terra*, meaning 'The Earth'. It contains most of the information we need, referring to music as it relates to our existence on this planet and the corresponding role of the Harmonie and the Désaccord."

I opened it at the centre. A pen-and-ink drawing depicted billowing clouds head-to-head with each other, one of them line-shaded into ominous darkness, the other white and untainted, musical notation and Hebrew letters interspersed throughout. I glanced through the rest of the pages. The drawings were stunning, but it was as incomprehensible as the first book. I placed *Terra* on the table and slumped into the sofa. "All I can say is, I'm glad you're familiar with them. It must have taken you forever."

"A couple of years' hard graft."

"Then please enlighten me, what is *Terra* all about?"

He picked up his glass and sat back. "*Terra* describes

ways in which music can soar to the most lofty heights. It contains the mathematics which prove Rémy's claim that an orchestra can produce the best music when tuned to A at 432 hertz. It explains that this tuning reflects and even links with the Harmonie, creating resonance with the universe. It also details the Désaccord, how in principle it shapes music, providing contrast that reflects our experiences of life."

I thought of the seething darkness on the pog. "How can the Désaccord do that?"

"When discordant notes are used to counteract harmonies, music reflects the interplay of forces we encounter on a daily basis—good and evil, light and dark, male and female. But the Désaccord has an unruly power all of its own, a dynamic strength to enrapture. Perhaps the Désaccord is only everything we reject embodied in music to become the dark seducer of the senses. *Terra* reveals how the Désaccord may be utilised to create compositions of unprecedented power to this end. It also details how the Désaccord may be brought into balance."

"Through playing key songs at sanctuaries."

"Exactly, but—"

A knock sounded at the door.

I pushed myself up. "You were going to say?"

Alex rubbed his forehead. "It occurred to me I may have another way to retrieve Rémy."

"Hold that thought." A thread of hope twisted through me as I headed to the hall. I opened the door and took the paper bags from the delivery girl, then carried them to the coffee table and set out the cartons. Alex had put one of the books away and was scanning the other.

I went into the kitchen, found a bottle of Rémy's Merlot, two glasses, a corkscrew and everything else we'd need for the meal. I piled it onto a tray and carried it in. Alex looked up as I set everything between us.

"Shall I?" He nodded to the wine.

"Be my guest."

He ran the knife around the foil and removed the cork, confidence clear in his fluid movements. I lifted the carton lids, revealing pot au feu with Dijon mustard, choucroute saucisson, little croque monsieur bites, a cheese selection and crepe slices with honeyed apricots and roasted almonds. There was also a demi baguette in one of the bags. It was a complete melange, but hopefully Alex would find something he liked. He poured the wine then we helped ourselves to the dishes.

"It looks delicious." He raised his glass. "Santé."

I lifted mine, wondering what Alex had been going to say before the meal arrived. "Santé," I replied, and took a sip, almost choking as an explosion of maroon filled my senses. This was new. Well, not entirely new, but I'd not experienced taste as colour for a long time. No doubt it was the result of opening to Rémy. I took another sip and braced myself. The effect repeated, but I could push it away at any time—there was no reason to worry. I kicked off my shoes and curled my legs under me, balancing the plate on my lap.

Alex forked up his dinner at a swift pace. "Hungry?" I asked with a smile, thinking of Rémy at Les Fonts.

"Professional hazard, for me at least. I get so wrapped up in my work I don't eat. My last meal was... probably yesterday." He broke off a chunk of baguette.

I couldn't wait any longer to ask him, "Alex, you said you may have another way to retrieve Rémy."

He nodded. "I've been turning over why the key song

wasn't successful. *Terra* is adamant that it should work. I wonder if it's because of what we did with the Désaccord."

"How so?"

"The Désaccord is a force of the Earth—it exists everywhere all the time—but through the rituals we focussed part of it into a powerful concentration that somehow linked with Rémy. Perhaps what we did made it too strong to be neutralised in the usual way."

"That makes sense," I said.

"There's a ritual in the books with the purpose of rendering the Désaccord harmless. I always presumed it was included as a failsafe should a sanctuary not be available, but perhaps it was included for this kind of situation."

"When you say ritual, what do you mean? I have visions of satanic worship in pentagrams." I grinned and took a mouthful of choucroute, savouring the sourness.

He smiled. "Not exactly, but you are probably more right than you know."

"Oh?" I narrowed my eyes.

"A ritual uses a setting and specifically chosen words to open the mind to the task at hand, be that a satanic ritual with a pentagram or a eucharist celebrated in a church. Small details act as signals to the subconscious minds of the attendees, bringing them into a collective state of receptivity and intention."

"So what are the details of this ritual?"

"*Terra* is specific. It requires a venue with certain geometric dimensions, it necessitates the symbolism of a knife to represent cutting away the inflated proportions of the Désaccord, and it requires a small amount of blood to be drawn from one individual, showing that those present are willing to sacrifice their own needs for that of the hoped-for outcome."

I placed my fork down, a dry laugh escaping me. "That sounds..." I couldn't think what to say.

"Dramatic?" Alex offered.

"Definitely that."

"That's the point—to build meaning and emotion into action. Without it the ritual won't work. Believe me, we messed around enough to know."

"But the blood is a bit drastic." I gazed at the corkscrew on the table, the foil knife still extended.

"Just one drop is enough. It's not anything extreme."

The whole situation was extreme.

"If we carry out the ritual," he continued, "I would take the blood from my palm. A small incision."

"And would I need to be involved?" I wanted to help, of course, but this wasn't exactly my comfort zone.

"As the person in contact with Rémy and one of the few who actually know what's going on, it would aid the ritual to have your understanding and your intention."

I nodded slowly, trying not to grimace. "I'll need to run it past Rémy."

"Absolutely." He looked around the room. "He's not...?"

"No, he's still not here."

He let out a breath. "If Rémy wants to go ahead, I could arrange everything quickly." He glanced at the cartons. "Do you mind if I take some more?"

"Please do." I placed my plate down. I wasn't hungry. What had Rémy been involved in back then? Shifting in my seat, I rubbed my arms. There was little left of the fire and the temperature had dropped. I stepped over to the hearth and piled logs onto the embers. "If the internet is anything to go by," I said, hoping to lighten the conversation, "I wonder how you and Rémy found the time to get up to so much when you were holding down demanding jobs and attending every party in town."

Alex laughed. "We worked hard and played hard. It was all about the beauty of music and our passion for creativity, which spread to other areas—sensual pleasures, experience after experience. We never stopped." He took another mouthful. "But Rémy's disappearance was the end of it for me. It was passion and creativity driven to a destructive frenzy. I took off my red shoes and knuckled down."

It was all so bizarre, I couldn't restrain my curiosity. "So, what actually happened back then, if you don't mind me asking?"

He placed his plate on the table and examined my face. "I wouldn't speak about it to anyone, but you already know most of it." That vulnerability appeared in his eyes once more. "We followed the guidelines in *Terra*, performing rituals that added power and depth to discordant notes specifically written into Bénédict's composition. After the first attempt we had such acclaim for the performance that night, it bolstered us to enact the ritual again and again. Where initially the music held edge and depth, as we continued, the composition took on a beguiling intensity. That was when Bénédict and the orchestra were affected." His voice wavered and he gazed into the flames. "I began to have doubts at that point, but Bénédict was completely off his head with it and Rémy wouldn't listen—they thought they could control the Désaccord, but I think it was controlling them. They were wrapped up in the music and taken with the prestige—it was well known that the orchestra was tuned to 432, guided by Rémy, and part of the success of Bénédict's piece was attributed to the tuning." A flicker of anguish crossed his face. "Rémy wouldn't stop. He practised ritual after ritual, high on the power of it. He wouldn't let go."

That didn't sound like Rémy. Passionate, yes, but there was something so gentle and accepting about him. I supposed it made sense if he'd been controlled by the Désaccord in some way, but he'd caused so much pain, he'd had a part in his friend's death, and he'd put his family through hell. It left me cold. Yet I'd seen the agony in his eyes when he'd told me about Bénédict, the regret he'd obviously carried for years.

"When Bénédict died," Alex continued, "Rémy began to see sense. He tried to finish what we'd started and the Désaccord attacked him."

"Attacked?"

Alex glanced at me, his face haggard, the weight of what they'd done clear. "Not exactly a physical attack, although the Désaccord does have an unpleasant physical presence."

I shivered, thinking of the pog again.

"It was mental agony," he said. "His mind was torn apart. We were in regular contact—I remember calling him the morning of his disappearance." Alex's voice trembled. "He wouldn't answer, he didn't turn up for work, no one had seen him, and I was frantic. After a few hours I called the police, explaining that his mental state was fragile. The police contacted his family and his car was found soon after. Search parties went out and the rest is history." Alex rose abruptly. "If you'll excuse me." He strode into the kitchen.

I released a breath. Alex and Rémy had put themselves and others through so much. I could hear Alex running the tap. After a few minutes he came back in, his face and hair damp, his eyes rimmed with red, yet his confident bearing had returned. "I'm sorry. It's been a long time and it's not easy."

"I shouldn't have asked."

"No, you shared and I did the same." Alex picked up the Merlot in an offering. I held out my glass. He poured then added a little to his own.

"So what about you, Violette?" he asked as he sat down.

I raised an eyebrow. "I'm not sure what there is to tell."

"I don't think I know anything about you, apart from that you live in Sarrat, you previously lived in Paris and you have synaesthesia. I'm intrigued."

"I, uh... I grew up in Sarrat and returned recently after seventeen years in Paris. I presume my synaesthesia enabled me to see Rémy. We'd known each other as children and we..." How should I put it? "Got to know each other again."

Alex nodded. "It sounds like Rémy was lucky."

"Perhaps."

"But what about family? Are you married?"

"No." I shook my head. "There's only Rémy, and that's very new."

He frowned. "I didn't realise."

"It's not something I've been advertising, for obvious reasons."

He looked at me intently, his eyes flicking between mine. "Be careful, Violette. He can be passionate and persistent, but it's mostly a surface act, a foray with one person and then another. He must be desperate to leave the Harmonie, and you're the only one who can help."

I stared at him, wondering if we were talking about the same person. "What are you saying?"

"Based on my past experience of Rémy, who I know in

every way, and who was and I hope still is my closest friend, I'm saying that it might be prudent not to get too involved or you may end up his latest indulgence."

Indulgence... I gaped at Alex, unable to speak. The picture he'd painted was of someone careless who threw away people's emotions in pursuit of his own gratification. Rémy had always been so patient, so gentle, so considerate. Yes, the passion was there, but it was tempered, restrained by... kindness. Yet when I'd had lunch at the Rabastens, Yves had said that Rémy was completely wrapped up in himself. That and what I'd seen on the internet fitted Alex's picture.

My heart throbbed in my throat. I'd allowed myself to be so caught up in Rémy—his patient confidence, his intensity, the shared experience of our synaesthesia. I'd felt Rémy through and through and he'd felt me too. There was a connection I couldn't have imagined. But had I deluded myself into thinking our relationship was more than the reality? I'd been vulnerable when I'd returned to Sarrat. I could have shaped Rémy in my mind to be what I wanted, rather than seeing the truth.

Alex gazed at me, waiting for a response. "I'll bear that in mind," I managed, looking away and draining the last of my wine. I took a deep breath and pulled myself together. Rémy and I had something. How could I doubt that? I needed to focus on the reason Alex was here. "Indulgence or not, we have to get Rémy and Théo out."

"Agreed," Alex replied.

But I really didn't feel comfortable with the ritual. "Apart from what we've discussed, do you have any other ideas for retrieving Rémy?"

He shook his head. "Reacquainting myself with the

books today brought most of it back. I'll keep reading, but apart from the key song and the ritual, I'm not aware of another option."

Chapter Nineteen

Alex's words cut through me as I sat at the piano, staring at the keys. Alex and Rémy had been close for years, so Alex's experiences should count for something, yet his description of Rémy was completely at odds with the man I'd come to know. I rubbed my forehead and scraped my hands through my hair. No matter my confusion, I couldn't sit here all evening. I needed to call Rémy and tell him what Alex had said.

Pulling myself up, I placed my hands on the keys, the ivory cool under my fingers. I played, allowing myself to perceive the colour of the music, but all the time I was aware of a hollow deep within created by Alex's words.

Within moments Rémy's shoulder pressed against mine as he sat on the stool next to me. I drew my hands to my lap and turned to him, taking in the curve of his shadowed jaw, the play of his lips that broke into a smile, the softness and fervour in his eyes. My senses were full of him as he kissed me. This was the Rémy I knew, and yet the hollow remained.

"What is it?" That blue I could drown in.

I frowned. I should ask him about what Alex had said, but... perhaps I was afraid of the answer.

Concern covered his face. "Tell me."

"There was a lot to take in from Alex."

He rose and took my hand. "Let's sit somewhere more comfortable, and you can tell me all about it." I let him pull me to the sofa.

"Why did you go?" I asked as we dropped into the cushions.

"I have absolutely no idea. I wanted to be there." He kissed the top of my head. "So, what did Alex say?"

I laid my head against his chest, my fingers playing with the top button of his waistcoat. "The method the books recommend, apparently, is the playing of a key song at a sanctuary, just as your family do."

"But it's not working." Rémy tensed under me. "Was there anything else about it? There must be something Joël is doing wrong."

"Alex said not."

"Has he left the books?"

"He said he wouldn't. It's obviously hard for him to trust this strange woman who claims his long-lost friend is alive—although he heard you playing, so I think he's convinced now."

He nodded. "But there has to be something else."

I sat back a little to make eye contact. "Alex said there was another way... the only other way he could fathom."

His brow raised. "Yes?"

"A ritual where the Désaccord is rendered harmless."

He stared at me. "The ritual requiring a knife and blood."

"That was it."

"No," he said flatly.

"What do you mean, no?"

He sat up. "What I mean is absolutely and unconditionally no." There was hardness in his voice, rigidity in his colours.

"Why?" I scanned his face. "The whole thing sounds unnerving, but if the Harmonie is holding you because of the danger posed by the Désaccord, we need to put the Désaccord out of action. Then we can get Joël to play in the chateau and call you back."

"No, we can't do it... you and Alex can't do it. The ritual would require calling the Désaccord into the circle before attempting to render it harmless. It's too risky."

I tensed, my eyes hard. Was this Rémy's self-centredness speaking? "It's not only about the risk to you, though, is it?"

"What do you mean?"

"This whole situation is not just about your safety. There's Théo, of course, not to mention the effect it's having on your family and Alex—and me."

He took my hands in his, his fingers warm. "But I'm not saying it for fear of something happening to me. I'm saying it because of you and Alex. I understand the rituals. It's clear to me what's at stake, and it's dangerous, extremely dangerous. The Désaccord messes with your mind, and before you know it..." He shook his head. "We can't risk making the situation worse."

My brow furrowed. This was the Rémy I knew. Why was I second-guessing him?

"Tell me what's wrong," he said. "I know there's been something up since you called me"

"Noth—"

He placed his finger on my lips and shook his head. "Violette, I can sense it. I've always been able to sense you a little. But after the piano..." He made a small half-smile. "I'm completely open to you, and I know that since seeing Alex you're confused."

I studied his face. I couldn't sense him to that extent. But then, his synaesthesia was more developed than my repressed version. My eyes settled on his lips. Despite everything Alex had said, I could almost forget it all in Rémy's draw. I wanted to kiss him, to be lost in him.

His mouth curled into a grin. "So you still want me."

I started. "What? You can read minds now?"

"Not minds, just synaesthesia." He kissed me and, once again, I could feel something of him. Of course, we had more than what Alex called an indulgence, so why did Alex's words form an emptiness within me? I needed to be straight with Rémy. I pulled myself away. "You're right, there is something."

"Tell me," he said.

"I think I know you, and what we shared earlier was... unbelievable. But other people have given me a different impression—Alex and Yves mainly. I guess I'm scared I've been wrong in some way."

He raised an eyebrow.

"You're having a relationship with the one person who can see and help you." I took a breath. "You have a vested interest in me."

"Are you asking if I only want you because you can help me?"

I shrugged.

"Come on, Violette. You know me better than that. And I know you. We wouldn't have to have a relationship for you to help—you'd do it anyway."

"Of course I would." There was no question.

"Well then."

"You know you appear a bit... libertine on the internet," I added.

"Libertine?" He laughed and shook his head. "And the internet is so reliable."

"I got the impression from Alex that you indulged in a lot of brief relationships, and that you were quite..."

"What?"

I shifted against him. "Wrapped up in yourself." There, I'd said it, and I had no idea how he was going to react.

His face set into a frown, then his mouth pursed, a sparkle lit his eyes and he laughed.

"What?" I asked.

"I don't know. It's so me and so not me."

"That clarifies everything," I said, my tone flat.

He leant forward and kissed me, a brief, soft kiss. "There were times when I was like that, especially when I was younger, but my focus is music. Most of the time I was completely wrapped up in my work—I guess that's self-indulgence. Alex had to drag me away in an attempt to hook me up with some one-night wonder. But that was more him than me—he loved to be with people, especially if he got to take them home."

"Well, if the internet is anything to go by, since his promotion he's been a good boy."

"That I'd like to see."

"But what about Yves?" I asked.

Rémy scowled. "Yves never had a good opinion of me. There was always a lot of sibling rivalry, particularly with our music. I beat him in a few recital competitions and he hated to lose." He sighed. "It's just family stuff."

Was this his own version of events, or the reality? I studied his face, drawn to the depth of his eyes, and I could feel the truth of him. My distrust was ridiculous. I touched his cheek, the roughness of his stubble scattering colour in all directions. My problem wasn't him, it was me. "My senses tell me you are completely trustworthy," I said, "but for some reason it seems I have trouble trusting myself."

"Hey," he replied softly, grasping my hand. "You're having a relationship with a phantom. We can't interact with the world and play ourselves off against other people. It's not exactly a normal relationship."

I smiled, feeling a little lighter. "Not everyone would have taken what I said so easily."

He grinned. "But you do still have to get me back. I have something to come back for."

"But won't you consider the ritual? I have a strange picture of chalk pentagrams and mysterious cloaked figures with evil intent, but we have to do something about you and Théo."

"No," he said, his voice rock hard again. "Unequivocally, no." He rubbed his forehead then fixed my gaze. "Alex means well, and of course I would do it if I thought there was a good chance of Théo and I getting back safely, but the danger of calling the Désaccord into a ritual is too great. I'm not going to risk anyone else getting hurt."

"Well, we'd better find another way, then," I replied. And we really had.

"There must be something else in the books about using the key song at the sanctuary," he said, "something the musicians aren't doing right. If Alex can't find anything, do you think you could ask him to leave the books? Or if he won't, perhaps you could photograph the pages?"

"Yes, of course. I'll phone him first thing in the morning." I sat back and released my shoulders, feeling rooted to Rémy once again as though a haze had lifted. My eyes followed the contours of his face, the delicate mottle of his skin, the angle of his cupid's bow. It was ridiculous how he drew me.

He smiled.

"What?" I asked.

"You don't have to ask me what. You know."

I shook my head. "How much can you actually sense of me?"

"Oh, a fair amount." He took my hand and ran his fingers over the soft skin on the inside of my wrist, flooding me with shimmering blue. I drew in a sharp breath, ignoring my urge to hide from more sensory bombardment. It was different with Rémy.

"I felt you completely when we played the piano," he said, his voice low and unhurried. "I felt every part of you, and I know you felt me too. Violette, that's never happened to me before."

I drew my thumb along the edge of his palm. The piano had meant something to him, although deep down I was already aware of that.

"You know," he continued, "Plato said we all have inner music, a sort of pattern created by the cohesion of our bodies. He called it our musica humanum. This pattern is often reasonably neutral with those around us, although we know when it clashes. But what makes up you, your music, it's sublime... I could never have too much of it." He stared at me steadily. "When we met again, it wasn't long before I was completely gone. I knew we had something—a harmony, a resonance. What we felt at the piano just confirms it, and I think perhaps our resonance caused us to meet."

"I like that thought very much," I whispered, shivers running through me at his words, at how I felt the same way.

The corners of his mouth turned up a little, then he shook his head. "It's not just the synaesthesia, though, it's everything—how easy it is to be with you, how we see the world the same way, how despite the fact you're so controlling of yourself, you're letting that go to help me."

I raised my eyebrows in mock consternation at the mention of my control, a smile playing at my lips. He had me there.

He laughed. "I'm completely undone. I've never felt this way. I know we've only shared a short time together, but I don't want to spend another moment away from you."

My shivers coalesced into everything I felt for this gentle, intense, wonderful man, the serendipity of him taking my breath away. "I'm utterly caught in you," I whispered. "It feels like you're a part of me, a part I need to exist. You bring so much into my life, and I don't want it to end." I pulled him toward me and kissed him fervently. He reciprocated, then he broke away, sprang up and lifted me into his arms. I kissed him again and again as he carried me into the bedroom and placed me gently down at the foot of the bed.

He stood there staring at me, shaking his head, a bemused smile on his face as though he couldn't believe his luck, then he brushed my cheek tenderly and silver burst through my skin. It rushed over me, one sensation too many. My stomach folded and my throat stuck. But I chose him over some irrational response. He'd already shown me I wouldn't lose myself experiencing him, so what did I have to be afraid of?

Letting out a steady breath, I pushed my uncertainty away and reached up, drawing my fingers over the sinews of his neck. His skin shuddered. I ran my hand to his collar, tugged at the knot of his tie and pulled the length of silk to the floor, then unfastened the top buttons of his shirt. His mouth was parted, his arms holding me against him.

I unbuttoned his waistcoat then the rest of his shirt, and as my fingers worked the fabric, I could sense him—he could barely contain himself, but at the same time he was savouring every moment. When I'd undone the last button, I drew my hands across his firm abdominals and up over his chest. I couldn't get enough of him—he was sublime, his colour something else. He gasped at my touch, his fingers pressing into my back.

My hands brushed his shirt apart, catching upon a soft ribbon. The harp key hung at his chest. I ran my fingers over the small piece of metal that had been so much a part of my life.

He wrapped his hand around mine, closing our fingers against the iron. "It will always be with me."

I smiled, my eyes sinking into his. I let the key fall to his chest, stole my hands across his collarbone and pushed his shirt and waistcoat from his shoulders. He grabbed the fabric and pulled his arms out, then took the bottom of my polo neck and drew it up over my head. Grasping my waist, he pulled me close, our skin touching, my sense of him blending with myself. He was warm, solid, his heart pounding, his breath ragged. He trailed his fingers over my back, rousing plumes of colour and rivulets of fear. But I didn't care for the fear. I wanted him.

Clasping the back of my head, he kissed me again. This time slowly. I savoured the velvet-dark taste, my fingers tangled in his hair. Then, as if he could no longer wait, he kissed me with a fierceness that made me want him even more. He pulled away and lifted me up. I wrapped my legs around his middle and he climbed forward onto the bed, lowering me gently into the centre, the key swinging between us.

We gazed at each other, our senses mingled. We were utterly bound, and there was nothing I wanted more. He lowered himself forward to kiss me, and my hands passed through his body.

"Rémy," I gasped.

He launched upright, releasing a cry, my hands drawing out.

"Your skin... your body," I whispered. The chandelier was visible through him, and the lounge beyond. He was translucent, a spectre. I shifted back, my heart thumping.

He stared at me, his breath heaving.

"Why?" I shook my head, unable to pull my eyes from his tenuous form. "I could feel every part of you—I'm feeling more than I have for a long time. What happened?"

"I... uh... I don't know." His voice was jagged, anguished.

"We have to get you back," I said, desperation gripping me.

"I know." He met my gaze and I could hardly bear the look in his eyes. "Violette, I have no idea what's going on or where this will lead, but I need you to remember something."

I nodded, still staring at him.

"I'm yours. I always will be."

He reached out to touch my cheek and I jerked away.

I lay in Rémy's bed on the side nearest the windows, the covers pulled tight around me. The curtains hung open and I stared over the roofs into a sky mottled with hazy moonlight. A little ice had formed at the edge of the glass—it would be biting out there this late, or this early, depending on which way I looked at it. I should have fallen asleep hours ago, but not tonight.

No, tonight Rémy was fading. We'd just found each other and now he was leaving me. Nausea turned my gut—I couldn't lose him. Even after these short weeks, he'd become so much.

He was still here. I could sense him lying awake on top of the covers next to me, but at some point he would go. I'd opened myself to him and it hadn't been enough. It had worked after the pog, so why not now? Yet I couldn't deny that, apart from with Rémy, I wasn't completely open to my synaesthesia. I held most things away and perhaps that mattered.

My chest tightened at the thought of opening further. I couldn't get past the sensation of being overwhelmed, being suffocated. But if it weren't for that, wouldn't I want to experience the world in the dynamic, sensual way that was normal to Rémy? Despite everything, I was more accepting of the idea than I'd been in a long time.

A car pulled into the street, the engine growling above the murmur of sleepless Paris. I let the grey barbs fill my vision. The noise grew in intensity, the ugly colour crowding me. I hated this so much, but I had to be able to manage it, I had to try to help. The car pulled to a stop not far away and voices, clamorous in the night, thanked the driver and made small talk. I let those sounds in too, a man and a woman conversing a little too loudly. It was late, couldn't they get a move on into their apartment? But that would only be so I wouldn't have to endure their colours. No, I needed to face this. The woman released a ragged, dragging laugh and the man spoke again, his voice lurid and heavy. Another car rumbled in the next street, the wind scraped at the windows, the indistinct noise of the city reverberated, buzzing, pressing inward, stopping up my senses, covering my face, pulling on me, pulling...

"Violette?" Rémy sat up.

Fighting the urge to push the sensations away, I forced my breath to remain deep and regular. I had to be able to do this. But still it pressed in, tightening, thickening, smothering, and... there was something else there too, something underneath it all, tied to the colour, shaping it, giving it form, something I dared not touch. It lay at the margins of my mind, black, nebulous, abhorrent, a wraith of fear and horror that I couldn't quite grasp. It coagulated and filled my throat. I thrust upward, gasping, my heart pounding wildly.

"Violette, what's wrong?" Rémy reached out a filmy hand, then thought better of it. His face creased in frustration. "What happened?"

I couldn't go any further. I focussed on what I could see of the bedcover and pushed all the impressions away, the voices on the street, the wind, the horror, all of it but Rémy. The heaving of my chest slowed.

"Violette?"

"I'm fine. It's just my synaesthesia." I lay down and pulled the covers up around my neck, trying to ignore the dread that remained. Rémy settled next to me and I turned to face him, his familiar features like the clear night sky.

"You still can't sleep?" he asked softly.

"No," I whispered. "I'm terrified of losing you."

He made a grim half-smile. "I know. But it's more than that, isn't it?"

"Rémy, are you in my head again?"

He smiled. "I always want to be inside your head."

I longed to reach out and touch the curve of his cheek, but I didn't dare.

"Violette," he said.

"Hmmm?"

"What are you so scared of?"

I hauled myself onto my back and stared up at the chandelier, the crystals catching the moonlight, casting faint shards across the ceiling. He was right—I was scared of something. Underneath it all, dread circulated within me. It lay beneath my colours, raw and excruciating, forming them into a nightmarish blanket of fear that overwhelmed me every time I tried to open myself, and I hadn't been able to get past it to help Rémy. What was this horror, this... pain? I turned toward the window and curled up, tears trickling down my face. All I knew was that I couldn't lose Rémy.

Chapter Twenty

As I opened my eyes to the stark morning light, I noted the pillows, the tangled duvet and nothing more. He was gone.

I sprang up and wrapped Rémy's robe around me, panic pulsing through my veins. Of all the days to oversleep. I strode to the kitchen and grabbed my phone, the time flashing up. It was still reasonably early. I tapped dial on Alex's contact details and walked to the window by the piano. The sky was mottled grey, the clouds high and racing, the pavement beneath patched with snow.

"Violette," came Alex's structured, grounded black, "how are you?"

"I'm fine, but Rémy isn't. I don't think I'll be able to see him for much longer."

Alex was silent for a moment and then, "What do you want to do about it?"

"Rémy was adamant he didn't want us to perform the ritual. I know it's only a matter of hours since we spoke, but do you have any other options?"

"I'm sorry, I spent half the night going through *Terra*, but I couldn't find anything."

I drew a sharp breath.

"Look," Alex added, "it's understandable Rémy is nervous about the ritual after everything that happened, but it's not in the same category as what we did back then. If we went ahead, we would be rendering the Désaccord harmless, nothing more."

I couldn't just let him fade. "So what are the risks—the worst that could happen?"

"Worst possible scenario, the ritual doesn't work and Rémy is still trapped. Then we would have to think again. But I have to say, in the past the rituals were extremely effective."

"How quickly could we do it?"

"I could get out of a couple of work commitments today and prepare the place we used to use. I'm not conducting tonight, so I could have everything ready for this evening."

"Alright," I said. "Let's go ahead." There was no other option.

"Great. The sooner we get him back and safe, the better. Can you meet me on the front steps of the Palais Garnier at nine?"

"Yes, definitely."

"Alright. We'll take it from there."

"Thank you so much, Alex. I really am very grateful."

"No trouble at all. I'm just waiting for the moment we get him back and I can see the look on his face. See you then." He disconnected. I pocketed my phone and exhaled slowly. This would have to work. I couldn't allow myself to consider any other possibility.

I stepped to the piano and ran my hands along the ebony

rim, wanting to call Rémy, wanting to be with him, wanting to reassure myself he was still... visible, but he was so perceptive, I couldn't risk him guessing my plans and trying to talk me out of them.

After dressing, I opened my laptop on the dining table and sat down to work, attempting to think solely of my clients. I stopped for a croque monsieur from Les Demoiselles at lunchtime—food had seemed like a sensible idea, but I couldn't eat. As the day wore on my insides knotted as I considered if I was really doing the right thing. Rémy was firmly opposed to the ritual and Alex had been sure it was our only option, but I hardly knew Alex.

The light faded outside and still I worked. A couple of hours later I closed my laptop. Not being with Rémy was like denying a part of myself. I had to call him, even if it was only for a few moments before I left. I could keep my intentions hidden for that long, and besides, there was something I wanted to ask him.

I played *Lo Boièr*, the melody taking me up in spite of my worries. In fact, it was strangely comforting. I played through twice and had to stop myself continuing. It would be easier to remain wrapped within those familiar notes rather than face what lay ahead.

As the colours faded, I glanced around the apartment. He leant against the wall by the bedroom doors, his arms folded, his body lighter again, little more than a shadow. He walked over and stopped a few feet away, no doubt sensing I could barely handle seeing him like this.

"Hello," he said softly, his mouth curved into a pained smile.

"Hello." It was like being children again, neither of us knowing how to handle the situation.

His eyes narrowed. "Violette, what's wrong?"

"You mean apart from you fading?"

"Yes, of course I mean apart from that, you know I do."

I shook my head. "I wanted to see you." How long would it be until I never saw him again? It was too much to contemplate.

"Have you arranged to get the books?" he asked.

"I'm going to see Alex now. I'll sort something."

He nodded.

I studied his diaphanous face. "Can I ask you a question?"

"Of course."

"Do you trust Alex?"

He laughed. "Completely. We've been through hell and back, and I, uh, mean that literally. I'd trust him with my life."

That settled it, then. My last inkling doubts faded away.

"Why?" he asked. He peered at me for a moment, then his eyes opened wide. "Violette, don't even consider it."

Damn him, he was way too sensitive. This was a mistake. I glanced at the door.

"Don't do the ritual." His voice was hard, demanding.

My heart thrashed. What could I say?

"There's no way you can do it," he insisted. "It's too dangerous, you have to trust me."

I stared at him, feeling his desperation, his sincerity, his utter belief that the ritual was the wrong thing to do—but I had to get him back. I couldn't let him change my mind.

Taking a deep breath, I darted to the table and grabbed my bag. He stood staring at me for a moment, as though he couldn't work out what was happening. I dashed to the hall and pulled on my outdoor things.

He strode in. "Violette, please don't do this. You mean so much to me."

I ignored him and left the apartment, pulling the door tight and running down the stairs, my heels clicking against the stone with burst after burst of impenetrable grey. There was a movement in the corner of my eye. He was behind me.

"What can I do to change your mind?" he called, anger edging his words.

I couldn't speak. I didn't trust myself.

He was close now—I could feel him a stair or two above. I glanced back and he lunged for me, his hands passing through my body, achieving nothing more than shuddering my bones.

"Violette, don't go, you can't do this. I need you not to do this," he yelled. I turned my head to glance at him one last time. His face was wrought with desolation.

Picking up speed, I spiralled around and around the stairwell, focussing on my footfalls to block out the sound of his voice and the sense of him—everything I'd come to cherish so dearly. I refused even the slightest sensation and, as I pushed through the door to the street, he was gone.

"I'm so sorry, Rémy," I whispered into the wind.

I stood before the ornate facade of the Palais Garnier, surrounded by thrumming traffic. Colour scraped across my vision in intimidating swathes. I pushed it away, but I really didn't want to. As much as I disliked the invasion, I wanted to hold on to what I shared with Rémy.

The relentless north wind filtered through my coat, chilling every part of me. I tugged my scarf tighter, then pushed my gloved hands into my pockets and paced on the spot, taking in the countless busts and medallions of composers set amidst the grandiose pillars and sculpted divinities of the opera house.

"Violette." Alex strode toward me from the metro, a friendly smile upon his face. We exchanged kisses.

"Let's get him back, shall we?" he said.

I nodded. "Absolutely."

"It will be warmer inside." He indicated toward the entrance.

We headed to the far corner of the building, where gold-tipped gates stood open. Angels loomed from plinths on either side, one female—her body draped in plentiful robes, her hand raised in supplication, her face soft—the other male, brandishing a scroll and a lyre, his lines sharper, his features dauntless. When Alex said to meet outside the Palais Garnier, I'd presumed it was because he was working there, not because we would be entering.

We passed through the gate and the double doors beyond, Alex inclining his head to the attendant at the side of the vestibule. Shreds of music drifted around us in a flickering spectrum as we made our way to the grand staircase.

"There's a performance of *Don Giovanni* in progress," Alex said.

I nodded as I absorbed the interior. Sweeping stairs split left and right to form a balcony around the atrium, the painted ceiling above supported by colossal marble columns. The intricate masks of gods and goddesses peered down from sculpted arches, and decorative figurines supported countless candelabra. All of it glowed in opulent marble and gold. I'd always loved this place, coming early for performances to take in the architecture as much as the music.

I followed Alex down the stairs and through a corridor, passing a number of attendants. He guided me around the side of a red rope cordon and led me down a comparatively plain staircase.

"Are we doing the ritual here?" I asked in a hushed voice.

"The access to the venue is here," he said softly.

"I guess it's fitting."

We reached the bottom and turned into a narrow corridor of painted brick and wooden doors, one of which stood open to a large room filled with dressing tables, mirrors and clothing scattered about.

"The building stands on one of the old sanctuaries of the Harmonie," Alex said as we strode along. "Garnier knew exactly what he was doing when he designed the place, incorporating perfect geometrical proportions to create a temple of music."

That was encouraging. "So we'll be using a place dedicated to the Harmonie?"

"Unfortunately, no, that would be the auditorium in this case. We have something more specific for our purposes."

He pulled open a door at the end of the corridor and we entered a large storage area filled with props, *Don Giovanni* echoing around with surprising volume. We passed a decorative woodland scene and stopped by a metal staircase set into the floor.

"Hold tight," he said. "There's not much grip on the steps."

We descended into a cold basement lined with electrical boxes and rows of pipework, then headed to a low wire cage in the middle of the room. A dark opening yawned from the floor inside the meshwork. Alex drew out a key, unlocked a padlock and swung up a grille. He fished in his pocket, pulled out his phone and clicked on the torch, shining it into the blackness to reveal water underneath.

I looked at him. "The underground lake? I thought it was an urban myth."

"Completely real. Used in the old days as a reservoir in case of fire."

"We have to go down there?" I shivered at the dark waters.

"Yes, we do." Alex took the steps backward, then paused halfway down and held out his hand.

I hung my bag across my shoulders and clasped hold of him, glad of his strength as I trod down steps that were little wider than a ladder. If it had been anyone else but Alex with his secure colours and his friendship with Rémy, I would've had serious doubts. "Please tell me there's something other than water down here."

At the bottom Alex stepped to one side and shone his phone for me to see. At the side of the steps a ledge extended, broad enough for a person to walk along comfortably. The expanse of water continued beyond, difficult to make out in the limited light.

Alex supported my arm as I stepped from the stairs to the ledge, pulling me into him as my completely inappropriate city boots slipped on damp rock. For a moment we were a little too close.

"Alright?" he asked, his voice reverberating off the walls.

"Yes, fine," I replied, gaining my footing. I tried to see out over the lake, but all I could distinguish was the reflection of light from the basement. "I have to say, I presumed you would be doing the ritual somewhere private, but this is a little extreme."

He laughed. "Completely. But you have to see it through

our eyes. We were searching for a place that could be adapted to the specifications in *Terra*, somewhere away from onlookers and anyone who might be able to hear us. There isn't much real estate in Paris like that." He turned back to the stairs. "Hold tight for one second. I have to pull the grate back over. It's highly unlikely anyone will come down to the bottom level tonight, but in case they do..."

By the time I'd taken out my phone and tapped on the torch, Alex was back on the ledge. He indicated along the walkway. "Why don't you go ahead? That way I can be sure I don't lose you in the lake."

"There will be absolutely no chance of that." I stepped forward and followed the ledge. A little way ahead a flickering glow emanated from the wall. As we drew closer I could see what it was. "A flaming torch. More drama?"

He grinned. "I'm the music director of the Paris Opera. I have a sense of drama."

I let out a laugh.

"But really," he said, "it's in preparation for the ritual. Everything must be just so, including our own inner readiness. Props such as natural lighting aid the transition from the outer world to the world of the ceremony. It's the same in theatre. Garnier's opera house was designed to pull spectators into another realm, one open to all possibilities."

"Another reason you couldn't have rented a flat?"

He laughed, his eyes sparkling in the guttering light. "Oh yes. The torches would've been against fire regs."

I shook my head. "As long as we get Rémy and Théo back."

He nodded. "Exactly. I want to do everything possible for this ritual to have maximum effect."

Stepping carefully onward, my fingers trailed over the

damp brick for balance, the sharp tap of our footfall and the occasional drip of water casting stark colour. Once past the torch, there was more light beyond—a series of torches, their reflections flickering in the lake, illuminating the giant limestone buttresses that supported the weight of the opera house. The place was surreal, a shimmering river Styx, a transition to a world that was, for me, completely unknown.

"Beautiful, isn't it?" Alex said. "It's surprising what appeal can be found in dark places."

"It's stunning."

"We must carry on. We need to start soon."

I tucked away my phone, Alex's lighting doing more than it could manage. Continuing along, the ledge passed torch after torch until the buttresses merged with an end wall. A tunnel, lit in the same way, led into the bedrock of Paris.

"There are a few steps up," Alex called.

I took them carefully and entered the narrow passage. The walls were rough, cut into stone, the going a little uneven with water pooling in places, yet it was safer than the lakeside shelf. Even so, the rock closed around me. My breathing grew shallow and the back of my neck prickled, but Alex's shuffle echoed from behind, his presence encouraging.

The composition of the tunnel walls changed, seeming to have some kind of textured regularity. I studied the surface and my breath stuck. The building material was bone—the ends of long bones from countless bodies, the flesh rotted away hundreds of years ago. "We're in the catacombs, aren't we?"

"I didn't want to say anything to put you off."

He was right, it would've unnerved me. It was unnerving me now. I continued along and the bedrock changed, my boots slipping and crunching against the ground. I stopped, my mouth dropping open. Thousands of bones littered the floor—I stood upon the remains of countless lives. My heart beat in my throat and I tried to swallow it away.

"I'm sorry to put you through this," Alex said. "It's not the most pleasant of places."

I pulled myself together. It would be worth it. It had to be.

Stepping forward, my feet grated in grey lacerations, nausea spreading through me. But the bones dwindled and we walked once again upon compact earth and rock, although the walls still held their macabre lode.

"It's just ahead now," Alex said.

We emerged into a circular chamber, two tunnels extending from the far side. The low roof was supported by four pillars, and a stone plinth stood in the centre, all of it lit by hundreds of candles wedged into bone walls, the pattern of which was different here. I peered more closely, my breath quickening. The architect certainly had grim artistic flare, incorporating three rows of skulls into the construction. Most of the fleshless heads faced down, with only the curved crowns visible, but here and there a face gaped outward, the candlelight draining into the eye sockets and the nose hole, the jaw bones absent. Where did they put the jaw bones?

"So, what do you think of our location?" Alex smiled, appearing boyish once again.

"It's horrendous. Utterly unsettling." My ears rang and the room swam a little.

"Exactly the point," he said as he strode to the plinth.

I stepped over to the nearest pillar and propped myself up, blinking in an attempt to regain focus. Alex opened his overcoat, pulled out *Terra* and a large knife with a mother-of-pearl handle and placed them carefully on the stone. I forced myself to breathe, but the dusty, deathly air stuck in my throat. An icy sweat spread over my body and my knees buckled. I had no choice but to sink to the ground.

Alex rushed over and knelt by my side. "Panic attack?"

I nodded, unable to speak.

"Deep breaths," he commanded, his face reassuringly alive amidst so much death. "It's just a load of old bones, nothing will hurt you."

He was right, yet the chill felt like something more. I needed to focus, like I'd always done to control my synaesthesia. I thought of Rémy as he'd been prior to last night, his arms solid around me. Gradually my breath evened, and I looked up into Alex's concerned eyes.

"How is it now?" he asked.

"Better."

"You're not the first person to lose it down here." Alex held out his arm. I took it and pulled myself up, feeling reasonably stable.

"If you're ready," he said, scanning my face, "I'd better explain what will happen during the ritual. Obviously, we don't want any interruptions."

He meant me. "I'll be fine," I said. I had to hold it together. "Tell me the details."

"I'll be reading from *Terra*." He glanced at the plinth. "You saw the knife?"

I nodded.

"We'll be using that for the blood. And we have a few people coming to support us, some guys who were involved before. They want to help retrieve Rémy, and their presence will improve our chance of success."

"Alright."

"How are you feeling now? We could wait a few minutes."

"No, let's get on with it." The quicker we got out of here, the better.

He walked over to the plinth and positioned himself. "If you stand on the other side."

I obliged.

He opened the book and placed his hands on the corners of the stone. "Ready?"

"Yes," I said. "Let's do it."

Alex nodded, then glanced to his side. A group of men dressed in orchestral-black shirts and trousers trod in from one of the tunnels. They formed a circle around the pillars, their backs to the candlelit walls, their faces in shadow. A few people was an understatement. There had to be at least twenty.

Alex took a deep breath. "O Désaccord," he read out. "O dynamism of music, force of the world, resonance of death, I entreat you." The Middle French was made a little more comprehensible by his articulation. "Be with us in our temple of bones. Come calmly into our midst and be tempered for those who serve you."

We weren't serving the Désaccord, but I supposed Alex had to read what the book specified.

"For we celebrate your unending glory," he continued, "the glory unto despair and destruction."

As he spoke the chamber darkened, the air shifted around me and... I could hear it, almost imperceptible at first, a sort of unnerving background disquiet. Rémy said the Désaccord would have to be present before it could be rendered harmless. Well, I'd experienced it before, I could manage it again.

"Désaccord, come into our midst," Alex called, and with his words the air thickened in great swathes, an uneasy keen scraping through me. Panic rose in my throat. I grasped the plinth, focussing on the stone to force the hideousness away.

The sound intensified to a piercing clamour that pervaded my colours and my senses, and the air grew dense until it was black as night. I stiffened as I breathed, sure it would suffocate me, and in it came, stirring what I'd felt last night as I'd lain beside Rémy—the excruciating agony and dread that had always hidden beneath my colours. My skin prickled with sweat and my breath heaved. Whatever this dread was, wherever it had come from, it was too much—yet I could push it away. I had to.

I shut everything from my mind but the rough stone under my hands, the cool surface, the grit shifting under my fingers. Taking a breath of rank air, I forced myself not to choke and held the darkness from my centre, yet still the dread remained.

"Désaccord be tempered," Alex said. "Allow the one who raised you and opposed you to be here. Allow the one who is guarded and protected by the Harmonie to be with us." I stared at Alex, attempting to comprehend his words through the distortion of my senses and the unearthly cacophony. His colour, his steady black, was somehow different, and I didn't like it.

"Allow yourself to be calmed," Alex continued, "so we, in serving your ends, may manifest the one who defied you." He was talking about Rémy, surely. But the plan wasn't to call Rémy here, it was to neutralise the Désaccord so Rémy could return to the chateau.

"Rémy Rabasten," Alex pronounced, "we call you to our circle."

The contaminated air to our side seethed and roared then broke apart, revealing a glimmer of unadulterated white light, the candles paling to nothing. The luminosity opened out until it extended from ground to ceiling, and the Désaccord congealed around it as if to restrain its lustre. Amidst the radiance an outline became visible—the curve of a shoulder, the length of a leg, the angle of a cheek. And there he stood, translucent amidst the brilliance.

"Rémy!" I cried.

His head shot toward me, his eyes wide and blinking as though he were attempting to see, then he gazed about, taking in Alex, the chamber and the men who were shuffling at their stations. Had Alex managed to call Rémy back? Was this a change of plan? But Rémy appeared more wraithlike than ever.

"Alex, what's happening?" Rémy yelled.

Alex stared at him, his jaw slack, his body motionless.

Rémy attempted to step forward, but the Désaccord forced in on him like a cage, the clamour building to a multitude of dissonant tones that combined to a deathly shriek. I glanced back and forth between Alex and Rémy, confusion stupefying me, dread twisting in my chest. Something was terribly wrong.

Alex took a breath and returned to *Terra*. "Because Rémy Rabasten dwells in the Harmonie under its protection, you, O Désaccord, cannot harm him."

Rémy thrust his hands against the darkness, but the darkness held firm.

"Yet I beseech you, O Désaccord..." The murk condensed and the howling built. "Banish him. Banish Rémy Rabasten from the world so he may never manifest here again."

"Alex. No!" I yelled. "What the hell are you doing?"

His face creased into a sneer. "Exactly what it looks like. Finishing what should have ended five years ago." His voice was lifeless now, a sinkhole of light. It repulsed me.

"Violette, get out of here. Now!" Rémy yelled, thrashing against the twisting blackness to no avail. I stared at him as the reality sank in, horror dripping through me, rooting me to the spot. Now I could see it, the vile murk oozing through Alex's nostrils and into his mouth, his eyes black with it.

"O Désaccord," Alex continued, "we offer in exchange for this banishment a sacrifice of blood."

"Get out of here!" Rémy shouted again.

I shook myself. I had to get away, but I couldn't leave Rémy to whatever Alex was attempting. Yet surely if Alex didn't have the book, he couldn't continue with the ritual. I lunged forward to grab *Terra*. Alex shot out his palm, slamming it into my chest, hurtling me to the floor.

"Violette, forget the book!"

I looked up from the dust, pain shooting through my ribs. Rémy's face was creased with frustration, yet his eyes still held that unmistakable softness. He'd said not to do the ritual —perhaps I could listen to him this time.

"Go!" he yelled.

I turned toward the tunnel through which we'd arrived, my heart racing. Alex's assistants stood almost shoulder to shoulder before the passage, but a small gap lay open. I charged for it. One of the men stepped across and shoved me back. Regaining my footing, I tried to ram through the human barricade. A fist struck the side of my face, pain searing down my neck. I stumbled and fell to my knees.

"Violette!" Rémy cried.

Blood pooled in my mouth, metallic, raw, as dark as the

earth. I had to get away, but all I could do was peer into the dirt. Two polished black shoes stepped before me. Alex grabbed my arms and bent them behind my back.

"Get up," he growled, and pulled my wrists, streaking fire through my sinews. I had no choice. I stumbled as I rose, my head spinning. He shoved me toward the plinth and we stood before *Terra*, me clamped to his side. I tried to twist away, but he only tightened his grip, pulling me closer so I could smell his acrid sweat.

"Our blood sacrifice," he called out, "to honour you, O Désaccord, to empower you, to serve you."

"Violette!" Rémy was thrashing at his cage with every part of his body.

Alex tore open my overcoat. I tried to pull away again and again, but he held firm. He grabbed the knife from the plinth and raised it above us, the blade gleaming.

"Désaccord," he yelled, his voice as black as death, "by this sacrifice we banish Rémy Rabasten." He plunged the knife into my gut.

I stared at the handle, unable to believe the blade lay within me, unable to comprehend what Alex had done, unable to feel anything at all as I watched my blood pool into my clothes. Then pain took me in streaks of unbearable agony. I gripped the knife and tried to pull it out, but Alex released me and I dropped to the ground.

In another time and place, far away from myself, I registered Rémy kicking at the sides of his prison, screaming my name. The Désaccord densified and pressed in on him, obliterating my view, then it dissipated, leaving a void where he'd stood.

After that, there was nothing.

The illusion cannot maintain itself for long. If there is a beginning, there is an end, and this is the end. I burn with your loss. I am torn, broken, reduced to nothing. I bear each discordant note of my life and every shard of pain I engendered through my actions, but my inability to save you weighs too heavy for my soul. My only grace, the grace I do not deserve, will be my oblivion in this sublimity.

Chapter Twenty-One

"Rémy!" I screamed, flinging myself up, my gut searing, bright lights and raucous colours blurring around me.

"Violette, listen to me." A woman's voice cut through the fog. "You're in hospital. You've had an injury to your abdomen and I need you to lie down."

"No. I need to find Rémy. I need him now." He swam before my mind's eye, the Désaccord forcing him away once and for all. I had to get to his apartment to play *Lo Boièr*. Electricity flashed through my middle as I tried to get up.

Hands gripped my arms and pushed me back down. "You can't go anywhere at the moment. We need to get you better." The voice streaked across my vision in ugly grey.

I winced at the colour, but it wasn't just the voice. There was so much noise—shuffles, clatters, whirrs, hums. The din grated in my ears and denied me most of my sight. But no matter, I needed to call Rémy. "I have to go." I twisted around to slide off whatever I sat upon, but something pulled at my wrist. Raising my arm, I peered at the hindrance, my eyes struggling to focus through the mass of colour—a wire or a tube—no, a cannula. I tried to pull it off, but hands seized me from behind. What was wrong with them? Why did they have to hold me here?

"Let me help," a familiar voice boomed in copper and bronze, shades of Sarrat in the autumn. The colours came together to form Joël's face—those brown eyes, that always jolly turn of mouth.

I grasped at him. "Joël, we have to help Rémy, we have to get him back." He would understand. But no, he thought Rémy was gone. "Joël, he's not missing. We have to help him —he's trapped in the Harmonie."

"She's confused from the anaesthesia," the woman's voice rasped.

"I know, Violette," Joël replied, his colours thundering. "I know. But right now, we need you to lie down. You have a wound to your abdomen. It's been stitched up, but if you're not careful you'll undo all the doctor's handiwork."

His words jumbled. I tried to piece them together. "But we have to help Rémy. He's fading." I pushed up again.

He placed his hands on my arms amidst all the other hands that clambered over me, but his touch was soft and reassuring. "You're not going to be any use to Rémy if you collapse walking down the corridor, which is most likely what will happen if you get up. The quickest way out of here is to relax. You need to trust me on this."

I took him in through the colour—always that honest look. "Like when you told me to get off the pog," I mumbled.

"And was I right about that?"

He'd been absolutely right. If only I hadn't returned. I sat back, pain cutting across my tummy. The hands supported my body as I lay down. The pain wasn't so bad like this, but I ached for Rémy. I felt as though I would break.

"Do you mind if I talk to Violette in private?" Joël asked the woman—the nurse—she had to be a nurse.

"Of course. Ring the buzzer if you need anything at all. We'll be just outside." She left the room with another attendant.

Joël hauled over a chair.

Feeling overwhelmingly tired, I closed my eyes, but old bones and a knife appeared before me. My heart pounded and nausea rose in my throat. "Alex," I whispered.

"He's not here," Joël replied, "and I won't let him hurt you again."

"How do you know?" I murmured. "How did I get here?"

"I'll tell you about it, but not now."

A clatter from the corridor stripped my vision to black. I gasped and flung my hands over my ears. "Can't you tell them to be quiet?" I hissed.

He got up and closed the door. It made a slight difference, but not much. "Joël, what's going on? Why is this place so noisy? I can't stand it."

"It's not noisy, it's quiet," he said softly.

I gripped my hair with my fingers as if I could tear the sound and colour away. "Don't be ridiculous, I can barely think."

"What's the noise doing to you?" he asked.

"The colours, there are too many colours."

He narrowed his eyes. "You're a synaesthetic, like Rémy."

I nodded, Rémy's soft gaze before me, tearing me up.

"Then it's the medication. It happened to Rémy once." He squeezed my hand, his touch soothing. I closed my eyes, wanting everything to go away, and despite it all I could feel sleep tugging at me.

"Violette," Joël said, "before you rest, I need you to listen."

I forced myself to look at him.

"I've made sure you're safe from Alex for the moment, but it's not easy to protect you here. The doctor said you're doing well. If I make arrangements for you to be moved to private care with all the provisions you require, will you sign the release papers?"

"Anything. Just turn the volume down." I couldn't keep my eyes open any longer. I yearned for oblivion without noise, without despair.

"Alright. I'll sort it."

Jolting back at Joël's words, his colours hammered me once again.

He studied my face. "Concentrate on getting better and know you're completely safe."

I grunted acknowledgement and drifted away.

My dreams formed an endless blur of spooling images woven with unease. As I awoke, I felt as though I were pulling myself from a deep shaft to meet an onslaught of colour and sound. Peering through the commotion, I took in the railed bed, the alarm button and my cannula. I was in hospital. I'd come here after Alex... I drew a deep breath and clutched at the cellular blanket that lay over me, my heart racing, my memory surreal as if it hadn't been me, but it had. He'd tried to kill me. Yet Joël said I was safe—Joël, he was here somewhere, or at least he had been.

I shifted, my middle aching, my head numb, my face and chest sore. I could barely think, and I felt sick—sick with myself. I'd tried to make things better, but everything had become so much worse. I glanced through the window. The pale clouds indicated morning, but all I could see were skulls, inky blackness, a knife flashing in the candlelight and Rémy's desperate face as Alex banished him.

I needed Rémy, I needed to feel his presence, but how could I? Yet for all its hideous pomp, what was to say the ritual had actually worked? Perhaps I could still call him.

Closing my eyes, I released a breath, allowing my thoughts to drop aside, but colour forced in on me, colour that was only the surface of that deep, unfathomable dread—the synaesthesia was awful but the dread was worse. It submerged me, my throat tightening, my stomach clenching in an excruciating spasm. Without thinking I stared at the threads of the blanket bunched between my fingers and pushed the torrent away. It wouldn't go—not all of it. Joël had said something about my medication. Whatever the cause, I couldn't call Rémy like this. Everything was terrible in here. I had to get to his apartment to play *Lo Boièr*, or back to Sarrat and the harp. But Rémy was fading—there was a chance I wouldn't be able to see him anyway. The whole situation was a mess.

As I gazed around the room, I fought my colours and my disorientation. After a while a nurse entered and removed my cannula and an orderly brought in some toast. I had no appetite but I ate a slice knowing the faster I recovered, the faster I could figure out some way of helping Rémy. The food grounded me, making me feel almost human.

The doctor came in. "It appears that you're doing well,"

she said as she studied my notes, her voice much too loud. "How are you feeling?"

"Sore, groggy."

"I need to examine your wound. It shouldn't take a moment."

I adjusted my gown and flinched as she peeled back the dressing, the pain triggering a flash of Alex's face and a flare of terror. He was out there somewhere. "I have to speak to the police," I said, cringing at the volume of my voice.

"Of course," she replied, not looking up.

"I know who attacked me," I said more softly.

She rose and flicked through the notes. "The crime was reported when you were brought in. The police will be here this morning. You can update them then."

I tried not to wince at her words and nodded. She started writing, the pen scraping across my vision. "How did I get here?" I asked.

She flicked through the papers. "You were brought in by ambulance with Joël Rabasten the night before last." She turned another page. "And it looks like you've been very lucky. The knife slid between your large intestine and missed your infrarenal aorta by a few millimetres. If it had cut through either, you would've been in much worse shape. In addition, there's an absence of contusion due to the sharpness of the blade, so the wound is actually quite small. You were stitched up successfully, and as long as you take it easy and keep the area clean, we don't foresee any problems. You can go home to rest in a couple of days."

"Thank you," I said.

With a brief smile she headed out, nodding to a suited figure in the corridor.

"Violette," the blackened shards of a voice called, a

balding head peering around the door. Philippe. My stomach sank.

"How are you?" He strode over, flowers cradled in his arm.

"Hello, Philippe," I murmured.

He kissed my cheek and handed me the bouquet of ranunculus.

"Thank you," I said. "Could you put them on the table?"

"Of course." He moved the flowers and adjusted his jacket. "What on earth happened?" he asked, his voice loud and authoritarian.

How was I going to explain this one? "I have no idea. A random attack, I guess." My brusqueness did little to hide the lie. "How did you know I was here?"

"I was called as your next of kin. Isabelle and I have been terribly concerned."

I groaned inside. I'd made that arrangement years ago. He'd been the sensible option when Eveline had taken a turn for the worse. "I'm sorry. I'd forgotten. I should have updated it."

"No problem. I came in yesterday, but you weren't conscious. Isabelle has been in too."

They always did the right thing, although it never felt as though genuine sentiment lay beneath. "That's kind," I replied.

"And the police are dealing with it?"

"They'll be in later to talk to me."

"If you require help in that department, let me know. Is there anything you need? I have to get back to work, but I'm sure I can find time later."

"I've someone taking care of me," I said, wondering if Joël would turn up again. If not, I'd contact a friend. "The doctor expects a speedy recovery. I really am fine, Philippe. I know how busy you are, and Isabelle too. Please don't worry. I'm sorry to have troubled you."

He nodded. "Alright. Do call if you need anything. And... I've not mentioned this to Eveline. I didn't want to worry her. Is that alright with you?"

"Yes, absolutely. Please don't. There's nothing to be concerned about."

"Well, then, get better soon." We kissed, then he patted my arm with a half-smile and left.

I stared at his bouquet, the ranunculus wilting ever so slightly. Why hadn't I changed my next of kin? I could have asked any number of friends. Talking of friends, I should check my phone—and my clients would be waiting for replies. I glanced around for my overcoat. I'd tucked my phone into the pocket when Alex had guided me toward the chamber. Alex... I blinked the image away. But where was my coat... and my bag?

"Good morning," a voice called softly.

I turned to the sound, the first warm colours since waking.

"Joël," I whispered.

He strode in. "How are you doing?" he asked as he pulled up a chair and sat down without a sound.

"The noise is terrible, but I'm a bit more myself."

"Good to hear it. And your wound?"

"It's sore, but nothing more."

He nodded.

"Joël." I took a breath. "Alex Chaufourier—Rémy's friend—he stabbed me."

His face darkened. "I found you in the catacombs, unconscious and covered in blood. I wondered if something like that had happened. I told the police I saw you enter the opera house with Alex."

"You saw... and you found me? How come you're even in Paris?"

He glanced down at his hands, then looked me squarely in the eye. "I followed you."

"Followed me... where?"

"To Paris initially," he said. "Then when you stayed at Rémy's apartment, myself and others monitored your movements."

"I saw you... in the street around the corner."

"My tracking skills aren't particularly honed. I'm not cut out to be a spy—too much bulk." He rubbed his middle and chuckled under his breath. "I'm surprised you didn't see me more often."

I scrutinised his face, trying to make sense of his actions. "But why?"

"You called Rémy's name on the pog that night—you were in hysterics. I guessed you'd seen him. Sylvie said you were going back to Paris for a few days and... I just had a feeling. I wanted to find out what was going on."

"You were watching me." My fingers dug through the holes in the blanket, the indignation I'd felt when he'd dragged me from the pog reasserting itself. "What gave you the right, Joël? It's an invasion of my privacy."

He stared at me. "Considering everything that happened with Rémy, I was concerned."

I scowled at him. But then, how much did he actually understand? "Yesterday, you said you knew Rémy was in the Harmonie."

"I always wondered if that was a possibility," he said,

"seeing his body was never found. We weren't certain, though."

"We?"

"My family, the musicians, the Société."

"What society?" I was struggling to make sense of this.

"Some musicians and like-minded people who are aware of the Harmonie and the Désaccord."

Rémy said his family and some others had known. "But even so, you could have spoken to me about it." I sat myself up a little more and winced as my middle burned.

"I didn't know how much you knew. It's not exactly an everyday topic of conversation, and we've had our suspicions about Alex for quite a while. When I saw you go into the opera house together, I guessed it wasn't to see *Don Giovanni*."

I shook my head. "How did you find me?"

"We've known about the chamber since Rémy messed about there. I called for some friends to help and we entered the catacombs by an entrance much further away. By the time we reached the place, all that remained was you unconscious on the floor."

"I'd been left there." I shuddered.

"We applied a makeshift bandage to stop the bleeding and made a stretcher from a couple of planks we found in a nearby tunnel, then carried you out and called an ambulance."

My annoyance drained away. "If you hadn't come when you did… if you hadn't come at all… that would have been it."

"You would've made a nice surprise for the next cataphile to pass that way."

It was beyond contemplation. "Rémy told me not to do the ritual. I didn't listen—I wanted to get him back, and now he's... I don't know what. Banished?" My heart thumped—he couldn't be banished. "We have to get him back."

Joël put his hand on my arm. "The first thing we need to do is get you somewhere safer."

My stomach turned. "How much danger am I in?"

"Alex attempted murder. He's not going to want his actions known, so I'm not taking any chances. Was he using the Désaccord when he attacked you?"

"He was completely consumed by it."

"Then he has more power than he knows what to do with, and you're vulnerable."

Alex's voice, his colour, it had changed to something hideous. I'd trusted him—I'd liked him. What the hell was wrong with me?

"I've made arrangements to transfer you somewhere safe. My doctor contacted the hospital and reassured them that all measures will be in place for your care. If you're still happy with it, as soon as you've spoken to the police, we can go."

"Go where?"

"Private accommodation with a nurse available at all times."

"Is it quieter than here?"

He glanced out at the corridor where visitors trod past. "Guaranteed."

"Alright." Anywhere would be preferable to this noise.

He drew something from his pocket and passed it to me. A phone. "I thought this might come in handy. Your things were taken for evidence."

"That is so thoughtful of you, Joël—all of it is." I studied him. "But why are you doing this for me?"

"Rémy started this mess. Besides, you're a friend and our families have always helped each other—"

There was a knock.

"Violette Romèu?" A formally dressed woman stepped in, her blond hair cropped short, an efficient look on her face. She was followed by a short man overstuffed in his suit.

"Yes?" I asked, blanching at another onslaught of colours, my head throbbing.

"I'm Officer Bernas and this is Officer Lafleche," she said, her voice hard-edged. "We need to ask you a few questions."

"Come in," I replied.

Joël stood up. "I'll be right outside."

They strode over and displayed their identification. I glanced at the photo cards. Lafleche took Joël's chair, clattering the legs. Bernas remained standing. "How are you doing?" she asked.

I winced at her words. "I ache and the noise in here is terrible. If you could lower your voice, I'd be grateful."

"Joël Rabasten reported what he thought was a stabbing," she said quietly. Even so, her colours blared. "The hospital confirmed the incision in your abdomen was made by a knife. We'd like to get your version of events."

My version—how many versions were there? "I... uh..." This was going to sound ridiculous. But it was, after all, the truth, and I didn't necessarily have to include all the details. "Alex Chaufourier and I were in the catacombs. He stabbed me." The images crowded in once again. "There were others, men. I tried to get away, but they stopped me."

"What were you doing in the catacombs?" she asked. "Surely you know access is prohibited."

I nodded. "Alex took me there through the Palais Garnier. There's access through the basements, past the lake."

"The lake," Lafleche interjected in an ugly blast, his eyebrows raised.

"Yes, the lake." I glared at him.

Bernas's face remained impassive. "Why did he take you there?"

I drew a breath. "We were going to perform a ritual."

Lafleche rolled his eyes.

"What kind of ritual?" Bernas asked.

How was I going to explain this? Perhaps a lighter version. "We planned to... honour a friend. But Alex didn't stick to what we'd arranged. Something came over him and he went at me with the knife."

"And the other men, can you identify them?"

"They wore black... shirts and trousers. For that reason, I thought they were members of an orchestra, but I couldn't see their faces. One of them punched me when I tried to escape. I was desperate to get out—the details weren't important."

She glanced at my cheek and nodded. "I have to inform you, Violette, Alex Chaufourier was backstage watching *Don Giovanni* from the wings and talking to various cast members the whole evening. His movements have been verified."

"But... that's not true," I stammered. "He's lying."

"It has been confirmed by security footage."

"Don't be ridiculous, he was with me." They had to be mistaken. I scanned through my memory of the night, fishing for any detail that would help. "We passed a doorman on the way in, and a few ushers—they must have seen me."

She studied me for a moment. "How do you know Alex?"

"He's a... friend of a friend. I met him for the first time a few days ago."

"Violette, Alex said you'd harassed him since you turned

up at the opera house on Monday. He said you were a fan who had a thing for him, and he couldn't brush you off. Because of your behaviour he wondered if you have mental health problems."

My hands trembled. Of course he did, it made perfect sense. Much better to discredit me than to physically attack again and risk being caught. The scope of Alex's actions was bewildering. He'd planted doubts in my mind about Rémy and sown the idea for the ritual. I could hear Rémy's voice imploring me not to go ahead with it as I ran down the stairs and pushed him away. And then Alex had been so helpful, leading me carefully past the lake to my ritual death. He was a possessed madman.

"Alex said you were obsessed with a friend of his who disappeared five years ago. You wouldn't let the matter drop and you followed him to the opera house. When security wouldn't let you in, you left."

I shook my head. "He's lying. All of it. It's complete untruth." But it was obvious how this was perceived by the police.

"What were you really doing in the catacombs?" Lafleche asked, not making any attempt to keep his voice down. "And how did you come to be attacked?"

"I've told you everything I know. There's nothing I can do if you don't believe me."

Lafleche shook his head. Bernas scanned my face. "At this point you're looking at a sixty-euro fine for trespassing in the catacombs," she said. "Although considering your injuries, I think we can let it drop—on your assurance you won't go there again."

"Of course I won't be going there." I glared at them.

"But, Violette," she continued, "we need to follow up on

who actually attacked you. The perpetrator is free to do the same again. So please, when you find it within yourself to tell the truth, get in touch." She placed her card on the table and nodded to her partner. Lafleche rose.

I remembered my belongings. "My phone and my bag were taken as evidence. Is it possible to have them back?"

"We have the clothing you were wearing when you were attacked," Bernas replied, "but no other possessions were found on your person or at the scene. It's possible they were stolen. We'll contact you when we can release what we have." She and Lafleche left the room.

Did Alex have my things? I sank back into the bed and shivered. Perhaps he'd disposed of them to hide evidence of what had happened. That was preferable to the thought that he might hack my personal details. Either way, I'd lost my phone and I had no access to my bank account. But that paled in significance to the web of lies Alex had spun.

"Everything alright?" Joël stepped in lightly.

I swallowed. "The police thought I was crazy. They have surveillance footage of Alex in the opera house at the time of the attack. How is that even possible?"

"I don't know." He shook his head. "I'm sorry, Violette."

"Well, I don't think you need to worry about my safety. If Alex hurts me again, he'll blow his cover."

"Even so," he said, "I'm not taking any risks."

A shout blasted in the corridor, scalding my vision. It really was too much. "I need somewhere quieter," I said.

"I'll sort it." He headed out.

I drew the phone from the bedside table, synced my contacts and accessed my email, tapping out generic messages informing clients I was in hospital and would resume their projects as soon as possible. After my recent slump, this wouldn't go down well. A little later the nurse came in with the release papers. I signed, and once I'd eaten a few mouthfuls of lunch, I struggled into the jumper, sweats and pumps Joël had produced from somewhere. Eventually the nurse brought in a wheelchair.

"I'll be fine," I said. "I can walk."

She shook her head. "Hospital policy. We wouldn't normally release you for a couple of days."

Anything to get out of here. I sat down. She passed me Philippe's flowers and I thanked her for my care. Joël took the handles and pushed me out the room, down the corridor and into the lift. I felt like the invalid I was. On the ground floor we emerged into the bitter air by the taxi rank and the city descended, colour slamming into me, noise splitting me apart. I grasped my head.

Joël pushed something under my fingers. A transparent case containing earplugs. I squeezed his hand.

"Comes of having a brother with synaesthesia," he said.

I pressed the foam into my ears as I was unceremoniously wheeled up a ramp into the taxi. It was only as we pulled away I realised I'd been at Hôpital Necker, opposite Eveline's maison de repos. I hadn't even questioned where I was, and even now I hadn't a clue where we were going.

The streets passed by and we crossed the Seine. Rémy and I had walked the bank only days ago. We turned into an avenue of detached townhouses, immaculate railings and pristine gardens. The taxi pulled over by a stunning building and I was wheeled to the ground.

"I can walk from here," I said, pushing myself up. "It's really not that bad."

Joël placed his hand on my shoulder. "Let's do what the doctor orders."

I shook my head and sank back into the chair. Joël wheeled me up the path between sculpted box hedges. Four storeys of elegant limestone rose above us, the windows topped with gabled pediments. A large wooden door stood in the centre between two columns, a bronze plaque fixed to one side. Joël wheeled me closer and I read, *Société Philharmonique.* A society for the lovers of harmony.

The door opened and a slender man in nurse's scrubs propped it back, a warm smile lighting his youthful, open face. A ramp had been placed over the steps. Joël wheeled me up and through the entrance, bringing me to a halt in a broad corridor with sturdy oak doors and stairs sweeping upward. The corners of the ceiling mouldings were decorated with guilt lyres, but apart from that, the decor was uncomplicated, the walls white, giving the hall a sense of space. I pulled out my earplugs. Our noise aside, the place was pleasantly quiet.

Joël stepped over with the nurse. "This is Luc. He'll be helping you out for a few days."

"Good to meet you, Violette." Luc spoke softly with warm Bretagne colours. There was no doubt he'd been briefed about my synaesthesia.

"Hello," I said, and turned to Joël. "What is this place?"

He stepped behind the wheelchair and pushed me along the corridor, Luc's footsteps following.

"The headquarters of the Société Philharmonique is the gathering place for all those who wish to promote the Harmonie, to keep its songs sounding in the sanctuaries and to perpetuate its spirit. The building itself is a focus of the Harmonie, so there's no way Alex, tied up with the Désaccord as he is, could have access."

"But Alex works at the Palais Garnier and that's a sanctuary—and the chateau, the Désaccord is rife there."

"Both places used to be foci of the Harmonie," Joël replied, "but not anymore. Things change."

We stopped before a lift and Joël pressed the call button.

"So the Harmonie and the Désaccord are common knowledge now?" I stared up at Luc, who smiled as though this were an everyday topic of conversation. "I'd thought the stories were myths. Surely most people think the same?"

"Most people," Joël said as he pushed me into the elevator and made room for Luc. We rose two floors with me grimacing at the noise, then Joël wheeled me through the door opposite. The bedroom was warm, the decor comfortable with an old chest of drawers, an armchair in the corner and luxurious curtains at the window. Luc raised the back of the bed and lowered the whole thing down. I gazed at it, wanting the plump duvet and pillows around me.

"I'll leave you to get changed," Joël said. "I'll pop in afterward to check you have everything you need." He left the room.

"Alright, Violette, let's get you sorted." Luc took pyjamas from the wardrobe and laid them on the bed. "Do you need help changing?"

"No, I'm absolutely fine." I wedged my hands against the wheelchair and levered myself up, my stomach burning. Luc shot over and supported me.

"Really, I'm fine," I said, finding my feet.

"I'll give you a minute to get sorted, then." He walked out and pulled the door closed.

Bending cautiously, I eased on the pyjamas. Someone had considerately bought a loose size so I could adjust the waistband away from my wound. Then, barely able to hold my eyes open, I slid into bed and sank into the soft mattress. The journey from the hospital had taken it out of me.

There was an almost imperceptible knock at the door.

"Come in," I murmured.

Luc entered. "Your medication." He handed me a paper cup and a glass of water.

I swallowed the pills and my eyelids fell.

"You sleep," he said. "I'll be in the room next door. Call anytime you need me, day or night. There will be food later and the doctor will be along in the morning."

I nodded, but I wasn't really listening. I was back in Sarrat, sitting at the hearth with Rémy.

Chapter Twenty-Two

My wound stung as the doctor's gloved hand palpated my tummy. Seeming satisfied, he replaced the wadding and folded down my pyjama top. "You're doing well, Violette. How are you feeling?"

Rémy wasn't here. He'd been with me all night in ragged, desperate dreams, but he wasn't here now. I felt like a shell, half of myself. But that wasn't what the doctor asked. "A bit sore," I said. "I slept through and missed my evening medication. Luc didn't want to wake me." And because of it my colours had almost returned to their usual intensity.

"And the memory of the attack," he added, "how are you managing?"

The echo of Alex's distorted features had been different since arriving here—there was something about this place, something warm and comfortable, and the attack had stopped burning through my head. It was still there, waiting in the shadows, accompanied by the indeterminate dread that lay beneath my colours, but gossamer hung between me and the memory. Rémy was another matter. I hadn't listened to him... The despair on his face... I swallowed and glanced at the doctor. "I'm doing alright."

He nodded. "Your stats are fine. Are you eating?"

"Yes, I've had breakfast." Well, nibbled some apple and bread.

"Good. Make sure you move around as much as is comfortable, and I'll be back in the morning." He packed up his bag and left the room.

I stared out the window, wondering what to do. Snow-dusted branches hung across a sky that burgeoned with leaden cloud, but the view wasn't going to keep me occupied for long. Debilitation was not my preferred state. I needed to forge on with something to keep my mind from the pangs that threatened to well up. I couldn't even work—my laptop was at Rémy's. But they'd said only a couple of days, then I could go home. Surely there was a chance I could call Rémy then, a chance that whatever Alex had done hadn't worked. Even if Rémy were a phantom, to see him, to speak to him, would be something. But more than that, I had to figure out a way to get him back properly. Rémy thought my best chance was the books. Alex's volumes were copies, so if I could call Rémy, I could ask him about the originals.

Footsteps strobed before me as my morning medication began to take effect. Luc entered the room.

"The doctor was happy," he said as he cleared away some gauze and tape from the top of the chest of drawers. "Do you want something to read or watch?"

"No. I need to move around. I'll get dressed."

"Sure."

I studied the side of his face as he rummaged inside a drawer. Were the Harmonie and the Désaccord an everyday part of his life as they had been for Rémy and presumably Joël? It was so strange to perceive life that way.

"Luc, how do you know about the Harmonie?" I asked.

He glanced over his shoulder and smiled, then went back to the drawer. "I grew up with the knowledge. My family always played at one of the sanctuaries in Brittany. I guess it was a way of life. And you?"

"Uh... pretty much the same, only in the Pyrenees." Except no one told me the stories were true. "Have you been here before, to the Société?"

"Yeah, we used to visit when we came to Paris occasionally. We'd meet other musicians here."

The Société Philharmonique... Musicians... The Harmonie... There had to be some kind of musical instrument here. I should have thought of it sooner.

"Luc, tell me there's a piano in this place."

He nodded. "Of course. In the lounge—first floor at the front."

I pushed myself up and swung my legs off the bed.

"Whoa there," he said. "What's the rush?"

"The piano. I need the piano."

"Perhaps you should take it a little more slowly?"

"The doctor said I should move around as much as possible." I searched the room for my clothes. They hung over the armchair. "I need to get dressed."

"Alright. I'll be back in a bit." Luc headed out and closed the door.

I winced as I pulled on my sweats too quickly—rushing wasn't going to help. I drew a deep breath and finished dressing, then stood up and attempted a few steps. My head swirled for a moment and my tummy panged a little, but nothing more, and the pain would go when my medication had taken full effect.

The stairs down a flight weren't much trouble. I headed to the front of the house and pushed open the door. The lounge extended across the building, the light from three floor-to-ceiling windows reflecting in the polished parquet, the pure white walls decorated with various musical instruments—a couple of lyres, a lute, a violin, a viola. In the centre of the room a modern seating area framed an understated fireplace, to one side stood a meeting table and chairs, and at the back, open and ready to play, was a grand piano.

I walked over and sat gingerly upon the piano stool, my lacerated abdominals twinging. Trying to relax my middle, I placed my hands gently on the keys, closed my eyes and played *Lo Boièr* one finger at a time, opening myself to the melody, trying not to flinch at the intense colour and the simultaneous wave of dread. And the notes were... odd, ringing out in indistinct smudges. The blend of indigo and orange was unmistakable, and yet it was different to when I'd played on Rémy's piano and my harp. The colours were dull, lacking purity. But perhaps it didn't matter. I had to try anyway.

Playing on through the verse, I endeavoured to absorb myself in the music, but I just felt stiff and uncomfortable. The refrain always caught me, though. I played it slowly, singing the vowel sounds, each one a different timbre. A, E, I, Ó—I stopped. It wasn't working. The colour was off, very slightly, but it made such a difference. I tried again, humming the whole verse. *Lo Boièr* grated and jarred. The tuning was out. I couldn't call Rémy like this.

"It's always good to hear *Lo Boièr*," Joël said from the doorway.

I turned my head, tensing as my wound twinged. "The tuning is out."

He came over and leant against the side of the piano. "It sounded fine to me."

"Is it tuned to 432 hertz?"

He stared at me. "Of course."

"It's still out, Joël." Urgency hardened my voice. "It's not tuned. Could you please get it sorted?"

"You sound like Rémy."

"Well, Rémy would have said the same thing."

He studied me for a moment. "Alright, I'll get someone around to tune it."

"When?" I asked.

He raised his eyebrows. "We're quite particular who we admit here. It's not a case of calling any tuner, but I'll get someone as soon as I can."

I took in Joël's amiable face. He'd already gone to so much trouble for my sake and now I was asking more of him. "Thank you," I said. Feeling my middle, I stood up and shuffled toward the seating area.

Joël shot to my side. "Let me help."

"No, really, I'm fine." I lowered myself onto the couch, appreciating the back support. "This all seems like an awful lot of trouble to help out a friend," I said. "A full-time nurse, a private doctor and use of this place."

He sat down in the armchair opposite. "I'm not going to let you become another of Alex's victims. It was bad enough what happened to Rémy and Bénédict, but we've suspected there have been others. Anyway, the Société will always intervene in matters concerning the Harmonie and the Désaccord."

"Société? As far as I can tell, there's no one here but the three of us."

"The Société meets here regularly."

"And they're okay with me staying here like this?"

"We," he said, "not they. We want you to stay."

"What about your bar? You're taking time off to help me."

"I've some great staff who can manage fine, and this is more important." He paused for a moment then sat forward, resting his elbows on his knees. "Violette, you saw Rémy. I... uh, I have so many questions—how did you see him? How long has it been happening?" He shook his head, the pain clear in his eyes. "The fact he's not dead... Part of me hoped desperately that there was a way for him to be alive. How is he?"

It must have been hell for Joël—for them all. "He's fine. He says he has a peaceful existence, although the Harmonie is not his place and he wishes to return." I felt like I was giving a seance.

Joël let out a breath and drew his hand over his beard.

What else could I say? "I saw him for the first time the day after I returned to Sarrat, and then he continued to turn up. He was acting strangely, as if he didn't know where he was, which makes sense now. He tried to tell me in a round-about way what'd happened to him. I didn't get it, although I knew something was going on. It wasn't until we went to the pog that evening..." I rubbed my face and winced as I pressed on my cheek.

"What happened then?" Joël asked.

"I was so confused by his behaviour and he wouldn't tell me the truth. He didn't want me to go to the chateau, but I was mad at him. I stormed there. We were near the top and the Désaccord surrounded him, tore at him... He vanished." I took a sharp breath. "He appeared again later at home, but he was translucent. He said I needed to focus on my synaesthesia so I could continue to see him. I did, and he... solidified."

Joël nodded.

"And Théo, Théo is there too, with Rémy," I added.

"Théo Guérin?"

"Yes."

Joël closed his eyes for a moment and exhaled. "I wondered if the two disappearances were connected. They happened on the same day, although Rémy's was made known almost a week later." He lowered his head and rubbed his fingers across his scalp, then said, "Go on."

"Rémy explained that the key song wasn't working at the chateau and he didn't know why. We came to Paris for Alex's help. Alex had these books, copies Rémy made from somewhere. They detailed all kinds of information about the Désaccord and the Harmonie, and Rémy was convinced we'd find a solution in the pages. Alex mentioned the ritual, and when Rémy began to fade again, I was convinced we had to do something fast, so..." Regret cut through me. "Against Rémy's wishes, I asked Alex to go ahead."

Joël studied my face. "I can't believe you would've gone into something like that without serious persuasion. Alex is manipulative."

I readjusted my position. I'd been desperate with worry for Rémy, and obviously Alex was devious, but there had been another option—not a solution, but an option that might have granted more time. If I'd been able to get past my colours and the fear that lay beneath, I might have been able to solidify Rémy and give us a chance to work out a proper solution. Bile rose in my throat, staining my vision lurid green. If I was completely honest with myself, I couldn't deny I'd chosen the ritual because I couldn't face whatever it was that lay within me.

"Violette...?" Joël said. "Are you alright? You've gone pale."

"Uh, yes, I'm fine." But I'd chosen myself over Rémy and Théo. I'd been scared, so damn scared, but that didn't feel like an excuse.

"As I was saying, you weren't the first to be persuaded by Alex." Joël's friendly face gazed at me with concern.

I dragged my attention back to the conversation. I needed to focus on the situation at hand, and Joël obviously knew a lot about it. "But why did Alex want to get rid of Rémy?" I asked. "I thought they were friends."

"They were. All I can guess is perhaps Rémy had a change of heart about the Désaccord and Alex didn't agree."

"Rémy said he'd wanted to put a stop to what they were doing."

He nodded. "I'm guessing Alex perceived—still perceives Rémy as a threat."

"But what does Alex have to gain by manipulating the Désaccord?" I shifted against the sofa, sitting myself up. The medication had kicked in and I couldn't feel a thing in my gut. If only it could take away everything else.

"Control. Power," Joël replied.

"Over what?"

"People. As far as I understand, he wouldn't have been offered the post of music director without the Désaccord's influence. Pretty much anyone who comes into contact with Alex is under his sway, certainly the staff at the opera house. The Palais Garnier is his kingdom now, and I'm sure that has something to do with his alibi. I believe he's made a lot of money from his ability to influence too." Joël's eyes narrowed in thought. "Alex always was such a strange character. I remember when Rémy brought him back to the farm, they were besotted with each other. When Rémy broke up with him, apparently Alex was pretty twisted up. I always wondered if he held it against Rémy."

My mouth dropped. He and Alex... Why hadn't he mentioned the relationship? Perhaps he considered it dead and buried—and we hadn't exactly got to the point of scrutinising each other's pasts. There was so much I didn't know about him. But dry facts about a person's life couldn't compare to what we'd felt at the piano. I'd known him completely.

"You look surprised." Joël examined my face. "I don't know if I'm going out on a limb here, but you've been so concerned for Rémy. Are you two... together?"

"We were drawn to each other. It seemed right." That was an understatement.

Joël's mouth drew into a smile. "And I guess it is right—you obviously see the world in the same way."

If synaesthesia was anything to go by. "I guess we do." I thought of our hands as we played the piano—and my hands as they sank into Rémy's body. There had to be a solution. "Rémy said the key song should call the Harmonie to the chateau—he was sure of it. You play up there all the time. What's wrong?"

Joël sat back and shook his head. "I haven't got a clue."

"Then there must be some other way to get Rémy back.

What about the Société, do they have any ideas?" There had to be something.

"If there was a way, we would have tried it."

Losing Rémy was not an option. "The books—Rémy was sure they held the answer. Do you know anything about the originals?"

Joël rose. "Wait there a minute."

I wasn't going anywhere in a hurry.

He strode out the room, and from the sound of his shoes tapping on the stairs, he headed upward a couple of floors. My gaze settled on the grand piano. The sooner it was tuned, the sooner I could try again.

A minute later Joël came back holding what appeared to be a bundle of ragged leather in his gloved hands. He strode to the table. "Will you be alright sitting over here?"

"Absolutely fine." I looked at him quizzically as I rose and walked over. He split the bundle into two tattered books, placing one on a reading plinth and the other on the table, then pulled a pair of gloves from his pocket and passed them to me. "Handle with care."

I glanced at him, unable to believe what I was seeing. "They aren't... are they?"

Joël drew out the chair in front of the plinth and gestured to it. I sat down carefully and pulled on the gloves, gazing at the book before me. The leather was crafted into a repeating floral impression, the edges frayed. I opened it at the first plate, my heart pounding. Above the ornate violin scroll was written *In Musica Sphaerarum*, and beneath it, *Terra*. "I can't believe it," I said, my voice trembling. "Rémy copied these?"

He nodded. "There's also a recent transcript in modern French, if that's any use?"

I stared at him. "Uh, yes. Completely." Perhaps now

there was a chance. I turned the foxed page. "There has to be something here to help."

"Violette, we've looked and looked again," he said, a furrow sunk between his brows. "You're welcome to study the books, but I doubt there's anything to find."

I shook my head. No way. There had to be something.

Chapter Twenty-Three

THE BOOKS OCCUPIED ME FOR THE REST OF THE DAY. I read whilst constantly shifting position to alleviate pressure on my stomach. Luc brought food at intervals and clucked around with cushions and medication. The place was so peaceful that even drugged up my synaesthesia was not nearly as bad as at the hospital, but my nerves were on edge, my stomach churning in the hope that I could do something for Rémy and Théo. It helped having the transcript in modern French. I read through *Terra* in a few hours, then examined passages that showed some potential, comparing the archaic French to the translation. The diagrams were more of a challenge, their meanings arcane, evoking bewilderment more than anything else. Eventually Luc forced me to bed, my stomach sore, my back stiff.

After a deep sleep I rose early and, even though I couldn't tear my thoughts from Rémy, part of me felt a bit better—my colours were less intense and I could barely feel my wound. This place was doing me good. The doctor pronounced me very well and authorised my discharge for tomorrow under the condition I saw my own doctor regularly. After everything that had happened, I yearned for the barn—for that old familiarity. I'd taken photos of the books and the transcript so I could continue my search at home, but I would miss the nurturing atmosphere of the Société.

As the day wore on, combing through the same passages again and again grew tedious. I walked around the Société to refresh myself, managing the steps pretty easily, returning to the books a little more awake. Yet no matter how many times I scoured the yellowed pages, I found absolutely nothing.

I was surveying a passage on the inherent interaction between the Harmonie and the Désaccord when an aged man entered the lounge, his body lean and straight, his head crowned with white curls, a carpetbag in his hand. The piano tuner. Finally.

"Bonjour." I nodded to him.

"Bonne après-midi," he said with a clipped voice, his birdlike eyes on the piano. I needed a break. I'd leave him to it.

I headed out and paused at the top of the stairs, catching Joël's steady bass rising from the kitchen as he sang *Se Chanta* in a hushed voice, probably so I wouldn't hear. His colours were intense, yet the old Occitan hymn was almost as much a part of Sarrat as *Lo Boièr*, the familiarity comforting. I sang along under my breath as I headed down, watching the colours of individual notes as they eddied before me. But unlike Joël's earthy ochres that formed the basis of his voice, or Rémy's constant midnight blue, I couldn't see anything of my own unique colour—the colour beneath the melody. I'd never thought about it before, not even as a child. Perhaps seeing your own colour was like hearing the intonation of your voice—it was so commonplace it wasn't noticeable.

I entered the showroom-perfect kitchen, *Se Chanta* and Joël's raw mountain colours not quite fitting the surroundings.

He broke off his rendition and beamed, a kettle in his hand. "Violette, how's it going?" The scales rang down from above as the tuner tested the piano. Unlike Joël's singing, the sound jarred. I forced away the colour and the disquiet as much as I could.

"I'm keeping at it," I said as I headed for the central island and slid onto a stool.

Joël nodded. "Tea?"

"Yes, thanks." I took in the enticing smell of something baking in the oven, possibly butternut squash. "You know I'm perfectly able to help with meals—or anything."

He poured and handed me a cup. "You need to focus on getting better. And anyway, you're reading the books to get my brother back. I couldn't ask for more." It was the answer I wanted to hear.

He turned away, poured another tea and brought it over with a bowl of lemon slices, then he leant on the worktop, his face creased, almost frowning. "We have to talk about Alex," he said.

"What about Alex?" I gazed into my tea, pressing my fingers against the burning ceramic as I tried to prevent his face from appearing in my mind's eye. The attack had been mostly absent from my thoughts here, and I wanted it to stay that way.

"I don't know how safe it is for you to be at home alone," Joël said. "You're possibly the only person outside Alex's sway who knows the real him—although I think he suspects some of us. I honestly don't know what he'll do about it."

I glanced up. "I've already considered that. Alex has a

perfect alibi. He's not going to ruin it by harming me. After all, the police know our position. If he tried anything else, he would be the first under suspicion." I placed my cup down, took a slice of lemon and squeezed it into my tea.

"With his ability to create a coverup?"

"What else can I do? I have a life to live." I had to help Rémy and Théo. I took a sip of tea and glared at Joël.

He shook his head. "I don't like it."

I shrugged, the repeated notes of the piano marbling around me. I didn't like it either—it was terrifying. But I wasn't going to let it stop me trying to get them back.

"I'll drive you," he said.

"That's kind, but my car is at Rémy's apartment and I'll need it in Sarrat." Plus he'd done so much already, too much.

"It's a long journey, and with your injury—"

"I'll manage," I snapped.

He pushed himself up, staring at me. It was hard to tell what he was thinking. He was so open and friendly, and yet there was a depth there too. He drew something from his pocket and slid it across the table. A credit card and a PIN written on a scrap of paper. "Take this—it's my spare. We can settle the balance later."

Staring at it, I was struck anew by his thoughtfulness. I'd been going to call Philippe this afternoon to arrange funds for travelling home. A call I hadn't been looking forward to. He was the last person I wanted to ask for assistance. I met Joël's gaze. "Are you sure?"

"Completely sure," he replied.

"Thank you," I said, wanting to express so much more but not finding the words. I pocketed the card.

Joël walked over to the oven, opened the door and stirred

the source of the aroma. "I'm sorry, but the books can't leave the Société," he said over his shoulder.

"I thought as much." I sipped my tea.

"I'm guessing you would have told me if you'd found anything." He closed the oven door and returned to the island.

I rubbed my forehead. "What, apart from how to manipulate the Désaccord in five hundred different ways, most of them pretty gruesome? Including how to perform Alex's ritual, with the specification of human blood made by a deep incision to the centre of the abdomen." Exactly where he'd plunged the knife. Nausea rose in my throat, and I placed my tea down. It had been nice not thinking of Alex. "You know, I was wondering why he'd gone for my stomach, when my throat would have been much more effective."

Joël squeezed my arm. "I don't know what to say, Violette, but there are people you can talk to…"

"And they would believe me—about the Désaccord?"

"We can find someone with a connection to the Société."

I squinted as the notes from upstairs irritated me. "Maybe. But what I don't understand is that the books are full of rituals for manipulating the Désaccord, but when it comes to the Harmonie, there's only one thing reiterated over and over."

Joël fixed his eyes on mine. "The key song played at the sanctuary."

"There's nothing else," I said. "It's like a reset button, evoking the Harmonie, which has the power to bring the Désaccord into balance. A sort of cure-all."

"Agreed," Joël replied.

"Then why won't it work?" I scanned his face. "Why doesn't it work for you lot when you play in the chateau?"

"I don't know," he said. "There was a real sense of peace up there on the pog, before all this happened, but I'm not sure we ever managed to call the Harmonie directly as Rémy must have—at least to say, there was never any chance of us lot getting caught up in it. Rémy achieved something I'm not sure we ever did."

As I tried to focus on Joël's words, the notes of the piano chafed at my nerves and pulled at the unease deep within—there was something about the sound ringing down from above. Staring into nothing, I focussed on the colours, seeing dullness where I should have glimpsed vitality. But if the notes weren't tuned properly, what chance would I have of calling Rémy?

"It's not right," I said, stepping off the stool, my middle throbbing. Ignoring it, I headed out the room and took the stairs, forcing myself into a sensible pace.

"What's not right?" Joël strode up behind me.

"The tuning."

I walked into the lounge, Joël following. The tuner was leaning into the piano in much the same way Rémy had. He lifted his head then stretched an unsteady arm to the keyboard and played an interval.

"Pardon, monsieur," I said as I walked over, "is it possible you could adjust the tuning slightly?"

He rose and faced me, peering along his nose. "I'm sorry. Is there a problem?"

"I... uh, need the tuning to be very precise. I wonder if you could readjust it?"

The man's mouth hung open for a moment, then he glanced over my shoulder. "Hello, Joël," he said.

"Frederick," Joël replied as he stepped beside me. "Violette, Frederick is one of our most skilled tuners. I'm sure what he's doing is more than adequate."

They couldn't see it. Of course they couldn't, or Frederick would've tuned it the right way to start with. "I do appreciate that," I said, "but I need it to have a specific colour."

Frederick looked as though he'd never heard anything so ridiculous.

I turned to Joël. "I need this to be right," I hissed. "It's a small adjustment."

He scoured my face. "Why?"

I didn't want to raise Joël's hopes that I could call Rémy —or perhaps I didn't want to raise my own hopes. "Just, please... Rémy would've said the same thing."

He nodded. "I'm sorry, Frederick, but Violette is very specific about her tuning. Could you please accommodate her?"

Frederick pulled himself up straight, his dark pupils staring at me. "Very well. Let us commence, then, from the beginning."

I let out a breath.

He played A. "Is this satisfactory?"

The colour was dull, lacklustre. I shook my head. "Could you adjust it ever so slightly, please?"

"Higher or lower?" he asked.

I didn't know. I only knew when it was right. "Uh, higher."

He reached into the piano and made an adjustment, then played the note again. The colour lacked even more clarity. "No, sorry, lower. A little lower than before."

Frederick raised his eyebrows at Joël and made another

adjustment. It was brighter than the original. "Yes, that's better. A little more."

He made another adjustment, tapped the key once again, and the note shimmered across my vision, lit with its own intensity. "That's it," I said. "Perfect."

Frederick released a sigh. "So now I have to retune the rest."

"Thank you," I said. "I'm very grateful."

He got to it without acknowledging me.

"Thanks, Frederick," Joël said. "I appreciate it. How's Cecile, by the way?"

"Much better," Frederick called from the depths of the piano. "She sends her love to you and your family. Do tell them when you see them." He came out and played another interval, looking only at Joël. They continued their conversation and I walked over to the table and settled in front of *Terra*. After a few minutes Joël strode past, squeezing my shoulder before heading out.

I tried to focus on the text as Frederick tuned the rest of the piano to my A, but the radiant notes forced into my thoughts as I reread the same pages again and again. Eventually the piano stopped ringing. I turned to see Frederick packing his bag. He zipped it closed, gripped it in his gnarly hand and strode past, nodding curtly to me with the barest of glances.

Staring at *Terra*, I could only see the click of Frederick's shoes upon the stairs, his call goodbye to Joël and the slam of the front door. The colours stilled. I walked over to the piano, pulled out the stool and sat down, my heart pounding. Finally, I had my chance. Taking a breath, I placed my fingers on the keys and pressed A. That glow rose before me, simple yet radiant. I played on, the blend of orange and indigo effulgent, the notes drawing me. A twist of dread rose from my depths at the colour, but I ignored it and the melody took me up, the room dropping away, my existence consisting of *Lo Boièr* and nothing else.

Completely lost in the melody, I repeated the verse a few times then drew to a close, my reason for playing rushing back, my breath sticking in my throat. I scanned the room, twisting around painfully, studying every space, every corner—the seating area, the meeting table, the door, the windows. The room couldn't be empty. I rose and searched again, turning around and around. Rémy had to be here, but there was no sign of him.

I sat down and gazed at the keys. Alex's banishing couldn't have worked. No, Rémy would come. I played *Lo Boièr* once more then examined the room afresh—nothing. I played again, frantic desperation replacing my ability to experience the music, and still nothing. I carried on and on as evening drew in. He would come—of course he would.

"Violette, dinner's ready," Joël's voice called from the door, breaking my barest thread of a connection to *Lo Boièr*.

"I'm not hungry."

"How about a break then, at least for a few minutes?"

"No, Joël, could you give me some space?" I turned back to the keys and picked up where I'd left off, my chest tight, my body aching. A while later Luc came in with my medication and a glass of water. He turned off the lights, all apart from a lamp near the piano, and said goodnight. I gulped the pills down and continued.

I kept at it until my unsupported middle was too uncomfortable to ignore, then I pushed the piano stool away and dragged an armchair under the keyboard and played again. At one point I heard Joël climb the stairs, probably to bed. I dismissed his colours and focussed on the melody.

Tiredness welled up, fogging my mind and my vision, causing me to ruin the tempo and hit wrong notes, and with each mistake I grew more tense, my heartbeat rising until I couldn't even think where to place my fingers. Every part of me was ready to snap. I snatched my hands away. There was no point—*Lo Boièr* wasn't going to work like this. I glanced around. Surely he was here. Surely.

The room was still, the night a rich midnight blue tinted with moonlight. His colours, but not him, not his gentle voice, not those eyes that could see into me, not that pull, that inexplicable draw.

I slumped back, my breath shallow, a lump in my throat. He wasn't here. He wasn't coming. Alex's ritual had worked. And not only that, there was nothing in the books. There was nothing—nothing but cold, gnarling dread. I stared at a patch of moonlight reflecting off the floor, stark, white, devoid of warmth. I'd found him and now he was gone.

Tears came, then. I couldn't stop myself. I didn't want to.

I opened my eyes and scraped my tear-damp hair from my face. The moonlight was gone and I had no idea of the time. A blanket lay over me—someone must have been in. I sat up gingerly, but my middle was fine—the medication doing its work.

The piano keys lay before me, an invitation to play once more, but there was no point. He wasn't coming. I had to go home in the morning and carry on with him in my memory, yet without him by my side. It was the possibility I hadn't allowed myself to consider until now.

I pulled the blanket tight around me. I couldn't conceive what it must be like for Rémy and Théo stuck in the Harmonie, yet Rémy said he had a good existence there—I supposed that was something. I could see Rémy on the lane outside my house when he'd first appeared. He'd not known where he was. A hint of a smile pulled at my lips, then I let out a sob. My return to Sarrat had been completely coloured by him. Not just our meetings, but visiting his family and seeing the musicians on the pog. They'd been playing to call him back. So much of it had involved him.

Tears pricked in my eyes. Why wasn't the key song working? The books were emphatic that a specific key song should be played at a specific sanctuary to evoke the Harmonie and reset the balance between the Harmonie and the Désaccord. The musicians were playing the key song, so what was wrong? I stared at the piano, lamplight glinting off the gloss. It was ridiculous that one of the Société's most experienced tuners hadn't been able to hear the tuning to bring the notes to life. Not that it mattered in the end—I hadn't been able to call Rémy anyway. Although, at least I'd had the chance to try—*Lo Boièr* wouldn't have come alive without the adjustments. But, then, if the adjustments had made a difference...

I shot upright, my middle pulling, my heart pounding.

That was it. That was the problem. All of them—Joël, Frederick and no doubt the rest of the Société, whoever they were—they couldn't see the tuning. The musicians had played on the pog for years not achieving anything, hadn't Joël said? No doubt they'd tuned their instruments to 432, just like Frederick today—but the colour came alive at an ever so slight variance. I got up, walked to the window and gazed at the grey clouds scudding across the velvet sky. They were playing the right song, in the right place, with the wrong tuning. That was why they hadn't been able to invoke the Harmonie, that was why they hadn't been able to call Rémy back.

Chapter Twenty-Four

I had to get to the chateau. Now.

Yet the thought of climbing up there alone sent shivers through me. I could ask Joël to come, but he'd marched me off the pog without a stab wound. He was even concerned about me driving back. No, I had to put this right, and I couldn't risk the possibility of him hindering me. I drew my phone out. Two o'clock. He and Luc should be fast asleep. I had my chance.

I ensured I still had Joël's card and PIN safe in my pocket then stepped into the hall, padded up the stairs and headed into my room. Endeavouring not to make any noise, I opened Luc's medication drawer and took out several packets of pills and some earplugs, dropping them into a carrier bag. On second thoughts I collected tape, gauze and a wad of dressing. It would last me until I made it to the doctor's in Ax. Luc's notes lay on top of the dresser. I tore off a blank sheet and scrawled, *Joël, Luc, thank you*, then folded the paper in half and placed it on my pillow. Luc wouldn't be in until seven at the earliest.

Without a sound, I trod down to the front door, put on my pumps and Joël's overcoat, and grasped my bag. Clicks echoed through the hall as I released the deadbolts. I froze, straining to listen, but all was silent above, and after a moment I slipped outside.

It was bitterly cold on the street. Hardened patches of snow clung to the pavement here and there and clouds scudded across the clear sky, driven by an icy wind. I turned into the main thoroughfare and stumbled as the commotion of late-night traffic descended. Supporting myself against a shop wall, I focussed on the signboard and followed the curves of the cursive lettering, pressing away the insidious unease that rose with the roar. The colour dulled a little, but not enough. It was leaving hospital all over again. But thinking of hospital... I rummaged in my bag, pulled out the earplugs and secured them in. The sensory overload cut by half. It wasn't completely better, but it was better than nothing. I stepped out to the kerb and raised my arm. An oncoming taxi slowed to a halt. "Rue Margueritte, please," I said as I climbed in.

Five minutes through the empty-for-Paris streets, me doing my best to ignore the grind of the engine and the dull ache in my middle as the taxi shifted this way and that, and we drew up outside Rémy's apartment. I paid the driver then headed inside and took the elevator, wincing at the grating and shaking of the mechanism. The society had been so peaceful. As the lift opened, I shut out the image of Rémy's desperate face as he'd torn down the stairs after me. I'd been so stupid, but I could do something about it now.

I tapped the code into Rémy's door, pushed inside and turned on the light. Everything was as I'd left it the day I'd headed out to meet Alex—the open piano, my laptop on the table, the not-very-well-made bed—the bed we'd lain in together. I walked over to the piano and traced my fingers along the rim. He'd told me not to go.

I turned away. Dwelling on it wouldn't help.

It didn't take long to gather my belongings. I pocketed my keys, so thankful I'd stowed them in the apartment for safekeeping rather than in my bag. After taking one last look around, I closed up and headed downstairs with my case.

The dim lighting in the garage pulled shapes from the dark cavities between the cars. A thread of ice ran down my spine as I loaded the boot. I drew out my earplugs, turned around and scanned the shadows. The garage lay silent but for the distant rumble of the city and the soft drip of water—both cast too much colour before me, but that was all. Satisfied, I shrugged off Joël's overcoat and laid it on my case, then shut the boot, wincing at the echoing slam. The sooner I was out of here, the better.

I climbed carefully into the car and organised myself, adjusting the seat and pushing the earplugs back in. My medication sat in the top of my bag. I stared at it for a few moments before pressing out a dose—I really didn't want to intensify my colours, but I needed to get to Sarrat. I threw the pills to the back of my mouth and took a gulp from a bottle of leftover mineral water.

My fingers were already cold. I turned on the ignition, swung the car around and waited for the garage door to roll up. Something moved in the corner—an overcoat-clad silhouette shifted and merged with the darkness, and the blade of a knife gleamed. My heart pounded. I clicked on the full beam, flooding the gloom with light. Nothing. I really didn't need to do that to myself. But after everything, I supposed it was to be expected. The door mechanism clicked fully open and I pulled out, scanning the car park in my rear-view mirror. But I was being ridiculous—I'd barely thought of Alex in the Société and I wasn't going to start now.

I headed south through the street-lit Paris night. In minutes I was over the Seine and past the arrondissements thanks to the late hour. But even with earplugs, the engine rolled through my head, the horror that accompanied it making me sick. The focus of the high-speed drive forced some of it away. That and the constant thought I really might be able to help Rémy and Théo. At Châteauroux, just over halfway to Sarrat, I stopped for fuel and bought a chocolatine and a coffee, glad to unfold my cramping middle. I took more pills and headed onward.

My phone buzzed as I picked up speed on the autoroute. I flicked my eyes to the screen. "No way, Joël, I'm not answering you." Damn him. He must have woken and checked on me. But what could he do? He didn't know where I was going, although it wouldn't take much to guess. He would think I'd gone home, but the fact I'd left in the middle of the night was suspicious. The phone stopped buzzing—then it started again. I pressed my foot down on the accelerator just in case.

The hours passed, hope spurring me forward. Once past Cahors the icy patches of snow became a thin covering, the dawn scattering rays of luminous red and turquoise across the blank canvas. And on I drove, my wound aching, the phone ringing occasionally, the engine blaring with increasing intensity, causing my temples to ache and my throat to stiffen. Yet despite my discomfort, the constant monotony of the autoroute and my lack of sleep weighed heavy on my eyelids. I pressed my hands into the wheel as though that small exertion might keep me awake. When it did nothing, I shifted around, causing my stomach to burn. Eventually a jagged line appeared on the horizon and the mountains rose before me, the sight cold water on my face. Home.

I sped onward, my middle tender, my colours pounding. I joined the route national at Tarascon, then turned off onto back lanes from Ax. The sky grew leaden, and by the time I reached the descent to Sarrat, snow was sweeping through the valley, the pog only discernible as a vague outline, the meadows blanketed in white, the river barely distinguishable from the land.

Relief surged through me as I pulled up outside the barn, the walls and hedges bound in drifts, the hornbeams iced. I turned off the ignition and relative silence descended. The noise had been too much and my tummy was by no means comfortable. I rummaged in my bag for the medication and pressed out more. Stopping now because of my wound was out of the question. I pushed out an additional couple of pills and swallowed the lot down with some leftover coffee, then opened the door and climbed out steadily.

The chill wind stole through my clothes, casting curling streaks around me as I headed to the house and unlocked the door. The hall was only a little warmer than outside and yet it smelt familiar—a hint of fresh paint, linseed floor soap and the aroma of garlic. I stepped into the lounge and glanced at the chateau just visible through the snow. Rémy.

"I won't be long," I murmured.

I hastened to my bedroom and pulled on thermals and skiwear, my middle hurting as I bent double. Was I really going to be able to do this? I stared at my bed as I tucked my sweater in. The last time I'd lain there, he'd stroked my hair as I'd drifted to sleep. I had to try—the medication would take effect soon.

Downstairs, I found a universal socket wrench in the utility and zipped it and my phone into my pocket, then I strode to the harp and trailed a finger across the strings. The glissando rang out in a spectrum of vibrant colour. Rémy's tuning had held.

I tipped the harp sideways and unscrewed its legs to make for easier carrying, then dropped the cover over the burnished frame. Finding a grip on the soundbox and the column through the floral calico, I drew the harp into my arms. It was lighter than it looked due to the hollow soundbox—even so, pain cut through me. I carried it to the hall and placed it upon the tiles, then zipped up my jacket, pulled on my boots, hat, hood and gloves, and took a deep breath. This had to work.

Taut with nerves, I opened the door, hauled up the harp and stepped outside. Performing a balancing trick with the frame on my foot, I locked up the house and tucked the keys under the mat. Despite my earplugs, a blast of wind scoured my vision, swirling greys barely distinguishable from the snow. My breath caught. I forced air into my chest as I peered through the colour and hoisted the harp up, shifting it around to find a less painful hold close to my body.

I headed onto the road and hurried past Sylvie's without seeing any sign of life, then I descended onto the drover's track, the trees arching above. In spite of the branch cover, snow lay thick on the ground. With each step I hauled my boots high and grappled with the harp, splinters of pain radiating from my wound.

As I stepped out of the trees and made my way across the meadow, the snow drifted in thick swathes, a veil between myself and the steely walls where, somehow, Rémy waited. The gale whipped up a deluge of colour and froze my cheeks, but the rest of me was hot with the effort of each step.

At the start of the old cobbled track, I kicked snow from a boulder and placed the harp down, my arms trembling, my belly burning. The medication wasn't doing anything, but more likely I was doing too much. I could sit down for a moment but I wasn't sure I'd get up again. My middle panging, I lifted the harp into my arms and trod up the meandering path.

Once through the scrawny box and blackthorn that clung to the lower slopes, the snow lay in a thin cover, most of it blasted off the face of the pog by the wind. Eddies of white swirled on the gale, blending with my colours, forcing me to search for the real amidst the distortion. I made my way gingerly, wedging my boots on exposed rock where I could. My foot slid and I tensed up to balance myself, pain shooting through my middle. It was too risky carrying the harp before me like this. I wrestled the bulky frame to my side, gained a firm grip on the column with one hand, and extended my other arm to support myself on the rising rock. The harp scraped against my leg as I slipped and twisted upward, but I was steadier.

As the path grew steeper my breath heaved, my arm burned with the weight and my stomach smarted with each step. Through the blizzard I could make out the stand of box where Rémy had disappeared, the boughs whipping to and fro. The surrounding air was shrouded now, cast with a grim pallor, and foreboding trickled through my blood. I pushed myself onward, catching a barely perceptible undertone in the wind, a low moan that bore darkness, hate and cold, dripping fear. My skin crawled—but I knew what I was dealing with.

Swathing pain extended outward to encompass my whole body as I hauled myself up the last incline—too much pain, but what option did I have? If I couldn't make it back down, I could always call someone to help—perhaps Noé. He'd understand.

As I stepped upward, the air became rancid, as though it possessed nothing to sustain me, its texture like mucus in my throat. I forced myself to breathe steadily, once in and once out, for each agonising footfall. The air sank in cold and lifeless, draining me of hope and the will to continue. The moaning grew to a screech as though all the notes in existence had coalesced to a piercing dissonance—it scoured me with wretched shards, a wretchedness that held pain and distortion and hate, and it tore on the horror that lay deep within, prying beneath my colours, gnawing at me, gnawing at the dread I couldn't face.

I focussed on the icy slope to hold the Désaccord back as I took a step, but still its colour swallowed my breath and my senses. I took another step and drew onto the level rock before the chateau, then another and the ground slid away. In one endless, desperate moment as I fell, I managed to twist and position the harp safely on top of me, then I slammed into jagged stone. Pain lacerated through my body and dampness bloomed from my wound. I lay still, attempting to breathe away the agony, cold panic rising in my throat, dark wraiths of wind and snow whipping around me. But I couldn't stay here. I would freeze. I slid the harp aside and slowly levered myself to sitting, my middle blazing.

The back of my neck prickled. I was being watched. Someone stood before me, veiled by snowfall. I sat rigid, the harsh beat of my heart counting out the seconds, my heightened senses humming as I waited for Alex to make his move. But nothing happened—it was the Désaccord unnerving me, that was all. Bracing myself, thinking of Rémy and Théo and nothing else, I staggered up amidst gouging pain and took hold of the harp. I was so close now, I had to carry on. With deep, foul inbreaths, I trod along the length of the chateau and pulled myself through the stone arch.

Within the shelter of the walls the wind dropped a little, but the shriek of the Désaccord continued. I peered through the abhorrent colour, searching for a suitable position, my nerves raw, my gut searing, every part of me saturated with terror. The musicians had sat at the narrow end where the bedrock rose. I trod over. The ground was relatively level in the centre. I cleared the snow with painful sweeps of my foot, then set the harp down and drew off the cover.

Wind gusted through the courtyard and the harp teetered to the side. I grabbed the frame and wedged the wood against me, trying not to slip on the ice. Then I tugged off my gloves, took out my earplugs and zipped everything into my pockets—and there was nothing but sound and colour, a deluge, a ceaseless tumult. Gasping, I clutched the harp, mooring myself to the bleak reality in which I stood. The gale buzzed the strings and flickers of pure colour daubed the vile air, a relief to the constant darkness, something to focus on, something to draw me out of the hideousness—I needed that colour.

I drew my fingers across the strings. The glissando rang out just audible above the howling, casting tones before me, some fresh and flawless, others tired and flat. I peered through the murk and plucked the strings I would need for *Lo Boièr* one at a time, my fingers already bitten with cold.

The F was dull, the B too, but the other notes blazed out. As if in response to the shimmering colour, the darkness densified. I fumbled with my pocket and pulled out the socket wrench, glancing around the courtyard for that flashing blade. "It's just the Désaccord," I mumbled, my words stolen by the storm.

Supporting the harp against the wind, I placed the wrench over one of the tuning pins where the key had fitted perfectly. I turned the handle, plucking the corresponding string repeatedly until the note rang out in clarity, then I repeated the process for the other string, the gale ramming into me and the snow blasting around. Satisfied with the colour, I lowered myself down to sit on the nearest rock and, gritting my teeth at a violent spasm in my gut, drew the twisted wood toward me.

I clasped the wavering harp between my knees and plucked out the first tentative notes of *Lo Boièr*. Pure colour rose around me, swirling about the chateau amidst the darkness. The Désaccord condensed, the air pervaded with malice. I played on but the A was now dull, and the F again. The combination of the cold and my playing was interfering with the tension of the strings. I pulled the wrench from my pocket, forced myself up and adjusted the pins again, tears beading in my eyes at the brutal throbbing in my middle. Then I sat back down and played once more, desperately trying to ignore the sense that I was so vulnerable—that my colours or the Désaccord or my pain would consume me.

As I played again, I focussed on the notes. Fiery orange merged to celestial indigo, a daybreak glow that cut through the storm and rose amidst the chateau to become clearer, more resonant, more intense, as though the chateau itself were amplifying the music.

The Désaccord howled and twisted. I braced myself against the harp as it rocked in the tempest, clamping my legs hard around the frame despite the pain. Although my fingers now had no feeling and only muscle memory enabled me to pluck the strings, I kept the tempo and the notes rang out unadulterated.

The cacophony intensified and the Désaccord released a deafening wail as though it had been torn. I risked a glance upward as I played. There, in the centre of the chateau amidst the bleakness, was a thread of luminous, flawless white. I stared at it, drawn to its opalescence—*Lo Boièr* was working. The Désaccord thrashed ineffectually against the purity then gathered into a dense mass around the light, the pressure in the courtyard building like the air before a thunderstorm amplified a hundredfold. With a mighty roar, the mass rolled out in a hurricane lash of darkness. The blast hit, sending me to the ground and thrusting the harp into the wall. The light faded to nothing.

I peered at the harp's remains through shudders of pain. The soundbox was shattered, the column snapped. The wood undulated against the chateau wall. The strings flailed in the gale. That was it then, that was my chance gone—that was my chance for Rémy smashed against the rock.

I let out something between a choke and a sob, my hopeless, dusky grey mingling with the dark strands of the howling wind. There was no chance now. But... I stared at the colour I'd released with my cry... I'd always hummed along to *Lo Boièr* when I'd played the harp or the piano—I'd harmonised with the melody, shaping my voice to equal the colour of the notes. If I'd done it then, surely I could do it now. After all, I knew the words and I knew the melody. I'd played it often enough.

"*Quand lo boièr ven de laurar,*" I attempted, my colours flickering with a vivid edge, not quite there but close. Trying to ignore the Désaccord's howling, I prised myself up to sitting, my middle searing. "*Quand lo boièr ven de laurar.*" I recited the words again and again, studying the colour of each note, modulating my voice, allowing myself to sink into the melody. As I continued, the notes gained more quality until they rang out with the radiance of Rémy's tuning. The Désaccord battered into me with renewed vigour, but the words lent me strength.

"*Planta son agulhada.*" I continued through the verse. The Désaccord bawled and screeched, pulling up despair from deep within—but it couldn't take hold. The key song resonated through my body. "*Planta son agulhada,*" I repeated, then sang on to the refrain, "*A, E, I, Ó, U.*" Each vowel formed in a different part of my mouth, lending a unique timbre to the individual letters. My voice was a dynamic instrument able to shape the melody with more than pitch alone, and the colour scintillated with an edge I'd not seen before. The Désaccord released a desolate shriek and an exquisite lustre broke through the darkness. *Lo Boièr* merged with the luminosity once more, the Désaccord protesting in a wailing fury. The Harmonie grew in intensity, and with an ear-splitting boom, a shockwave thundered through the chateau, thrusting me down.

Then silence.

And from the silence arose a barely perceptible sound, a song almost beyond hearing, as though it wove the fabric of the cosmos, as though it were life itself. Warmth blossomed around me, my fingers began to thaw and the pain in my gut waned to a mere ripple. I opened my eyes and sat up carefully. Shimmering white-gold suffused the chateau, the serene air permeated with delicate snowflakes. At the end of the courtyard the light grew to a brilliant incandescence, and from the centre of the lustre, two silhouetted figures emerged—a tall man clasping the hand of a small boy. They stepped onto the courtyard, crystal snowflakes settling in their hair as they peered around, their faces uncertain.

I rose slowly, my chest pounding. I didn't dare believe what lay before me. "Rémy," I called, my voice trembling.

He fixed on me and his eyes grew wide. "Violette?"

Even here, even now, there was something about him, something that drew me unequivocally. I pulled back my hood.

His mouth dropped open. "Violette," he whispered, "you're alive." He stood stock still for a few moments, then turned to the boy and knelt down. "You alright?" he asked.

Théo nodded and grinned, his messy blond head bouncing, catching the golden light.

"Alright." Rémy ruffled Théo's hair as he stood up. "Looks like it's time to go home."

Hand in hand, they strode toward me.

CHAPTER TWENTY-FIVE

Darkness struck Rémy from the side, blasting him across the chateau onto the rocks. Théo stumbled back into the luminescence. The white-gold pulsed, closed in on itself and was gone, Théo with it. The deluge returned, bellowing and shrieking, raising hairs across my skin, but I couldn't understand it—how could the Désaccord be back?

Debauched air forced in on Rémy as he writhed on the ice. I ran toward him and a bolt of wretchedness rammed into my chest, hurtling me into the snow. Grimacing in agony, I prised myself up. Something moved in the shadows through the arch. A man in a black suit and a white shirt strode into the chateau, oblivious to the elements, his face boyish yet horrific, his lips forming archaic words that soared through the courtyard, borne by the Désaccord.

Alex's eyes lingered on me for a moment, and then, still chanting, the Désaccord seething around his form, he strode toward Rémy. I stared at Alex, dumbfounded, alarm constricting my throat. I was back in the chamber and I could feel the pinch of his fingers, see the glint of the blade.

Alex extended his arm and the Désaccord surged out, slamming into Rémy who screamed and bent double. I had to do something, but my senses were afire with the chamber, the smell of old bones and Alex's sour sweat before he'd plunged the knife in. Alex raised his arm and Rémy rose above the ground until he hung before the keep, writhing and twisting, crying out through bared teeth as darkness bore in on every part of his body.

What was wrong with me? We weren't in the chamber now, and this time I was by no means defenceless. I forced the images away—I could do this. I had to do this. "*Quand lo boièr ven de laurar...*" My words cut through the blackness.

Ceasing his chant and laughing, Alex turned toward me, his hand still raised at Rémy, somehow holding him aloft.

"*Quand lo boièr ven de laurar...*" I sang on with luminous colour.

Alex's lips formed a twisted smile and the Désaccord thrust in on me with its unrelenting cacophony, its clamour. I fought to focus, to push away the hideousness, but its scraping filled my vision and my mind. I tried to sing, but opening myself to see the notes allowed it in further.

"I don't need to hurt you, Violette," Alex said, his words cutting through the storm. "You do it all by yourself."

The Désaccord seeped into my veins, into the core of who I was, and as if greeting an old compadre, its rancour met what I didn't want to acknowledge, what I didn't dare touch—the Désaccord found resonance with the tangle of unbearable dread that lay beneath my synaesthesia, and it pulled at the threads.

Through shards of colour and horror, it drew out fragmented impressions... Eveline, her car on the autoroute... the mountainside not far from Les Fonts... Maman's perfume... My breath quickened and I gasped for air. I couldn't face these images—they would smother me, they would break me—but more impressions came, Sylvie's stricken eyes, my toy-strewn bedroom, Maman and Papa as I said goodbye.

Grasping my head, I dropped to my knees, each recollection an individual torture, a scouring pain. I couldn't go where the Désaccord wished to take me. Through strangled breaths I pressed my colours and the memories away with everything I'd learnt over the years, yet still the impressions came, one after another. I stared up at Rémy who contorted in agony as Alex and the Désaccord tormented him. I had to sing.

I gulped in as much air as I could and tried to release the melody, but in my mind's eye Maman stood before me wearing her crepe dress, the dress I hadn't allowed myself to think of for so long. My hands, my arms, all of me trembled as I pushed the image back and attempted to form the words of *Lo Boièr* once more. The memory of Sylvie's harrowed face unfurled—that expression I could never see again. I forced her from me, I forced my colours from me—I couldn't do it, I couldn't open myself to my synaesthesia to sing or it would all unravel.

"I tried so hard to banish you." Alex's voice jarred through my head as though it were a part of the impressions that assailed my mind, yet he wasn't addressing me. He stood before Rémy, his hair whipped up by the Désaccord, his eyes dead. "I really did try hard to drive you away, not only in the ritual, but before."

I endeavoured to shut out his voice, but it was indistinguishable from the Désaccord and the horror within me.

"We created music that undid souls," Alex continued,

"music that reduced people to their bare parts and revealed life for what it was, yet you wanted it to end."

"We were hurting people, Alex," Rémy yelled. "It couldn't go on."

Alex raised his hand and the Désaccord wrapped nebulous bonds around Rémy's body, forcing him still. "You're right," Alex replied. "It couldn't go on as it was. We were attracting too much attention, especially when Bénédict died. It had to become more discreet, but it had to continue. You weren't going to prevent me."

Alex's words drew out more images. If I could only shut out that voice, that colour, surely the memories would stop.

"It didn't take much, not by then," Alex continued, "to follow you to the chateau and provoke the Désaccord. It wasn't the Désaccord that had taken a personal dislike to you. It was me." He closed in on Rémy, only a breath away. In an instant his hands shot through the murk, grabbed Rémy's waistcoat and shirt, and tore the fabric apart, then he wrapped his fingers around Rémy's neck and squeezed.

I had to sing—but I couldn't.

"We were friends," Rémy rasped, glaring at Alex.

As if thinking better of it, Alex released his grip and ran a hand over Rémy's chest. "I do miss you," he said, "but..." He took a step back, reached inside his jacket and withdrew a large knife with a mother-of-pearl handle. The knife.

I stared at the glinting metal that had almost taken my life. It was unreal, a part of something that couldn't have happened to me, and yet it had. Memories from long ago mingled with the horror of that night to drag hopelessness from my depths—I'd been powerless then and I was powerless now, unable to resist Alex, unable to help Rémy, unable to do anything but fight myself.

Alex drew the blade to Rémy's chest.

Rémy attempted to thrust away, barely managing to move at all. "Don't be ridiculous, Alex. We can sort something out."

A twisted smile formed on Alex's lips as he placed the point under the centre of Rémy's collarbone and ran the blade diagonally downward, blood beading in its wake. I wanted to cry out, I wanted to yell for Alex to stop, but I could only hold back the memories.

Sweat trickled from Rémy's temples as he strained against his swathing ties. Alex repositioned the knife to the edge of Rémy's chest and carved another incision across the first, a blood-red cross over Rémy's heart. Then, grasping the handle with both hands, Alex drew the knife back over his head.

I had to do something... anything... I couldn't lose Rémy again. This felt like a repetition of the ritual—the same players, the same knife. I'd ignored Rémy's advice and followed Alex to the chamber then, because I'd been too afraid to lay my colours wide open and face what lay beneath—and now I was doing exactly the same thing. I stared up at Rémy—he was strength of conviction, he was passion, he was colour, he was part of me. I had to sing, but the images were terrifying.

I sat there shaking violently, staring between Rémy and Alex, the Désaccord whipping around us all in a merciless fury. The knife was poised above Alex's head, a thick stream of obsolescent French flowing from his mouth, words I'd read over and over in *Terra*, words from the darkest rituals.

Rémy's eyes flicked to mine. They held so much and, despite the Désaccord, despite the memories, I could feel him, I could feel an acknowledgement of the bond we held, of the brief but incomparable relationship we shared. I'd found something in him, something more than I'd expected from life, something more than the colour that overwhelmed me and the pain I didn't dare touch—but I had to dare, I had to dare for him. I'd been afraid before the ritual, and look where it had led. If I sang, no matter what it did to me, at least there would be a chance for him.

Alex adjusted his grip upon the knife as the grim words flowed from his lips, his chant rising to a crescendo.

I had to try.

"*Quand lo boièr ven de—*" I opened myself and the Désaccord sank into me, its shrieking becoming one with the tangled agony inside my chest, pulling up memories—all of them in a second and an eternity.

My words dropped away and my breathing grew shallow. I was on the autoroute, the landscape passing in a monotonous stream, the hum of the engine boring into me, grey and grating, blending with the colour of Eveline's voice when she occasionally spoke. But my colours weren't for her, this ghastly woman, and they weren't for the dull repetition of the road or the wraith of Paris that loomed before me. No, my colours were for Maman and Papa and home. Yet all of that was behind me, endless kilometres behind, and no matter what I did, no matter how I pleaded with Eveline, she wouldn't take me back.

I couldn't go back.

A gasping dismay filled me. This couldn't be true, this couldn't be happening. I would wake up soon and I would be tucked in bed at home. Maman would be downstairs preparing breakfast and Papa would be singing in the garden as he shovelled snow. Eveline said something, words I couldn't make out, words that were black and sharp and hideous. I didn't want to see her colour anymore. I didn't want to see any colour.

The Désaccord prised further in, further back. I stood on the side of the mountain a little way from Les Fonts. Sylvie was there, and Eveline holding a silver casket, and Rémy's parents, and Nico and his wife. There were others too, the musicians and friends from the village all huddled in their thickest coats. The colours of Sarrat rippled with the breeze, swirling over the mantle of snow that covered the landscape. I observed Eveline with a wary eye as she spoke, then she removed the lid of the casket and shook the contents into the breeze. The wind carried the ash upward, over the twisted box and the limestone crags to disappear into nothing. I wanted to cry out, I wanted to scream, but there were so many people around me. I forced myself not to make a sound, not to move, not to feel.

Further back still. I was in the living room of the barn as it was then—cluttered, messy, lined with bookshelves, packed with furniture and toys. It was morning and Maman and Papa weren't back yet. Sylvie's eyes were red and she looked as though she were going to choke. She sat down next to me on the sofa and her words echoed around. "I'm so sorry, my darling, your parents were involved in a car accident last night." A strangled sob escaped her throat.

I stared at her.

"Your parents died."

My head buzzed and a sinking feeling engulfed me as my world drained away to nothing.

The Désaccord drove deeper, and there they were, Maman and Papa standing in the hall. I never liked it when they went out without me. What if they never came back? I clasped onto Maman first. She looked beautiful in her crepe dress and delicate shawl, and she smelt nice when she dressed up, like springtime despite the snow outside.

She stroked my head. "Promise me you'll be good for Sylvie at bedtime. We'll be back late, so no waiting up."

I glanced over at Sylvie and smiled. She was such good fun. She grinned back, her face playful. There was no doubt about it, we would have a great evening. I pulled myself away from Maman and sprang onto Papa, wrapping my arms around his waist. I laughed as he clasped me in his arms and wrestled me from side to side, his suit jacket swinging open to reveal a glimmer of red silk beneath.

I gasped. My world had ended.

Pain tore through me, raw and excruciating. I braced myself against the desolation, against everything I hadn't dared to feel for so many years, against all the defences I'd raised and all the times I'd had to act as though I were fine, when nothing could have been further from the truth. With slow, deep breaths, I breathed through my devastation. I'd suffered so much, but my grief wasn't something external to fight—it had always been there underneath, unacknowledged and desperate. It was obvious now—I hadn't been able to bear my colours because they were Maman and Papa, the barn, Sarrat and my whole life before that moment. I hadn't been able to bear the agony that my life had been torn from me. I'd had to push away the memories, my colours and the torment in order to survive.

Everything hurt so terribly, but now that my pain lay clearly before me, it lacked the power to rise like a demon and persecute my existence. It was part of who I was. The Désaccord drove in once again, but there was nothing hidden for it to exploit and it sank back toward Alex. I had to act— before Alex noticed.

I took a deep breath and sang. I sang my favourite part of *Lo Boièr*, I sang loud and I sang from everything that made up me. "*Quand serai mòrta enterratz-me*"—When I am dead do bury me. The colours were more vibrant than ever.

Luminescence streaked through the courtyard.

Alex, still bearing the knife aloft, turned to face me, his eyes wide. The Désaccord struck my body, forcing me to support myself in the snow to keep upright. Its hideous threads attempted to sink in once more, but there was nothing for it to goad.

"*Quand serai mòrta enterratz-me*," I repeated, and the Harmonie surged out, dispersing Rémy's dark bonds. He struggled against the last of the dissipating strands, gaining more and more freedom.

Alex gathered himself, turned back to Rémy and thrust the knife down. In a swift movement Rémy twisted away and threw his fist into the side of Alex's head. The knife fell to the ground and Alex stumbled to his knees, the hideousness bawling with indignance. Rémy's gaze linked with mine for a moment then he sprinted toward me through the fury.

Pulling himself up, Alex raised his arms in supplication, blood trickling from his forehead, the foul air a part of his warped features. The Désaccord melded into a deadly mass then rammed into Rémy, hurling him to Alex's feet.

Panic rose in my chest as the murk raised Rémy up and bound him again. I sang on. "*Al pus fons de la cròta*"—At the depths of the cave. The Harmonie grew in intensity. On the edge of my vision I caught a movement through the archway —several figures held back by the Désaccord, one of them a blot of orange.

Alex began chanting again, this time his voice forceful and formidable. He seemed impervious to the luminosity that almost entirely filled the courtyard. The Désaccord grew around him until it was a massive sickening shadow, a grotesque blight in the brilliance.

"*A, E, I, Ó, U,*" I cried, each letter aglow with its own timbre, sealed with the U, which rose up from my being, the sum of my life, the sum of all the pains and pleasures, the agonies and joys, all I'd lost and loved. It poured out, resplendent and radiant.

Alex brought his arms down and thrust the Désaccord toward me.

The Harmonie responded, sweeping outward, propelling the onslaught away. Alex's face contorted with rage, his eyes blazing. He dove for the knife, sprang up and plunged it into Rémy's chest at the centre of the blood-red cross.

A part of me acknowledged that the Harmonie continued to expand, that what remained of the Désaccord railed against its lustre, but I could only stare as Alex withdrew the knife from Rémy's flesh, releasing a surge of blood— too much blood. Rémy's eyes grew still, his body stiff, his mouth agape. He slumped down lifeless, and the world exploded in light and darkness.

I opened my eyes and, through splinters of pain, pushed myself up to sitting. A dull light suffused the chateau, the grey cast of the Désaccord wavering on a cold breeze, subdued yet still present.

But Rémy... what I'd seen, it couldn't be... Alex couldn't have.

But I'd seen it, I'd seen the knife drive into Rémy's chest, I'd seen the life withdraw from his eyes. I scanned the courtyard, my head spinning. I needed him, I needed to hold him once more, to tell him I would always be his, but the chateau lay empty.

I twisted around. My harp lay smashed at the foot of the wall—there was nothing left but pain, memories and the broken harp. Colour flickered across my vision at the faint disquiet of the Désaccord, but the dread that had accompanied it was gone, replaced by heart-wrenching despair.

"Rémy?" Through almost unbearable pain, I stood up and turned around. "Where's Rémy?" He had to be here. I had to be able to hold him, to say goodbye.

"Rémy?" I called again and again, my chest throbbing, my middle searing as I stumbled to where he'd fallen.

He was gone.

I dropped to my knees, my hands sinking into the snow, my world falling away once again. All I could do was stare at the white nothingness beneath me.

An arm wrapped gently around my shoulder. "Come on, Violette, we need to get you home." The colours of Sarrat. Joël.

He pulled me back to sitting and brushed the snow from my unfeeling fingers. I vaguely registered blood on his hands.

"Stretcher, now!" he yelled, then more hands shifted my body and laid me down.

U

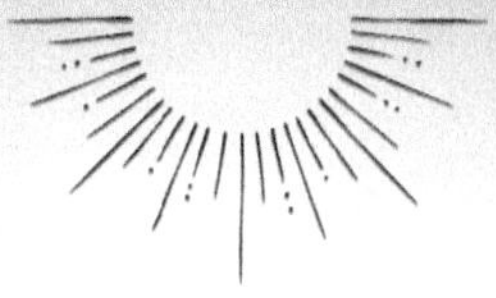

Through the interplay of opposing forces, I have found perfection. You drew me back. You gave every part of yourself for me. I cannot cheat death, therefore my continuation occurs only in you, the other half of me. In you, I have found unity. In unity, there is eternity. In unity, there is harmony.

Chapter Twenty-Six

I was dry, parched, empty.

The doctor visited, Sylvie brought food, Joël checked in, and all of it chafed like sandpaper. The events of the past weeks seemed unreal. Joël told everyone I'd been attacked in Paris, and after I'd returned home, my wound had opened whilst out walking. It was almost easier for me to believe that. Yet as I sat up in bed with the duvet wrapped tightly around me, the chateau stood there beyond the window, wreathed in pallid cloud, a testament to all that had passed.

The musicians searched for Alex afterward, just as they'd searched for Rémy's body, but they'd found neither, and although Joël said I was safe, I didn't care. Yet occasionally I would see the knife slashing toward me only to miss and pierce Rémy's chest. Then my breath would stick in my throat. Everything stuck in my throat—I'd found a missing part of myself and he'd been taken from me. I was arid. I couldn't even cry.

We returned to the chateau three days after losing Rémy. Joël and I wanted to call the Harmonie to retrieve

Théo—and Rémy's body too, if it were somehow possible. We discussed the matter functionally, never touching on our grief. On Joël's questioning I explained that a slight variance in tuning from 432 was necessary to call the Harmonie. Joël talked of measuring the frequency so the musicians could return without me, but I wanted to be there. Joël reluctantly conceded, knowing, I think, that I needed closure as much as him. Sylvie protested, unable to understand why I'd want to risk myself after having been stitched up again. I'd had to make up something about the Paris attack having brought up memories of the time I'd spent at the chateau with my parents, memories I needed to lay to rest. She only backed down when the doctor, who played with the musicians occasionally and was informed of everything, explained that he thought it would help me recover.

Joël drove us through snowdrifts to the parking area where Rémy left his car years before, then he launched the four-wheel drive along the track to the base of the pog. Surrounded by the musicians and supported by Joël's arm, I picked my way painfully up the icy flanks. A dull howling enveloped us as we approached the chateau, the weight of the Désaccord still draped about the walls, but I didn't care for it or the colours it provoked.

The musicians tuned to my specification and played *Lo Boièr*. The wind rose and with it the Désaccord brushed its murk around us, but its zeal had seeped away with Rémy's life. The Harmonie broke through, its luminosity blending perfectly with the melody. I braced myself for the sight of Rémy's body and watched hawklike for Théo, yet there was nothing but rock, snow and grey walls lit with the sublime shimmer of the Harmonie. As the final notes of *Lo Boièr* faded, the luminosity closed in on itself and the Désaccord took possession of the chateau once again.

We returned in silence.

After that I spent my hours in the armchair, wrapped in my robe and covered with a blanket. I stared at the chateau through blizzards and drifts, as though the view of the dark walls could anchor me to my memory of Rémy—his presence, his smile, his laughter, the way I could never take my eyes off him.

And the world continued as though nothing had ever happened. Birds scraped at the snow, cattle wandered through the valley, cars passed on the lane, and Sylvie buzzed around despite my protesting. I wanted to be alone. My wound was mending and I could do most things myself, but still she came.

A couple of days after we'd returned from the chateau, I sat in the armchair as usual. The evening had drawn in, the sky a deep, saturated blue. There was something about that moment before nightfall proper, as though so much lay beneath. The fire crackled, casting a streak of luminous orange across my vision. Another snap and this time the glow was almost a physical thing, my skin tingling with its hue. I'd not given a thought to my colours since losing Rémy. Apart from using synaesthesia functionally when we'd returned to the chateau, I'd ignored all of it, not because it bothered me, but because I didn't care. The flames spat and sparks burst before my eyes, and it wasn't just the fire—the range hummed a deep brown like the depths of the earth and the wind played at the doors in pearly flourishes amidst the unfathomable twilight.

Without thinking I rose and, ignoring the ache in my stomach, took my boots from the hall and pulled them on.

Then I wrapped the blanket around my shoulders, slid open the glass doors and stepped into the snow, submerging into the inky darkness. The wind was louder here and silver enswathed me, fusing with swirling snowflakes and rippling vortices of midnight blue. The colour was so intense, so alive, so visceral. It sank into me, and there was nothing between the world and my senses. I turned around, gaping in wonder —this was what I'd denied myself for so many years, this profundity, this beauty. And I knew this was how Rémy had seen the world.

Tears welled up from my depths and trickled over my cheeks—tears for the child who used to feel... this, tears for the woman I'd become, the woman who'd held so much away. The air chilled my damp skin and nipped my fingers. Half laughing for the beauty of it all and half gasping for the pain that surged through me, I stumbled inside, shook the snow from the blanket, closed the door and hurried to the fire. As I held my frozen hands as close to the flames as I dared, deep sobs took hold of me, shuddering through my chest. He wasn't coming back.

I flung the duvet up, feeling a faint pull at my middle. The cover floated down and settled over the bed. Before we'd gone to Paris, he'd lain there watching me sleep. He'd said sometimes it scared him that he might slip away, and now he had. Now he would never return. My chest was open, exposed, raw. I almost dove back into bed, but Sylvie was downstairs. She'd only worry.

"Do you want parsnips in the cassoulet?" she called from the kitchen in staunch forest green. My colours were fully open and they always would be. Through them I was connected to Rémy, Maman and Papa, and everything I loved.

"I don't mind," I replied as I headed downstairs. She didn't have to prepare another meal for me. I was perfectly capable and I needed to make that clear. I appreciated her help, but it had been two weeks now.

As I crossed the hall, morning sunlight streamed through the window by the front door, revealing all the imperfections I'd missed whilst decorating. The crack by the study caught my eye—I'd filled the hole but the putty had shrunk. I ran my fingers over the broken surface and the image of a cup hurtling into the wall flashed through my mind—a white ceramic breakfast cup, the one Papa always used. I stepped into the living room and turned around just inside the door. I'd stood here when it'd happened. Maman had been coming down the stairs and Papa had pushed passed me, the cup in his hand. I could see them now through my ten-year-old mind, a mind alive with the colour and sensation that had been my daily reality. Papa paused in the doorway. They were quarrelling a little and then it became heated. I hated it. I hated that they fought, but I couldn't look away. Papa was different somehow, he'd been short-tempered for weeks, almost nasty. He hurled his cup. Maman stepped to the side and the ceramic smashed into the wall, casting coffee all over the paintwork, the coats and shoes, the floor. Maman had been livid—she would always meet a challenge. They argued and argued then, until Papa closed the study door in Maman's face and she retreated to the kitchen, crying.

I'd forgotten the memory completely—and they'd fought so much before their deaths, I was sure of it. I surveyed the crack. Was it possible I'd only remembered the good times?

I stepped over to the kitchen doorway and leant against the frame. Sylvie was peeling potatoes. She glanced at me over her shoulder and smiled, then turned back. "The cassoulet is nearly prepared," she said as she worked. "I'll pop it in the slow oven and it will be ready for dinner." She placed a peeled potato in the sink and picked up another. "Armel dropped over the fourth meal from Clémence. They really have been very kind. I've put it in the fridge and it will do for tomorrow." She looked over her shoulder again and frowned—she must have seen something in my face.

"It wasn't a happy place, was it?" I asked.

She put down her knife and turned to me, her eyebrows raised. "What was that?" But I think she'd heard.

"When they died. I had this memory of them, of Sarrat, of everything—it was so perfect. But it wasn't. They were shouting all the time, then acting as if everything was fine amongst friends."

She stood stock still for a moment, then drew herself up. "It wasn't the happiest of homes. They were arguing more and more, particularly before the accident."

I let out a dry laugh. "I'd forgotten, or blanked it, or both. I just remember Maman's encouragement, Papa's enthusiasm and so many good memories—so much warmth and fun. But there was more, wasn't there?"

She wiped her hands on a tea-towel. "It's coming back?"
I nodded.

"They were having marital problems," she said, "and you were stuck in the middle. I felt for you in that last year. The atmosphere wasn't pleasant."

I snorted. "I expect that added to all the reasons I liked being at your house so much."

"Come here, my darling." She walked over and wrapped

her arms around me. I encircled her in return, blinking away tears. How could I hold it all in, feeling her affection like this?

She pulled back and studied my face. Her eyes were glassy too. "I'm sorry. I didn't know how much you remembered and I never wanted to bring it up. But the good memories, they were there too, and there were plenty." She smiled. "Your maman and papa loved you very much."

I swallowed. I knew they had, but now there was more to come to grips with.

She shook her head. "The attack obviously threw you. You know, you can always talk to me about it if you need to."

But there was no way I could. "Thank you," I said.

She rubbed my arms and turned back to the cassoulet.

I walked over to the glass doors and stared out over the valley as more memories unfurled—the argument Maman and Papa had barely contained when we'd had guests for dinner, Papa bawling at Maman for no reason I could gather as I hid in my bedroom, Maman crying as Papa climbed into the car for work. There had been so much tension, but there were pleasant recollections too—I'd loved to crawl into Papa's study and hide under his desk. Of course, he'd noticed. He would pull me up onto his lap and show me his latest acquisitions.

Wanting to trace the contours of the memory, I headed into the study and closed the door. I'd not been in here since I'd left for Paris—I hadn't been able to think about work.

My modern table was pushed against the side wall, adorned with a wide-screen display, a keyboard and a mouse. A filing cabinet stood in the corner, and apart from that the only furniture was a storage cupboard with a printer on top and a chair. It was a far cry from Papa's book-lined study, his mahogany desk a megalith in the centre. I'd sat there with him and I could see the lines on his face as his eyes narrowed at an incomprehensible passage in the book he held. I could see his gloved finger trace the script across the yellowed parchment. I could see a wolf-like creature on the facing page, its body composed of strange interlocking spheres and a staff decorated with musical notation. My vision closed in and my heartbeat grew heavy. The books. They'd been here.

A knock rapped at the front door in bursts of burnt umber, and the tap of Sylvie's footsteps strobed in sepia, but all I could think of was the wolf. The door clicked open and the hearty ochres of Joël's greeting burst forth, pulling me away from the image. I'd told Joël I needed a little space, so we'd not made contact for over a week, and we'd still not broached what had happened.

I took a deep breath and opened the door. He stood on the other side of the hall, pulling off his snow-encrusted boots. He looked up and inclined his head.

"Violette, dear," Sylvie said, "I've put the cassoulet in the range. Are you alright now?"

"Yes, I'm absolutely fine."

"Good. I'll pop in sometime tomorrow."

"Sylvie, you really don't have to."

"Well, I'll see if I have the time," she said dismissively.

But she would come.

She put on her boots, wrapped an extensive scarf around her shoulders and left the house, leaving Joël and I staring at each other.

I had to say something. I had to say something so I never had to say it again. "I'm so sorry—"

"Violette, don't—"

"I tried to save him. I tried to bring him back. I wanted him back so much."

He gazed at me for a few moments, his face fixed, then he strode over and wrapped me in his arms. I let tears stream down my cheeks, and by the shaking of his chest, I knew he was doing the same.

Eventually he pulled away and grasped my shoulders in his broad palms. "Don't be sorry. If it hadn't been for you, we never would've known what'd happened to Rémy. You tried to help him and it didn't work, but that was more than anyone else managed."

"But I... If I'd waited for you..."

"Don't, Violette. This whole thing was Alex's doing. Don't turn it around."

I nodded and wiped my cheeks, but there were so many what-ifs.

He stepped back, drew a tissue from his pocket and wiped his face. "Maman and Papa asked me to express their gratitude for what you did. They'll tell you in person when they see you, but they didn't want to intrude."

"You explained?"

"Yes. We're planning on holding a memorial service at some point. I'll let you know the details."

A memorial was so final. I tried not to cry again. "Uh, come in," I managed. I led him into the living room. "Do you want a drink?"

"No, I'm fine." He perched on the sofa and I propped myself up on the hearth.

"I thought you might like to know about Alex," he said.

"Oh?" I pressed my palms into the stone slabs, the ridges digging in. I'd not wanted to think about that twisted face, but now bitterness rose within me.

"He turned up in hospital the day after it all happened and we've had people keeping an eye on him to ensure your safety. His illness was kept quiet but his family have just released a press statement explaining that he's in intensive care with an unidentifiable ailment. He's not expected to live." Joël's mouth was set firm, but there was a glint in his eyes.

"What happened?" I was curious now.

"He was messing around with things he didn't understand—how could he have any real grasp of the Désaccord from what he'd read in a book? And"—Joël glanced out at the pog, its walls barely visible behind a shroud of falling snow—"you sure as hell gave him a beating."

I frowned. "I didn't do anything to him."

"I got the impression that whatever he was doing with the Désaccord, he had to do it a hell of a lot harder with you calling the Harmonie. He used everything he had and it took too much out of him. He gave himself a death sentence."

I let out the breath I hadn't realised I'd been holding. Alex was no longer a threat. I looked up at Joël's warm brown eyes. "Thank you."

He raised his brow. "What for?"

"For letting me know. For taking me to the quiet and safety of the Société. For saving my life."

He shook his head. "I'm just glad I was there to help. But really, no thanks needed. We were both wrapped up in this."

He was so unassuming. I managed a small smile.

"So, you've had Maman's puy lentil cocotte?" he asked.

But I was only half listening. Something else played in my mind. "Joël, the books... I saw them when I was a child. Here, in Papa's study."

He raised his chin for a moment and his broad chest expanded as he took a deep breath.

"Papa had them here, didn't he?" I said.

He looked me straight in the eye. "Yes."

"And you didn't say anything."

"I didn't want to upset you," he replied.

"About what? My parents died a long time ago."

He shrugged.

"But why did Papa have the books?"

"He found them in a house sale. He was the first to study their contents and realise their significance to the old traditions."

"Oh," was all I could say as I took in the information. "Uh, he wasn't exactly... he had quite a temper toward the end."

A look of weariness drew over Joël's face. "I remember. He became... not at all like himself. We believe he experimented with the books, with the Désaccord."

I tried to link my memories, old and newly revealed, to what he was saying.

"Your maman eventually persuaded him to give the books to the Société for safekeeping," Joël continued. "The night they died, your parents were going to play in Toulouse. Afterward they'd arranged to meet a member of the Société to pass on the books, but of course, they never made the meeting. The books were retrieved from the wreckage of the crash and given to Eveline. We appealed to her for them, explaining how they were destined for the Société in the first place."

I thought of Eveline's suspicions about the crash. "Did the books or the Désaccord have anything to do with the accident?"

Joël's forehead furrowed. "Your papa was pretty worked up because of what he'd been doing... but there was black ice. I don't think it's possible to know exactly what happened that night."

"Then Maman and Papa knew about the Harmonie and the Désaccord." I sat back against the limestone beside the fire.

"Of course," he said.

My eyes narrowed. "But why didn't they say anything to me?"

"They told you the stories, right?"

"Yes, but most kids around here know those."

"They would have explained when you were older, I suppose, as my parents did with me and my brothers. What else could they have said to you at that age?"

He had a point, but I was going to have to get used to this new version of my parents and my life.

Two days later, Roselle stood on the doorstep, a covered dish in her hands. The sun, as high as it could be this time of year, spilled through the hornbeams and glittered upon the snow. In contrast, Roselle's face was stone. I wasn't sure I could handle her. It was enough dragging myself through the barest requirements of life.

"I heard about your attack," she said, her words a grey fog. "I made this. I hope it means you won't have to cook for a meal or two." She passed me the dish.

I stared at her, thinking of Théo, wanting to be able to say something—that Théo was alive. And then what? There was nothing I could say that wouldn't make her think I was mad.

"Uh, thanks." I forced a smile. But I really was grateful.

"How are you?" she asked. "It must have been awful."

"Yes, it was." I could say that truthfully. "But I'm almost better now."

She nodded and her lips pressed together. "Well, when you feel up to it, let me buy you a coffee."

"That would be great," I said. "I'll hold you to it."

Her eyes lit for a moment. "You betta."

I gaped. She'd spoken in English with a ropy American accent, just like she used to when we were children, and for the briefest moment, there had been a hint of something other than grey in her colour, the faintest touch of olive. I shook my head and smiled, trying not to cry.

Her mouth curled at the corners. "Look after yourself then."

We exchanged kisses, and as she headed up the path, a pickup pulled in behind her car. Noé jumped out and called a greeting to Roselle, then strode to the back of the truck and pulled out a triangular frame wrapped in an old blanket. He hauled it into his arms and headed down the path.

I waved as Roselle drew away, then I stared at Noé, my brow raised in question.

He met my gaze—his eyes so similar to Rémy's, although a different light lay behind them. "All fixed," he said in earthy colours a little darker than Joël's.

"What?" I said. "How can it be?"

"Are you going to move and let me take it indoors?"

I stepped to the side and gazed at the blanket as Noé walked in. The harp had been in pieces. I'd presumed it had been dumped. "Someone repaired it?" I asked.

"Yep. I did," he said with a grin. "Where do you want it?"

"The living room. In the corner."

As we walked over, I prepared myself for a bad repair or for it to look completely different. It had been destroyed—how much hope was there? And, after all, Noé was a farmer, not a musical instrument maker.

He set the frame down, lifted the blanket and stood back.

I took in the curved crown, the honey-grained wood, the twisted array of branches as organic as anything outside. I stepped closer and ran my hands over the shoulder, feeling the wooden twines under my fingers. It was perfect. It was just as it had been. "I can't see any damage," I said.

Noé's grin grew even wider. "It's my little hobby, instrument making. Hopefully I've returned it to its original condition. But as I hadn't seen the thing for years, I had to use some guesswork."

Letting out a sharp laugh, I knelt before the sound box, my middle aching faintly. I pulled the harp toward me and drew my fingers across the strings. A mix of dull, clashing colours sprawled out.

"I thought I'd leave the tuning to you," he said.

Gratitude welled up within me and I realised that deep inside I was feeling something other than grief for the first time since losing Rémy. I placed the harp back on its feet, jumped up and wrapped my arms around Noé. He reciprocated.

"Thank you so much," I said in a muffled voice from somewhere amidst his chest and arms.

"It was the least I could do," he replied.

I pulled away from him. "Can I offer you a drink or anything?"

"No, thanks. I need to get back. We have to shift the herd and it's going to take some time."

We made our way to the door and exchanged kisses.

"See you soon, I hope," he said, and strode up the path.

"Noé," I called.

He turned around.

"Thanks again."

He grinned and headed for his truck. I closed the door and walked over to the harp, running my eyes over the polished grooves, the almost seamless joins, the new set of strings. The aroma of beeswax exuded from the wood, casting my colours with gold, and no, I really couldn't see where it had broken. I plucked at middle A and a dull indigo F scattered out. That could be sorted.

I found an adjustable spanner in the utility and, with some fiddling, fitted the head to the shape of the pins, then attempted to tighten the A string. The spanner slipped, narrowly missing marking the wood. Readjusting my hold, I maintained the angle of the handle with both hands. The pin turned. I plucked the string and it rang out deep carnelian. Turning the spanner a little more, the colour changed to crimson, more still and it transformed to incandescent amber with the depth that meant it was tuned to the Harmonie. I set to work at the other pins, seeking that undeniable lustre. The spanner was awkward, and some of the strings were loose and needed rethreading, but after a while the harp was ready.

I pulled up the stool, sat down and wrapped myself around the wood. I knew he wouldn't come, but I played *Lo Boièr* anyway, absorbing the vibrations of the melody, shaping my lips to the refrain, feeling the strings under my fingers and acknowledging the beauty of the music before me. Now that my colours were unencumbered by the pain of the past, they shone with a fullness that flooded my mind and my body, a fullness that spoke not only of pure sound but of endless possibilities.

Watching the last colours ripple through the air, I drew my hands from the strings and placed the harp down. I stared around, more out of habit than hope. Of course he wasn't here, he never would be. But he was here in the music and the colour.

The next day I picked up the threads of my life. I faced work because I desperately needed to pay my bills, but I faced it with heavy functionality. Some clients had waited patiently, but most, including Aubépine, had moved on. My business was a shadow of what it had been, but it would build up again in time.

In spare moments, I would rest on the sofa and stare into the fire, or gaze out over the valley to the chateau, delicately fishing within myself, seeking who I was amidst the reverberations of the previous weeks and the memories of my past. Sometimes I would speak to Rémy and tell him about my day or how I was feeling. His absence was a desolate void, but I couldn't deny that our time together had pushed me through the boundaries of what I'd thought was myself. I'd ventured beyond the fiction I'd created to cope with the life I couldn't face, and I'd discovered a world illuminated with colour, vibrating with the music of every living thing.

Glancing through the window at blizzards and leaden sky, at effulgent blue and pristine white, the days passed from November to December, and I thought that perhaps the mist wreathing the pog was lighter, the chateau itself a little less obscure.

Chapter Twenty-Seven

No matter how I reorganised the graphics for Sablier, the proposal wouldn't come together. They wanted something by the second week in December and it was already that. My gaze crept from the screen to the window for the tenth time since sitting down at my desk. Even though the sky burgeoned with barely restrained snowfall, the chateau appeared to shimmer. The swathing gloom of the Désaccord had seemed to melt away over the past few days and the place looked... more pleasant.

I clicked on my phone and placed it face down as a barrage of messages came in. Being incommunicado was suiting me, although this moment every morning was not pleasant. But the deluge could wait a few more minutes. I pulled over my sketchpad and pencil and added lines to one of yesterday's designs, the sensation of paper under my fingers reminding me of how I used to enjoy working with raw materials. Perhaps it was time to return to my roots.

The phone rang. Colour washed over me—my synaesthesia was becoming a common part of life, but I couldn't ignore the intrusion. It was probably a client. I grabbed the phone and checked the display. *Joël* flashed up. This wasn't the best time. It took enough effort to get started in the mornings without distractions, but there was also a list of texts from him, most of them saying, *Call me.*

Well, then, I'd better answer.

I swiped the phone. "Joël. How can I help?"

"Violette, finally. I've been trying you constantly," he blustered. "I was about to drive over."

"What is it?"

"They're back. Noé found them."

"Who?"

"Rémy and Théo. Violette, he's alive!"

I drew in a sharp breath and attempted to assimilate Joël's words. Théo was alive and Roselle would have her son back. I could barely believe it. Something good had come from all we'd been through. I was happy, of course I was, but it would mean seeing Rémy's body, and that would make everything final. It would be the end of all we'd shared. "That's wonderful, Joël," I said, my voice tight, the room swaying. "Absolutely wonderful for Roselle and Pascale."

"Do you want me to pick you up?" he asked.

"No, it's fine. I'm coming straight over."

Everything around me was overexposed—the swirling snow in the lane, the blanketed village and the drape of white covering the Rabastens' farm. I drew up next to the doctor's four-wheel drive and climbed out, my head numb, an icy cold creeping through my sinews. The ramshackle farmhouse sheltered more than I could bear to see, and yet I needed to say goodbye—I needed that more than anything. My breath was ragged as I strode to the entrance and knocked. The door opened immediately.

"Violette," Joël said, a broad smile spread across his face. His expression was completely inappropriate—Théo was back, and that was great, but the return of Rémy's body didn't warrant this. We exchanged kisses, his hands clasping my arms. "Come on in."

I stepped past him and removed my outdoor gear in the entrance hall. As Joël took my things I caught the rumble of another car drawing up outside.

"Just a moment." Joël pulled on a pair of boots and headed out.

I entered the broad room and there was that fuzzy golden head. Théo lay on the sofa close to the roaring fire, an expansive grin rounding his cheeks. The doctor sat by him, talking softly. Perhaps it had all been worth it—Théo had a life in front of him now. The memory of him and Rémy emerging hand in hand from the Harmonie tore at me. I closed my eyes for a moment and breathed through the pain. I wanted to go home, but I had to pull myself together and get this done.

Noé, Orianne and Yves sat at the dining table, their hands harbouring cups, their eyes fixed upon me. Of course, this was a terrible time for them too. I needed to say something—

The front door opened and Joël strode in, kicking off his boots, scattering lumps of snow and ice across the flagstones. Pascale followed, a worn fragility upon his face, then Roselle burst forward. She stopped as she caught sight of Théo, her mouth agape, her eyes wide.

"Maman!" Théo cried. He raised his arms to her, his grin somehow wider.

A small strangled noise broke from Roselle's throat.

"Théo?" Pascale asked.

"Papa!"

Then desperate hope unfurled upon Roselle's face. She took a step toward Théo and paused again.

"Come on, Maman," Théo called. "Hurry up." In an instant she rushed over, bent down and gathered him in her arms, repeating his name over and over through choked sobs and Théo's protests and giggles. The doctor stood up with a satisfied smile. Pascale took his place, wrapping himself around his family, burying his head amongst their arms.

My eyes stung with tears. I turned away and tried to swallow down the emotion before I could no longer restrain myself. I needed a distraction. The doctor and Joël were engrossed in a quiet conversation by the door—no help there. Yves caught my eye. He rose from the table and strode over, beaming and shaking his head. We exchanged kisses.

"Good to see you, Violette," he said softly, no doubt not wanting to disturb the reunion. He was still smiling—with it all so raw, I couldn't take more misplaced cheerfulness. "We are exceedingly grateful for what you did," he added.

Noé and Orianne joined us, their faces beaming. I stared stupefied at them. They moved in and we kissed.

Orianne placed her hand on my arm. "Thank you very much for everything."

"Absolutely," Noé agreed. "There really aren't words."

"I'm so glad Théo is back," I replied as I tried to interpret their reactions. Perhaps they were relieved now they had finality with Rémy.

Emmie and Seb ran through the kitchen door. Seb darted over and tugged at my jumper. "Aren't you going to come and see Uncle Rémy?" He dashed away, giggling with his sister.

This was too strange.

Joël came over and hung his arm around my shoulder. "You did it," he said, still grinning. "He's alive."

This was ridiculous. I had to say something. "It's wonderful that Théo is back, but at the same time I, uh... it's going to be hard to see Rémy's body."

Joël managed a scowl on his smiling face. "What do you mean, Violette? I told you, he's alive."

"Yes, Théo's alive and I'm glad."

He shook his head. "Théo and Rémy—they're both alive."

My mouth hung open. I was unable to comprehend his words.

He glanced toward the door that led to the rest of the house. "He's in one of the back bedrooms, resting up. The doctor's seen to him and he's absolutely fine."

I couldn't take my eyes off Joël. His words were so callous. "Don't be stupid. He's dead. We saw him die."

"I don't know how it's possible," he said, "but he's alive and kicking, and he's been asking for you ever since he was found."

Yves, Orianne and Noé nodded in agreement.

I let out a brief, shallow laugh. "This would be a cruel joke, Joël Rabasten."

He studied my face. "It would be, and you know I would never do that."

Of course I knew. But he couldn't really be alive. Even hoping for such a thing was beyond me. And yet... "What happened?" I managed.

"I was doing cattle checks in the meadows at sunrise," Noé said. "I saw someone walking down the pog with a child in their arms. It was unusual that early, and after last night's snow, so I parked and walked up. And, well, the rest is history."

I nodded dumbly. I couldn't put this together—it didn't make sense.

"Come on." Joël tugged at my sleeve. "I'll take you to him."

He pulled me toward the door by the fire. I followed, unable to grasp what was happening—Rémy was gone. We'd shared so much in such a short space of time, but it had ended.

"He's along here," Joël said.

We stepped into the hall, Joël leading the way. I vaguely registered the paintings that hung upon the walls, the rug under my feet, but all of it was distant and unreal.

Joël halted a little way before an open door. "Maman, Papa, come here," he called.

Clémence appeared from the room and caught sight of me. Her face lit and she walked over with short, sprightly steps, her eyes sparkling. Armel followed, closing the door behind him.

"My dear," Clémence said in warm, nurturing tones, "I do not have the words. You brought our son back to us." She wrapped her arms around me and held me close, her delicate scent and maternal warmth enfolding me, yet I couldn't respond. I was frozen between what had been and what might be. She stepped back, took in my expression and glanced at the door. "I wouldn't have believed it myself before I saw him."

I managed to nod.

Armel came forward and grasped my shoulders. "We are forever in your debt, Violette. Thank you." He lowered his head then stepped past Joël and me, grasping Clémence by the hand and drawing her along the corridor.

Joël studied my face. "Come on then." He opened the door and stepped in.

My heart pounded as though my chest could barely contain its violence—I couldn't entertain the possibility that he was alive, yet I had to know. I stepped through the door and stopped. The room pressed in on me—the roaring fire, the outdated furniture, the floral decor, the snow swirling at the window—then the impressions retreated, leaving only him, my imagination brought to life.

He sat there supported by pillows, a duvet pulled up to his chest, those eyes holding so much gentleness and fervour, those lips playing a little as though he were contemplating what to do next. He wore a grey round-neck T-shirt but he looked the same—and still there was that something about him. His eyes flickered, searching mine. I could sense his need for me, just as I had when we'd played the piano, but I didn't dare move. I didn't want to shatter this reality, lest it were only an illusion.

"Well." Joël grinned. "I think I'll leave you two to it." He stepped away and the door clicked closed.

We stared at each other for a few moments, then Rémy broke the silence. "There was an end to the story I told you... the story of the musician." I gazed at his midnight blue rippling around me, the colour I'd never thought I'd know again.

"After the musician had been trapped in the sublimity of the Harmonie for many years," he continued, his voice low and melodious, "after he'd reflected for what seemed like an eternity on the events he'd brought into play, and after he'd experienced the pain he'd caused like a burning scourge in every fibre of his being, the musician was called forth from the radiance by a beautiful maiden."

I couldn't help myself—I let out something between a breath and a laugh.

"A beautiful maiden," he went on, "with unwavering determination and great bravery, who resolved to help the musician return. The musician and the maiden realised they were two of a kind, two people who could see music, who could experience it in the very core of their beings, and they became entangled, as if their music had been made to accompany each other.

"Through courage and personal sacrifice, the maiden called the musician back to the world—the world where the Désaccord measures out the rhythm of life through death, the world where the Harmonie ever waits for all that is discordant to merge once again into the Great Song." He pushed himself up and sat forward, the duvet sinking to his waist. "The musician declared he would never part from the maiden for all of his days, and they lived happily, bountifully and joyously ever after. The musician's exile had ended."

He smiled—a glorious, beautiful thing, a thing I had missed so terribly. I shook my head, tears pricking my eyes.

"Violette..."

My body trembled. "You can't be alive. You can't."

"I'm here," he said softly.

I couldn't be apart from him any longer. I strode over, jumped on top of the duvet and took his face into my shaking hands. In a desperate attempt to confirm his reality I ran my fingers over his cheeks and around his jaw, then back through his hair and across the ridges of his neck, then down the musculature of his arms and over his hands. The sensation of his warm skin under my fingers rippled his colour through me, and all the time he watched—I could feel him taking me in, understanding my need to assure myself he was solid and real.

I drew my fingers over his left hand. It was balled tight. He turned his fist over and unfurled his palm. The harp key lay there, strung on the faded blue velvet ribbon. I stared at the twisted metal—it was still with him. My eyes flicked to his for a moment. He smiled. Then, still wanting to be certain, I pulled up his T-shirt and ran my fingers over his heart—the place where Alex had carved his macabre cross, the place where the knife had sunk. There was no sign of a wound.

"What happened? Alex... the knife... you...?" I whispered.

"I was taken up into the Harmonie once again. I healed in timelessness and waited to be with you, to be able to touch you. I missed you every moment." He brushed a strand of hair from my forehead. "Because of what you did at the chateau, the balance between the Désaccord and the Harmonie reset. The Désaccord gradually dissipated to the point where Théo and I could return."

"I missed you so damn much." Tears spilled down my face. "I caused you so much pain—I drew you to the pog, to the Désaccord, when I didn't know what was going on—I initiated the ritual—I brought you out of the Harmonie, leaving you exposed to Alex."

He ran his fingers over my cheek, his eyes not leaving mine. "You saved me."

My skin shivered with the colour of him, that saturated dusk, that unfathomable intensity. His lips flickered upward —he could feel me too, and he could sense me sensing him. It was an endless circle of emotion, sensation and colour.

Needing him closer still, I pulled him to me, our lips almost touching. We stayed like that for a moment, breathing each other in, then we drew together and kissed tenderly. He was here, he'd returned to me, and our musica humanum blended—his midnight blue and my...

I pulled back a little and laughed, our faces still close. "Violet," I murmured—I could see it now, the colour that made up me, the colour that had always accompanied me, although I'd been unable to recognise it. I watched the stippled strands twist and twine, mingling with Rémy's darker, more impetuous tone.

He kissed me again. "Yes, Violette."

Bonus Chapter

Thank you for reading *The Piano Tuner's Song*.

The bonus chapter is available to download here...

Enjoy!

*I would be extremely grateful if you could rate and review this
book on Amazon, Goodreads or anywhere else!*

With heartfelt thanks,
Karenza

Where the fae and human
realms meet...

FOLKLORIC

THE FOLKLORIC SERIES
BOOK ONE

KARENZA GRANT

Acknowledgments

Thank you to everyone who dared venture into the world of *The Piano Tuner's Song* at various stages throughout the writing and editing process.

I'm hugely grateful to Viktoria Dahill, Katie Mouallek, Rachel Schmidt and Abhivyakti Singh, whose feedback was constructive, thought provoking, supportive and at times hilarious. Your individual perspectives have been indispensable, and together you form one amazing writing group. To Stuart Bache for the stunning cover. To copyeditor Toby Selwyn for absolute professionalism combined with patience as I queried him yet again! To all my beta readers, for your keen eyes and useful comments. To Lorraine Wilson, who has been an inspiration on my writing adventures. To Octavia Denning, without whom I wouldn't have gotten so far so quickly—actually, I might not have gotten out of the starting blocks at all without you. I'm always indebted to Dorine Maine for being there with such kindness and love.

Particular thanks to Rillian Grant, my intrepid first reader, tech support bar none and voice of encouragement. Special thanks to Minerva Grant, who inspired me to keep writing, even on the toughest of days. Last of all, thanks to Mina, whose generous heart is a blessing.

Karenza Grant writes folklore-inspired fantasy of all kinds with delectable slow-burn romance.

Her early years in Cornwall were largely the source of her fascination with all things mysterious. She lived below a hill reputed to be the Cornish residence of the Unseelie Court, and the local myths got their claws in. Now she's inspired by a broad range of creators, from Jim Henson and Arthur Rackham to a whole host of amazing authors.

She has three black cats known as The Three Guardians who supervise from various corners of the writing desk (yes, there's a lot of fur).

Karenza loves hearing from readers, so make her day and get in touch by email or socials. Find her at www.karenza grant.com. Subscribe to her newsletter for all the latest.